BLACK
ORCHID

A THRILLER

VAUGHN C.
HARDACKER

Skyhorse Publishing

Skyhorse Publishing books may be purchased in bulk at special discounts for sales promotion, corporate gifts, fund-raising, or educational purposes. Special editions can also be created to specifications. For details, contact the Special Sales Department, Skyhorse Publishing, 307 West 36th Street, 11th Floor, New York, NY 10018 or info@skyhorsepublishing.com.

Skyhorse® and Skyhorse Publishing® are registered trademarks of Skyhorse Publishing, Inc.®, a Delaware corporation.

Visit our website at www.skyhorsepublishing.com.

10 9 8 7 6 5 4 3 2 1

Library of Congress Cataloging-in-Publication Data is available on file.

Cover design by Jane Sheppard
Cover photo: iStockphoto

Print ISBN: 978-1-5107-0531-9
Ebook ISBN: 978-1-5107-0532-6

Printed in the United States of America

1

There was a young woman standing in the threshold of Ed Traynor's office. At first Traynor thought she looked as timid as a gun-shy retriever, but then he realized she was debating whether or not she should come in. It was August and business was slow, and he'd been enjoying a quiet Friday morning at his desk—sitting with his feet propped up on its corner and reading a crime paperback. He'd gotten through several pages before even noticing the woman, and when he finally had become aware of her presence, he'd thought to himself: *Real observant. If I was her, I'd walk away.*

Now, he dropped his feet to the floor, stood up, and studied her. The short, royal-blue skirt she wore made her look more like she should be leading cheers for her college football team than standing in the doorway of a private investigator's office. Her appearance was neat—a look that

Traynor thought many young women today disdained, or seemed to. Her brown hair fell to her shoulders in soft waves. She had the darkest eyes he'd ever seen—almost obsidian. The mercury was supposed to push past the ninety-degree mark, but one would never know it to look at her. She looked and more importantly, smelled as fresh as if she'd just stepped out of the shower. He thought that maybe she stood in his office door hoping to sell him candy to support her school's yearbook or athletic department.

"Can I help you?" he asked.

"Are you"—she glanced at the lettering on the door—"Mr. Edward Traynor?"

He took out his wallet and looked at his license. "This official document from the great state of New Hampshire says I am—although, you'd never know it from the picture. Call me Ed. Edward sounds too stuffy."

Her face reddened. Sometimes Traynor's sophomoric sense of humor left people cold. He realized that they needed to know each other better before he could be his usual flippant self. Suddenly, he felt foolish, almost ashamed of his behavior. He threw the novel on his desk and stood up. "I'm sorry. Sometimes—usually when I'm alone too long—I get smart-mouthed." He circled the desk and offered her a chair. "Have a seat, Miss . . ."

"Hollis, Deborah Hollis. Please call me Deb."

"Okay, Deb it is." He waited until she was seated, her bag demurely placed on her lap and both legs clamped tightly together. He dropped into his chair and swiveled it around to face her. "So, Deb, what brings you to my office?"

"I'm told you're a private eye."

"The best there is in New Hampshire."

"I believe you're the *only* one in the state—at least the only one listed in the phone book."

He chuckled and thought: *No one's putting anything past her*. He decided to stop the smart-mouth attitude and get serious. "That term is a bit dated. These days we're called detectives or private security consultants. What you call me depends on what you pay me to do."

"I need you to find someone."

"Then it's 'detective.' Who do you want me to find?"

She stared at him, almost as if testing his sincerity. Her eyes weren't black—when the light hit them just right, he could see they were a dark blue. "My sister. Her name is Mindy, Melinda actually."

"And she's missing?"

"We haven't heard from her in almost two months."

"Missing persons are usually best handled by the police. They have more resources and cost you nothing."

"We contacted the police: they found nothing."

"These things take time."

"I don't believe they're looking." Her nostrils flared.

"Hiring a person like me can be expensive."

She took out a checkbook and said, "How much?"

"My rates are five hundred a day plus expenses."

She quickly wrote out a check, for what he assumed would be one day, two at most. She ripped it out of the book and handed it to him. Traynor took it and glanced at it: five thousand dollars. "This is enough for ten days, less my expenses."

"It's good. You can call the bank before you do anything."

He wasn't questioning the validity of the check, but he *was* surprised. Most women her age would not have such easy access to so much cash. They'd probably have to ask if he took credit cards.

He glanced at the address on the check; it was a New Castle address, in the neighborhood of the Wentworth Hotel to be exact. In New Castle, they called brand-new million-dollar homes the *projects*. Her address wasn't in the projects. She was in the exclusive part of town—waterfront property.

She was one of *those* Hollises; they were old money—lots of old money. The state of New Hampshire has eighteen miles of seacoast, and at one time the Hollis family owned almost three-quarters of it. Today, it was common knowledge that they only owned about a quarter of it. About thirty years ago, old Elias Hollis sold off most of his property for megamillions or more. He doubted her check would bounce. In fact, he doubted if a check for ten times that amount would be large enough to put a dent in the balance.

"Deb, I know this may sound as if I don't want your business, but I need to know. Why would a young woman of your obvious means choose me?"

"You come highly recommended."

That was a new one. "And, who was it gave me this stellar recommendation?"

"Sheriff Buchanan."

There was a time when Earl "Buck" Buchanan and Traynor had been friends. They'd been New Hampshire State Police homicide detectives together. These days, Buchanan was the Rockingham County Sheriff, which Traynor believed was just another way of saying a politician. No doubt the Hollis family was a major contributor to his upcoming reelection campaign. Nevertheless, Buck hadn't needed to mention him; as a matter of fact, Traynor was surprised that he had. A couple of years ago, Traynor got involved in one of Buchanan's cases. The sheriff never bought Traynor's resolution, as accurate as it was. Still, he knew Buck would not have sent Deb Hollis to him if he had any doubt about Traynor being up to the job. It looked as if he had a case.

"When did you last see or hear from your sister?"

"Two months ago. She called me."

"Where was she then?"

"California. She's always wanted to be an actress and went out there to get some experience. She said she was building her resume." She hesitated, and then said, "Truthfully, I believe she went out there because it's as far from here as she could get without leaving the country."

Traynor knew he had to be careful with his next question, but it was *the* question that he needed answered. "Deb, are you sure your sister wants to be found? She wouldn't be the first twenty-something to get upset with the family and run off."

"I understand, but that isn't the case here. Mindy takes great pleasure in calling my parents and rubbing it in their faces . . ."

"So there *is* some type of family feud taking place—"

"It's more rebellion than feud," she said. "However, her problems were with our parents. She and I got along fine. We were very close."

"You have an address for her?"

"She was living in some place called Simi Valley. She and another woman were sharing a place." She wrote down the address on a piece of notepaper and handed it to him.

He looked at it. Traynor was a born-and-bred, live-free-or-die New Hampshire man and didn't much like the West Coast. However, he was familiar with the Los Angeles area, having spent time there while in the service. As a young Marine, he had roamed the area, looking for college women—even met a few. So he got to know his way around quite well, though of course, that was long ago. No doubt the place was a lot different than he remembered—but at least the general geography would not be completely alien. One thing jumped out at him, though: her address. It was near the San Fernando Valley; he would have expected a young woman with access to the Hollis fortune to be in the more affluent suburbs, such as Brentwood. His face must have telegraphed his thoughts, because Deb said, "Mindy and Daddy haven't spoken in over a year. She wouldn't ask him for a glass of water if she were dying of thirst."

"So she was trying to do it on her own?"

"Yes."

"What about you? Do you get along with your father?"

"Even though Mindy's three years younger than me, I'm Daddy's baby—his favorite. But if he knew I was here, he'd be livid. Mindy gets her stubbornness from him."

Traynor pondered the probability of successfully locating Mindy; he knew it was low. Then his eye caught the check lying on the desk before him. For the past couple of months, all he'd had were a couple of small cases—neither of which brought in much cash. He picked up the check, reread it, and then looked at Deb Hollis. "Okay, Deb, you've got yourself an investigator."

Suddenly, she began crying. Traynor didn't know what to do, but then he never did when a woman cried. He wanted to comfort her, but wasn't sure how she'd react—after all, he'd never laid eyes on her until fifteen minutes ago. He did what he thought was the manly thing—he handed her a box of tissues and stared out the window, giving her some semblance of privacy.

Traynor watched a fishing boat struggle against the current as it pushed its way up the Piscataqua River. It passed the Portsmouth Naval Yard, which was really in Kittery, Maine. The fishing boat was almost out of sight by the time she stopped sniffling. He turned back to her as she was wiping her eyes. She blew her nose, Traynor held up the wastebasket, and she threw the tissue in it.

"Do you have a picture of Mindy?" he asked. "I need one I can keep."

"Yes. It's a couple of years old, but she hasn't changed much—at least she hadn't the last time I saw her." She rooted around in her bag, pulling things out, and placed them on a corner of his desk. The contents of her purse soon covered the surface. She removed used tissues, makeup, more used tissues, lipstick, and a condom. She hesitated for a second, staring at it as if she had no idea where it came from, then blushed and quickly stuffed the condom back into a side pocket. Once again, he turned to the window for a second, this time hiding his smile. It was like watching an inept magician try to find a rabbit in a hat. When at least thirty wads of tissues and sundry cosmetics were piled on the desk, Deb smiled significantly and took out a tiny wallet. She pulled a photo out of it and handed it to him.

The picture was of a woman in her mid- to late twenties with light brown hair cut just below her shoulders. She wore blue jeans, a white blouse, expensive sandals, and leaned against a late-model Corvette, —her broad smile indicative of what seemed to be a happy time. Her resemblance to the young woman sitting across from him was such that there was no doubt they were sisters.

Traynor focused on the photo, studying Mindy's face. Her eyes had a faraway look to them. He didn't want to say anything, thinking it was his damned old biases again. But he'd seen eyes like those a thousand times—on drunks and drug addicts. He got a bad feeling, one that gave him second thoughts about taking this case. The outcome might not be one Deb Hollis was going to like. He put the photo on the desk.

"I may have to speak with your parents. Is that going to be a problem?"

"I'd appreciate it if you didn't speak with them unless it's absolutely necessary."

"I think it will be *absolutely necessary*."

"How can you be sure?"

"Experience. Sooner. Sooner or later, your father's going to find out about me. I've always found being upfront from the beginning to be the best policy."

"Okay, but I want to break the news to him. I hope I can calm him down before you get there."

"I'd like that, too." He gave her what he hoped was his most reassuring smile. "I'd like to see him this afternoon, and then tomorrow I'll do some checking. How about three o'clock? Will that give you enough time to talk with him?"

"I guess it will have to, won't it?" She held out her hand.

Deb Hollis's hand was so tiny and finely sculpted that he was afraid to grip it for fear it would break. Her ring finger held a diamond that was large enough to let one know it was expensive, but not so large as to be considered ostentatious. Her nails were impeccably manicured and real. Traynor realized he was holding her hand longer than needed and let it go. "I'll do everything I can to find your sister," he said, trying to get back on safe, professional ground.

"Thank you. You'll never know how much this means to me."

"I'll do my best. I need as much information on your sister as you can provide . . . especially her social security number."

"I thought you might, so I put together as much as I could."

She reached into her bag once again and this time, found what she was looking for immediately. She extracted a folded sheet of paper and handed it to him. He unfolded it and noted that everything was organized and written in legible handwriting—there was even a photocopy of a credit card application with the social security number. "This is great. I'll get started immediately."

She stood and offered her hand again. "I'll be looking for you at three . . . The address is on the check."

After she left, he picked up the phone and called Charley Giles. Charley was the most technical friend Traynor had. He and Max Thurston owned an auto body repair shop, which doubled as a command center when Traynor was on a case and Charley had done a lot of online research for him. Charley had ways of getting data that bordered on the amazing. Max, on the other hand, provided additional muscle and backup on those rare occasions when Traynor needed it. Charley answered the phone on the second ring.

"I need anything you can find on Melinda Hollis, aka Mindy. Last known address for her is in Simi Valley, California. Her social is . . ." He read off the number.

"What's this all about?"

"I'm employed," Traynor said.

"It's about time."

The PI is a trained investigator, not a professional counselor, though many clients seeking the former actually need the latter
    —*Private Eyes: A Writer's Guide To Private Investigators*

2

Before Traynor went to see the Hollises, he wanted to talk to the person who had recommended him: Sheriff Buck Buchanan. Traynor was more than a little nervous when he was shown into Buchanan's office and held his hand out. "Buck, it's been a while."

"Hello, Eddie. Yeah, it has been." Buchanan stepped aside and motioned for Traynor to sit in one of the chairs that fronted his desk. Like Traynor, Buchanan was a big man, over six feet tall and wide shouldered. However, unlike Traynor, not all of Buck's bulk was muscle. Since he had retired from the New Hampshire State Police and became desk-bound, his already substantial stomach had grown. Still, he was an imposing figure. "I hear you moved your office out of Manchester."

"Yeah, I'm in Portsmouth now."

"So, that means you're doing business in my county now."

"That sounds as if you're still pissed at me."

"I was never pissed at you . . . Disappointed is more like it."

"Buck, it came down just like I said."

Buck held up a large hand. "I ain't going down that rathole, Eddie. You know what I think, and let's leave it at that."

"All right." Traynor did his best to keep cool. He had never been very graceful when chastised.

"What brings you here?" Buck asked. "It obviously isn't a social call."

"I got a client this morning, someone you recommended. Given all that's gone down, I never thought that would happen."

"That would be Deborah Hollis . . . great kid. You'll probably have to go out to California."

"That might present a problem," Traynor said. "Like you, I've got no authority out there. The last time I checked, my license was issued by the state of New Hampshire."

Traynor followed Buchanan with his eyes as the sheriff circled his desk, pulled out his chair, and dropped his huge frame into it. "Eddie, let's get things out in the open and cut the crap, okay? You're right about one thing, I don't like the fact that a perp who should have been taken into custody is dead and you helped make that happen. Anyone who knows anything about you knows how nutso you get about pedophiles and perverts; however, if you can live with it, I can. You're still the best goddamned investigator I know, and you don't usually worry about the small stuff, like a valid license in another state."

Traynor's defenses went down. "Okay, Buck. Suppose you tell me what you know about the Hollises and this case?"

"The kid and her old man have been at odds for years. She walked on the wild side—a real party girl. The type you and I fantasized about when we were kids—sex, drugs, and rock and roll—that sort of shit. My people busted her a few times, although it never got to court. We know all too well what happens when big money gets involved with the legal system."

"Yeah," Traynor commented, "same thing that happens when it gets involved with government. She have a record?"

"I ain't at liberty to say much—let's just say that the courts have sealed her records. As for whatever it is that Deb hired you to do—all I know is the case ain't in my county."

"Am I safe in assuming this is the same family that owned half the oceanfront real estate in Rye at one time?"

"Same bunch."

Traynor studied his old friend for a moment, trying to pick up on any body language that might tell him more than Buck was able, or willing, to say.

"How much resistance am I going to get from the family?"

"Can't rightly say. You'll have to go over there and see." Buchanan stood up. Suddenly, he smiled. "Knowin' you, the Hollises may have met up with someone who isn't impressed—or intimidated—by them."

"Are they intimidating?"

"I'm not gonna say anything that will prejudice you—go find out for yourself."

Traynor stood and said, "Maybe when this is over we can get together and have a beer, sort of clear the air?" He held his hand out. "We friends again?"

Buck grabbed Traynor's hand and smiled, creating a wide, broad gap that filled his face. "We never stopped bein' friends, Eddie. We just had a difference of opinion. It's not like it was the first time we ever disagreed. What is it about your scurvy ass that makes me unable to stay pissed at you?"

"Maybe it's my wonderful smile, sparkling white teeth, and dynamic personality?"

———

Some of the most expensive real estate in New Hampshire could be found on New Castle Island. It was a part of Portsmouth, but Traynor knew the residents would never admit to that; they believed that the island was an empire itself. He drove along Route 1B until he saw the *new* Wentworth Hotel perched on a bluff, which gave every room in the place a waterfront view. Built in 1874, the *old* Wentworth had been a posh hangout for the elite set for a good part of the late nineteenth and early twentieth centuries. In 1905, it had housed the delegates to the negotiations that ended the Russo–Japanese War. But by the 1970s, it was closed, abandoned, and in such a state of disrepair that it looked like the setting for an Edgar Allen Poe tale. Several years ago, Traynor mused, one of the major hotel chains bought the wasted building and restored it—though "completely rebuilt it" was probably a more apt statement. The hotel looked now as it did 130 years ago—only now with all the amenities modern society demands. As he drove past it, Traynor thought: *Maybe I'll use the money from this case to spend a night—even though I'm sure it will take most, if not all, of it.*

Traynor crossed the bridge onto the island and turned down a narrow lane, heading toward the yacht club. Before leaving Portsmouth, he had programmed the Hollis Estate into his GPS. It was a good thing he did so, or he'd never have found the way in. Traynor turned off the public road and followed a paved drive through a thicket so dense it reminded him of the hedgerows he'd seen in Normandy when he'd toured the coast of France the year previous. Like those in Europe, the bushes had woven themselves into an impenetrable wall. The thicket opened and he found himself traveling through landscaping so incredible he was tempted to stop and measure the grass, and he wouldn't have been surprised to learn that every blade was cut to exactly the same height. In the center of the lawn was a gigantic flagpole, designed to look like a ship's mast. At the top of the center-mast, the Stars and Stripes flew and on the arms, two other flags—one the New Hampshire state flag and the other, he learned later, was the Hollis family pennant. A brisk offshore breeze blew across the property, snapping and flapping the ensigns in the afternoon stillness.

Traynor followed the curving drive until he was in front of the huge colonial house. It was white with black trim, and on the second story, a widow's walk wrapped itself around the house. Traynor had no doubt that the original occupant had been a sea captain—no, make that the owner of a fleet, probably whalers—and the walk was built so his wife could watch for his return from years at sea.

He parked his car, and the door opened before he could even get his hand on the handle. It startled him. He hadn't seen the guy. Not wanting to look stupid, he stepped out, doing his best impression of Prince Charles. Trying to sound like British nobility—an accent he'd always thought sounded as if the speaker had a tangerine stuck up his or her ass—he said, "Sir Edward Traynor, to see the lord of the house."

The guy looked as if he were in danger of rupturing his spleen, trying to keep from laughing. He pointed to Traynor's bruised and battered Durango and said, "As soon as I saw those wheels, I knew someone of great wealth and taste was about to descend upon us."

A wide grin spread across Traynor's face. He could take a joke as well as the next fellow. He studied the man for a second. He had a muscular build and appeared to be about ten years Traynor's junior, which put him in his early to mid-thirties. It didn't take Traynor long to decide that this guy was someone who could probably handle himself well in a fracas.

Still playing the game, the man said, "You'll find his lordship in the back, on the deck, sire."

Traynor was shocked and more than a little let down. A house like this shouldn't have a deck—it should have a *veranda*. He decided that his bonny Prince Charles routine needed more work. He said, "Around to the left?"

"Yeah, it's the side opposite to your right. Even a personage of such in-grown bloodlines can't miss it—just follow the walk. They're expecting you. Leave the keys in the ignition and I'll park it."

Traynor followed the path he had indicated, admiring the roses and flowers that lined the paved lane. When he turned the corner of the house, Traynor was treated to a gorgeous view of Seavey Island—or more accurately, the old Portsmouth Naval Prison. The island was home to the Naval Shipyard and the prison, which closed in 1974. The past few years had seen increased activity at the old military slammer; developers were considering remodeling it into expensive condos. It beat the hell out of Traynor why anyone would spend a fortune on a condominium in which the master bedroom was once a jail cell. They could fix and paint it up all they wanted, but to him, it would always be one big, beige eyesore. He liked the view from his office better.

When Traynor turned the next corner, he saw the house was shaped like a U. Sometime in its history, someone must have added wings to the main house. When he could see inside the U, he saw a stone veranda and patio combination that led to an Olympic-size swimming pool, with a retractable enclosure that allowed year-round use. The Hollises were sitting on patio furniture that Traynor was sure cost more than the apartment building in which he lived. But Traynor decided he wouldn't hold their wealth against them. Being rich had to be a nasty job, but someone had to do it. Traynor figured that if someone had to save him from the burden of being affluent, it might as well be the Hollises.

Traynor stopped short of stepping onto the deck. For some strange reason, he felt like a junior naval officer reporting to the admiral's flagship. It only seemed appropriate to wait until he was given permission to come aboard by the officer of the deck. The problem was that he wasn't exactly sure who was in charge. There were four people seated around a huge table, the top of which sparkled in the sun like it was made of polished marble—possibly because it was.

Of the four people, he knew only one by sight: Deborah Hollis. She sat next to a svelte woman, probably in her mid- to late fifties. He assumed it was her mother, *the* Mrs. Hollis. The other two occupants were male. One appeared to be about sixty, the other much younger—at most forty. The older man was speaking in a voice much too loud for the environment, and Traynor immediately knew he was an alcoholic.

Deborah was the first to see him, and she got up and walked to the edge of the veranda, beckoning for him to enter—which he interpreted as being granted permission to come aboard. If there had been ensigns flying, Traynor would have saluted the colors.

Deborah had changed clothes since she had been in his office. She was in a less businesslike pair of tangerine-colored pants with a matching striped top and an obviously expensive pair of white sandals. She took him by the hand, and the older woman, who was dressed for lunch at

Tiffany's, glared at him like he was her daughter's date from the wrong side of the tracks. Her look was so scathing it made Traynor feel as if he were from the wrong side of the universe. He caught himself wanting to salute the old woman and the house, but refrained.

Traynor didn't know whether it was money or the people that had it that brought out the smartass in him. He did, however, believe that whatever it was, it went back to his parents. They had nothing but disdain for anyone better off than they were. He'd often thought that God had known what he was doing when he made his father a working-class stiff; if he the old man had money he would have been a real pain in the keester. Even without money he'd been a bit much.

"Welcome to our home, Mr. Traynor," Deborah said. "Would you join us for tea or coffee?"

"Coffee, please. It's always been my opinion that the best thing that ever happened to tea took place in Boston over two hundred years ago." Over her shoulder, Traynor could see her parents looking uneasy; he thought, *They must have an aversion to dining with the hired help.* Traynor let Deborah guide him to her parents.

"Mother, Father, I'd like you to meet Mr. Ed Traynor. He's the security consultant I told you about. He's assured me he'll find Mindy."

Traynor's mouth fell open; he didn't recall making any guarantees. If anything, he had tried to impress upon her that there were two chances of finding her sister: slim and none. And if Mindy did not want to be found, slim had already left town. Deborah ignored his surprised expression and kept right on with the introductions. "Ed, this is my mother, Marsha, and my father, Cyril Hollis. This gentleman"—she indicated the younger man—"is Byron Moore, our family attorney and financial advisor."

Unsure what to say, Traynor offered his hand to Mrs. Hollis. She lightly grasped it, looking as if one of the thousands of ever-present seagulls had shit in her palm. He had no doubt she would sterilize her hand at the first opportunity. For a woman with a 1960s beehive hairdo, she definitely had an attitude. As soon as she dropped his loathsome appendage, Traynor offered it to Cyril, who ignored it completely. Then his ancestral dislike of rich snobs made an appearance. He reached for his wallet, intending to hand Deborah's check back to her. Traynor was fully prepared to tell her not to use it for toilet paper—the ink might come off on her ass. But he didn't get the chance. Deborah's face was red with embarrassment as she led him to a stuffed chair, which at least looked inviting.

Not to be put out, he offered his hand to Moore. If he copped an attitude, Traynor was out of there. To his surprise, Moore grasped his hand and said, "Please, have some coffee. We're in dire straits."

Dire straits? Traynor took in his impeccable business suit and then glanced at Cyril, who was dressed in what one would expect a wealthy wino to wear—even though the remnants of breakfast and/or lunch were evident on the front of his ruffled white shirt.

He studied the elder Hollises; contrary to Moore's comment, they didn't strike him as being in dire anything. *But*, he thought, *what do I know about obnoxious, rich assholes?* However, being the consummate professional, Traynor assumed he might be mistaken and decided to hear them out. "Just how *grim* is the situation?" he asked, directing the question to Moore. Two could play at their little game.

"My daughter is missing." Cyril must have been at least three drinks beyond sober, and his booming voice was inappropriately loud.

Traynor turned his attention to him. There was nothing about Cyril Hollis that would assuage his preconceived bias against rich assholes. Hollis's eyes seemed to have no whites and were so bloodshot they looked pink. His nose was bulbous, swollen, and tiny red veins formed a fine net along the surface. The pores were so stretched they looked like manholes. Traynor thought if he were to sneeze, he'd hemorrhage for at least an hour. His red face ended abruptly at a receding hairline of snow-white hair.

He used both hands to guide the martini glass to his lips and made a slurping sound as he downed the liquor in a single gulp. No sooner did he finish the booze than a butler built like a linebacker for the Patriots magically appeared and refilled the glass. He wore a tux, like that guy Jeeves in the movies that played on the classic movie channel at two in the morning. The phrase "gentleman's gentleman" came to his mind, but then

Traynor looked at Cyril Hollis again and decided that valet was more appropriate. There was not much evidence that Hollis was a gentleman. Once his employer's glass was full, the servant quickly retreated and Traynor returned his attention to Cyril Hollis. He wondered what it must be like to spend your golden years in an alcoholic haze, being catered to in a mansion filled with paid codependents. Traynor opted to ignore the slovenly behavior of his host. "I understand that, sir. Can you tell me when you last heard from her?"

Cyril looked at him as if he'd said something inane. Maybe he had—either way, it had gone over Hollis's head. Traynor knew that the old man had one, at most two, drinks left before he'd suffer a major crash and burn. His estimate was off by two. Cyril took a big gulp of his martini and missed the table when he tried to place the glass down. It hit the deck and shattered into hundreds of pieces. Cyril stared at the broken glass, as if he had no idea how it had gotten there. When he raised his head, he looked as bewildered as a lion cub meeting its first snake. More servants appeared from the ether and flocked around, cleaning up the spill. The butler reappeared, and he delicately placed a towel in the old man's soaking lap, fussing over him. Hollis might have been loaded, but he was still sentient enough to know he had screwed up and he excused himself. As soon as the butler stepped away, one of the staff—a dark-complexioned man dressed in black slacks and a tight T-shirt that emphasized his bulging biceps—effortlessly lifted Hollis and carried him inside the mansion. Seemingly concerned for his welfare, Mrs. Hollis said, "Take him to his chambers, Manuel." She then darted off after her husband and his entourage.

Traynor was left alone with Deborah and Byron Moore. Which didn't bother him in the least; it didn't take an Ivy League degree to know that they were the real decision-makers around the Hollis Manse. It was suddenly quiet on the veranda. The only sounds were those of the sea, wind, and the calls of gulls.

Traynor slid his chair farther under the shade of the parasol and turned his attention to his companions. He directed his first comment to Deborah. "I'm not sure you need a detective as much as you need an addiction counselor."

Moore clearly took umbrage at this, and Traynor held up a hand, stopping him before he could speak. "I've got half a mind to hand back your check and leave you two to this circus. Are you sure your sister is missing, not hiding out?"

"She's missing, Ed. I know what you must think about my parents, but I can explain."

Moore butted in, voicing his opinion. "Deb, it's not your problem— it's theirs. They, not you, should be apologizing for their actions." He elevated himself several notches in Traynor's book.

She sat in silence for several seconds, her eyes lowered, staring at her hands, which were busy smoothing her skirt. Finally, she looked at Traynor and said, "Mindy had her disagreements with Mother and Daddy, but in spite of everything else, she and I were close. She'd call me weekly. I did warn you that you should talk with my parents *only* if it was absolutely necessary."

Traynor had no comeback—she was right. He turned to Byron Moore. "Where do you enter into this?"

"Along with being the family's attorney, I'm also a CPA and the CFO of Hollis International. In a nutshell, I manage the people who are responsible for the Hollis estate's finances."

"I see."

Moore continued, "I, too, want to know that Mindy is all right. I couldn't have stronger feelings for these girls if they were my own."

That statement could be taken many ways, and Traynor sure as hell didn't want to delve into that any deeper.

"Please forward all your future monetary requirements to me." He slid a business card across the table.

Traynor picked it up and tucked it away in his shirt pocket. "Fine. Let's get down to business." He turned so that he could see both of them without having to look back and forth. "Quite frankly, Deb, I believe someone has been lying—whether it was your sister or someone else is irrelevant. But, if an attractive young woman is looking to make it as an actress, I doubt she'd head for the San Fernando Valley. The type of films they make there usually come out solely on DVD. In fact, the valley's the Hollywood of the porn industry."

Deborah looked uncomfortable. "I know. But that's what she told me and Vincent backed her up."

"Who is Vincent?"

"Some guy she was dating out there . . ." Her face reddened.

"*Just* a boyfriend? The look on your face says there's more to it."

"I think she was sleeping with him. He's supposed to be some sort of movie producer."

Traynor noted her ruddy hue and thought her embarrassment over a sister sleeping with a man was a bit odd, when she herself carried a condom in her purse.

"Does it bother you that she's been sleeping with someone?"

"Heavens no. But to lower herself to sleeping with some so-called producer—that pisses me off more than it embarrasses me."

Traynor was starting to like Deborah, and her candidness made him all the more determined to help her. "Fair enough. That gives me a place to start looking. I need a list of all of her friends, both local and any you know of in LA or Simi Valley—as well as any addresses and phone numbers you have."

Deborah sniffled again, and Moore handed her a handkerchief. It looked as if it had never been used; Traynor couldn't stop from thinking that he probably carried it in case a damsel in distress needed something to blot her tears. Traynor thought it made him look like an ass-kisser and realized that he didn't like the man. A short time in the presence of Mr. Byron Moore, attorney at law, would be more than Traynor wanted. He believed that Moore probably felt the same about him and that neither would make it to the invitation list for the other's next backyard barbeque and beer bash.

Deborah said, "I'll get you something to write on."

Traynor didn't know why, but he expected her to go after it. As if some telepathic order had been sent, a young woman in a maid's uniform— a functional American maid's uniform, not one of those sexy French ones popular in sexual fantasies—appeared with the required tools: a flat, rectangular tablet computer. Traynor wondered just how many people were employed to keep the Hollises living in the manner to which they were accustomed.

Moore and Traynor sat in silence as she tapped the screen of the tablet. The silence finally got too loud. Traynor smiled at Moore. "How 'bout them Sox, huh?"

Moore looked shocked. Traynor fought to keep from laughing; obviously the corporate lawyer didn't do a lot of male bonding. "I'm sorry?"

"The Red Sox, they're a baseball team in Boston. . . . You might have heard of them?"

"Oh, of course, those Sox. What about them?"

Traynor was about to make some smartass remark, but Deborah stopped tapping the tablet and said, "There, that's done." She turned to the maid. "Anna would you go into my office and get the printout from the printer?"

Anna nodded and said, "Of course, Miss Deborah." It was the first time that Traynor had noticed any of the hired help address her in a formal matter. It brought out a different aspect of her personality . . . one he had heretofore not seen. In short time Anna returned, handing a sheet of paper to Deb.

"Thank you, Anna," Deborah said, and she then handed the sheet to Traynor. She turned to the maid and nodded, and the young woman left.

Traynor took the sheet and saw five names printed on it. He folded the sheet of paper and slid it into his shirt pocket.

"I'm sorry I don't have more than that," Hollis said.

"Actually, Deb, I've had cases where we had a lot less than this at the onset." He believed he'd gotten all he was going to get that day, so he stood. However before leaving, Traynor needed to get something out in the open. "I'll get on this right away," he said. "However, I feel it would be unethical if I didn't tell you both I'm not licensed in California. If you hired someone out there, you might get faster results—not to mention that if I have to go out there, less expensive ones. A local investigator will know the turf better."

Nevertheless Deborah seemed sure of herself when she said, "I want *you*, Ed. I want someone from around here, someone I can trust." Once again, she swept her hand around, encompassing the estate. "As you can see, expense is not an issue."

"I'll do what I can."

As he walked around the house, Traynor couldn't help but hope that Deborah Hollis's trust in him wasn't premature. But the fact that Buck had recommended him for the job was reassuring. It made him feel good that regardless of their personal situation, Buchanan still valued his abilities as a detective. Traynor hoped this case could help get things between Buck and him back to the way they were before they'd had their most serious disagreement.

Traynor walked slowly, analyzing what he'd learned that afternoon. That the Hollises were richer than he'd ever imagined was a given. Although how they stayed that way, what with Cyril's being smashed all the time, was at best a miracle. It was evident that despite her youthful appearance, Deborah Hollis was very likely an astute manager and businesswoman. Just how much influence Byron Moore had with the Hollises, Traynor had no clue. One thing was certain though: Moore was more than just hired help. As he turned the corner of the north wing and put the Atlantic Ocean at his back, Traynor began to think about the guy out front. Who was he? What was his function? Why did he have a nagging feeling that this guy probably knew more than anyone around this place?

His car pulled up and Traynor picked up the pace. It was time to get some answers.

Interviewers observe verbal and nonverbal responses to recognize whether an individual is being truthful or deceptive.
—*FM 3-19, Law Enforcement Investigations,*
January 2005, Department of the Army

3

The same fellow who had greeted him stood beside Traynor's car. The chauffer, if that's what he was, gave off an aura that immediately warned anyone not to screw with him. He was over six feet tall, with well-developed arms and pectoral muscles. There were several scars on his face that served as an additional testament to the violence he had no doubt seen and been a part of. Traynor couldn't help but wonder what this guy's position in the Hollis pecking order was. There was something about his demeanor that said he was more than a driver. Traynor held out his hand. "Ed Traynor."

The man gripped Traynor's hand firmly, but not with enough strength to make it an obvious test of wills. "Jack McMahon."

Traynor studied him for a second. There was a cop-like aspect to his stance. "My pleasure." Traynor glanced around for a second and asked, "What's your function around here?"

"I'm the *would-yuh.*"

"What in hell does a would-yuh do?"

"At least one hundred times a day someone asks, Jack, would yuh do this for me?" He grinned.

"Gotcha. Must make for long days."

"Officially, my job is security. Truth is, I'm mostly a chauffeur, a bodyguard, and the babysitter for the old man when he gets in his cups—and of late, that seems to be my main malfunction, if you get my drift. Manuel is the real security around here . . . He's the old man's primary babysitter."

"Babysitting the old souse must be a full-time job."

"There are worse jobs around this place. If nothing else, it pays well."

Traynor thought that McMahon had a point there—he could be cleaning bird shit off the walks. The thought made him glance at the sky, at the seagulls flying above. When he saw McMahon staring at him, he felt his face redden and said, "Nice day, huh?"

Jack chuckled. "I know you're not just passing the time of day. Before I moved here, I was a cop on the LAPD. Ask me what you want to know."

A man after Traynor's own heart—and it had been said that he was as subtle as a kick to the groin. "If you do a lot of their driving, you must know the family well."

"I can see that I'm not gonna put anything past you."

"Sometimes I amaze even myself." Traynor raised his arm and pumped his thumb toward the house. "They're quite the menagerie, aren't they?"

McMahon must have thought one or more of the Hollises could read lips, because he turned his back to the mansion before speaking. "Between you and me . . . the old man belongs in a nuthouse."

"It's easy to see that he's an alcoholic—not necessarily crazy," Traynor said. "I mean if he belongs in an institution, why isn't he in one?"

"Wouldn't do a damn bit of good. He'd get up one morning, buy the place, and turn it over to the patients."

"What about the wife?"

"That one's all bitch. She wears the Hollis money well." Even had he not said anything, the way his smile fled and his flinty eyes narrowed let Traynor know that *the* Mrs. Hollis was not one of McMahon's favorite people. He said, "Always treats me like I'm something she found on her shoe after walking across a barnyard."

"The girls?"

"Deb is the brains of the family, but she's okay. Not as personable as Mindy, but still treats everyone with . . . what's the word I'm looking for? Dignity, she treats everyone with dignity."

"So I gather that you find Mindy the most likable?"

McMahon didn't have to think about his answer. "Yeah. The way I see it, she only has one flaw."

"Which is?"

"Trust. She's too damned trusting. She'd give Willie Sutton a million bucks and ask him to deposit it in the bank for her."

Something didn't make sense to Traynor. If Mindy was so likeable and trusting, why was she the one who had problems with her father? He would need to delve deeper into that. "Seems to me that things are a little backward," he said.

"Right about now, if I was you, I'd be asking myself: why did she and the old man have problems?" Evidently, McMahon thought like Traynor—who quickly decided that McMahon had to be a genius.

He said, "It crossed my mind."

"Like I said, Mindy was trusting, but not stupid. If you let her down enough, she'd walk away and never look back."

"And she did . . ."

"Ole Cyril let her down one time too many. I'm told he went from idol to shit-bum in about two years," he said.

"Care to divulge your source?" Traynor asked.

"Nope, but you might ask Manuel—Manuel Vegas, the old man's right hand."

"I think that I saw him, but didn't have a chance to speak with him. What is his relationship with the girls?"

"Manuel's been here longer than I have. Sometimes I feel that he had a lot to do with raising those girls, possibly more than either Her Majesty or Cyril."

"How's he taking her disappearance?"

"That's hard to say. Manuel is one of those people who wouldn't say shit if he had a mouthful. Still, it wouldn't surprise me if he's concerned about her, but is keeping his mouth shut."

"The ideal employee."

"You got it. Just keeps quiet and does anything the family tells him."

"Like cleaning up after the old man?"

McMahon gave Traynor another of his lopsided grins. "Noticed that, did you?"

"How could I not?" Traynor recalled the way Manuel handled the drunken Hollis. "Seems to me, he has to deal with all the affluent drunks on the grounds. Does Manuel have an address?"

McMahon pointed at the mansion. "He has an apartment in the castle's basement. Not a bad deal: rent, food, and utilities are all included."

"I'd like to talk with him. I doubt I'll be able to do it here, though. Does he ever leave the estate—you know, hang out anywhere?"

"Well, nobody's perfect, right? Manuel likes the girls, though not the way you'd usually think of it. He's a voyeur, not a user. He gets Wednesday nights free and can usually be found down at the Golden Coconut."

Traynor knew the place—a strip joint across the border in Massachusetts. It was Friday, and if he was going to make any headway on this case, he couldn't wait five days to get Manuel alone. "That's the only time he leaves here?"

"On Saturday mornings, he usually runs into Portsmouth to do a few personal errands."

"Why didn't you tell me that?"

"You asked where he hung out. That's a lot different from where he goes." A true cop . . . Traynor was beginning to like this Jack McMahon.

"If I wanted to accidentally bump into Manuel, what time and where should I be tomorrow?"

"Around ten in the morning, I'd be in front of the post office. The first Saturday of each month, he sends a care package to his relatives on the island."

"The island?"

"I think he's Puerto Rican or maybe Dominican—one of those islands down there." He glanced at his watch. "Look, as much as I'd like to stand around chatting all day, I got things to do." He nodded toward the manse. "After all, they do pay my salary."

"I understand. I may want to talk with you again. In the meantime, if you come across anything that will help me find Mindy, call." Traynor gave him one of his cards, climbed into his Durango, and left.

Instead of old-fashioned legwork and long, patient research, the
PI simply visits an old friend, the computer hacker.
—*Private Eyes: A Writer's Guide To Private Investigators*

4

Traynor drove along Route 1B, following the twisting, narrow road through New Castle. Driving through the village was like driving through colonial New England. The settlement was as old as New Hampshire itself, and at one time, the main street had most likely been a narrow cart path. Expanding the thoroughfare to accommodate modern vehicles took away many of the front lawns, leaving nothing but a narrow gravel shoulder between the houses and the street. Through the narrow drives, the Piscataqua River was visible, revealing commercial fishing boats lined against piers. He wondered what the original occupants would think if they learned how much their once-humble property was now currently valued. He wound down out of the village and crossed over the causeway into Old Portsmouth. The street branched right, and Traynor drove through the city to I-95.

Forty-five minutes later, he was in Charley and Max's auto repair shop north of Manchester, in Hooksett.

Charley was in the office, and as usual, he was bent over a computer, oblivious to anything that responded to anything other than zeroes and ones. When Traynor entered, he intentionally slammed the door.

Charley heard the door bang shut and looked up, his eyes narrowed at the unwanted interruption. He was the antithesis of good health. He was anything but the image of computer hackers most people had. Now upward of fifty, Charley had jumped onboard the virtual express almost at the very beginning. He was about forty pounds north of where he should have been, and his thinning, long hair was unkempt, as usual. If Traynor didn't know that he was as ambivalent to women as he was about everything else nontechnical, he'd have thought Charley had that "morning after" look people joke about. The only way a woman would ever get his attention, though, would be to have a couple of gigabytes of RAM and a super hard drive.

Charley's scowl disappeared when he recognized Traynor. "Hey, Ed."

"It talks!"

Charley shook his head. "You know, Eddie, sometimes you're like my first wife."

"Really? How's that?"

"Like her, you're seldom photographed with your mouth closed."

"I used to wonder why every time I came in here there were no customers." Traynor aimed a thumb over his right shoulder. "After that, I'm not wondering about it anymore."

"So what brings you into my world?"

"This morning, as you might recall, I used an antiquated electronic instrument to call you." Traynor made a point of looking around as if seeking something. "You might have one. What was that thing that guy named Bell invented a few years back?"

Charley leaned back and chuckled. "I know you're technically challenged, Ed. It's called a telephone."

Traynor snapped his fingers. "That's it. One of these days, I'll get caught up on all this newfangled stuff."

"As computer and technology illiterate as you are, how in the hell do you expect to make it as a detective in an electronic world?"

"That's why I have you, old buddy." Trading barbs was an integral part of their relationship; if Traynor didn't do it, Charley was sure to think something was seriously wrong. Their ritual observed, Traynor got down to business. "Okay, enough BS. You find anything?"

Charley handed him several printed sheets of paper. "I got what I could on short notice—her social was a big help. There's her address, place of employment, driver's license, and anything else I could find."

Traynor scanned the sheets, looking for anything new. There wasn't much he didn't already know. "This is it?"

"Pretty much."

"Define 'pretty much.'"

"I Googled . . ."

"Be careful with that stuff, googling at people could get you arrested." Traynor's joke didn't register. "Google . . . it's like ogle—you know, staring or peeping?"

"Funny. Pathetic, but funny. Anyhow, I Googled her name, found nothing new. Then I got hold of a friend of mine who lives out in Silicon Valley. She . . ."

"She? All right, Charley! You have actually gotten to the point where you've learned there are two genders."

"Screw you, Ed. May I continue?"

"Go ahead. I'll try to control myself."

"Sarah, my friend, gave me what I needed to hack into the LAPD computers . . ."

"Really? What did you find?"

Charley picked up his ever-present bottle of soda and sipped from it. "I came across an interesting tidbit in the LA papers. They got a Jane Doe out there." He paused.

"And?"

"It's pretty brutal."

"Charley, tell me what you know for crying out loud."

"What really caught my attention were the similarities to Elizabeth Short, who was mutilated and murdered in 1947. They dubbed her the Black Dahlia."

"Okay."

"I just found it very interesting. You got a missing New England girl who went out to LA to live and fell out of sight. Short was from Medford, MA and went out there to make it. She was found in a vacant lot. I won't go into detail, but she was cut up pretty bad. The case was a real sensation back in its day. This Jane Doe was found in an undeveloped area where the Reagan Freeway runs through Santa Susana Pass—the entrance to Simi Valley."

Suddenly Traynor became interested. Deborah had told him that Mindy was living in Simi Valley. "When did they find her?"

Charley took the papers from Traynor's hand and leafed through them. When he found the sheet he was looking for, he passed it back. The date was just under a week ago. Traynor's heart sank.

"You find out where they buried her?"

"To the best of my knowledge, they haven't yet. Most likely they got her on ice someplace. Refrigeration, Ed. It's another modern day invention you may have heard of."

Traynor gave him a light tap on the jaw. "I got one more job for you."

"Okay."

"Find me a flight to LA."

Nonverbal responses will either support or contradict the spoken word.
—FM 3-19, Law Enforcement Investigations

5

That night, Traynor called Deborah Hollis, explained what he'd learned, and got her immediate approval for the trip. Before hanging up she said, "I'm going to call in a favor or two—if they haven't buried or cremated that woman, I want you to look at her."

Then Traynor called Charley. "You get me a flight?"

"Yeah, Jesus, airfares have skyrocketed, Ed."

Fortunately, Traynor didn't have to worry about that. "When do I leave?"

"One twenty-five in the afternoon, tomorrow. Boston to Burbank via New York and San Francisco. With the intermediate stops, you'll arrive around ten at tomorrow night left coast time. Your fare is almost 300 bucks."

"First class?"

"Economy."

Traynor shrugged his shoulders. "What the hell, Hollis can afford it."

On Saturday morning Traynor was perched in front of the post office, sipping from a cup of takeout coffee and doing his best not to look like a vagrant or a stalker.

Manuel was obviously a creature of habit. Traynor couldn't have been in place more than fifteen minutes when a Lincoln limousine pulled up with Jack McMahon at the wheel. The "would-yuh" made it a point to ignore Traynor as Manuel stepped from the backseat and walked around to the rear of the car. The trunk popped open, and he removed three medium-sized packages.

Traynor tried to remain inconspicuous as he watched him stack the boxes and walk toward the entrance. It was a waste of effort. Manuel's head was cocked to the side, and the packages blocked his view of anything to his left—including Traynor. The door closed behind him, and Traynor glanced back at the car. McMahon beckoned him over. The side window slid down and McMahon said, "He'll mail those packages and then head for the Funky Fox restaurant."

"I know it."

"I'm heading back to the estate . . . He'll call when he wants a ride back."

"Thanks."

Traynor stepped back onto the curb, waved, and watched the Lincoln pull away from the curb, quickly merging into the traffic. Traynor waited for a couple of seconds and then started on the three-block stroll to the restaurant. The Funky Fox was a retro place—its décor could be described as 1960s chaos, and the inside looked like a flea market, with the wares hanging from the walls. At first glance, one would call it a dive—and by most standards, maybe it was. However, Traynor thought, that it had the three most important features of a successful low-scale restaurant: the food was above average, the portions were large, and the prices were inexpensive.

It took Traynor less than ten minutes to get there. The Fox was primarily a breakfast place, and on weekend mornings the line stretched out the door and onto the sidewalk. He must have been just ahead of the rush, because in less than five minutes, a table opened up near the door and Traynor grabbed it. Two or three minutes later, Manuel walked in. He stood by the entrance, searching the interior for a place to sit, but there were none to be found.

Manuel was obviously a clothes horse; even on his day off, he wore a black suit, white shirt, and tie. His indigo hair was slicked with some type of oil, and it glistened in the morning sun. Traynor motioned to him and indicated one of the empty seats at his table. "I don't mind sharing if you don't."

Manuel shrugged and sat down. He stared at him for a second and said, "You're the man Ms. Deborah hired to find Ms. Mindy."

"That's right. I was sitting at the table yesterday when you helped your boss into the house."

His face reddened. "I'm sorry you saw Mr. Hollis like that."

"I don't know what Hollis pays you, but I'll bet it isn't enough for you to have to make excuses for him." Traynor offered him his hand. "Ed Traynor."

For a moment, Manuel hesitated—Traynor assumed he was surprised that someone would want to shake hands with a lowly house servant. However, it didn't take him long to get over the shock. "I'm pleased to meet you." He released Traynor's hand and sat back. He appeared to be assessing the situation. "This isn't a coincidence, is it?"

"No, Manuel, it isn't. If I'm going to find Ms. Mindy, I need to know as much as possible about her. Who she hangs with, the type of places she goes, does she party, things like that."

"I don't know if I should tell you anything."

"If you're worried about Ms. Deborah, don't be. She knows that I'll probably be talking to everyone on the staff."

Traynor placed his cell phone on the table. "I'll make you a deal, okay?"

Manuel stared at the phone, then at Traynor—his eyes piercing and brows narrowed. "What kind of deal?"

"You use that phone to call Ms. Deborah. If she says it's okay to talk to me, you tell me what I need to know. She says no, I buy you breakfast and we go our separate ways."

He seemed to ponder the offer. "The family hired you?"

"Ms. Deborah did. She's very concerned about her sister."

Manuel seemed to come to a decision. He pushed the cell phone forward and leaned back. His face suddenly looked younger than before, and Traynor realized that this was the first time he'd seen him at ease. He said, "I suppose one could say that it's my duty to answer your questions."

A server approached the table. She had more piercings than a barroom dartboard. Silver balls and studs lined both ears, and there was a small silver ring in each corner of her lips. She dropped two menus in the center of the table and said, "Coffee?"

Traynor nodded. Manuel, ever the proper gentleman, said, "Yes, please."

When she turned away, Traynor returned his attention to Manuel. "Tell me about Mindy. According to Deborah, her relationship with her father was, at best, strained."

"She's the youngest child and grew up in the shadow of her sister. All the family's attention goes to Ms. Deborah. She's the rising star."

Traynor soon came to the realization that Manuel was very well spoken, and most likely highly intelligent. But then, he would have to be if he wanted to survive in the Hollis menagerie. "How did she cope?"

"By rebelling . . . She would do anything to get attention."

"Mindy walked on the wild side?"

Manuel didn't have to think about his answer. "Very. She was the party animal in the family—boys, booze, drugs, anything went. Then in college, she got serious about becoming an actress. She told me that she was going to be the biggest and best in the movies. She also said she was going to do it on her own without help from Mr. Hollis."

"That's why she went west?"

"Most likely. The Hollises are a big name on the East Coast, but not so big out there."

"When you say she got serious, do you mean she went . . ." The right phrase eluded him, so Traynor settled for the first that came to mind. ". . . clean and sober?"

"For the most part. She'd still party occasionally, but not like she did when she was younger."

The server returned, and when she banged the coffee mugs on the table, some slopped over the sides. "You know what you want?" she asked. The early-morning sun reflected off a stud in her tongue. Traynor ordered a ham and cheese omelet, and Manuel ordered eggs over easy, bacon, home fries, and toast. She jotted their orders down and left.

When she'd once again disappeared, Manuel said, "I don't know how much more I can tell you. I'm just one of the household help—invisible to them, until they need me."

Traynor studied Manuel. When you've spent as much time investigating people as he had, you develop a sense of when people are lying to you, and more importantly, when they're holding something back. Traynor felt that Manuel fell into the second category. For some reason, Traynor got the feeling that being a rich asshole's right-hand man was, for want of a better way of describing it, a cover. During four years as a Marine and twenty as a police officer, he had encountered very few people in the physical shape Manuel was in. Up close, it was evident that the suit he wore hid a muscular, wiry frame, and he was not as old as Traynor had expected.

Manuel met his stare with an unflinching one of his own. It was not the type of behavior one expected from a man who made his living kowtowing to a bunch of spoiled, rich people.

Traynor sipped his coffee, set the mug on the table, and said, "Why do I get the feeling that you aren't exactly what you want people to think you are?"

Manuel never battered an eye. A knowing smile spread across his face, and he said, "You got me."

"I do?"

"Yeah, I'm really a spy on a mission to weaken the US government by being a professional codependent to a bunch of drunken millionaires who own businesses that cater to the defense industry."

"Really . . . how's that working out?"

Another smile and Traynor realized that he liked Manuel. "Not so hot. Seagulls keep interfering—people feed the damned things too much."

Traynor was still laughing when the waitress returned and slid their breakfasts in front of them. She walked away, then returned with a steaming carafe and topped off their coffee. "You guys all set?"

"Nothing more for me," Traynor answered.

Manuel nodded, which she apparently took to mean that he too was fine.

———————

Traynor went from the meeting with Manuel to his apartment. He grabbed his carry-on luggage and arrived at the gate fifteen minutes prior to boarding. Jack McMahon was standing there. He waved to him.

"What brings you here?" Traynor wondered if maybe Deborah didn't trust him as much as he thought she did and had sent her staff to check up on him.

"I convinced Deborah to let me go with you."

Traynor's face gave away his question.

"I know the area, still have contacts with the LAPD—and I'm licensed to carry a gun out there. Deborah agreed that it might make the job easier. Then there's a couple other things . . ."

As he listened, Traynor noted that McMahon was the only employee who dropped the Ms. title when he spoke of Deborah Hollis. He decided to check into that at a later time. He asked, "What might they be?"

"First, Mindy knows me. You're a stranger and she may not feel very comfortable talking with you. Then . . ."

Traynor knew what he was getting at, but decided to let him say it first.

McMahon said, "If the worst has happened and we have to ID her body, we won't have to rely on a two-year-old photograph."

"Welcome aboard," Traynor said.

"By the way, they need you at the counter."

"Why? I already have my boarding pass."

"You've been upgraded to first class. You're representing the Hollises now."

"I'm mildly surprised that they don't have their own jet."

"They do, but since it's only the two of us and we're just hired help, it's cheaper to fly us commercial, even first class."

"Well, all things considered, I guess it's better than being in economy with the riffraff."

A guilty person['s] . . . voice may change pitch or waver
and the speed of his response is usually drawn out as he takes additional time
to formulate his response.

—*FM 3-19, Law Enforcement Investigations*

6

Traynor stared out the window and watched the ground fall away. He settled back into the comfortable seat, thinking that if one had to fly, first class was the way to go. McMahon was in the aisle seat, sipping on a beer. "This the first time you've gone back?" Traynor asked.

"What?"

"Is this your first trip back to LA since you left?"

"Yeah."

Traynor probed further. "Why'd you quit?"

For several seconds, McMahon seemed reluctant to answer. But then he took a drink and said, "I needed a change of scenery." McMahon's demeanor told him that there was more to it than he was letting on.

Traynor changed tack. They had a five-hour flight ahead of them, and there would be plenty of time to return to the subject. "Did Mindy have any friends in LA?"

"Not that I'm aware of. But she's young and many kids still believe California is Mecca. They think it's where they'll find romance, adventure, and success. Lord knows, I've met hundreds of them—kids on the prowl for the fast life."

"From what I've learned so far, she doesn't seem like the type to be easily impressed or led."

"She isn't—at least not in the way you usually think of it. But she still had what I thought were unrealistic expectations."

Traynor turned his attention back to the window and studied the billowing tops of the clouds. They looked like majestic mountains against the bright blue sky. They looked as if you could walk on them.

"You have a plan?" McMahon asked.

Traynor faced him. "A plan?"

"How you want to go about finding her?"

For the first time, it dawned on Traynor that he had no plan whatsoever.

"I guess we'll just touch base with the local police and hope they lead us in the right direction. I've learned that they have a Jane Doe in the morgue—maybe we can get a lead there."

He chuckled. "Not much of a strategy."

"No," Traynor replied, "it isn't."

"I think I can help."

Traynor turned back to the window again. After a few seconds, McMahon took a magazine out of the pouch on the seat-back in front of him and thumbed through the pages. He closed it and put it back. Without fanfare, he said, "I got my ass in trouble a few years back."

"Oh?"

"I used excessive force on a perp."

"Been there, done that."

McMahon gazed intently at his companion. Traynor began to feel that McMahon's eyes were lasers burning a hole through him. He felt compelled to offer an explanation. "I was a New Hampshire state cop.

We got a call about some redneck asshole who'd been terrorizing his family. When it became evident that he'd been sexually abusing his fifteen-year-old daughter . . . I lost it."

"Was it worth it?"

That made Traynor pause as he pondered his answer. "Yeah, every second of it."

"Must have been pretty bad."

Traynor remembered the incident vividly. "The perp had been battering his wife for years, which I didn't like, but I could take it."

Traynor knew that McMahon was assessing him. When Jack said, "You look like you can handle yourself in a scrape."

"I do okay . . . I don't usually start them, but I usually finish them. I walk away the victor more times than not."

McMahon nodded, indicating that he was satisfied with Traynor's answer. "Sorry I interrupted, finish your story."

"We responded to a domestic abuse call, and I walked in on the sonuvabitch molesting his fifteen-year-old daughter. I exploded and beat him senseless in front of his family. It wasn't nice."

McMahon seemed to ponder that. "My story isn't much different," he said. "The captain felt it would look better if I resigned rather than got fired."

They didn't say much for the rest of the flight.

When the police arrived on the scene, they found the body of
a young woman who had been bisected.

—Crime.about.com

7

No matter where Traynor traveled, Sunday mornings felt the same: slow and laid-back. He stood on the small balcony outside his hotel room and listened to the quiet. It was just seven in the morning, warm with low humidity, and the only sounds were those of an occasional car passing by and the chirping of birds. It would have been truly beautiful if it hadn't been for the air quality. Smog hung over the mountains like a dirty gray blanket. Bad enough—but when the southern California smog mixed with the smoke of who knew how many brush fires, the result was a caustic atmosphere that burned Traynor's nose and eyes. The smell of burned wood and airborne ash permeated everything.

His phone rang and he went inside to pick it up. "Traynor."

"It's me," McMahon said. "I took a chance you'd be up. I know from experience that it usually takes a couple of days to adjust to the three-hour difference in time."

"My biological clock thinks it's ten in the morning," Traynor said. "I've been thinking that since you know the area, I'll leave the itinerary up to you. What's our game plan?"

"I'm going to make a few calls. Maybe I can call in some markers."

"Okay. What can I do in the meantime?"

"Hang tight, it won't take me but a half hour or so. Why don't you grab something to eat?"

"I'll be here. Call as soon as you get done."

McMahon called forty-five minutes later. "Meet me out front." His voice sounded terse, not at all happy.

"What's up?"

"We're going to be given a tour of the LA morgue. I got us in to see the Jane Doe."

"How'd you pull that off?"

The line was silent for a moment. McMahon finally said, "I called an old acquaintance who told me this Jane Doe has an unusual tattoo. They didn't release the info to the public. They wanted to weed out serious suspects from the usual array of nutcases who confess to every crime in the news."

"Okay, how does that tie in to Mindy Hollis?"

"Mindy had a tat that could be considered unusual."

"These days all the kids have tattoos—what does it take for one to be considered unusual?"

"Either way, *the* Mrs. Hollis would have shit a razor blade if she knew one of *her* girls had gotten tattooed. So Mindy had it in a place where her mother wouldn't see it."

Strange visions passed through Traynor's mind. "Where was it?"

"Wait and see."

———

McMahon's contact on the LAPD met them in the parking lot. He introduced her to Traynor as Angela Engle. It was obvious to Traynor that there was history between McMahon and Engle. He wondered if they'd been in a relationship—they made a good-looking pair. Traynor caught himself studying the two of them. She was tall—five eight or nine—but shorter than McMahon, who Traynor estimated to be just over six feet. Her light brown hair had a slight reddish tint and was cut short. Like McMahon, she obviously spent a great deal of time outdoors, and her face and forearms were tanned. The edges of their eyes showed small crow's feet from staring into the sun too long and like his brown eyes, her blue ones were piercing. It was easy to visualize them boring through a suspect until they got the confession they sought.

She was in uniform, brogans, and a short-sleeve shirt on which she wore sergeant's stripes. If anyone could look good in a police uniform, Angela Engle looked good. More importantly, Traynor decided, she had to be good at her job. Even in the enlightened second millennium, police departments were still testosterone-driven paramilitary organizations; women didn't make sergeant unless they were better than average—a lot better. Law enforcement at the street level was still a man's domain. There was a hardness about her that would make anyone think twice before taking her on, and for some reason, whenever she looked at McMahon it was especially evident. The way she looked at McMahon bordered on hostile, and Traynor got the impression that she could hold her own against any man.

McMahon approached her with a nervous smile. She looked at him for a split second and then turned away as if he were a piece of trash blowing past. She seemed to relax and get whatever angered her under control. She was the epitome of professional. "I'll warn you guys up front," Engle said. "What you're about to see is not nice."

Traynor's sensors went off. How bad was this corpse that even she was forewarning two experienced police officers? He began to steel himself for the worst-case scenario.

Over the years, he'd been in a lot of morgues, and he'd figured that they all must have been designed by the same architect. This one, like all the others in his experience, was a functional place—a meat locker for the unfortunate—with cold tile floors and a wall covered with refrigerated drawers. The morgue air had a dry, artificial quality to it—similar to the inside of an airplane.

The attendant was a big guy, taller than Traynor's six one and a good fifteen inches thicker through his midsection—and it wasn't a healthy fifteen inches. After Engle introduced them, she stood off to the side as he led Traynor and McMahon deeper into the morgue. The attendant pulled out one of the drawers and paused before pulling the sterile sheet back. "This one ain't pretty," he said as he slid the sheet down the body.

It took all Traynor's strength not to turn away. The corpse was that of a young Caucasian woman, but that was about all that was discernable. Whoever had done this was one sick bastard. They'd cut the corners of her mouth back to the hinges of her jaw—leaving her to go through eternity with a perpetual grin. Her face was battered so badly he doubted that her mother would recognize her. He became enraged. "What sadistic . . ."

Before Traynor could complete the sentence, the attendant chimed in. "This ain't the worst part. They cut her in half, sliced off her breasts, and removed all of her organs. You want to see?"

"That's not necessary," he said as he turned to McMahon. "Is it?"

"Normally, I'd agree. However, she's been battered so badly I can't be sure if it's her or not. I need to look closer."

"Closer! Christ, man, haven't you seen enough?"

McMahon said to the attendant, "I need to see the inside of her left thigh."

"What?"

McMahon stood tense with clenched fists. "Just show me her fucking thigh."

The attendant slid the blanket down past her trunk. Her body must have shifted when the drawer had been opened; the upper and lower halves did not line up exactly. Her stomach and abdomen, lacking internal organs to support them, had sunken inward and some type of white cloth had been shoved into the cavity—a corner of it was visible along the jagged line where she'd been severed in half.

"You'd need a chainsaw to do something like that," Traynor said.

The attendant glanced up at his fury. "The ME thinks whoever did this used a bone saw to sever the body . . ."

"A bone saw? You saying a doctor did this?"

The attendant shook his head. "The ME's almost certain this killer has more knowledge of human anatomy than some neighborhood butcher. The cuts are too precise—if I had to guess, I'd say they were more surgical." As the attendant continued to move the sheet down to the victim's thigh, Traynor looked at Engle. Like McMahon she was heavily in cop mode.

McMahon stepped forward. He made a quick inspection, snatched the sheet out of the attendant's hand, and drew it back over the victim's body. His face was ashen, and for the briefest of moments, his guard fell and he looked distressed. "It's her." He stormed past Engle and out the door.

Traynor paused for a second, watched him leave, and then curiosity got the best of him. He grabbed the sheet, studied her thigh for a few seconds, and then lowered it again. There was a tattoo of black orchids circling her upper thigh. He looked toward the door and saw Engle's face. Her tan complexion was tinted red, and he was certain it was not from embarrassment. Her eyes were narrow and her mouth a tight, straight line. While he'd been surprised by McMahon's knowledge of a tattoo in such an intimate location, she was pissed. Traynor hoped, for his sake, she didn't get McMahon alone until she had cooled down. Several times in his life, he'd seen people with a desire to inflict physical pain on someone, and when Engle glared at McMahon, she had that look.

Some minutes later, Engle, McMahon, and Traynor were back in the parking lot. Without saying a word, she stomped over to her police cruiser and leaned against the front fender, arms crossed as she glared at McMahon.

"Well," McMahon said to Traynor, "I guess you'll be on the next plane back."

"I think I'll stick around for a couple of days," Traynor said.

"You did what you were hired to do and found Mindy."

"Deborah paid for a few more days of my time . . ." Traynor paused, wanting to avoid saying the wrong thing.

He needn't have worried; McMahon seemed to be tuned into the same station. "Any sonuvabitch who'd do that to another human being needs to be brought down."

"So," Traynor said, "where do we start?"

"The boyfriend?"

"Okay." Traynor stood in place and stared at him.

"What?"

"The tattoo."

"What about it?"

"How'd you know where to look?"

McMahon walked away, without looking back.

"McMahon!" Traynor followed after him. "Goddamn it, Jack, what are you keeping from me?"

Suddenly, McMahon spun on Traynor, leaning forward and hunching his shoulders. The effect was so aggressive that Traynor braced for an attack. Suddenly McMahon relaxed. "We were lovers for a while."

"And?"

"That's it. She ended it and I moved on."

"Okay. Are you going back to Portsmouth?"

He looked at Traynor as if he were from another dimension. "*No fucking way*. At least not until we bring down the sadistic bastard who did that."

"Ever feel like killing some motherfucker?" Traynor asked.

"Before now? No, never."

"Me neither." He looked at the morgue entrance. "At least not since that one time when I was a cop—then I saw that . . ."

McMahon's jaw torqued tight and his eyes narrowed, like gun slits on a tank. Traynor had seen that look before. It was the look an enraged man gets when he's about to kill something—anything. He glared at the mountains to the north and said nothing.

Traynor nodded toward Engle and said, "I think you got other problems, Jack."

He followed Traynor's gaze. "Shit."

"Why is she so pissed?"

"We were married. Divorced before I went back east." He didn't wait for a reply, which was good because Traynor didn't have one. He was too busy wondering how many more goddamned surprises were in store for him.

Traynor held back and watched Engle glare at McMahon as he walked toward her. Her arms were wrapped tightly around her chest. She shifted slightly and stared off at the mountains in the distance. Traynor heard her say, "I see you still let the small head rule the large one." Without looking at McMahon, she said, "Why is it that you insist on acting like a life support system for your penis?"

"Jesus Christ, Angela . . ."

"She was a kid, Jack. What did you do? Regale her with stories of your daring adventures on the LAPD?"

Traynor went over, breaking up their domestic dispute by leaning against the car. "You want I should let you two alone to kill one another?"

Engle unfolded her arms and rocked away from the cruiser. "If I'm going to kill anyone, it will be somebody worth killing." Her demeanor suddenly changed, returning to stoic professionalism. The metamorphosis was more dramatic than switching on a light in a dark room. Her complexion returned to its normal ruddy tan, and her shoulders and arms relaxed. "You want to see where we found her?"

"The crime scene?" Traynor inquired.

"The dump scene. We're certain she was killed somewhere else. There wasn't a drop of blood where she was found."

"You have any idea where she was murdered?" McMahon asked.

"The closest we can narrow it down is to someplace west of the Rocky Mountains," Engle said. She walked around her car, stood by the door, and looked at them across the roof. "Follow me in your vehicle. By the time we get there, my shift will be over. The scene is closer to my precinct, and I'm not about to drive back here to drop you guys off."

Traynor exhaled with relief. The last thing he wanted was to be in close quarters with her and McMahon—especially with Engle wearing a nine millimeter pistol.

In the car, McMahon seemed distracted; his knuckles were white where they curled around the steering wheel. After several minutes passed, it was evident that he was not about to break the silence. So Traynor did. "Can I ask you a personal question?"

McMahon looked at him. "If I said *no* would it stop you?"

"No . . ."

"So ask," he said like a man resigned to facing execution.

"If you and Engle are divorced, why's she so pissed about you and Mindy?"

He stared at the road and Traynor was about to accept the fact that he was not going to answer the question when McMahon said, "She still loves me."

"That's it?"

"I still love her too."

"So why the divorce?"

He inhaled deeply and then exhaled. "There were a couple of reasons. First, she caught me . . ."

"Screwing around?"

"More than once."

"Okay, I can understand her reaction."

"We could have survived that," McMahon replied. "But, the second reason is the real killer."

"What can be more damning that adultery?"

"We were a toxic couple—we love each other as much as any man and woman can, but for some reason we mix like gasoline vapor and a lit match."

That brought a picture to Traynor's mind—that of his own brother, John, and his wife, Jo-Ann. They were as toxic a relationship as he could think of.

The Black Dahlia case was never solved and is still considered open.

—Author's note

8

They followed Engle to the 101, got off in Woodland Hills, and turned onto Topanga Canyon Boulevard. They passed by a couple of upscale malls and then things changed: expensive retail outlets gave way to three or four miles of mom and pop shops and restaurants. They were about a mile north of the Los Angeles city limits when she turned onto the Reagan Freeway, stopped halfway up the grade that climbed through Santa Susana Pass, and turned on the light-bar on top of her police car. She got out and waited on the shoulder behind her cruiser until they joined her.

"About one hundred yards up there," she said. Without another word she began climbing through the brush and rocks.

McMahon and Traynor followed her, weaving their way up the sandy slope through scrub brush and small boulders. It was difficult for Traynor to make his way up, and he marveled at how easily Engle scaled the steep slope. She was obviously experienced at climbing Los Angeles's myriad hills. She stopped about a quarter of the way up the incline and waited for them to catch up.

Reaching her, Traynor took a second to look at the view. A layer of smog and smoke sprawled across the San Fernando Valley, creating a mesmerizing, albeit ghostly, panorama. He thought that it looked like an artist's rendering. He let his gaze drift south along Topanga Canyon Boulevard and watched the cars snaking their way through the tangle of traffic. To his left, he saw a secondary road twisting away from the freeway. "Where's that go?" he asked.

"That's the Santa Susana Pass Road. Before the freeway was built, that was the only way into Simi Valley from Topanga Canyon," Engle said. She pointed to a solitary building. "Fifty years ago this area was nothing but boulders and brush. That's all that's left of the old Spahn Movie Ranch."

It meant nothing to Traynor, but he turned to see what she was pointing out anyway.

"The Spahn Movie Ranch is where they made a lot of B westerns after World War II. *The Lone Ranger* TV show and a lot of movies were filmed here in Simi Valley." She moved her arm to the right to show him a sprawling view of a bedroom community. His first impression was that it consisted of nothing but light brown houses with dark brown roofs.

Traynor turned his attention back to the immediate area, studying the stunted brush, sand, and boulders that covered the valley below. "When I was a kid, I thought the entire west looked like this," he said. "At least that's the way it always looked in the movies and television."

"It isn't all pretty," Engle commented. "There's a dark side to Santa Susana. People around here love to talk about the Reagan Presidential Library and the movies that were filmed here. But they don't like to talk about the other stuff."

She had piqued his curiosity. "What other stuff?"

"In 1969, the Manson Family lived on the movie ranch. During that time, they killed Sharon Tate and the LaBiancas." She nodded toward the San Fernando Valley. "And down there is the porn capital of the world."

"So I've been told."

Engle turned and got back to the business at hand. "Part of the corpse was found over here."

"A part of it?" Traynor asked.

She motioned for him to follow and wove her way through some small bushes, then around a medium-sized boulder. "A couple of hikers found her torso here. The other half was about ten or fifteen yards over there." She pointed up the slope. "The scene was clean. No blood and no trace evidence—not even a footprint. It was like she'd been dropped from the sky."

That got his attention. "Maybe they wiped their tracks."

"That's doubtful. There'd still be traces of where they smeared everything with a bush or whatever."

Traynor noticed McMahon intently studying the area. "Be awfully hard to get up here and back without leaving some kind of sign," he said.

"Not if you have access to a chopper," Engle answered.

"Are you saying," Traynor queried her, "they dropped her from a helicopter?"

"They probably hovered a few feet off the ground—otherwise we'd have found impact marks."

"If that's the case," he commented, "why separate the parts?"

"Maybe to throw us a curve. It's the only thing I can think of that makes sense." She glanced at her watch. "You guys seen enough? I'd like to go home and take a long, hot shower."

"Need your back washed?" McMahon asked.

Traynor couldn't believe he'd said that. He gawked at McMahon for a few seconds before turning his attention to Engle. She snapped her head in McMahon's direction and glared at him; it was evident that all he had to do was bat an eye the wrong way and she'd shoot him. She settled for saying, "If I do, you'll be the last person I'll call." She pushed the bushes aside and stomped away.

"You're one silver-tongued devil," Traynor said.

"Yeah, but any fool can see she's still crazy about me."

"Judging from her body language, she's living proof why the primary suspects in most homicides are spouses and ex-spouses."

McMahon laughed. "You probably got that right. Let's be cops and go talk to the roommate."

By the time McMahon and Traynor stumbled down the steep hill and reached their car, Engle had pulled onto the freeway and was headed over the rise. They stood on the shoulder until she disappeared.

"What you think?" McMahon asked.

"I think that someone with a lot of money perpetrated this . . . choppers don't come cheap . . ."

"I thought that too. But I'm not talking about that."

"Then what are you talking about?" Traynor asked.

McMahon nodded in the direction Engle had driven.

Traynor saw where McMahon was looking and said, "Oh, her. I think she's a lot more woman than I could handle."

McMahon sounded wistful when he said, "She was for me too."

*. . . often times what the suspect "does not" say is as important
as what he "does" say.*
—FM 3-19, Law Enforcement Investigations

9

Simi Valley looked and felt like hundreds of other south California suburban towns. There was no business district to speak of—just one strip mall after another, interspersed with small businesses and then subdivision after subdivision. They followed Los Angeles Avenue, which was as close to a main street as there was in the city, going west. Palm and yucca trees lined the streets and brought back memories of Traynor's days at Camp Pendleton.

McMahon was familiar with the area and didn't even have to consult a map to find Simon Street, a small artery off Sequoia. He stopped in front of a tan split-level and peered across Traynor's chest, studying the front door.

"What's the name we want?"

"Doerr, Celia Doerr."

He notched the gear lever into park. "This must be the place."

Traynor glanced around. "Riiight. Where are we anyhow?"

McMahon gave him a light tap on his left biceps. "Hell," he said, "everyone knows that. We *are* where we *are*."

"Three million comedians out of work," Traynor said, "and I got to get the reincarnation of Henny Youngman. Don't quit your day job, okay?"

"Take my wife . . ." McMahon said. ". . . Please," quoting one of the old comedians more famous jokes.

Traynor glared at him and got out of the car. However, he couldn't help but smile when McMahon came around from the street side, giggling at his own stupid joke.

Traynor rang the bell. After a few moments of silence, he wondered if anyone was home, but then the door opened and a woman who looked to be in her late thirties or early forties stood before him. "Celia Doerr?" he asked.

"Yes, can I help you?"

"I hope so. I represent Mindy Hollis's family."

"Represent them?" Her words were directed to Traynor; however, she stared past him. He knew she was studying Jack McMahon, whose demeanor was probably transmitting *cop* to her. Her gaze returned to Traynor. "What do you mean?"

He pointed over his shoulder with his right thumb. "Her family hired my colleague and myself to find her."

"I don't know if I can help you. I haven't seen her in weeks."

"We know," Traynor said. "We also know where she is."

"Thank heaven, I was worried."

Her mouth said one thing; her cold eyes and expression something else. Traynor went for the kill. "She's in the morgue."

A sudden transformation swept across Celia Doerr's face. Her mouth opened and her eyes widened. "The morgue?" Traynor watched her closely and decided that Celia Doerr was acting as if she was surprised—and it wasn't good acting. He was certain that she'd already been aware of Mindy's death.

"Yeah," McMahon said from behind Traynor, "the morgue. It seems Mindy went out and got herself dead."

Doerr took a step back. "I can't believe that."

"Believe it," Traynor said, studying her closely and looking for any indication that she was shocked by the news. "Look, it's awkward standing here on your porch—can we come in?"

"Of course. Forgive me, but the neighborhood has been infested with door-to-door evangelists of late. Apparently, God told them Simi Valley is in need of salvation."

When she stepped back, Traynor walked through the door into a comfortably furnished, but by no means lavish, living room. There was a small fireplace that he doubted had ever seen a fire. On the mantle were pictures, one of which was of Mindy. Doerr led them to the couch and when they were comfortable, asked, "Would you care for something to drink?"

"I'm fine," Traynor answered.

"Me too," McMahon said.

"Ms. Doerr . . ." Traynor said.

"Call me Celia, please."

"Okay, Celia. I'm intrigued. You seem—"

"Kind of old to be Mindy's roommate?"

Her candor surprised him. "Yes."

"We worked together at a place in the valley. She lived in a hotel and her funds were running out. I know how tough life can be when you're young and far from home and offered to rent her a room. It's so easy for a young woman to get into trouble out here."

Mindy's fate was ample proof of that. Traynor glanced at McMahon to see if he wanted to ask anything, but he seemed content to let him lead. "Was she seeing anyone?"

Doerr tensed and Traynor knew she was debating whether or not to tell them something. "Well, I hate to tell tales . . ."

"Celia, Mindy is beyond being hurt." He nodded toward McMahon. "My friend and I want to see whoever murdered her brought to justice." *Or*, he thought, *just plain brought down*.

"Well, there was this one guy. However, she was very secretive about it."

"Secretive?" Traynor reached into his coat pocket and took out his notebook and pen. "Can you be a bit more specific?"

"That's the problem—I can't. She never brought him here."

"Did she ever mention his name?"

"No, that's what I'm talking about. Mindy always went to him and sometimes I wouldn't see her for days."

"Did he ever pick her up at work or someplace where you might have seen him?" McMahon asked.

Doerr seemed surprised that he had interjected himself into the interview. "Well, I did see her get into a car once, but I can't be sure it was his."

"What type of car?" Traynor asked.

"One of those expensive sports cars. I think it was European."

"A European sports car," McMahon repeated, "so we're probably looking at somebody with money."

That made sense to Traynor—after all, Mindy was accustomed to being around people with money. Lots of money.

"Where did she meet this guy?" Traynor asked.

"I can't be sure, but she spent a lot of time at a club."

"What sort of club?"

"A health club—although I think it's a stretch to call any club with a bar a *health* club." She pulled open a small drawer on the table beside her chair and took out a book of matches, which she handed to Traynor. "I mean what type of health club gives out matches? To me, that seems to endorse smoking."

He read the name and address from the matches and handed them to McMahon before turning back to Celia. "You're going to be visited by the police. Until today they had her listed as a Jane Doe. That, however, ceased when we identified her this morning."

"I understand."

Traynor said, "The cops will be asking many of the same questions we did. They'll be especially interested to know why you haven't reported her missing."

Doerr's complexion suddenly turned ashen, making it obvious that she was nervous—possibly scared. Traynor didn't think Doerr had killed Mindy, but he believed that she either knew who did—or at least had a good idea of who had. He wondered if she realized that she had screwed up by not placing a missing person report. Either way, he was certain that she knew one hell of a lot more than she was letting on.

He turned to his partner and asked, "You got any questions?"

"Would it be possible for us to see her room? Maybe there's something in her things that will lead us to her mysterious boyfriend."

"Well." Doerr seemed embarrassed. "I have to be honest. Mindy didn't exactly disappear. She moved in with Mr. Anonymous. She took all of her things, and I haven't heard from her since."

Back in the car, McMahon said, "Mr. *Anonymous*? I think we were just fed a lot of bullshit."

Traynor said, "That may very well be the case, but Deborah told me she was seeing some guy named Vincent. How many Vincents do you think there are in southern California?"

"A couple million, and that's if you don't count all the Vinnies."

"How many do you think hang out there?" Traynor nodded at the matchbook he held.

He looked at the embossed type. "At least this gives us a place to start looking for the mysterious Vincent—that'll narrow it down to only one million." He flipped the matchbook into Traynor's lap. "Next stop the Body Boutique. Sounds like a pick-up joint to me."

"Aren't all those places the equivalent of the bars we trolled for women in our younger days?"

"Yup. Although it's a matter of taste. In one, you get the smell of stale beer and whiskey and in the other, sweaty bodies . . ."

"I'm already getting turned on," Traynor said.

10

The Body Boutique was one of those functional new buildings with the aesthetics of an assembly line. The first thing Traynor noticed when he walked in was the artificial smell of whatever they used to cover up the odor of sweat. A row of treadmills was lined up across from a line of televisions, all with the sound muted. They were all occupied by twenty- and thirty-somethings, who, Traynor thought, would probably tell you that they enjoyed working out. However, one look at their red, dripping faces was enough to bely that. Traynor had to wonder: *How could anyone enjoy an activity that makes you look as if you're about to drop from exhaustion?* He said, "These people look like survivors of the Spanish Inquisition."

"Obviously, you have no idea of fun," McMahon replied.

"Fun?" Traynor called his attention to the row of television screens. The runners were working hard to get nowhere; they were all wearing headsets that plugged into audio jacks on the treadmills and stared at the screens before them. "If it's so entertaining, why do they need TV to get their minds off it?"

He grinned and said, "You may have a point."

"Ironic, isn't it?"

"How so?"

"These days, the way to meet a woman is by ensuring that you'll have no energy left to do anything once you do."

He looked at Traynor and shook his head. "I gather you aren't a runner."

"Hell, before ten in the morning, I'm not even a stander . . ."

Before they reached the check-in counter, a refugee from Muscle Beach confronted them. "I'm sorry, guys, but unless you're members or a guest of one, I can't allow you in."

"Really?" Traynor said. "And just who the hell might you be?"

"Darrell Duncan, I'm the day manager."

"What if I want to join?" McMahon asked.

Duncan paused and looked at McMahon and then at Traynor. "Do you want to join?"

"No," McMahon said. "But thanks for askin'."

"Then . . ."

McMahon grabbed the front of Duncan's sleeveless T-shirt and his voice was barely audible when he said, "Listen, dipshit. We aren't here for a workout." He flashed a badge. Even though the shield appeared official, it was anything but. Traynor recognized it as one you can order from any number of catalogs, saying you are licensed to carry a concealed weapon. "You're sticking your nose into an official investigation, and if you don't back off, I'm going to break it in front of all these little girlies that you want to impress with those gym-developed muscles." He pointed to Traynor. "Right about now, my partner is deciding whether or not he should dismantle you. I ain't sure I can hold him back much longer."

The confused manager looked warily at Traynor, who did his best impression of menacing, giving him what he called his *don't tread on me* scowl. "Maybe we should talk in the office," Duncan said.

"Yeah," Traynor said, staying in character. "Maybe we should."

The manager led them deeper into the sweat factory, past the locker rooms, to a small windowless office that was furnished with only three chairs, a couch, and a cheap desk with a computer and printer on it. Traynor wondered what sort of activities might take place on the cheap vinyl couch. Still wary of them, Duncan placed the desk between him and the two of them and sat down. "How can I help you?"

"Do you know a woman by the name of Mindy Hollis?"

His brow furled. Traynor thought he was making a valiant effort to make them believe he was thinking. "Not off the top of my head." When McMahon presented him with the picture that Deborah had provided, he took it and stared at it for a second. "Oh yes, *her* . . ."

McMahon and Traynor exchanged a quick glance between them. "Suppose," Traynor said, "you elaborate."

"She came in two, three times a week—we haven't seen her for the past week, though."

"She come alone?" Traynor asked.

"At first she did. Then she connected with Vincent."

"Vincent?"

"Yeah. Several of our members tried to warn her about him."

"Warn her?" Traynor was suddenly very interested in this conversation.

"He's a movie producer . . ."

"What sort of movies?" McMahon asked.

"Not the type you'd ever want Mom and Dad to see you in."

"Porn?" Traynor asked.

"Of the worst kind." He stood up and rounded the desk, making sure the door was secure, and returned to his seat. "Rumor has it that he has connections with a producer in Mexico, who's involved in the drug business."

"Go on," McMahon said.

"I've heard the Mexican specializes in a particular type of film . . ."

Traynor got the feeling that he wasn't going to like where this was headed.

"Each time one of these women hooks up with Vincent, they stop coming in."

"Tell us more about this Mexican," McMahon said.

"Keep in mind that this is all hearsay, but I heard he doesn't want big names in the porn scene. He wants *new* talent for his movies."

All of a sudden, Traynor got a horrible premonition and felt his stomach sink. "Why's that?" he ventured.

"He makes films for a select audience. Most of the stars know about him and won't go within ten miles of Vincent. Not to mention, the Mexican goes in for reality."

"There's no such thing as a realistic porno," McMahon said.

"There is if you arrange things so the woman doesn't know what's in the script . . ."

"Are you telling me," McMahon said, "somehow they set these women up and film them being raped?"

"That's what I've heard."

Traynor said, "Where can we find Vincent?"

Duncan's brow broke out in a sudden sweat. "Look . . ."

McMahon leaned forward and rested his fists on the desk. "No, asshole, you listen. Mindy Hollis is in the morgue. Someone brutalized her and then mutilated her. My partner and I are going to find the bastard or bastards who did it. Now either you tell us how to find this piece of shit or we're going to think that maybe you're in on it. You with me on this?"

He swallowed hard. "Look, if my boss finds out that I gave out information about a member, I could be fired."

"Or," Traynor added, "if you don't, we could take you apart one piece at a time."

Duncan's eyes darted between them, and he must have decided that being fired was the better fate. He began typing on the keyboard. In a few seconds, he printed out the information they wanted. Traynor snatched the paper from his hand and read the name Vincent Beneventi and more importantly, an address and phone number.

*If there's anything more important than knowing what you know,
it's knowing what you don't know and where to find the answer.*

—Author's note

11

B oth lost in thought, McMahon and Traynor did not speak until
they were on the 101. Traynor tried to erase visions of Mindy's
final hours from his mind. To anyone other than a sadistic
psychopath, envisioning what she must have endured was anathema.
Still, the one thing that bothered him more than anything else was what
and how he was going to tell the Hollises about Mindy's death. Finally,
the silence became too much to bear. "Where is this address?" he asked.

McMahon pulled the GPS from its holder and handed it to him.
"Enter it in."

Traynor programmed the device, and when it brought up the route,
he handed it back to McMahon, who glanced at it and zoomed out the
display before saying, "Off the 101, not far from Echo Park. I know the
area. It's not the best area in the city, but then it's not the worst either."

"I'll take your word for it."

McMahon reached around and took a nine millimeter pistol from its holster on his back. "Take this."

"I don't have a carry permit."

"Ed, we've just learned that we are about to stir up some shit with some *flaming hemorrhoids*. Before this is over, you won't be worrying about anything as trivial as a permit to carry a handgun. We're talking about people who may have murdered and mutilated at least one person that we know of—need I say more?"

Traynor checked the Glock's magazine and action. "At least I finally feel dressed."

They lapsed into silence again. After fifteen minutes had passed, McMahon said, "You seem to be trying to get your mind around something—what's eating you?"

"You know what sucks?"

"I know a lot of things that suck. Can you narrow it down some?"

"How about having to break the news about all this to the Hollises over a phone?"

"Yeah," he agreed, "that's gonna be a giant life-sucking vortex."

3143 Doctors Drive turned out to be a palm tree in front of a vacant lot. McMahon and Traynor stood beside the rental car and watched the breeze carry a piece of newspaper across the knee-high brown grass. Traynor turned to McMahon and asked, "Is there such a thing out here as green grass?"

"You know what they say about the seasons in Maine?"

" . . . Nine months of winter and three months of lousy sledding."

"Well, out here the two seasons are brown and green."

"Humph. When does the green season happen?"

"After El Niño and mudslide seasons . . ."

"So, they *do* have four seasons out here."

"I guess. Shit."

"What?"

McMahon looked as if he'd just eaten a large, hairy insect. "I didn't want to have to do this, but . . ."

"Do what?"

"Ask Angela for help." He looked as forlorn as a kid whose puppy had just run away.

"It could be worse. The cops don't have to tell us anything about an on-going investigation."

He stared off into the smog. "Something like this she'll jump in with both feet—even if it means she could lose her badge."

———————

Forty-five minutes after McMahon had explained what they had learned to Angela, she met them in the parking lot of a big box store. One look at her and Traynor was certain that she was at best reluctant to offer help. "You got no business pursuing this," she said. "It's an LAPD case."

"C'mon, Angela, if it wasn't for us, you'd still be looking at a Jane Doe. Gimme a break on this, okay?" It was apparent to Traynor that groveling was not one of McMahon's strong suits, but he was certain that if anyone could make him do so, it was Angela Engle.

She sighed and looked at Traynor in exasperation. "I'd quit any job that made me work with this reprobate," she told him.

"Hell," Traynor said, "compared to some of the people I come in contact with he's a pillar of respectability."

"Those people," she quipped, "must have the intellect of a one-celled animal."

What could he say to that? Anyone who has been a cop long enough believes that they've come in contact with people who scraped the bottom of the gene pool—then along comes some idiot you're sure is a new life form.

Engle leaned back against the fender of her police car, crossed her arms across her chest, and sighed. "Okay, I'm in." She extended a finger and pushed it to within an inch of McMahon's nose. "But if you pull some crap that is gonna jeopardize my career, I'll do time for murder—yours."

Traynor wasn't sure about McMahon, but he believed her.

She settled back and asked, "What do you need?"

"Who you know that works vice?" McMahon asked.

.... successful detectives are catalysts. In an investigation they can cause reactions on the part of the other individuals involved.
—*Private Eyes: A Writer's Guide To Private Investigators*

12

Traynor thought that Dick Lebow looked like anything but a vice cop. Rather than a sloppily dressed burnout, he was—like Manuel, Cyril Hollis's body guard—a clothes horse. His suit must have cost him a month's pay and the creases in his trousers were sharp enough to make a Marine drill instructor proud. Lebow looked as if he visited the barbershop each morning on his way to work. He must have seen the questioning look on Traynor's face because he offered unasked, "The Department pays for my suits. Times have changed. Drug dealers try to look like businessmen today—hell, since the dot-com craze of the nineties, they dress better than most."

They sat in an upscale coffee shop near Hollywood Boulevard and sipped on five-dollar coffees. Lebow looked across the table at McMahon and Traynor and said, "I hear that you guys are interested in Vincent

Beneventi, but can't find him. Well, that ain't a surprise. He doesn't exist. I guess you could say that like all would-be players in the movie biz, it's a stage name. You should be asking about Vernon Skidgel—a small-time piece of garbage who wants to be big-time." He took a photo—a mug shot—from his inside jacket pocket and slid it across the table. "We busted him for soliciting once, but it didn't stick."

"What about the Mexican producer?" McMahon asked. "You got a line on him?"

"I can't be certain, but you're probably looking for Giuliano Olivas Toledo. We usually refer to him as Holy."

Traynor could not help but ask, "So, how would one go about finding *Holy* Toledo?"

Lebow chuckled. "I got to confess . . . you go asking for him that way, all you'll get will be a painful exit from this world. One of his flunkies made the mistake of calling him that where Toledo could hear him. They found the guy crucified head-down to a cross in the desert. He must have been out there for over a week. Wouldn't surprise me if Toledo didn't film the entire thing—he's into that type of shit. He's psychotic and sadistic." Lebow drank some coffee and watched a couple of young women in short skirts parade by the window. "Only way you'll find him is to go south. The closest to the US he's ever been—at least to our knowledge—is Tijuana. You want to do business with Toledo, you go to his backyard. That way he's in control."

"Next question: where should we look for Skidgel?"

"Anywhere you can find unsuspecting young girls. You might want to watch the Greyhound bus station on South Los Angeles Street and of course, the workout joints. Personally, I'd hit the bus station first."

McMahon nodded to Traynor. "Looks like we've got a lead."

They stood up and Lebow said, "Guys, if you kill the bastard, dump him outside of LA County. Orange County would work—that way we won't have to waste any more time and energy on the scumbag."

It was late afternoon when they arrived at the Greyhound bus station. It took them less than ten seconds to identify Vernon Skidgel, a.k.a. Vincent

Beneventi, and it didn't take them much longer to figure out why he was so successful at luring women into his trap. He looked like the hunks you see on the covers of romance novels. He was muscular—most likely from spending hours on the machines at the Body Boutique—and his long brown hair was pulled back into a ponytail. "He looks like he can handle himself in a brawl," Traynor commented to McMahon.

McMahon never took his eyes off Skidgel. "I wouldn't worry about him. He's a pretty boy and a con artist—those muscles are for show. In a fight, he'll be as useful as a tire pump in a canoe."

They observed Skidgel as he prowled the waiting area, weaving through the room, in search of susceptible young women. The announcement of a bus arriving from Denver came over the public address system, and like a hawk diving at a rabbit, Skidgel headed for the door through which the arriving passengers would enter.

"Look at him," McMahon said. "He's like a jackal following the scent of a carcass."

"It's no wonder he preys on the young and inexperienced," Traynor commented. "Anyone who's been around the block at least once should be able to figure out his act."

"Obviously," McMahon said, "he's not with the times. These days, these assholes use the social websites to lure their prey."

"Social websites?" He'd have to ask Charley about that when he got back east.

"Yeah, Craigslist is one of the best known. You can reach thousands of these young, innocent girls online. The odds of meeting some sweet, tender thing are much greater there."

"I'll have to take your word for it. What's our plan?"

"I'm curious. Let's watch the scumbag work."

Skidgel looked like a throwback to the seventies. He wore a blazer, no tie, and the top three buttons of his shirt were open. He leaned against the wall beside the door, eyeing each of the passengers. When two attractive but obviously very young women (Traynor doubted that they were of legal age) entered and stared at the room with wide eyes, he pounced. They looked warily at his approach. Skidgel was smiling like a movie star as he closed in on his prey. First, he spoke to the blonde and then to the brunette for a few seconds. He reached into his shirt pocket, handed each of them a business card, and then guided them to seats that were away from the main flow of traffic, wasting no time going into his spiel.

"You know," McMahon said, "he belongs in Hollywood as a character actor."

"You can't be serious," Traynor said.

"Oh, I'm serious all right. Whenever he shows character, he's acting ..."

"You know, Jack, you do have a way of putting things in perspective."

"Okay," McMahon said, "I've seen enough of this sitcom ..." He crossed the room with Traynor on his heels. As he passed by Skidgel, McMahon stopped, stared at him for a few seconds, and then exclaimed, "Vernon? Vernon Skidgel! Hell, man, I haven't seen you in years."

Skidgel looked at McMahon as if he were a madman. McMahon, however, was not to be deterred. He grabbed Skidgel by the hand and began pumping it like he was trying to get water from a dry well.

The girl with light brown hair looked at Skidgel with obvious suspicion. "I thought your name was Vincent?"

Skidgel became flustered and said, "It is. I ain't got a clue who in hell this crazy man is ..."

McMahon lifted him by the arm and pulled him away from the girls, saying, "Of course he does. You always were the joker, Vernon."

Traynor decided it was time for him to get in on the act and he grabbed his other arm. "Yeah, Vern. Next you'll be saying you don't remember me."

They ushered Skidgel across the waiting room and down a corridor to the men's room. As soon as they were inside, Traynor released his grip and looked around for something to secure the door with. He didn't find anything. As he turned back, Traynor thought, *I hope nobody walks in on us.*

Meanwhile, McMahon pushed Skidgel the length of the restroom, opening stalls as he went. They had the place to themselves. At the end of the room, McMahon shoved Skidgel into the cinder block wall. "You were right, Vernon, you don't know me. However, in the immediate future, you and I are going to be more intimately involved than you are with your proctologist." McMahon spun him around and buried his fist in Vernon's gut.

Skidgel grunted, wrapping his arms around his midsection, and lurched forward. But McMahon grabbed him by his chin and raised his head until he could look him in the eye and through clenched teeth, said, "Now, do I have your undivided attention?"

"W-what the hell? Who the fuck are you guys? Vice? I'm gonna file charges against you for excessive force."

McMahon grinned. "Go ahead—for all the good it will do you."

Skidgel looked quizzical.

"We aren't cops."

Skidgel deflated. "Then why the fuck are you pushing me around?"

"Tell us about Mindy Hollis."

"Who?"

Traynor stepped forward and thrust Mindy's picture at him. "Maybe this will jog your memory. You picked up the wrong one this time, Vernon—or should I call you Vincent?"

"I ain't got any idea what you're talkin' about."

"I think you do," Traynor said. "If you don't tell us what you know, I'm going to let my friend off his leash—and believe me, you don't want to be a part of that."

"Okay, so I went out with her a couple of times. So what?"

"She's on a slab in the morgue, that's what," McMahon said. He slammed Skidgel against the wall with each word. A hollow clunk sounded each time his head hit the cinder blocks.

"Now, before my partner spreads your pretty nose across your face, you better tell us about your producer friend, Toledo," Traynor said.

Skidgel paled and his knees seemed to go weak. "I don't know anyone by that name."

McMahon looked over his shoulder at Traynor. "I don't know about you, but I don't think this is going to get us anywhere. Why don't you step outside and let me and Vernon have a chat? When I get through with this pretty boy, he won't be able to pay a hooker for a blind date."

"I'll wait outside the door." Before turning away, Traynor said, "Well, Vern, it's been real . . ."

Sweat was dripping from Skidgel's forehead, and he reminded Traynor of a lost child. Unable to keep from getting in a last word, Traynor waved and said, "Be seeing you, Vern."

Traynor stepped into the corridor just as a man was approaching. He held up his hand and said, "Sorry, closed for maintenance. I think there's another restroom that way." He had no idea if this it was true or not, but he pointed toward the main waiting area. The poor guy paused as if he were about to have an accident, then spun around and trotted in the direction Traynor had pointed.

Behind him he heard McMahon speak, immediately followed by a muffled voice. He assumed that they were pleas for mercy from Skidgel. There was a brief commotion and then McMahon walked out of the rest-room with his prisoner in tow. "Vernon has offered to let us look at his place."

"Sounds as if that might be interesting."

"Yeah, especially his DVD collection."

As they guided Skidgel past the two young women, Traynor stopped before them. "Do you ladies have anyone in town?"

The one who had been suspicious said, "No."

"My best advice is that you catch the next bus home." They gave him a doubtful look, and he knew they were not going to take his advice. He pointed to Skidgel, who had lost his male-model look and was cowering at McMahon's side. "Let me guess," Traynor said, "you want to try and make it in the movies . . ."

The blond nodded.

"And ole Vern there told you he was a producer . . ."

Another nod.

"Well, in his own way, he is . . . but mostly he's a pimp. In no time you'll be working the streets. Oh, he might get you into films—but not the kind you'll ever see in the front of your local video store. They usually keep the adult films in the back." He was not sure this would be enough to convince them—after all, there was a segment of society that would *want* to star in any type of movie, even a porno.

Their eyes were as big as Frisbees and their mouths dropped open.

"Go home, girls. If you stay here with no jobs or friends, another pimp like that will latch on to you."

They looked at each other for a few seconds, and then the blond said, "We don't have enough money for return tickets."

"If you can't even afford bus fare, how do you expect to live?"

Again they looked at each other and he knew that they had never thought about it.

"Come on," Traynor said. "The trip home is on me."

"Why would you do that?" The brunette was suspicious again.

"Because I've seen this scam played many times." He handed each of them one of his business cards. "If it will make you feel better, you can pay me back. Mail it to the address on the card."

Still suspicious, she looked at the card and said, "Portsmouth, New Hampshire—where's that?"

Traynor wanted to make a wisecrack, something like, *go east until you smell it, then turn north until you step in it*, but didn't—this was not the right time or place. "It's about an hour north of Boston," he said. "We have our share of predators like him there, too. Now what's it going to be?"

They got up and followed him to the ticket counter where he bought two one-way tickets to Colorado Springs. He handed each of them a ticket, then reached into his pocket and took out a fold of cash. He peeled off four twenty-dollar bills and handed two to each of them. "That should be enough for you to eat on. Don't be foolish, girls, get on the bus and go home, before you regret it." Having done his good deed for the day, he turned toward McMahon and their prisoner. As they herded Skidgel toward the exit, McMahon said, "That was touching."

"Yeah, sometimes I even surprise myself."

"But don't be surprised if they return those tickets and keep the cash . . ."

. . . bodily reactions and postures occur as a subconscious protection mechanism and are generally more consistent with deception than truthfulness.
—FM 3-19, Law Enforcement Investigations

13

Skidgel lived in one of those apartment complexes that were as common in the San Fernando Valley as cactus in southern Arizona. The apartments formed a square that enclosed a patio area with an empty in-ground swimming pool, in which various types of detritus drifted with the breeze. They followed a portico that led from the parking lot to the patio area. Skidgel's apartment was on the first floor to the right of where they exited the short breezeway.

He unlocked a door beside a large sliding door in which the glass was shielded from the sun by long plastic louvers and stepped aside to allow them to enter first. McMahon grabbed him by the shoulder and pushed him inside, saying, "You think we're stupid?"

Skidgel stood in a small living room, rubbing his shoulder. "Hey, man, cool it. You ever consider anger management?"

McMahon pushed his way past him and said, "Don't need it—not as long as there are people like you I can take out my frustrations on."

Traynor entered the apartment and stood at the threshold, allowing his eyes to adjust to the dim interior. He wondered if Skidgel housed his prey here. The cheap discount-store furniture was not what one would expect from a successful movie producer. In fact, even an unsuccessful one would live better than this. The couch had a plastic finish, similar to naugahyde, only cheaper—the cuts and tears that were spread across the seat and back were repaired with duct tape, which did nothing to diminish the tawdry look. Even the chairs were garage-sale quality: plastic, scratched, and scarred. The coffee table was not exempted and was a collage of cigarette burns, round scars from moisture off beer cans, and crusted bits of food.

McMahon roamed down a short hall and stopped before a closed door. "What's in here?"

"Bathroom," Skidgel said.

McMahon looked at the state of the living room and then at the filthy kitchen—which was in even worse condition than the living room. He looked at Traynor and said, "I think I'll take a pass on the shithouse."

Traynor turned to Skidgel and said, "Does the Board of Health know you let the young women you con live like this?"

Skidgel shrugged.

Then Traynor noticed the one exception to the array of cheap furniture—a state-of-the-art entertainment system, complete with Blu-ray player, amplifier with 7.1 surround sound, and a fifty-two-inch flat-panel TV. "You watch a lot of TV?" he asked.

"Mostly I watch movies."

Traynor snorted and said, "I don't think I have to ask what type of movie you like." Along the wall opposite the couch were shelves constructed from two columns of cinder blocks with two-by-six boards suspended between them. The shelves were filled with DVDs, the majority of which were the sort most people hide. "I don't think I've heard any of these movies mentioned during the Oscars," Traynor said.

Skidgel watched as Traynor trailed his finger along the spines of the DVD cases, pretending to read the titles. As he approached the middle of the second shelf, Skidgel suddenly became agitated and got to his feet—all the time keeping a wary eye on the DVD shelf along which Traynor's finger slid. Seeing his sudden interest, Traynor began to search the titles in earnest. When he saw one titled *The Black Orchid*, he recalled the tattoo on Mindy's thigh. It was of a woman's sexy legs with a tattoo of a black orchid on her right thigh. The tat was similar to the one Deborah Hollis had on hers. He handed the case to McMahon, who studied the picture and then, without warning, punched Skidgel so hard Traynor thought he had broken the scumbag's jaw.

Skidgel backed up, stumbled over the coffee table, and collapsed onto the couch with his legs on the table. He spat a wad of blood onto the matted, urine-yellow shag rug.

McMahon waved the DVD case at Skidgel and said, "You said you only dated Mindy a couple of times."

"That's right."

McMahon turned the case over and read the credits. "Says here that Vincent Beneventi is one of the producers—isn't that your *professional* name?"

"Of course it is." He lightly touched his swelling jaw and slurred when he spoke. "See, you didn't believe I was really a producer, did you?"

"Who's the woman on the cover?"

McMahon bent over him and held the case close enough for Skidgel to read.

"When I found that movie, you looked like you were about to shit yourself," Traynor said. "Why?"

"Uh . . . that's a movie that you can't buy at the corner adult store. It's for special, limited distribution, one of the ones we only sell to *special* customers."

"It's empty," McMahon said. Traynor turned his attention away from Skidgel. McMahon held the case open, showing that there was no disc inside. Traynor turned back to their host. "So, where's the DVD?" For a brief second, Skidgel glanced nervously at the Blu-ray player. Traynor noticed. "That's one hell of an impressive entertainment system you got there, Vern. Why don't you turn it on and give *us* a look?"

Skidgel's face took on the air of a man pleading for mercy as he faced the death sentence. "No reason to be fussy," Traynor continued, "just play whatever's in there."

"I don't think you guys would like it . . ."

"You don't? Why in the hell not?" McMahon asked.

Skidgel began sweating, and he tried to avoid making eye contact with either of them.

McMahon grabbed him by the neck of his shirt and pulled him forward. "*Why not*, Vernon?"

"Because . . ."

"Then turn the goddamned thing on." McMahon bent forward until his face was within inches of Skidgel's. "Is there something on that disc that you don't want us to see?" His voice lowered to a sinister level. "*Is that Mindy Hollis on the cover?*" He smacked Skidgel in the forehead with the plastic case, and then grabbed Skidgel's shirt and shook him until he flopped back and forth so hard Traynor thought his neck would snap and separate his head from his body. "*Well, is it?*"

Skidgel tried to hide his head in his arms, but Traynor saw enough of him to see he was nodding his head yes.

McMahon shoved Skidgel back and stood erect. His fists were clenched, and Traynor would not have been surprised if he reached for his gun. He placed a hand on McMahon's arm, hoping to restrain him. He felt the tension leave McMahon; he turned to the cowering man and said, "Turn it on . . ."

McMahon stepped away from Skidgel and stood to his left. Once again, his hands were clenched into tight fists.

Skidgel's hands shook when he reached over to the end table and picked up a remote control. He gave Traynor another furtive look and then began beseeching each of them in turn. "Look, guys . . ."

"Play it," Traynor said. "No more games. I want to see what's in that player—and I want to see it right fucking now!"

Resigned to his fate, Skidgel turned on the television.

It took several seconds for the circuitry to illuminate the display, and Traynor saw the menu screen for *The Black Orchid*. "Select the chapters menu," he said. Skidgel moved the cursor down, and the screen changed, displaying thumbnail pictures of the various scenes on the DVD. Traynor scanned them and saw a series of pictures of Mindy Hollis. He saw stills of her being sodomized, and performing sexual acts that many people considered pleasurable—people who were willing participants. However, from the look on Mindy's face, he could tell that she was anything but a willing participant in the making of this movie. Seeing the degree of degradation to which this naive young woman had been subjected enraged Traynor.

However, those stills from the early chapters were nothing compared to the last five, which featured her murder and dissection. Traynor turned to McMahon and said, "Are you thinking the same thing I am?"

McMahon seemed as angry as Traynor. "I always believed that snuff films were an urban myth—but that sure as hell shoots that theory all to hell."

At that moment, Traynor knew that he himself was capable of subjecting Skidgel to the same tortures that Mindy Hollis had endured before the film's ultimate climax—her death and mutilation. Traynor looked away from the screen and glanced at McMahon. His complexion was pasty and his eyes had narrowed to slits. Then Traynor looked at Skidgel . . . He was staring at the thumbnails as if in a hypnotic trance. When Traynor asked, "You have a favorite scene, Vern?" his words were full of loathing and distaste.

Skidgel jumped up and turned his attention from the screen to Traynor.

Traynor tried to maintain control, but his voice was elevated when he said, "During my twenty-five year career in law enforcement and as a private investigator, I've come across scumbags who I thought were the lowest of the low." He pointed at the screen. "But, you're the first son of a whore I've ever wanted to take behind the barn and use a chainsaw on . . ."

He knew it took all Skidgel's strength to keep looking at him and not the screen. "All I did was . . ."

"Set up a beautiful young woman to be slaughtered for some sick perverts' entertainment," Traynor roared. He turned back to the screen and said, "I've seen enough, turn that fuckin' thing off."

"We can't," McMahon said.

"What?"

"If we're going to get the rest of these scumbags, we got to watch it all . . . whether we like it or not."

Skidgel pointed the remote at the HDTV, and when he hit play, *The Black Orchid* began.

———————

When the movie ended, Traynor felt like a voyeur. He doubted there was a shower capable of making him ever again feel clean. He strode across the room and pressed the eject button. When the DVD drawer slid open, he took the disc out and returned it to its case. Turning back to Skidgel, he asked, "How many more copies of this you got?"

"There's a couple cases in the bedroom closet."

McMahon had not said a word since the movie started, and when Traynor turned his attention to him, he saw that McMahon, too, trembled as he struggled to control his rage. Traynor realized that if they stayed in this room much longer, one or the other of them might kill Skidgel with his bare hands.

When McMahon said, "I'll check," his voice was under control, and Traynor knew he had passed his crisis point.

"I'll call Lebow," Traynor said.

"While you're at it, call Angela, too," McMahon said. "She deserves a piece of this bust. After all, if not for her, it might have taken us days to find this bucket of puke."

Traynor made the calls and then sat in one of the plastic chairs. "Well, Vernon, ole friend, seems we got some time to kill—you got anything you want to get off your chest?"

Vernon completely deflated. "I'm fucked either way, ain't I?"

"Yeah, I'd say so. Even if you skate the murder charge by turning state's evidence, her family has enough money to find you wherever in the world you try hiding. And if that job falls to us, I'm sure my friend and I will take it."

Sweat dripped from Skidgel's nose and chin, and his eyes darted from side to side like those of a cornered rat. Traynor wished that the young women in the bus station could see him now. He must have decided that he had nothing to gain by keeping his mouth shut and said, "Okay, what you want to know?"

"How did you get her to agree to this?" Traynor held the DVD case up.

"She didn't. Neither of us knew it was a fuckin' snuff. All I did was give her directions and tell her to meet me at the house—it's east of here, toward Death Valley—isolated and private. I didn't even go out there . . . I gave her directions and a key. The crew was already there, inside, all set up and waiting for her when she arrived."

"I want the names of every sonuvabitch involved. You lie about anything and I'll make sure that you'll get it worse than she did."

"I do that and I'm fuckin' dead . . . No way am I sayin' anything." He flopped back on the couch and sat with his arms folded across his chest and stayed that way until Engle and Lebow arrived.

. . . statutory requirements for victim and witness assistance . . . from initial contact with offenders through investigation, prosecution, and confinement.
—*FM 3-19.13, Law Enforcement Investigations*

14

They spent the next four hours at the police station, watching Skidgel deny any knowledge of Mindy Hollis's death. He did however slip and give them Toledo's name as the producer who had financed the film. While professionally done, the credits at the film's end told them nothing, and the only intro to the film was the title. No actor names had been credited.

Finally Traynor felt he had spent enough time staring at the monitor that showed them what was happening in the interrogation room and he beckoned for McMahon to follow him. They left the room and walked outside. It was hot, although the sun seemed muted as it tried to burn its way through the ever-present smog.

"I don't think we're going to learn anything. Even if the police do break him, they aren't going to share it with us. We may as well go get some rest."

"Maybe," McMahon said, "Angela will fill us in later. I can ask her anyhow."

McMahon and Traynor were silent as they drove back to their hotel. McMahon parked the rental and then turned to Traynor. "How you gonna handle this?"

He did not have to tell Traynor to which *this* he was alluding. It had been on his mind since they had left the police station. How was he going to break this to the Hollises? "You ever wish you weren't so damned good at your job?" Traynor asked.

"This is the first time for me. I'll make the call with you, if you'd like."

"You're more than welcome to be there, but it's up to me—it's what Deborah hired me to do."

"Don't forget that she sent me with you—that makes it my responsibility, too."

"Okay, point well taken." Traynor opened his door. "Well, we'll never get it done sitting on our asses."

They decided to call from Traynor's room. Ed glanced at the digital clock and noted that it was after ten o'clock. "Quarter past one in the morning back east," he said.

"I know Deborah," McMahon said. "She'll be pissed if we wait."

Traynor made the call. Without going into the details, he told Deborah that her sister was indeed dead. Before he could say more, she said, "Byron and I will be there in the morning. We'll have the corporate jet fly us into Burbank."

Traynor said, "We'll meet you at the airport."

"I'll call you as soon as I get an arrival time."

He hung up, turned to McMahon, and asked, "So, what do we do now?"

"Get some sleep and meet her at the airport. Unless we're told otherwise, our job is done. You were hired and I was sent out here to find Mindy—we found her. So, as of right now, you're unemployed and I'm back to being the would-yuh."

Within hours, they would learn how wrong McMahon was.

———————

The Hollises' Gulfstream G500 taxied to the general aviation terminal and McMahon and Traynor waited outside the entrance to the General Aviation Terminal for Deborah Hollis and Byron Moore to disembark. They held their hands against their ears to protect them as the jet engines turned down. The door opened and Moore came out first. He waited at the bottom of the short staircase for Deborah, and they walked side by side into the small terminal. She and Moore looked like a couple of high-powered executives on a business trip. Deborah was attired in a stunning gray suit, white blouse, and expensive high heels. Moore wore his ever-present navy-blue pinstriped suit, white shirt, and power tie.

Deborah immediately marched over to them; it was obvious that the past twelve hours had not been easy on her. Her eyes were red and puffy—no doubt she had been crying. "Thank you, Ed," she said.

"I'm not so sure that thanks are in order . . ." Traynor did not add what was going through his mind: that it might have been easier on everyone if they had never found her.

She turned to McMahon. "Considering things, how are you doing, Jack?"

For the first time since they had seen Mindy's body, the anger left his face and a deep-seated sorrow replaced it. "I'll be okay," was all he said.

"Have the police found her killer?" Deborah asked.

"That's a subject better discussed in private," Traynor answered.

She stared at him for a second, as if she were wondering what he was talking about.

"There are too many ears around here," McMahon added. He nodded to Moore. "Byron, good to see you—although I wish it was under different circumstances."

"Well," Moore said, "it's better that we know, rather than spend the rest of our lives wondering where she is and what happened to her."

"That's another topic to be discussed in private," Traynor said.

Deborah turned to Traynor. "What are you saying?"

"Let's discuss this in the car," he said, then turned away and walked through the gate in the fence that surrounded the terminal and into the parking lot.

McMahon and Traynor had driven to the airport an hour early and traded the midsized rental for a Lincoln. They entered the parking lot elevator, and Traynor pushed the button for the fourth level. No one spoke during the ride to their parking level, but Traynor knew that Deborah and Moore were staring at him and McMahon, no doubt wondering how much worse this was going to get. He was certain they were thinking that Mindy had been murdered—and what could be worse than that? Forty-five minutes later they entered the morgue—and then they knew.

None of them had eaten that morning, so they went to a restaurant that McMahon knew. He spoke to the owner and they were led into a small room usually reserved for overflow. While they were waiting for coffee, McMahon stepped away and made a call on his cell. He disconnected the call, closed the phone, and returned to the table. "I've asked a couple of other people to join us," he said. "They should be here soon."

Twenty minutes passed before Angela Engle and Lebow walked through the door. Traynor signaled and they made their way to the table. Once they were seated, McMahon introduced them to Deborah and Moore. Engle turned to Deborah and said, "I feel terrible about your sister."

"Thank you." Not one to chew around the edges, Deborah went right to the heart of the issue. "I'd like to know what you're doing about this guy down in Mexico City . . ." She could not remember the name and turned to Traynor.

"Holy Toledo," Traynor added.

Deborah glared at him, suggesting that this was no time for jokes and that she did not appreciate his lame attempt at humor.

He shrugged and said, "That's what the police call him. Besides it's easier to remember than his real name."

"Which is?" she asked.

Lebow answered, "Giuliano Olivas Toledo. Miss Hollis . . ."

"Deborah."

"Deborah, there are a couple of issues we have to overcome. First, neither Sergeant Engle nor I are assigned to this case. A crime of this magnitude will be investigated by the robbery/homicide division. Even they'll have their hands tied. Toledo and the rest of the bottom-feeders that hang around him are Mexican nationals and the government down there has its hands full with the drug cartels, who are getting a lot of media attention around the world. To them, as bad as he is, Toledo is small stuff. Then there's the problem of the Mexico City Police. If they aren't the most corrupt law enforcement agency in the world, they're in the top three. So I'm sure that you can see that neither they nor the government down there is going to give a damn . . ." He paused and his face flushed when he looked at Deborah.

"That's okay, Lieutenant. I'm well aware that in the overall scheme of the world, my sister's murder is not going to lead the news, except maybe in New England . . . and even then only for one or two days."

Lebow took a drink of coffee and continued. "Toledo is able to operate as he does because he greases a lot of palms, both down there and up here . . . the Mexico City PD is one of the best money can buy. They won't be jumping with joy about the prospect of turning over one of their major benefactors."

"So what recourse do we have?" Deborah asked.

"You can go home and try to find consolation in the fact that we got Vernon Skidgel."

"Who's he?"

"You know him as Vincent Beneventi, Mindy's boyfriend," Traynor said. "He's the guy who set her up."

"And," Lebow added, "you can hope that Toledo and his goombahs come here. But, I'd say that, given Toledo's history, we only have two chances of that happening—and neither are likely."

"Meanwhile," Deborah concluded, "the case gets put in the cold case files, and after a few weeks, months at most, Mindy is just another statistic."

"I'm sorry," Lebow said. "We can only do what we can do. Even if Toledo were to come to LA and we get him, there's no guarantee that he'll ever see a courtroom. Skidgel was the only one stupid enough to list his name as a producer on the DVD. To be truthful, he isn't exactly the sort of witness a prosecutor wants to go into court with. He'll piss off every juror who hears about the shithead's background."

Deborah sat quietly, obviously pondering what she had just heard. After a few moments, Lebow said, "You'll have to excuse Sergeant Engle and me. We have to go to work."

"Of course," Deborah replied, "thank you for all your help."

Lebow nodded and Engle smiled, and then they were out the door.

Deborah drank some orange juice and set her glass down. "Ed, do you have a passport?"

"Yeah."

"With you?"

"Since nine-eleven I use it as ID whenever I fly."

Her eyes were steely when she looked at Moore. "I have an idea," she said, "that may entice Toledo to come to north of the border. Byron, I want you to fly back home and send Manuel here."

"How does Manuel fit into this?" Traynor asked.

"You'll need someone who speaks Spanish while you're in Mexico City."

"Mexico City?"

"Remember the old saying about Mohammed and the mountain?"

"Of course."

"Well, in my plan, you and Manuel are going to be Mohammed."

"But," Traynor objected, "Manuel will only get in the way if things get intense."

"Oh, I doubt that. You haven't filled him in, Jack?"

"Didn't think there was reason to," McMahon replied.

She turned back to Traynor. "Manuel has a number of skills."

"Be that as it may, given his current position, they may have diminished," Traynor said.

Deborah stared out the window and seemed to have tuned him out; his arguments were getting him nowhere. She turned back to him, smiled, and said, "Don't worry about that."

Traynor wondered what she was keeping from him.

It is the spirit of the men who follow and of the man who leads that gains the victory.
—*George S. Patton (1885–1945), The Cavalry Journal*

15

They left the restaurant and drove back to the airport. In the terminal, Deborah shook Moore's hand and then walked back to them. "You aren't going?" Traynor asked.

"I'm staying with you guys."

"Until Manuel arrives?"

"Until the end."

Traynor rolled his eyes in exasperation and turned to McMahon. "Don't you have anything to say?"

"Nope. She's the boss and I make it a point never to question the person who signs my paycheck."

Traynor turned to Deborah. "This is not a tourist trip. I can understand you sending Manuel, but if you come along, there'll be two of you to watch over . . ."

"One," she interrupted. "I'm not going with you to Mexico City. My plan calls for me to do something else." She gave him another of her impish smiles. "Besides, don't be surprised if Manuel ends up taking care of you."

He stared at her. "What is it about Manuel that I don't know?"

McMahon interjected, "Manuel is a former mercenary. He worked extensively in Mexico and South America, and after that he worked for the DEA. He was undercover in Mexico for eight years—and survived. That should tell you something about his abilities."

It did. For a number of years, Mexico was long considered one of the most dangerous places on earth for businessmen or tourists—let alone an undercover narc. Traynor knew that Manuel must have some extraordinary skills if he had survived that long. "If he's so good, why in the hell is he wasting his time babysitting Cyril Hollis?" There were times when Traynor's mouth was like a runaway train—and this was one of them. He cast a nervous look at Deborah. "I'm sorry, that was uncalled for."

"I understand. No one knows my father's shortcomings more than me. To answer your question, Manuel has a considerable price on his head from a number of organizations—the sort of groups that would kill his entire family if they knew where he was. My father pays him extremely well, and Hollis International provides security for his relatives in the Caribbean. In return, from time to time, he takes on special assignments for the corporation."

"Still, I apologize."

"Accepted," Deborah said. "Now that we have that settled, let's go. I'm curious about the DVD you found."

That made Traynor's head snap up. "Deborah, I wholeheartedly advise you against watching it."

"Why? It may help me understand what happened out here. As loathsome as it may be, I believe I can handle seeing it."

"Are you going to tell her or am I?" Traynor asked McMahon.

"Deborah." McMahon paused and after a few seconds, said, "The movie is not *just* a porno."

"What else might it be?"

Another pause.

"A snuff film."

"What's a snuff film?" she asked.

"They filmed everything," McMahon said. "Mindy's rape and all of the things they made her do. Then they murdered and mutilated her on camera . . ."

At that moment, Traynor learned something about Deborah Hollis. She was an expert at hiding her emotions—possibly a skill learned growing up with a drunk for a father. He made a mental note to never get into a poker game with her.

Her eyes narrowed and her complexion reddened. "I'll handle it. But if I'm going to finance and manage this operation, I want something that will piss me off enough to let you guys do what you do best. I want my sister's butchers to pay." She glared at each of them in turn. "If the law will do it, fine—if not, then we will." She paused and took a breath. "Do you know what pisses me off?"

Everyone around the table remained silent.

"What really gets to me is that people actually buy shit like this . . ."

"And pay thousands of bucks for a copy," Traynor added. "These are people more in your class than ours. The average pervert can't afford it."

McMahon shuffled his feet and looked nervous. "Skidgel is known for enticing innocent women—those who have no idea that he's involved in an illegal side of the porn industry. We've been told that established porn stars steer clear of him. He and Toledo go in for realism. Their movies feature women who have no idea what they're walking into."

"Deborah," Traynor interjected, "Skidgel was lying to us when he said that he sent her to the site alone. The shoot was in a very isolated place and someone had to take her there. From what we've learned, the only person she knew who could do it was Skidgel. Either way, the truth of the matter is that she was led into a trap. They were waiting for her with the cameras rolling the second she stepped through the door."

The Gulfstream landed at six that evening, and when Manuel strode into the terminal, Traynor was amazed at the transformation in him.

In Portsmouth, he would have sworn that the man was what he appeared to be: an overpaid and underutilized bodyguard. As usual, he wore black—although now it was a pair of cargo pants with a tight T-shirt that showed off his well-developed chest muscles. His biceps stretched the sleeves until they looked as if the seams would burst. Back east, his hair had been long but conservatively cut; now, however, it was sheared off close to his scalp. He sauntered, rather than walked, to them and stopped before Deborah.

She hugged him and said, "Thank you, Manuel. I'm glad you came."

"Ms. Deborah, there is nothing could have kept me away." He pulled back and turned his attention to McMahon and Traynor. "Good work, men. When you came out here, I had doubts as to the success of your mission. I only wish it had happened a couple of weeks sooner."

Traynor was still amazed by the change in Manuel. Then he realized that he shouldn't be surprised; in order; to stay alive for eight years as an undercover DEA agent in Mexico, Manuel had to be one hell of an actor.

Manuel ignored McMahon and Moore, and looking at Traynor, he said, "Now, we should leave—there is much to be done before we venture to *Ciudad de México*."

Establishing and maintaining effective rapport with suspects during an interrogation is instrumental in obtaining their cooperation and getting them to expose facts they would not otherwise feel comfortable disclosing.
—*FM 3-19.13, Law Enforcement Investigations*

16

They were in Deborah's hotel suite, discussing the trip to Ciudad de México, which Manuel said was Spanish for Mexico City. Over the years, Traynor had dealt with his share of Hispanic gangbangers and had picked up enough of the language to get his point across in most situations. Nevertheless, no one was ever going to accuse him of fluency.

Getting to Mexico City was not going to be a problem; the Hollises' Gulfstream would take care of that. Traynor told Deborah that he thought flying on a private jet seemed a bit ostentatious. She quieted his reservations when she said, "The Gulfstream is one of the most crucial elements to my plan."

That left the main problem, as he saw it, to ordnance. Getting through customs with the weaponry he was certain they would need was going to be a problem. However, Manuel didn't seem worried. He addressed Traynor's apprehensions, saying, "We won't need weapons until we find Toledo. In fact, while traveling, they'd only get in our way."

"So," Traynor replied, "we're going to fly into Mexico and take on a drug lord with no weapons."

"We're not going there to take Toledo on, as you put it."

"Then why are we going?" Traynor asked.

"Have you ever sold or bought drugs?" Deborah asked him.

"Not of late."

"Congratulations." She smiled a demure smile and then said, "You're about to become a major player."

Now he understood her plan. He and Manuel were going to Mexico City to make Toledo an offer he would be a fool to ignore. They were going to entice him to make a drug deal with Traynor playing the role of a crooked cop looking to make fast money. Nevertheless, Traynor was still uncertain how they were going to get Toledo into the hands of American authorities.

When he returned to his room an hour later, Traynor poured a glass of bourbon and walked out onto the room's small deck. While he sipped the smoky liquor, he couldn't help but run the events of the last few days through his mind. Unbelievably, three days ago he had been in his office reading a mystery novel, no job in sight, without a care in the world. Now, he was about to fly into a foreign country to con a drug kingpin, who also led a gang of drug dealers and killers.

He stared up at the night sky, wishing that the smog and ambient light didn't block his view of the stars. Rather than the streetlights reflecting off the haze, he needed something serene and clean to look at. Something that might transport his mind away from a world inhabited by people who thought that there was nothing wrong with paying thousands of dollars to buy a movie in which a beautiful young woman was brutally raped, murdered, and butchered. The very idea that anyone would consider such a thing entertaining baffled him and made his skin crawl.

He downed the drink, went back into his room, and prepared for bed. He had to get up in four hours, because in six hours they would be heading into the desert to locate the scene of the crime. Before he slid between the sheets, his phone rang. It was McMahon. "Come out to the parking lot."

"Why? We're going to that cabin in a few hours."

"Hey, I'm just passing on the message, okay?" McMahon said. "All I know is that when the man says be someplace, we'd better be there."

McMahon parked the car on the street and Traynor looked at him and then at Deborah and Manuel with surprise. "How the hell did you get us into the jail to see Skidgel at two in the morning?" he asked McMahon.

"Lebow and Angela called in some favors," McMahon said.

"For a couple of street cops, they seem to have a lot of juice," Traynor responded.

"I don't know about that," McMahon replied.

McMahon led them away from the front entrance and around the building to a parking lot filled with police cars. They climbed a short staircase and he knocked on the door. A uniformed police officer opened the portal and peered at them. His gaze fixed on McMahon. He looked more than a little nervous when he said, "At least you're on time, Jack." He stepped aside and let them in. "I'm way out on a limb with this," the cop said, "so all I can give you is fifteen minutes. Don't waste it."

He led them down a flight of stairs into the bowels of the building. When he opened a door, Traynor saw that they were in the holding cellblock.

"Third cell on the right," the cop said. "I'll be back in a bit—you better be ready to leave by then."

McMahon nodded and said, "Thanks. This means a lot to us."

"If we get caught, I'm sure that will console me while I'm standing in the unemployment line. . . . Fifteen minutes." He walked away, leaving them alone.

They found Skidgel lying on a small cot in his lockup. He was asleep until Manuel rattled the door. Skidgel jumped awake. "What the fuck!" He saw them and immediately shut up. He peered through the bars with narrowed eyes. "How'd you get in here?"

When Skidgel saw Deborah, he made a mistake. "Hey, babe," he said. "You should be in movies . . ."

Traynor wondered if Skidgel was a sadomasochist. Because if he was, then he was about to be very happy. When Skidgel approached to get a better look at Deborah, Manuel reached through the bars, grabbed the front of his orange jumpsuit, and jerked him into the bars. Blood spurted from Skidgel's nose and he cried out. "I'm gonna sue you, asshole! You got no right to . . ."

"Shut your trap," Manuel hissed. "We only got a few minutes and you're going to tell us what we want to know."

"What do I know that you guys want now?"

"Holy Toledo . . ." Manuel growled.

Skidgel motioned with his arm. "Last time I checked, he wasn't here."

Manuel jerked him into the bars again.

"Shit, man, give it a break . . . that fuckin' hurts."

"How do we get in touch with him?" McMahon asked.

"He ain't even in the country. He's in Mexico. I ain't seen him since we met in tee-jay[1] and that was over six months ago."

By this time, Traynor felt like a bystander. His usual MO would be to take charge, but one look at the fear in Skidgel's eyes told him to let Manuel run the show.

Manuel jerked him into the bars again. "So, fuckhead, tell us somethin' we don't already know . . ."

"Okay, okay. There's this guy who owns a couple of strip clubs in Mexico City. I leave a message with him and he gets in touch with

---

[1] Slang for Tijuana, Mexico.

Toledo—by the way, if you want to keep on breathing, ditch the Holy shit—it really pisses Toledo off, you know?"

Manuel took a small notebook from his pocket. "I want the names of the club and your contact."

"It won't do you any good. They won't give you shit unless they know you."

"Are you suggesting something?" Traynor asked.

"Spring me and I'll take you to my contact. That's the only way to do it."

"When's your arraignment?" Manuel asked.

Skidgel glanced at the clock mounted above the door through which his visitors had entered. "At ten." A hopeful look came over him.

Manuel quickly put an end to that. "The names or you go to your arraignment in a wheelchair."

Skidgel's eyes widened. It was apparent that he believed Manuel's words. After all, he had gotten access to him at three in the morning. Traynor passed his notebook and a pen through the bars, and Skidgel wrote something on one of the pages and then returned it. Manuel looked at it and then handed it back. "You write for shit. Print it so I can read the goddamn thing."

"It won't do you no good . . ."

"Just do as I say." Manuel still maintained his grip on the jumpsuit and shook Skidgel to emphasize his words.

"Okay, okay, shit, man, you work in the post office or something?" He printed the information and passed the notebook though the bars again. Manuel glanced at it and must have found it legible. He released him with a savage push.

"You're wastin' your time," Skidgel whined.

"You got enough problems without worryin' about ours," Manuel said. "Oh, and there's one more thing."

"Jesus, you're worse than my ex-wife."

Skidgel tried to scamper away, but wasn't quick enough. Manuel reestablished his grip on the jumpsuit. Knowing that he was about to kiss the bars again, Skidgel said, "Okay, okay, what can I do for you?"

"The cabin . . . I want directions."

"I already gave them to the cops . . ."

Manuel gave him a violent jerk. "Well, you didn't give them to me."

"You got a GPS?"

"Yeah."

Skidgel held his hand out, and Traynor once again gave him the notebook, he printed an address. "That'll get you there. Now can I get some sleep? I got an appointment in the morning."

When they turned away and walked down the corridor to the cellblock door, McMahon said, "It's been nice knowin' you, Vernon. Let me know what the visiting hours are at Folsom. I may stop by and check up on you—you know, kind of make sure that Toledo's contacts inside haven't cut your throat. That would be a shame, wouldn't it? A piece of shit like you doesn't deserve to die quick . . ." He turned and walked after them.

Traynor thought Skidgel must have been suicidal, because he looked at Deborah one more time and said, "Hey, sweetheart, I'm serious . . . I can get you a starring role." His laugh was abruptly cut off when Manuel charged back, reached through the bars, grabbed a fistful of jumpsuit, and yanked him into the bars so hard that the doors of the empty cells rattled. Skidgel's eyes rolled up, his legs lost their strength, his head flopped back, and his mouth opened as Manuel maintained his grip. When he was certain that Skidgel was out, Manuel released him. The unconscious prisoner fell to the concrete floor and lay in front of the cell door like a pile of dirty laundry.

Manuel stormed out of the cellblock, and Traynor, for one, stared after him. Manuel said nothing as he stormed out the door.

Traynor looked at Skidgel and thinking about his own propensity for making wisecracks, decided that he would watch his words when he was around Manuel. After all, discretion had always been the better part of valor.

The perimeters of a crime scene may be easily defined when
an offense is committed within a building.
—*FM 3-19.13, Law Enforcement Investigations*

17

The small house was on a dirt road a two-hour drive from LA. The exterior was stucco, the front porch sagged, the roof needed to be replaced, the yard was hardscrabble and covered with dark spots where oil and other fluids had leaked from a multitude of vehicles. As the four of them approached the door, McMahon said, "Why the hell didn't Mindy get back in her car and leave as soon as she saw this dump?"

"Who knows what was going through her mind," Traynor said. "Maybe she felt flattered that a hunk like Skidgel would be interested enough in her to give her a shot at stardom."

Manuel looked thoughtful as he studied the structure. "This doesn't look like a place where she would feel comfortable."

"Even though he denies it, we're certain that Skidgel brought her here," Deborah said. "I know she wanted to get a job as an actress, but I find it hard to believe that she thought any reputable production company would film way out here."

Manuel said, "If there were cameras, sound trucks, and other filming equipment around, it might have encouraged her."

A gust of wind blew from the surrounding desert, whipping debris at them until Traynor felt as if he were being sandblasted. "What are we trying to prove here?" he asked.

"I need to see it," Manuel said. "It will help me get a feeling for the people we're dealing with."

As convoluted as his explanation was, it made sense to Traynor—although from the look he saw on Deborah's face, he knew that as much as she believed she needed to see the site of her sister's death, the thought of actually standing in it was a bit much for her. She held back by the car, an apprehensive look on her face. "Are you all right?" he asked.

"No."

"You can wait in the car while Manuel sees what he needs to see."

"I know you may not understand this, but I want—no, I need—to see this. Maybe it will help give me closure."

"It may do the opposite and just cause you more pain," Traynor replied. He looked to Manuel and McMahon for support.

They shrugged and McMahon said, "She signs our paychecks. In my book that gives her the right to do whatever she wants."

Traynor stepped onto the dilapidated porch and tried the door; it was unlocked and swung inward. The windows were shuttered and the interior was dark enough to keep him from discerning anything until his eyes adjusted. Once his vision returned, it took no time at all to see that they were looking at the place where Mindy Hollis had been raped, brutalized, and murdered. The furniture was covered with industrial-grade poly, which was coated with a thin film of dust from the blowing sand.

McMahon stepped past him into the miniscule living room and stated the obvious. "This is where it was filmed."

"It's been cleaned," Traynor said.

"Obviously," McMahon said. "What did you expect?"

"That means," Traynor added, "that they either cleaned it themselves or brought a cleaning crew with them from LA. Or they could have hired someone local."

"An operation like this wouldn't take chances," Manuel said as he walked through the room and stopped before a door that led into the bedroom. His fists were clenched and his face flushed with indignation and anger. "They'd bring their own crew. People they could trust to keep their mouths shut."

Traynor watched Manuel as he lifted the poly from the bed and studied the mattress. "I don't care how much you clean, given the degree to which she was butchered, there'll still be trace evidence." At that moment, Traynor realized why Manuel wanted to see this place—he was hunting, and like a hound, he needed to pick up his quarry's scent.

Traynor studied Deborah. She was as pale as a bucket of milk. She roamed through the room, touching the furniture and peering at the walls. "Does this look freshly painted to you guys?"

The three of them were mute. Traynor visualized Mindy's blood and tissue splattering on the walls and floors during her mutilation. It sickened him, and more than anything else, he wanted to bring down every last one of the bastards who had perpetrated this crime.

Deborah seemed to strengthen and said, "I had to see this place. If for no other reason than I needed it to piss me off enough to know that I'm doing the right thing by not leaving this to the authorities."

"At least we got Skidgel," Traynor commented.

"On *what*? Conspiracy?" Venom and righteous indignation filled Deborah's voice. Traynor noticed that she displayed nothing of the perky little cheerleader who had walked into his office five days prior. In her place was a businesswoman who was as strong as tungsten steel.

"There's no way but the lying bastard was part of this. He knew what was going to happen when he set her up to come here. If he hadn't, they'd have found his body with hers," Traynor said. "That's more than enough to make him an accomplice—that should get him a long stretch in prison."

"Anything he gets—short of death—is a more lenient sentence than my sister got."

She had him there.

They roamed the rest of the building in silence until Deborah said, "I've seen enough." She stormed out of the house.

When he heard the car door slam, Traynor looked at Manuel and McMahon. "Think she got pissed off enough?"

"Right now," McMahon said, "I wouldn't want to be one of the people who did this."

As Traynor walked out of the house and approached the car, he thought: *What was it that Kipling said? "The female of the species is more deadly than the male . . ."*

Forty-one of the top fifty most dangerous cities are located in Latin America.

—*Business Insider*

18

The sun had barely punched a hole through the smog when they gathered on the tarmac for Manuel and Traynor's flight south. Deborah said, "Anything you need, call this number." She handed each of them a business card. "That's Hollis International's man in Mexico City. He'll get whatever you need."

"Thank you, Ms. Deborah, but it will be better if I work through people I know down there."

"Keep that number just in case—you never know what might happen."

"That brings something to mind," Traynor added. "Is there any chance we'll meet someone who remembers you from your undercover days?"

Manuel seemed to ponder the question. "I don't think we have to worry about that. It has been more than eight years since I was last in Mexico City—and the sort of people I dealt with have the life expectancy of an insect in a pesticide factory." A predatory look came over his face. "I can attest to that . . ."

Traynor decided not to push that issue any further.

———————

As the Gulfstream descended toward the runway of Benito Juárez International Airport, Traynor stared out the window at the mountains that appeared to be only an arm's length away. He turned to Manuel and said, "I never realized how high Mexico City was."

"It sits on a dry lakebed in the crater of an ancient volcano. In fact, when the Spanish first arrived, it was a lake. It has its good points and bad."

Traynor waited for him to go into more detail.

"Because of where it sits, it shakes like a bowl of gelatin during an earthquake . . ." Manuel paused and added, "The September '85 quake killed ten thousand people and almost destroyed the city."

He fell silent and Traynor realized Manuel was not going to offer any more information. He asked, "It killed ten thousand people?"

"That's how many they found. Only God knows the true count—it was the highest death count on record until the earthquake and tsunami in Japan a couple of years ago."

Forty minutes later, they entered customs. Beside each aisle was a stoplight. So long as it was green all a traveler had to do was present a passport and they were passed through with minimum hassle. However, if it turned red—which it supposedly did on a random basis—customs officials inspected each and every piece of luggage. They got lucky—they hit it green.

When they walked out of customs and into the terminal, Manuel strode over to a tall, nattily dressed man, and they hugged, patting each other on the back. When they disentangled, Manuel turned and introduced him to Traynor: "Felipé Shoucar, Eduardo Traynor."

Traynor offered his hand and he took it with a firm grip. "*¡Encatado de conocerle! ¡mucho gusto!*" Traynor said, hoping that he had pronounced the Spanish for "my pleasure" correctly.

Shoucar smiled and said, "*Se hablar español?*"

"Only a little," Traynor replied, holding his right hand up with about an eighth of an inch between his thumb and forefinger, "certainly not enough to survive on my own."

Shoucar laughed and said, "Ah, but a little is better than none, is it not?" He motioned toward the exit. "Gentlemen, our car is this way."

Once they were in the car and the driver had merged into the congested stream of traffic, Shoucar turned and said to Traynor, "Your first visit to *Ciudad de México?*"

"Yes."

"I hope you won't find it too overwhelming. We are twelve millions of people living in a city that should hold six millions. Unfortunately, a large percentage of our people live in poverty."

Traynor believed him. Shoucar must have noted that he was looking through the window at a neighborhood of hovels built inside a stone wall. "As you can see," he said, "those huts are made of cardboard. Fortunately for them, it does not rain often."

The arid nature of the climate was evidenced by a layer of smog, which made the air in LA seem pristine, and the streets were littered with trash and debris. "Doesn't the city have a sanitation department?" Traynor asked.

"Of course we do, but when the population is twice what your city is able to support, providing services is . . ." He paused as if struggling to find the proper English word and then added, "difficult." Once again he motioned to the cardboard shacks. "Most of those people are from the countryside, where poverty is a way of life. The huts are illegal, but there are too many of them for the *policía* to deal with—many of our poor live in these shantytowns, much like the hobos of America's Great Depression did."

"Sounds as if you've read Steinbeck," Traynor said.

"Yes, one of my favorite American authors . . ."

"I found *The Grapes of Wrath* depressing," Traynor said.

"The book makes me think of the plight of the majority of my people," Shoucar said. "One could say that one of the few benefits of living in a country like ours is that, unlike other countries, we don't feel economic downturns—it is the norm for us. Now to the business at hand . . ."

"We're looking for Giuliano Olivas Toledo." Manuel spoke for the first time since they had entered the car.

"Ah, that one. I've been trying to get him for years. He's like smoke—no matter how tightly you grasp it, it slips through your hand. What is your business with him?"

Traynor looked at Manuel, unsure of how much he should disclose to this man. He had no idea who Shoucar was, nor did he have a feeling for how trustworthy he was.

Manuel said, "It's all right to tell Felipé everything. He's *Policía Federal*, similar to our FBI. I would trust him with my life."

Which, Traynor was sure, they were doing.

"Why don't you fill him in?" Traynor said.

Manuel and Shoucar spoke in Spanish, while Traynor stared out the window, looking at the sights.

When they finished some minutes later, Shoucar switched to English and said, "I cannot be a part of the murder of one of our people."

"That is not why we are here," Manuel explained. "We want to entice him to go to the United States, where the authorities can deal with him."

Shoucar did not seem entirely convinced. "Manuel, you wouldn't lie to me, would you?"

"No, Felipé, as much as I would like to put a bullet in this son of a *puta's* head, that is not why we are here."

Shoucar's eyes narrowed as if still unsure of them. Traynor could not blame him; he wasn't sure how he would actually react when he finally met with Holy Toledo.

"Meeting Toledo will not be as easy as you hope," Shoucar said. He turned and looked at Traynor as if he were reluctant to say something.

Traynor tried to put him at ease. "Say what's on your mind—I'm not easily offended."

"Toledo and men like him are like prairie dogs . . . They are curious and want to know everything, yet they are wary to the point of paranoia. They will not be open to meeting with . . ."

"A *gringo?*" Traynor said.

"Not so much that. May I be frank?"

"By all means," Traynor answered.

"*Señor*, one does not have to look at you very long to decide that you are *policía*. You wear the job—as do all of us who have been *poli* for a long time. Toledo will know you are not who you would have him think."

Traynor looked at Shoucar and said, "Even a cop who's fallen from grace?"

Traynor wondered if maybe Deborah should have sent McMahon with Manuel instead. After all, he had been there, done that, and bought the T-shirt.

"The DF (Distrito Federal—Federal District) remains safe, in fact safer than some American cities in terms of the homicide rate. Recent jumps in the rate of extortion and kidnapping are worrying tendencies."
—Duncan Wood, Director of the Mexico Institute
at the Woodrow Wilson Center

19

*H*ombre was not the worst strip club in Mexico City, but it was by no means the best. The strippers, Traynor thought, were a mixed group, spanning from the very attractive to the extremely homely. The lights were low, and two circular stages—one at each end of the room—took up more than a third of the available floor space and the bar took half of what remained. In his official capacity, Traynor had been in any number of these places, but this was the first time he'd ever been professionally frisked and patted down by a bouncer at the entrance. Fortunately, he and Manuel had left the weapons that the Hollises' man had procured for them in their hotel room safes.

They were led to a corner table, away from the crowd, but still had an open view of the stage. No sooner had they been seated than a scantily clad waitress appeared, asking for their drink order. Traynor looked at Manuel and said, "You know your way around down here much better than I do. What do you suggest?"

"Tequila. What else does one drink in Mexico? Drink it straight up. You may as well drink the water as have ice in a drink."

He turned to the waitress and spoke to her in Spanish. She smiled and rushed away to fill their order.

"What did you say that brought on that smile?"

"She wanted to know which type . . ."

"How many types of tequila are there?"

"Who knows? But I can take you to a shop that sells only tequila and the shelves will be full of different ones."

"Hardly seems like a reason for her to smile like she did."

Manuel grinned. "That was because I told her that you were a tequila virgin and to bring us something that was not too strong."

"Thanks a lot," Traynor replied. "It didn't take you thirty seconds to completely destroy my macho image."

"You'll survive."

The waitress returned with a bottle and two glasses that were slightly larger than a shot glass. After she placed it on the table, Manuel spoke to her once again; this time she did not smile. She was nervous when she looked around, and then she bent over, displaying more cleavage than Traynor had seen in a long time. She said something, and when Manuel handed her a roll of peso notes, she looked as if she wanted to run as far from them as possible. She stuffed the money between her breasts and almost sprinted away.

"Well, that reaction was different."

"Wasn't it, though? I asked her if she knew a man named Arquímedes Treviño. She told me that he was not a man we should be asking about. That's when I gave her the money. Unless I miss my guess, we'll have a visitor—or more—very soon."

Manuel knew his business. In just a few minutes, a large man in a gray suit approached the table. He wore a white shirt open at the neck, and Traynor thought he saw the flash of a handgun in a shoulder holster. "I think our man is on his way," he said. "Nice suit. He must have a good tailor. You can hardly see the piece he's wearing."

"Relax and let me handle this," Manuel said.

"All things considered, I don't see where I have a lot of say in the matter."

Manuel grinned. "McMahon said you were sharp."

Before Traynor could think of a wisecrack, the gun-toting tough was beside the table. "Good evening, señores. Marisol told me that you asked about Señor Treviño."

He looked at Traynor when he spoke, but when Manuel answered him in Spanish, he discarded Traynor like he was a pair of boxer shorts with a loose waistband. The thug sat in the empty chair beside Manuel and slid his chair close. They leaned forward as they spoke, and Traynor's limited knowledge of Spanish kept him from understanding most of their conversation, so he stared at the stripper who was performing on one of the two stages.

Suddenly, their guest rose from the table, walked through the cigarette smoke, and stopped beside a door that was on the back wall between the stages. He punched in a code and disappeared. Traynor turned and peered at Manuel through the dim lights and spiraling smoke. "What gives?"

"We have to wait and see."

"That's it?"

"Not quite. He was concerned that I would bring an *extranjero* with me—especially one who was a cop."

"First, what is an *extranjero* and second, what did you tell him about me?"

"An *extranjero* is a foreigner, an alien. I stuck with our story . . . you are a *policía* who was caught taking bribes. Now you are involved in other types of business."

"Do you think he bought it?"

Manuel shrugged. "Who knows? All these *matón* are paranoid."

"*Matón?*"

"Hoodlums . . ." He looked over Traynor's shoulder and added, "I think we are about to get an answer.

The hood returned and stopped beside their table, leaning over and saying something with his mouth so close to Manuel's ear that Traynor heard nothing. Manuel nodded and the messenger disappeared into the foggy room.

"Well?"

"Señor Treviño has agreed to speak with us."

Traynor looked at the door between the stages and saw there was no one there to enter the code and give them access. "We won't be meeting him here," Manuel said. "He will send someone to tell us where later. Until then, we enjoy the tequila and watch the show."

They were there an hour before the *matón* returned. Without saying anything, he handed Manuel a slip of paper and walked away. Manuel read the paper, shoved it into his shirt pocket, and stood up.

"Do we have a meet?" Traynor asked.

"In two hours. Before then, we have to go to our rooms and get something."

Not one to belabor the obvious, Traynor followed him out of the club.

———

The last place Traynor expected to meet with a member of Mexico City's mob was a church in a small village on the outskirts of the metropolitan area. As they drove down the unpaved street, he studied the adobe huts and hardscrabble yards. "Looks like someone modeled this place after a Clint Eastwood spaghetti western."

Manuel grinned. "Most of Mexico is small towns and villages."

In the headlights Traynor saw a tree with flat green leaves. "What type of tree is that?"

"It's not a tree, it's a paddle cactus." Traynor did not answer him, but he had always thought that all cacti were either a small melon-sized ball of thorns or like the Saguaro variety common in the Arizona desert. He turned his attention to the buildings. The headlights illuminated a cathedral-style church that was the most imposing building he had seen since they had left the city. "Are you Catholic?" Traynor asked Manuel.

"Why do you ask that? It's not relevant to anything."

"I don't know, I thought I'd ask to make conversation. I know a lot of people down here are Roman Catholic."

Manuel kept his eyes to the front and shrugged. "I'm a *none*."

Traynor almost laughed. "You don't look like a nun to me."

"But I am." Manuel's gaze was penetrating and Traynor was starting to feel uncomfortable. Suddenly Manuel smiled and said, "When it comes to religion, I got none, don't want none, and ain't about to get none."

Traynor replied, "Yeah, me too." He studied the puissant village and said, "Still, it amazes me how the Catholic Church builds these huge monoliths to Christ in the middle of all this squalor. Christ was a pauper, who lived on the charity of others. I can't help but wonder what he would think about these monstrosities. They could feed this village for years on what that cost."

"Would Jesus wear a $1500 watch?" Manuel said.

"What?"

"That was the question I asked when I saw my first television evangelist. He was wearing a Rolex."

While Traynor mulled over that idea, they stopped in front of the church.

Manuel put his pistol under the driver's seat. "They'll frisk us," he explained. "Remember they're all paranoid. We won't get in with our weapons, so we may as well leave them here rather than risk leaving them."

"Why'd you have us bring them?"

"This meeting is the easy part."

"You wanna explain that?"

"These assholes won't try anything in a church—it's sacred ground. But once we leave . . . it's no holds barred. So slide it under, but not too far back that it'll be a pain in the ass to get to."

Traynor also slid his Glock under the seat.

They exited the rental and climbed the stone steps to the church entrance. Two of Treviño's goons suddenly filled the doorway. When Manuel held his hands out to the side, Traynor did the same. The goons came out and patted them down. When Traynor felt hands pat the insides of his thighs, near the groin, he was inclined to bust the matón's chops and make some remark such as: "Ohhhh, I didn't know you cared ..." However, given the situation, he maintained his composure and kept his sarcasm to himself.

The goon stood up and glared at him. Traynor lowered his arms, now fighting back the urge to offer his hand to be kissed.

The matón must have sensed something and said, "*Etraño.*"

The pat-down completed, the hoods stepped aside. Once they were inside the door, Traynor asked Manuel, "What did Big Boy call me?"

He grinned. "He called you gay."

"Really?"

"Actually, he said you were queer."

Two men occupied the front pew, sitting before an array of candles—many of which were already lit—in front of a statue of Jesus Christ. Neither spoke nor looked their way. Traynor recognized one of them as the matón from the club. Manuel walked around the pew and stopped before the candles. He placed a bill in a small glass vase that was there for that purpose, then lit a long wax wick from one of the candles and used it to light a prayer candle. When he finished, he stood in the center aisle, genuflected, and then made the sign of the cross. Traynor thought it was a good act for a "none." The oblations completed, Manuel turned and sat beside the second man. Traynor flopped down beside Manuel, as far from the matón as he could get.

The man Traynor assumed to be Treviño sat between the hoodlum and Manuel and was a real Dapper Dan. His suit was impeccable and had to cost twice that of his bodyguard. His black hair was slicked back and glistened in the candlelight. He half turned sideways and looked at Traynor. "Señor, you have no loved ones for whom you would light a candle and say a prayer?"

"I don't see a need for it."

"But there is always someone who is in need of our prayers."

"It's been my experience that God is too busy with great things to listen to me—lighting a candle seems a waste of time to me."

He stared at Traynor for a few seconds and then said, "I am going to speak with your *compañero*. Unfortunately, I find it easier to talk business in our native language."

"I understand." Traynor smiled, hoping it came across as sincere. "I sometimes think that we North Americans are the most linguistically backward people on Earth."

Treviño returned the smile and then turned his attention to Manuel. For Traynor, the next ten minutes were like watching a foreign film without subtitles. He knew the discussion was serious, but had no clue how it was progressing. During the entire discourse the only word he understood was "Toledo." Finally, Manuel shook Treviño's hand and stood up. Traynor followed suit, except when he offered his hand, Treviño ignored it. Traynor assumed it was due to some papal decree against acknowledging a non-Catholic heathen and did not push the issue. He followed Manuel down the aisle and out of the church.

They got in the car and immediately retrieved their weapons. "Well?" Traynor asked.

Manuel turned slightly and stared at him for a few seconds. "What's eating at you?"

It surprised Traynor that Manuel had picked up on his disgust; he thought he'd been doing a good job of keeping it hidden. "How did you stand eight years of dealing with scum like this?"

"One does what one must—after all, it was my job."

"I take my hat off to you, man. I was a cop for over twenty years, fifteen as a homicide detective. I've dealt with killers, drug dealers, pedophiles, and just about every form of lowlife there is—or so I thought . . ."

Manuel started the car and pulled away from the church, where the Mexican mobsters stood on the steps staring after them. Manuel remained silent, letting Traynor vent.

"But these assholes are something else. They murder for their own profit and to entertain a clientele that should be exterminated—then they go to church, light a fucking candle, and pray like they're pious, God-fearing Christians, worthy of a papal audience."

"They're no different than the Italian mobsters of the thirties and forties. They would conduct *business* and then go to their victim's funeral and grieve over them."

"Yeah, but they were preying on each other, not innocent, naïve young women . . ."

"Ed, there's only one way to bring these sons-of-bitches down and that is to get in with them and tear their organization apart from the inside. In order to do that, you swallow your disgust and play their game . . . or at least make them think you are."

"Doesn't make it any more palatable."

"No, it doesn't. We're soldiers, Ed. Only our battleground is the streets on which we live. Like soldiers we have to be willing to make sacrifices—even if it means giving our lives."

Traynor knew he was right, but the conversation made him weary and he changed the subject. "What do we do until he contacts us?"

Manuel said, "Now we wait. He'll talk to Toledo and get in touch."

"And," Traynor asked, "in the meantime, how do we occupy ourselves?"

"Hang out at the hotel bar and bolster the local economy."

Outside of war zones, more Americans have been killed in Mexico
in the last decade than in any other country outside
the United States, and the number of US deaths jumped
from 35 in 2007 to 113 in 2011.

—*CNN,* June 9, 2013

20

The call came two days later. Traynor was eating breakfast in the hotel restaurant when Manuel entered and sat down. "We have a meet," he said.

"Where and when?"

"We're having dinner with Toledo this evening at a restaurant called *La Gruta.*"

"Doesn't *gruta* mean grotto? That's a strange name for a restaurant."

"Not in this case, it *is* a cave.... Actually, I'm sort of glad they chose it. It will give me a chance to introduce you to a culture that existed around the time of Christ and show you some of Mexico City's prime tourist attractions."

"Okay, let me finish eating and I'll be ready."

They drove from the hotel and wove around some twisted streets that had Traynor reminiscing about the narrow roads through the White Mountains of New Hampshire. As they passed a plaza, he noticed a statue with a large building behind it. "What's that?"

Manuel glanced and said, "The building is Chapultepec Castle."

"Really? Every Marine knows about Chapultepec. The red stripe that noncommissioned officers wear down the trouser legs of the dress blue uniform commemorates the blood of all the NCOs who were killed storming this place during the Mexican–American War. Is the statue a monument to the battle?"

"It's called *Monumento a los Niños y Castillo de Chapultepec.* In English it means Monument to the Young Heroes and Chapultepec Castle. I'll bet the Marines didn't tell you that most of the castle's defenders were children."

"I can't say they did."

After that they passed the city limits and the landscape changed to desert and small villages until they came to *Teotihuacan*—or what Traynor knew as the Aztec Pyramids—about forty kilometers from Mexico City. Manuel was quick to let Traynor know that the Aztecs had nothing to do with the dead city. In fact, he informed him, *Teotihuacan* was inhabited from 100 to 700 AD, long before the Aztecs founded what is now Mexico City. "If the Aztecs didn't build it, who did?" Traynor asked.

"That has been and is still being debated. Possible candidates are the Nahua, Otomi, or Totonac ethnic groups. Some scholars have also suggested that *Teotihuacan* was a multiethnic state."

They strolled along the main street, called the Avenue of the Dead, which Traynor thought sounded more than a little ominous, past the Temple of *Quetzalcoatl* (which Manuel said was one of their gods). They climbed sixty meters of stone steps to the top of the Pyramid of the Sun and looked over the valley. From his perch at the pyramid's apex, Traynor saw the stone foundations of thousands of homes that had existed long before people of European descent stopped living in hide tents.

"You wouldn't think there would be a city of this size here in the high desert," Traynor commented.

"It wasn't always a desert," Manuel replied. "There were even lakes then."

They dallied the afternoon away and as the sun set in the west, Manuel said, "Let's head for the restaurant."

"How far away is it?"

"It's part of the site," he said. "You can see the *Pirámide del Sol* from the parking lot."

As if the dead city of Teotihuacan was not enough, Traynor thought that the restaurant was incredible. They entered through a portico and down a set of winding stairs. He looked into the cavern and saw a dining area that, according to the brochure, seated eight hundred, as well as a huge dance floor on which the *Ballet Folklórico of Mexico* performed traditional dances from the various parts of the country.

"Impressive," Traynor commented.

"That's what Queen Elizabeth and President Kennedy, to name a couple of the more distinguished visitors, felt."

A maître d' met them and after Manuel spoke to him in Spanish, he led them to a secluded table ringed with multicolored chairs. They ordered drinks and waited for the arrival of Holy Toledo and whomever he brought with him.

Twenty minutes passed before they saw the maître d' lead two men to their table. Manuel and Traynor stood.

When the shorter of the two men studied Manuel for several seconds, Traynor thought that the meeting was over before it began. Suddenly, the man seemed to relax and he asked, "Señor Vegas?"

Manuel held out his hand and spoke in Spanish.

Traynor waited for Manuel to make the introductions in Toledo's native language with his impatience threatening to get the best of him.

If he was going to get everything secondhand, it was going to be a very long evening. He almost exhaled with relief when Manuel said, "My colleague speaks very little Español. Therefore if you have no objection, I would like to speak Inglés."

"That is fine," replied the short man. He was built like a brick wall, undersized but wide. However, it was evident to Traynor that he was not soft.

Manuel half turned toward Traynor and said, "Señor Giuliano Olivas Toledo, may I introduce you to Señor Eduardo Traynor."

Toledo held his hand out, and when Traynor gripped it, it felt cold and dry—like a snake's skin. He struggled to hide his loathing for Toledo. No matter how expensive his clothing and polite his speech, he was still a scumbag and predator. It was going to require his best acting job if he was to hide his distaste throughout the evening. He forced a smile and said, "My pleasure, Señor Toledo." Traynor applied as much pressure as he could to his grip, hoping to see him flinch. He did not.

Manuel nudged him and he released Toledo's hand and smiled. "Shall we sit?"

Traynor noticed that Toledo made a point of sitting across from Manuel during the conference. He knew that Toledo's choice of seating was intended as an insult and kept staring at him. Toledo sensed the attention, and every few seconds he would look at Traynor out of the corner of his eye. Traynor studied Holy Toledo and found himself making some assumptions about the drug kingpin. While he might be a dangerous man, he was clearly not the poster boy for courage. He was the type that would pay someone, like his companion—who looked like a bodybuilder—to do his *wet* work[2]. Traynor remembered the movie and knew Toledo had not been Mindy's leading man. If he survived, Traynor vowed he would find the actual killer, and when he did, the guy was not going to have to worry about legal fees. He wondered if Skidgel had been remanded or made bail and decided to call McMahon that night to find out.

---

[2] Slang for violent activity, up to and including murder.

Toledo made small talk for several minutes, inquiring about the state of the Los Angeles Dodgers (as a diehard Red Sox fan, Traynor did not give a damn, but Manuel played along). Finally, Toledo said, "I understand you have a business proposition for me."

Traynor sat up straight and hoped his excitement did not show as Toledo nudged at the bait like an inquisitive fish. Manuel glanced around, pretending to check that no one was close enough to overhear. "We have been told that you are a provider of a quality product."

Toledo sat back and stared at Manuel, then at Traynor. "Maybe it would help if you were a bit more specific." A schoolboy could see that he was suspicious.

"My companion and I represent a very wealthy investor, who has a problem that he has hired my companion and me to solve."

"What sort of problem does your investor need solved?"

"He has a need for cash . . . a lot of cash."

Toledo was still unsure of them and replied, "How much cash? I believe you said he was wealthy, did you not?"

"Yes. However, he has lately discovered that he needs a lot of money, fast. He has been told that you are a person who could be a great deal of help to him."

Toledo was not about to give them the benefit of an easy agreement. "I'm not sure I understand you."

Manuel looked Toledo in the eye and leaned toward the drug lord and whispered in his ear.

Toledo sat back and covered the lower half of his face with his hand as if he were in deep thought. He leaned back and said something to one of his bodyguards and then turned back to Manuel.

"I fear you have been misled by someone. I do not deal in such . . . a product."

Manuel sat back and looked at Traynor. "It seems that we have been misinformed, my friend."

"So it would seem," Traynor replied.

In unison, they stood and Manuel said, "I ask you to forgive us for wasting your valuable time."

Toledo remained sitting. "Please, sit down, gentlemen. Just because I haven't dealt with something doesn't mean that I am not interested in a viable business proposition." They settled back and he continued. "I have contacts who . . . shall we say, have resources that are available to a very, very discreet clientele. For a price they will provide a qualified customer with anything . . ."

"What might that price be, Señor Toledo?" Traynor was starting to get the hang of this banter.

"Like everything in life, that's negotiable."

Not wanting to distract his train of thought, neither Manuel nor Traynor said anything, allowing him to continue. "A deal like this is not to be brashly entered into. Let us meet in, shall we say, three days." He looked around the room. "Negotiations such as this require someplace a bit more private. I want to hear more about this wealthy investor and his role in this business." He and his soldier stood. Toledo shook their hands. Before departing, he said, "If I am able to arrange things, are you capable of providing . . . shall we say a portion of the price of the product when we meet in three days?"

"We are capable of bringing the entire amount," Manuel said. "Will one million American dollars be enough to purchase . . . shall we say two hundred kilos?"

Toledo tried to keep his greed from showing, but he did not succeed. Upon hearing the amount of the front money, he blinked and unconsciously licked his lips. He was like a buzzard at a massacre—crazy with lust to get his hands on his reward. "That should do." He nodded and left with his goon leading the way.

As they watched them depart, Traynor said, "Three more days. . . . What do we do until then?"

"I suggest we start by having dinner."

A reconnaissance of the neighborhood should be performed . . .
—*FM 3-19.13, Law Enforcement Investigations*

21

M cMahon watched Skidgel leave his apartment and stroll down the sidewalk. He started the engine and Deborah sighed when the air conditioning blasted her with chilled air. "How do you think he was able to raise bail?" she asked. She studied the rundown apartment complex. "You wouldn't expect someone who lives in a place like this to be able to raise a million dollars."

"He only has to put up ten percent. He used a bail bondsman most likely." McMahon pulled away from the curb and cruised slowly, keeping his quarry in sight. "For what it's worth, I thought the same thing. It definitely makes me think there's someone with money behind this."

They followed Skidgel for three blocks before he turned into a garage. "I wondered if he owned a car," McMahon said. They got lucky and found an empty parking slot across from the garage exit.

In less than ten minutes, a Porsche 9-11 convertible came out of the garage with Skidgel driving. "I'll be dipped in shit," McMahon said. "It looks as if ole Vern is worth more than we thought." He let the sports car get half a block ahead before pulling into the street.

"Do you know why street gangs never steal Porsche nine elevens?" McMahon asked.

"No."

"They think they're police cars . . ."

Deborah slowly turned her head in his direction and then began chuckling.

They followed the Porsche out of Los Angeles, skirting Beverley Hills, and into Brentwood. Deborah looked out the side window and said, "Now this is where I'd expect someone worth more than a million to live."

They passed a drive and McMahon said, "Yup. In fact, this next house is where O. J. Simpson lived."

Deborah turned in her seat and looked at the infamous house as it fell behind them. She smirked. "That's another one that finally got what he had coming to him." She turned to face the front and went quiet.

They followed Skidgel for a half mile and slowly passed by as he turned into a drive, stopped before a gate, waited for it to open, and then followed the long circular lane that led to the front of the house. McMahon stopped and they watched as he exited the Porsche and walked inside. "He didn't knock," Deborah commented.

"Yeah, says a lot, doesn't it?" McMahon checked his mirrors. "We need to find a spot from which we can observe this place. It won't be easy. I got this rental so it would blend into the other neighborhood. Around here it will stick out." He handed her a notebook. "Write down the address, would you? I'm going to ask Angela to find out who owns this place."

They drove around the neighborhood and found no place where a lingering vehicle would go unnoticed. "What now?" Deborah asked.

McMahon pointed to a road that meandered up the side of a mountain behind the house. "We'll watch him from up there."

"Okay. But we have no idea how long he'll be in there—what if he's only visiting?"

"There's no way in hell Skidgel is the head of this. I want to see who else is involved. But first we need to get some things. We'll need high-powered binoculars and a good—very good—video recorder. Skidgel is about to be the lead in another film . . ."

McMahon adjusted the screen of the car's GPS so that it zoomed out and showed a panoramic view of the area. They followed the map until it showed that they were at the entrance to the road leading up the ridge. He stopped the car and said, "I'm gonna stay and keep an eye on him." He jotted a list of equipment on a piece of paper and gave Deborah the name of a man he knew who would have the gear in his shop. "Tell him it's for me and he'll give you a discount."

"Does it look like I need a discount?" She perused the list. "What's this?" She pointed at the last item on the list.

"It's a tracking system, sort of like a GPS, only rather than telling us where we are, it will tell us where he is."

"How does it work?"

"The transmitter is magnetic. Once it's stuck on the car, it will send us a signal so we'll know his location."

"Looking at that place, I doubt our favorite shithead will have only one car . . ."

"You've been hanging around Ed and me too long. Your vocabulary has definitely gone south. Still, you make a good point," McMahon said. He retrieved the list and made a quick change.

Deborah saw that he had amended the tracking device to read six transmitters, looked at him, and nodded. "I have one last question. How will we get these on his cars?"

"That's my job. I'll sneak down there after dark and attach them."

"Jack, have you thought this through? An estate that large is certain to have a security system."

McMahon grinned. "I knew I brought you along for a reason." He thought for a moment and then said, "I know an exotic pet store that will provide us with what we need." Once again, he amended the shopping list.

He handed it back and again she quickly read it. "You're kidding me—aren't you?"

He stepped back and saluted her. "Nope . . . when you're on your way back, call me and we'll arrange a place to meet." He looked in the car and said, "You may want to change out of that skirt. We may be doing some climbing."

"Climbing?"

"You never know where we may have to go in order to be able to observe things."

Deborah nodded and drove off.

McMahon waited until she was out of sight and then walked up the winding dirt road. Even though the day was sunny and warm, he maintained a brisk stride, so that if anyone were to observe him, he would appear to be out for some exercise. In no time he was soaked with sweat, but he kept up his pace. Ten minutes later, he stood in the shade of the branches of a twisted tree and leaned against the trunk, staring down at the estate. He had found a location that gave him an unobstructed view of three sides of the house. He saw someone sitting in a chaise beside an Olympic-size swimming pool. His physique was similar to Skidgel's, but without binoculars, McMahon had no way of being sure it was him.

A woman walked out of the large house wearing a bikini—or at least the bottom half of one. She placed something on the table between the two lounge chairs and flopped down in the vacant one. Even without the aid of field glasses, McMahon could tell that she was well endowed.

He scouted the area, hoping to find a place where they could park the car without being seen from below. Once again, he got lucky and found a small picnic area about two hundred yards from his observation post. It was ideal. The dirt parking area nestled back into a grove of trees and bushes. He surveyed his surroundings and was satisfied that the mansion was not within the line of sight of the recreational area. Pleased with the location, he returned to his position near the slope.

He sat in the shade of the tree, leaned against the trunk and, despite the rough bark, settled in to wait for Deborah. He had been in place for almost two hours when she called his cell phone. He gave her directions to the picnic area and with a final glance at the now vacant swimming pool, walked to the appointed rendezvous.

McMahon was waiting in the middle of the lane when Deborah slowly approached their rendezvous. He motioned for her to park beneath the spreading branches of a large oak. When she turned off the engine and popped the hatch open from inside, he unloaded their equipment and placed it on a nearby wooden table.

He looked approvingly at her new attire. Instead of her usual skirt she wore jeans, a plaid shirt, and hiking boots. She was ready for climbing through brush.

"Anything happen after I left?" she asked.

He thought of the buxom, half-naked woman and said, "Nothing."

Deborah's brow curled. She said, "Do you know the looks I got when I bought every raccoon that pet store had?"

He smiled. "Speaking of which, we have to move them into the shade. We don't want the heat to kill our friends in there. C'mon, I'll show you our looking post."

As they walked out of the picnic area, she said, "Manuel called me while I was getting our stuff . . . They've made contact."

"And," he added, "Angela called. The estate doesn't belong to Skidgel. It belongs to Lawrence Provost, which could complicate things."

"How so?"

"He's very connected . . ."

"The mob?"

"The government."

Loose surveillance can be used to spot-check a suspect. It can be used
to compile long-term information on a subject.
—FM 3-19.13, Law Enforcement Investigations

22

Darkness blanketed the sky, and McMahon and Deborah had seen little, if any, sign of life on the grounds of the estate. "Time to go," he said.

"Are you sure? Maybe we should give it another hour?"

"By the time we get down there and get set up, it'll be close to an hour."

Deborah stood and brushed dust and debris from the seat of her jeans. She arched her back and stretched. "I can't believe that I've been sitting under a tree watching a house for over four hours."

"It's what we call a stakeout. I've sat for days . . . which we may do yet. Our boy seems content to hunker down."

"Safe within his fort."

"Yeah, something like that. C'mon, let's do this."

When they reached the SUV, McMahon opened the hatch and made one last check that all of their equipment seemed to be in order. He reloaded the caged and angry raccoons and then said, "You drive."

She walked to the driver's side door and when she opened it, stepped back a pace. "Whew!" She waved a hand in front of her face.

McMahon held the other door open and said, "Well, they have been cooped up in those little cages for the entire afternoon. When a coon has to go—it has to go."

Deborah held her hand over her mouth and nose, and then got behind the wheel. She opened all the windows and before McMahon was settled into his seat, began backing up. She said, "Before we return this rental, we'll need to air it out."

"Just a little longer and they'll be out of here."

Deborah hung her head out of the window as she drove down the sloping road. Twice, she had to yank the steering wheel to keep from driving off the road and down the slope. McMahon kept a wary eye on her, and although he wanted to tell her to pull her head inside before she killed them, he did not say anything. When they stopped near the side of the estate, she wasted no time exiting the car.

"There has to be a place where I can get over that fence without rock-climbing gear," McMahon said.

"Well, don't take forever finding it. This car smells like the dung pile at a zoo."

He grinned and got out of the car. "I'll only be a few minutes."

Before she could reply, he had disappeared into the darkness.

McMahon skirted the wall that surrounded the estate, thankful that the owner's paranoia was focused on keeping the inside of his compound secure rather than the outside. As a result, all of the perimeter lights faced inward, toward the house, and not toward the exterior of the walls. He circled around until he found the only breachable section of the ramparts. He stood beside a cyclone fence gate, which was obviously the entrance and exit for maintenance and sanitation workers. After all, even the most elaborate fortifications create garbage. He studied the buttresses and realized that there were no alarms on the top of them.

McMahon had surmised that if the estate had an alarm system, it was most likely dependent on motion detectors that would be strategically located around the grounds—which was why he'd had Deborah buy the raccoons.

McMahon returned to the car and quickly apprised Deborah of his findings. He directed her to drive along the barricade until they came to a tree whose lower branches pressed against the brickwork. They removed each of the four cages from the backseat and placed them on the ground. McMahon spoke so softly that his voice was barely louder than a whisper. "I haven't seen any roving guards and was unable to locate any sensors on the walls. That makes me believe that security is entirely within the walls."

Deborah nodded. "Okay, now I understand why we need the stench sisters."

He picked up the cages and one at a time, carried them to the base of the tree. "Think you can hand these up to me?"

Deborah lifted one of the cages. "I loaded them into the car, so I think I can handle it."

McMahon climbed the tree and perched on a thick branch about three feet below the top of the parapet. "Okay, give me the first one. Be careful you don't get your fingers inside those cages. Raccoons can be nasty suckers." To emphasize his point, as soon as she reached for the first cage, its occupant bared its teeth and sounded out a menacing hiss.

Deborah hesitated. "They're upset, aren't they?"

He grinned and couldn't resist saying, "If someone locked you up in a cage for hours, you'd be upset, too."

Taking great care to keep her fingers outside the bars, she lifted the first pen by placing her hands underneath the bottom. The angry occupant spun around, shifting the cage, and Deborah almost dropped it.

"Careful," McMahon said. "If you drop one and that pissed-off coon gets free, she'll attack the nearest thing—and you're it."

"Thanks. That's just what I wanted to hear."

"You're welcome." He reached down and when she lifted the cage, grabbed it. When he lifted the folding handle on the top, the animal tried to attack. Once he had the cage secure, he placed it on the top of the wall. When he put the second cage on the wall, the occupants of the small cells saw one another and hissed and fussed. *This might work out better than I'd hoped*, McMahon thought. In short time, he had all four cages aligned on top of the rampart.

"Thank God these things unlatch from the top," he said. "Okay, now the fun begins."

He balanced himself carefully against the wall and cautiously reached for the latches on the first two restraining cages. He flipped the latches and two whirling balls of fangs, claws, and fur exploded through the opening. They collided in midair and immediately became entwined, their hissing and growling filling the area. "Wow . . ." McMahon said as he released the final pair. In seconds, a free-for-all was being waged as the enraged varmints rolled, bit, and gouged each other. He watched them for a few seconds, passed the empty cages to Deborah, and then heard a loud bell ringing. McMahon turned his attention away from the melee taking place on the manicured lawn and hunkered down beneath the wall. He motioned to Deborah who passed a small satchel to him.

When he straightened up and cautiously peered over the top of the wall, he saw two men standing on the grass, engrossed in the battle of the raccoons. "I ain't goin' near them," one said.

"Me either. I don't know if my health plan covers injuries from this shit."

"Yeah, besides, as hard as they're goin' at each other, they'll either be tired or dead in a few minutes."

"Think we should turn on a water hose and wet them down?"

"What . . . and have them pissed at us? No way, man."

"We'd better get a shovel and wheelbarrow so we can pick up the losers."

As they turned away the first man said, "I've been to dog and cock fights, but never seen nothin' like that . . ."

"Yeah, we better turn the alarms off until they're gone. Otherwise, we'll be running back and forth all night."

"You get the alarms. I'll get the shovel and wheelbarrow."

23

"What are you guys going to do if Toledo won't go to LA?" Martin Harris, head of security for Hollis International in Mexico, sat beside Traynor and slowly turned his glass in the wet rings left on the table. He peered across the table at Manuel, as if he were awaiting word from on high.

"Haven't really thought about that," Manuel answered. "The DEA's got warrants for him. They been trying to either expedite or catch him on US soil for years—he's a smart sonuvabitch. We'll probably snatch him, fly him back in the company jet, and turn him over to the cops."

Harris slid a set of car keys across the table. "Then you better take this."

"What's this to?" Traynor asked.

"A company car—a Ford Excursion to be more exact. In the event you have to, as you say, *snatch* Toledo, you won't be able to turn in a rental, or park it in the rental return lot for that matter. Just leave the truck in the general aviation lot and give the keys to our employee in the terminal." Harris looked at Manuel and Traynor in turn. "You know, of course, that we . . . we being Hollis International . . . can't help you?"

"Isn't giving us a company vehicle helping us?"

"We can make the case that we were ordered to provide you with transportation—what you do with that truck is beyond our control."

Manuel scooped up the keys. "That should work."

"I'll return the rental tomorrow. You guys need anything else?"

Manuel patted the briefcase that sat to his left. "This is it. Thanks for everything."

"*De nada.* Hollis International pays me well to be their errand boy in Mexico. You guys watch your backs and cover your asses, okay? I know I don't need to tell you that this isn't a place where you should be running around with that." He nodded to the case, which held the equivalent weight of a million American dollars in newsprint, hidden beneath a top layer of Mexican pesos.

After Harris departed, Manuel seemed distant, lost in thought.

"You okay?"

"There's something bugging me. . . . It's about you."

Traynor sat up straight. "Which is?"

"Twice now, first with Treviño and later with Toledo, your feelings were obvious—so much that I was afraid it would blow everything. Can I trust you not to go nuts on me? We're too close to the end."

Traynor felt his face flush—but not from anger. He had tried to hide his feelings behind an aura of professionalism; still his loathing for the people responsible for Mindy's death got the best of him and it must have shown. "I'm all right," he said. "After a while even a skin-diver for a septic cleaning company gets used to wallowing in the filth."

Manuel smiled. "I don't like these *bastardos* any more than you do. I'd like nothing better than to give them the slow, painful death they deserve, but if we do that, we'll never get the rest of them."

"As much as I want Toledo," Traynor said, "I want the sonuvabitch who did the on-screen work."

"The actual killer . . ."

"I want the entire crew. The cameramen, and everyone who was in that house and did nothing to help Mindy Hollis."

"That might be a tall order," Manuel replied.

"Of course, but as we speak I'm sure Deborah and McMahon are working that end."

"So all we have to do is get Toledo north?"

"That's all. Although I think killing him will probably be easier . . ." Traynor mused.

"And more fulfilling, I'm sure. Still, that's not our mission. When I was undercover down here, I could have slit the throats of any number of assholes, but my job was to identify and locate them, not take them out. I know your frustration better than anyone."

"That doesn't make it any easier, does it?"

"Shit, like most things, if it was easy, everyone would do it."

Close surveillance requires continued alertness on the part
of the surveillance team.
—*FM 3-19.13, Law Enforcement Investigations*

24

McMahon gave the two men several minutes to get out of the immediate area and then poised himself to breach the wall when he heard Deborah hiss, trying to get his attention. "What?" he whispered.

She looked up at him. "What are you gonna do if those coons see you and decide to become allies against a common enemy?"

He paused for a second. "I could have gone all night without hearing that—there are times when you sound like the CEO of a major corporation."

"That's because I am one. As such, when I make a decision, I like to plan for all contingencies." She tossed him a can.

He caught it and saw it was pepper spray. "You do have a way of thinking about the things I either overlook or don't want to consider."

She grinned. "That's why I'm the boss. Be careful. I'm not sure the corporate medical plan covers raccoon attacks."

He smiled, gave her a thumbs-up, and went over the wall.

McMahon rolled when he hit the lawn and in one motion regained his feet. He checked to make sure he hadn't been noticed and dashed toward the garage. As he jogged, he heard the racket caused by the fighting raccoons. He hoped that they would keep it up for a while longer, but knew the odds were against it. They had to be getting fatigued and would soon disentangle and run for the safety of the surrounding brush.

In short time, he reached the garage and squatted in the shadows for a few seconds to catch his breath and listen for any signs that he'd been discovered. Then he slowly circumvented the detached garage. In the rear he found a door. He smiled when he turned the doorknob and it opened.

Once inside, he paused, this time to allow his vision to adjust to the darkness. Fortunately, the building had two large windows in the rear and side walls, which allowed enough ambient light for him to do what was needed. Attaching the magnetic transmitters to each car's undercarriage did not require precision—all it required was an area of metal to which it would attach.

McMahon duck walked to the Porsche he had followed to the house, attached the transmitter to the underside of the car, and switched it on. He quickly repeated the procedure on the other two cars parked there.

He scurried back toward the door and stopped suddenly when he heard voices outside. The voices stopped by the door and McMahon overheard the discussion. "Those damned coons gone?" a rough voice asked.

"Appear to be," remarked the second.

"It's gonna be a long night if they keep setting off every alarm in the place."

"We figured that, so the alarms have been turned off for a while. We'll have to make roving patrols for the next few hours. Skidgel is sure on edge tonight."

"That puke should be," a rough voice replied. "I have no idea why the boss keeps him around. From what I hear, he's into some perverted shit and there are some seriously bad dudes involved."

"What sort of perverted shit?" McMahon gritted his teeth when he heard the renewed interest in the speaker's tone.

"I ain't heard anything specific. You armed?"

"Yuh, as soon as the alarms went berserk, Provost put out the word that we were to get our pistols and enough ammo to hold off an army."

"All over some crazy fuckin' coons?"

"Hey, it's a job."

"Just the same, my next gig won't be for some paranoid nutcase."

"Makes you wonder what he's so damned afraid of."

"I know what he's scared of," a third voice interjected, "and it ain't none of your fuckin' business. Keep moving and watch the walls. You see those goddamn animals again, shoot them."

McMahon remained still as the voices faded and he hoped, disappeared into the night. He slowly opened the door and peered through the crack. Seeing no one in his line of sight, he stepped into the night. His heart skipped when he heard a voice say, "What the . . . who the hell are you?"

McMahon's mind raced and on instinct he said, "Mr. Skidgel's personal assistant. When the alarms went off, he sent me out to check the garage."

The sentry stepped forward and in the ambient light from around the swimming pool, McMahon saw that he was suspicious. "If you're Skidgel's assistant, how come I ain't seen you before?"

"Beats me," McMahon said, "but I'll be sure to mention your powers of observation to Mr. Skidgel when I get inside."

The guard hesitated, unsure whether or not he was in trouble. McMahon did not give him the chance to decide. He lashed out with a straight left fist and hit him in the throat, leaving him unable to speak. When the guard fell to his knees, choking and gasping for breath, McMahon followed up with a kick to the side of his head. The guard fell forward and hit the blacktop with a smack that McMahon was sure could be heard throughout the estate. His victim thrashed around for several long seconds and then went still. McMahon placed two fingers on the man's neck, checking for a pulse—there was none. "Damn it."

Knowing that he had no other choice, McMahon grabbed the dead man's arm and picked him up. As he threw the corpse over his shoulder in a fireman's carry, he was thankful that the security guard was small in stature. He moved away from the garage, and keeping to the shadows, McMahon carried the body to the spot on the wall where he'd entered the property.

"Deborah," he called, keeping his voice low.

"Yes."

"Step back from the wall. I'm going to throw something over."

He heard her say, "Okay, I'm clear."

McMahon stepped up on a large landscaping rock and strained as he pushed the body over the wall. It hit the ground with a dull thud and he quickly followed it over. When he landed, Deborah was staring at the corpse, her hand over her mouth and her eyes the size of pie plates. "Is that . . . ?"

"A dead man? Yeah, he caught me coming out of the garage—I tried to knock him out before he called anyone else. I guess I hit him harder than I thought."

"Jack, what are we going to do with . . . *him?*"

"Right now, we'll put him in the back of the SUV until we figure out a better solution."

"A better solution?"

"Yeah, like maybe finding a good cliff to throw him over."

"You can't be serious."

He reached for the body and hefted it over his shoulder again. "You have no idea how serious I am. You wanna open the hatch?"

McMahon and Deborah were silent as they drove along Topanga Canyon Road, west of the 101. He turned onto an unpaved secondary road and followed it through a series of hairpin curves until a turnout appeared in their headlights. After parking the SUV, he walked to the guardrail, stared out for a few seconds, and then returned to the truck. He stopped beside the passenger door and waited for Deborah to lower the window. "I don't suppose you have a flashlight on you?"

Still too shocked to speak, Deborah shook her head no.

"Okay, you wait here. I'll be back in a few minutes."

"What about . . . ?"

"Him? Don't worry, he isn't going anywhere—at least not until I get back." He returned to his vantage point and disappeared over the rail.

As he slid down the steep slope, he tried to remember the terrain from previous trips. "I hope it hasn't changed too much," he muttered as he descended the slope. Suddenly, he crashed into a bush. He peered around and saw that the rest of the hillside was still brush-covered. *Perfect*, he thought. He used his hands and feet to scramble back up the incline.

When he suddenly appeared beside the SUV, Deborah jumped in surprise and let out a scream that was muffled by the closed windows. He waved cheerfully, hoping to calm her, and then walked to the rear of the truck. A soft click told him that she had unlocked the doors. The hatch rose by itself, and he pulled the body out. In the dim interior light, he saw Deborah staring through the gap between her and the vacant driver's seat. Her face looked ghostly and pallid in the dim interior lights. He looked at the corpse and grunted as its full weight settled on his shoulder. He grumbled, "We got to stop meeting like this," and closed the hatch.

Reaching the railing, he looked back at the truck and although he could not discern her features, he knew that Deborah was staring at him through the side window. He waved again, hoping his casual attitude would offer her some comfort, and then dumped the body over the barrier. He placed one hand on top of the rail and vaulted over. The body had slid on the sandy loam and shale and it took him several seconds to catch up with it. He grabbed the guy by the shirt collar and pulled the body past the brush-line. He grunted and pulled until he determined he was far enough in the bush for the body to go undiscovered until some other hearty fool decided to scale the slopes of the Topanga Mountains. Once the dead security guard was hidden, he used both his hands and feet to scurry up the gradient for, what he hoped would be, the last time.

Back in the truck, Deborah stared through the windshield, intentionally avoiding making eye contact. "Deborah, are you all right?"

"I just realized that I'm an accessory to murder."

McMahon listened quietly, realizing that she was correct. He tried to put her at ease by lying. "It was self-defense, not murder." He pulled a pistol from his belt and placed it on the console. "He was wearing that and would have used it to defend one of the men who murdered Mindy. He gave me no choice—either I killed him or he would have killed me."

"But it happened during the course of a burglary."

"Actually, it was breaking and entering. Burglary is when you take something—I left stuff." He put the truck in gear.

"Don't try to mollify me with jokes, Jack."

He heard the concern and fear in her voice and tried to ease her apprehension. "All I can say is that anytime you get involved with people like Skidgel, shit seems to happen."

She reached across the console and touched his arm. "Jack, I know you wouldn't have killed that man if you had any choice. It's just that I've never been involved in anything even remotely like this. When I sent you and Ed out here to find her, I had no idea it was going to lead to people dying."

"Nor did we. In these situations, things have a way of going off on tangents. Ed, Manuel, and I have been doing this for years, and there is only one constant: you go where the investigation takes you. You just keep thinking about what happened to Mindy and eventually you'll be able to live with all of this."

She removed her hand from his arm and straightened up in her seat. "I hope you're right." She did not sound convinced.

"I know I am. Now let's get out of here. The sun will be up soon."

As they drove down the canyon, Deborah's exhaustion seemed to intensify. "I'm going to drop you at the hotel," McMahon said. "We're going to have to watch Skidgel 24/7, so we'll have to do it in shifts. You sleep until noon and then relieve me."

"I'll arrange for a rental car at the hotel," she said. He realized she was stating the obvious to keep her mind occupied, and so he let her talk.

It's an eerie experience to be surrounded by a roomful of the
most monstrous people on earth . . .
—Lee Lofland, retired police officer

25

Traynor's phone rang at seven in the morning. He snatched it from the cradle. "Yeah?"

It was Manuel. "Toledo's people called. They want to meet this afternoon."

"In broad daylight?"

"Obviously, he's paid up on his bribes and feels secure."

"What's our plan?"

"I'm still working on that. The only thing I know for sure is that he'll have a lot of security and they'll be armed to the teeth."

"What about your friend, Shoucar?"

"We can't risk it. So many of the Mexico City cops are corrupt that even he won't be able to keep this under wraps. Not to mention that what you and I are planning to do is against the law, even down here."

"So where are we meeting with them?"

"At Toledo's ranchero."

"His ranchero?"

"Yuh, that's why there will be security up to our asses."

"How the hell will we get him out of there?"

"That's what our mission for today is. We take no money with us, and we get an idea of the layout. If it looks as if we can take him there, we'll arrange a time to bring the money. Otherwise, we try to get him to agree to meet us at a place of our choosing."

Traynor hung up, feeling like he had just been given a pair of lead boots and ordered to walk through a minefield.

The smog was so heavy that the day seemed gray in spite of the cloudless, sunny sky. It felt as if the Earth needed a long shower to wash away the scum. Within the city limits, the street and thoroughfares were always congested and full of SUVs—most of which had started life in the possession of North Americans—and thousands of the lime-green, original Volkswagen bugs that served as taxicabs across the city.

There was little if any traffic on the country road as they drove south of Mexico City, only an occasional beat-up pickup truck. If the road had not been paved, Traynor could have believed he'd been transported over a hundred years back in time. They crested a hill and looked across a sprawling valley, whose primary occupant seemed to be a large stucco villa surrounded by a high wall, outside of which were acres of agricultural fields and pastures.

"Unless I miss my guess," Manuel said, "we're looking at *Ranchero Toledo*..."

"That what he calls it?"

"Hell if I know. The rich love to give their homes names."

"It could be because there's no mail service out here in the sticks—no street numbers."

Manuel chuckled. "I never thought of it that way."

As they drove down the curving road, Traynor grew tired of staring through the layers of desert dust and sand that covered the windshield. "My stomach feels as if I ate a bowl of snakes for lunch. It's like they're thrashing around in there."

Without taking his eyes from the road, Manuel replied, "I know that feeling well."

"How'd you stay undercover down here for so long?"

"Wasn't easy. There were many days that I was sure would be my last."

"So why do it so long?"

Manuel seemed to ponder the question. "This will sound nuts to most people, but you've been on the job and might understand. On those days where I thought I'd die, I experienced some of most intense highs I've ever had in my life. The wind rustling through the trees, even traffic noise, took on an intensity unlike anything I'll ever experience again."

"So, for eight years you were on an adrenaline rush?"

Manuel nodded. "It can be as addictive as sex or cocaine. I lived for the rush—I probably went out of my way to put myself in danger just for the high. I guess you could say I'm an adrenaline junkie."

"Are you feeling it now?"

"Not yet."

Traynor settled back in the seat. "Let me know when it happens so I can be ready. Okay?"

"Okay." He grinned. "But stay on your toes—sometimes it hits quicker than lightning."

"That's comforting."

When they reached the valley floor, Traynor got his first look at the hacienda's security—and it was daunting. As the road leveled and they passed the farthest extremity of the wall, he saw a series of towers spaced at equal distances along the parapets. "Am I seeing correctly?" he asked.

"Yeah, guard towers. In all probability equipped with machine guns."

"I believe that our friend Holy Toledo is more than a little paranoid."

"No comment needed there. Obviously this complicates things."

"Manuel, you have to be the king of understatement."

"I try. Either way, we got to adjust our strategy—and fast."

"I, for one, am open to any change in plans that won't result in my death."

"What about mine?"

"That's your problem. I got enough to do keeping my own ass alive." Traynor hoped Manuel knew he was joking. As in any combative situation, survival usually boiled down to the team that worked together the best. Manuel must have known he was kidding, though, because he was chuckling as he slowed before the heavy cast-iron gate that protected the compound's entrance.

There are two methods of mobile surveillance: foot and vehicle.
—*FM 3-19.13, Law Enforcement Investigations*

26

McMahon poured the last of the coffee from his thermos and sipped the bitter black brew. The early-morning sun peered over the crest of the peak behind him and warmed the night chill from his back. He glanced at his watch—five in the morning. Fatigue burned his eyes and he stood and stretched to alleviate the stiffness in his body. Several loud cracks came from his back and he groaned, "Gettin' too old for this shit." A man walked out of the house below, drawing McMahon's attention. He peered through his binoculars and immediately recognized Vernon Skidgel.

Skidgel sipped from a travel mug. He seemed to be searching the area, and McMahon dropped to his haunches behind a scrub brush. The sun was at his back so he did not have to worry about it reflecting from the binoculars, and as he peered through them, he intently studied his target.

Obviously, the asshole *must feel secure in his den*, McMahon thought.

One of the security guards came around the garage and stopped beside Skidgel, who lit a cigarette and listened as the guard spoke in an animated manner.

McMahon had no doubt about what they were discussing; a member of the security detail was missing. After several seconds, the guard walked away and Skidgel dropped his cigarette to the concrete surface of the walk. He ground the butt with his foot and walked toward the garage.

McMahon lowered the binoculars, letting them hang from the strap draped around his neck. He picked up the remote receiver from the ground and switched it on. The screen illuminated, displaying a large dot. He turned his attention to the garage and saw the door rise. Within seconds, a second dot split from the large one and began to move.

He ran to his car.

McMahon followed Skidgel as he drove into the San Fernando Valley. The tracking device made it easy, but McMahon still took extra caution in the event that his quarry had taken safety measures—such as having a member of his security team following at a safe distance to spot any tails.

Skidgel turned into the parking lot of a restaurant and looked in all directions before entering. McMahon swore under his breath. It was obvious that a meet was taking place, but there was nothing he could do about it. Skidgel would recognize him immediately and panic. Still, it was important to learn who he was meeting. The only option left was to park along the street and observe the restaurant, hoping that Skidgel would exit beside this new player.

McMahon saw a coffee shop across from the restaurant and turned into it, parking so he faced the restaurant. He went inside and kept his eyes glued on the establishment across the boulevard as he ordered a large black coffee and a bagel.

A half hour passed before Skidgel exited the restaurant alone and McMahon faced a decision. Should he tail him or wait and see who followed him out? The decision was made for him when another man walked through the door and stopped beside Skidgel. They chatted for several seconds before the man walked away in the opposite direction. Skidgel remained in place and lit a cigarette.

The transponder on his car would allow McMahon to keep track of Skidgel, so he opted to follow the new man. McMahon pulled out onto the street, slowly followed along behind his new quarry, and watched him get into a late-model Jaguar. He turned into the entrance of a gas station/convenience store and drove past the pumps, stopping at the exit and pretending to check traffic. His delay, as he allowed three cars to pass, raised the ire of one of the station's customers. The frustrated customer honked, and McMahon waved at him as if they were acquainted. The car's horn sounded again, but this time he ignored it. The Jaguar passed and McMahon drove out of the exit, cutting off a battered pickup truck so he could pull in behind his target. When they stopped for a red light, he jotted down the Jag's license plate number to give to Angela.

McMahon followed the Jag as it turned onto the Reagan Expressway and scaled Santa Susana Pass. When he crested the mountain, McMahon swore softly. "Shit, we're heading into Simi Valley again . . . and I'll bet that it ain't coincidence."

They drove into the city, and in no time at all, he had an idea as to where they were headed. His suspicions were proven correct when the Jaguar turned into a driveway. McMahon slowed as he passed the familiar house and watched the door open. Celia Doerr appeared in the doorway, and the man took her in his arms. Neither the embrace nor the kiss they shared was platonic. In fact, they were all over each other like two lovers who'd been separated for a long time.

Real-life mobsters are ruthless, treacherous, and deadly.
—Paul Doyle, retired DEA Agent

27

They were led into a very large and elaborate vestibule. The armed guard escorting them said something to Manuel in Spanish. "Gracias," Manuel replied, and the guard disappeared into the bowels of the house.

Once he was gone, Traynor asked Manuel, "What's up?"

"He's off to inform his *lord and master* that we're here."

"I thought we had an appointment with *the great man* and were expected."

"We do and are. This is just a game to put us in our place."

Traynor felt his anger growing again and swallowed hard, as if it were an odious hors d'oeuvre that had to be eaten in order not to insult the host. Manuel must have sensed his mood, because he looked at him reproachfully. "Don't worry," Traynor said, "I'm cool."

Rather than belabor the point, Manuel nodded and said softly, "Keep in mind these people are usually paranoid—they have to be to survive. Our every move and gesture is probably being monitored."

Trying to remain inconspicuous, Traynor scanned the room as much as he could without moving his head. Manuel whispered, "I'd bet on the painting."

Playing the role of a curious guest, Traynor strolled across the spacious foyer and stopped before a monstrous portrait of a Mexican don. The resemblance to Toledo was apparent. He noticed that one of the eyes seem to glisten and knew he was looking at a camera lens. Still playing his role, he said to Manuel, "Who you think this is?"

Before he could reply, another voice said, "Jose Maria Esteban Toledo, my grandfather and patriarch." Traynor turned. Toledo and his armed guard walked out of one of the hallways that ended in the antechamber. Toledo was dressed as if he were about to dine with the president of Mexico. He wore a tuxedo, complete with cummerbund. "In his time, he was *nobleza*, nobility—a king among men. He built this ranchero and hacienda when this valley was nothing but desert."

Traynor kept his response to a polite. "Very impressive." Still, he wondered how old Jose Maria would react if he knew what his grandson was doing to fill the family coffers. He looked back at the imposing portrait and studied the eyes. They appeared reptilian, cold, and lethal. Traynor supposed the old man would probably approve of anything his grandson did—so long as he grew the family's sphere of influence.

Toledo motioned with a sweep of his arm. "This way, gentlemen, if you please."

Traynor found Toledo's politeness patronizing but kept his contempt hidden. For as long as he could remember, he'd hated hypocrisy and those who thought he was too stupid to see through it. Here was a man who acted as civil and proper as one would expect the wealthy to be, but made his money dishing out misery and death. Traynor was really looking forward to bringing him down.

They followed him along a wide corridor. The walls were adorned with expensive artwork and the carpet was so plush it felt like they were walking on thick velvet. Traynor couldn't help but think that it was a shame that they were fouling it with their street shoes.

At the corridor's end, Toledo stopped beside a door and once again made a genteel sweep of his arm to guide them into the room. It was as breathtaking as it was massive. Leather chairs and couches were placed throughout, all facing the largest fireplace Traynor had ever seen. The hearth alone must have cost more than the average American home. It was constructed of white marble and the mantle held a collection of fine china vases. A number of firearms were mounted on the wall a few feet above the mantle—some antique and some modern. There were enough guns there to stock an arsenal.

Toledo noticed where he was looking and said, "Are you interested in firearms, Señor Traynor?"

"I wouldn't call knowledge of weapons an interest as much as a professional requirement."

Toledo smirked at him. "So you've used them in your work?"

"Both used them and have had them used against me—sort of an occupational hazard."

"Ahhh, so were you in the *servicio military?*"

"Yes, and I was a member of the police as well."

Toledo stiffened and gave Manuel a stern look. Before he could say anything, Traynor injected, "My superiors did not understand when they caught me with my hand in the cookie jar."

Toledo turned his attention from Manuel back to Traynor. "Cookie jar?"

"I was caught taking money from drug dealers for being blind to their activity."

His face lit with understanding. "I see. *Soborno*, or bribery as you call it, is a necessary part of doing business in my country also." He dismissed Traynor as just another crooked cop and turned to Manuel. "And you, Señor Vegas, are you also familiar with firearms?"

"For several years I was employed as a *mercenario*. Weapons were the tools of my trade."

Toledo looked as if he wanted to pursue Manuel's background further, but instead turned the conversation to business. "I have been in touch with my partners and they want to know more about your proposed project." He noted their empty hands. "You have brought the money, no?"

Manuel did not even blink when he said, "No."

"No?" Toledo was obviously not amused.

"No. You must pardon me, Señor Toledo, but with this amount of money, we do not feel comfortable driving around with it. After all, this is not our country."

Toledo reddened and Traynor knew he was upset. The man's reaction was so strong that it was evident Manuel had made the correct call in leaving the money behind. "I find it hard to believe that two men—of whom one is a trained mercenario—would be afraid to transport money."

"As trained professionals, we have also learned to minimize risk."

Traynor was not sure how Manuel's answer went over, but Toledo's eyes changed and like those in his grandfather's portrait, became reptilian with a glassy, lifeless appearance. Traynor glanced at the wall and wondered whether or not any of the weapons hanging there were loaded—not that it mattered. His luck was such that if all the guns were loaded except for one, that would be the one he grabbed.

After several tense moments, Toledo seemed to get his temper under control. However, he was not about to let them off the hook until he made his point. "Gentlemen, I must say that if we are to do business, there must be trust between us."

"Like having armed guards on your walls with their weapons pointed at us?" Manuel was not above throwing a barb of his own.

A sinister grin spread across Toledo's face. He knew that Manuel had him. "I guess we are at a stalemate."

"I wouldn't say that," Traynor said. "I'd rather say that we're just cautious men."

"Then," Toledo concluded, "I must ask what the purpose of your visit is?"

"We like to know something about the people with whom we do business," Manuel answered. "This *hacienda*, for instance, tells us that you are truly a man worth doing business with and not an opportunist hoping to steal a great deal of *dinero*."

Toledo did not seem impressed with the statement. "I'm glad that you find me worthy. I assume that you want to meet once more?"

"*Sí*, at a place of our choosing," Manuel answered.

"Then, I see no purpose in prolonging this meeting any further. You inform me of where you want to meet and—if it meets with my approval—we will meet. This time, gentlemen, you bring the million dollars and I'll bring your cocaine." With a curt nod, Toledo exited, leaving his guests in the hands of his security force.

Within minutes Manuel and Traynor were back in their vehicle and on the road back to Mexico City.

"Well," Traynor said, "all in all, I think that went about as well as we could have expected."

When Manuel smiled, his teeth looked blue in the light of the console. "Yes, as a matter of fact, I learned several things."

"Like we'll never get him out of his den—at least not alive?" Traynor interjected.

"That and the fact that we need to choose our next meeting place wisely. It has to be someplace public, but at a time when it is unoccupied. If we were to meet at . . . say Teotihuacan, it would be impossible to tell his security from the tourists. I don't know about you, but I, for one, like to know the odds I'm up against."

"Yeah, it's always comforting to know whether or not you've brought enough firepower."

Give instruction to a wise man and he will be yet wiser.

—Proverbs 9:9

28

Traynor called from his room. Jack McMahon answered on the second ring and updated him on what had been happening back in the good ole US of A. He was surprised to learn about Celia Doerr's involvement with Skidgel's associate.

"Have you learned the guy's identity?"

"The estate belongs to some political powerbroker, name of Larry Provost. I got Angela and Dick Lebow working that angle."

"It will be interesting to learn what his part in this is."

"Whatever it is, he's got money—at least that's what I usually expect when I see someone driving a shiny new Jag."

Traynor turned the conversation to their employer. "How's Deborah handling all of this?"

"Well . . . it was touch and go when I had the incident with the security guard."

"I'll bet. Is she all right?"

"She seems to be. But I'm keeping a close watch. The past several days have been quite a shock to her."

Traynor thought about the steel he'd detected in her character when she'd first arrived in LA and said, "Something tells me that she's gonna be all right."

"Yeah, I get that same feeling. What's goin' on down there?"

"We've met with Toledo twice."

"And?"

"We're trying to come up with a way to snatch him."

"Snatch him?"

"Manuel is of the mind that it's wasted effort to try and arrest him— especially down here. He'll just buy his way out and then we'll be targeted by his people and by the police."

"I've heard that the Mexico City PD has issues."

"Yeah, they're still trying to weed out the honest cops on the force."

"Well, keep in touch," McMahon said.

"I'll call you as soon as we know how this is goin' down."

Manuel was waiting when Traynor walked into the bar. Traynor was surprised to see that he was deep in conversation with Felipé Shoucar. He crossed the room and sat with them. Manuel nodded to him but kept talking.

" . . . We have met with Toledo twice now and still there is nothing concrete to give you. It isn't enough that he's a snake, but he's a snake with seemingly unlimited resources."

"And," Shoucar added, "one who has been very generous with his *contributions*. He is very well connected inside the police and government. Arresting him is one thing, keeping him in custody is another."

Traynor could not help but jump into the discussion. "Are you saying that if we were to turn him over to the authorities, they'd let him walk?"

"Eventually," Shoucar said, "they may send him to some posh jail reserved for the wealthy and VIPs. But it's more likely that he will be put under house arrest."

Traynor replied, "He may as well be given a get out of jail free card."

Shoucar looked quizzical, as if he was not familiar with the phrase. Manuel said something in Spanish. The only words Traynor understood was *monopolio* and *partida*, which he knew meant game. Shoucar nodded his understanding. "Not only will he, as you say, get out of jail free, but you may find yourselves under a lot of scrutiny. I'm afraid, my friends, that Toledo is as close to untouchable as one can get. You would have a better chance of taking *el presidente* into custody."

Traynor looked at Manuel, who returned his look. If Shoucar was correct, they would never get Toledo out of Mexico by plane or train. It looked as if they would have to abduct him. Easily said, but, given the level of security that Toledo had around him, not so easily done.

Shoucar motioned for the server and picked up his bill. "I must be going. I have not seen my children for three days, and I don't want them to start feeling fatherless." He shook hands and exited the lounge.

"So," Traynor said to Manuel, "where does that leave us?"

"As I see it, we only have one course of action left to us. We have to grab Toledo and run for the airport."

Traynor motioned for the server and ordered bourbon, neat, then turned back to Manuel. "Okay, given your vast experience in these matters, what do you think our chances of success are?"

"Two . . . zilch and zilch point shit."

"Not very encouraging."

"I know. We can only hope that it comes up zilch and not . . ."

"Power tends to corrupt, and absolute power corrupts absolutely.
Great men are almost always bad men."
—Lord Acton, English historian and moralist, 1887

29

---

ngela Engle called McMahon while he and Deborah were eating dinner in the hotel restaurant. "Jack, where are you?"

"Right now I'm eating dinner with Deborah. Why?"

"I got the information you wanted on the driver of the Jag. However, I'm not comfortable relaying it over the phone."

If Engle was leery of passing the info over the phone, McMahon was certain that it was extremely sensitive. "Can you give me a hint at what we're dealing with?"

"A scandal that could go all the way to Sacramento."

"Okay, where can we meet?"

"There's this bar in Thousand Oaks that I go to occasionally. We could meet there in two hours."

"Give me the address."

Engle passed on the location and then said, "You know anything about a body that was dumped in Topanga Canyon?"

"Why would I know anything about that?"

"Because the guy was an independent security contractor."

"So?" McMahon knew where she was going and did not want to give her any fuel with which she could stoke the fire of her suspicions.

"He was working for your buddy Skidgel. Now isn't that a coincidence?"

"It's a strange world, isn't it?"

When he hung up, Deborah asked, "What was that all about?"

Rather than scare her with the news that the body had been found, he replied, "That was Angela—she wants to meet with us in a couple of hours."

The bar was more of a restaurant than a watering hole and when McMahon and Deborah entered, they saw Engle wearing civilian clothes and sitting at a secluded booth near the back. Deborah slid into the seat across from her, leaving room for McMahon to sit beside his ex.

They ordered drinks and Engle said, "Jack, you guys may have opened up a real can of worms."

"Everything about this affair is a can of worms," he said.

"Yes, but . . . this *new* can contains the campaign manager of Mark Alioto, the Governor of the State of California—who just happens to be running for reelection."

"Really?" McMahon leaned back and allowed the server to place their drinks on the table. Once the waitress was out of hearing range, he turned his attention back to Engle. "Who's this campaign manager?"

"Lawrence 'Just call me Larry' Provost . . ." Engle paused and then added, "MD."

McMahon felt a major piece of the puzzle fall into place. "He's a doctor?"

"Yup."

McMahon glanced at Deborah and saw that her brow was furrowed. It was obvious that she too had made the connection between this new information and the surgical precision with which Mindy had been butchered. He turned back to Engle. "And he is apparently acquainted with our friend Skidgel."

"I checked into that after you asked me to identify the owner of the estate. It seems that Skidgel is in charge of security at Provost's estate."

McMahon held Engle's eyes with his. "Are you on the same channel as we seem to be?"

"If you're wondering if he was the cutter in *The Black Orchid*, then I am."

"Why would a doctor do such a thing?" Deborah asked.

"Who knows? Maybe we'll find out when we bring him down. There was a book written several years back—a former LAPD homicide detective made a strong case that it was his father, also a doctor, who killed Elizabeth Short ..."

Deborah looked at McMahon; her puzzled expression was all the encouragement that he needed to explain. "Elizabeth Short was from your part of the country, Medford, Mass. She was found in a vacant lot, butchered in a manner similar to Mindy—only it was never captured on film—at least not that I know of. They never solved the case, but this book pointed fingers at a lot of people—from prominent Hollywood celebrities to corrupt cops. The case is unsolved and still open."

"Do you think this Larry Provost killed her too?" Deborah asked.

"No chance of that," Engle answered, "The Black Dahlia murder was in the winter of 1947. To be Short's killer, Provost would have to be in his eighties or even his nineties."

"The Black Dahlia?" Deborah said.

"I know it's similar. Maybe the title is the killer's way of paying homage to the Dahlia," McMahon added. "In his book the author links his father and a popular artist of the day to over thirty killings, spanning from Elizabeth Short to an up-and-coming actress. He even believes the mother of a well-known writer was one of their victims."

Deborah took a drink of her cocktail. "You know," she commented, "I'm getting an entirely different view of southern California than that of the Mecca for surfers and aspiring celebrities."

"Yeah," Engle said, "we also have celebrities like Caryl Chessman, the Zodiac Killer, and the Hillside Strangler."

"Don't forget the local legend: Manson," McMahon said.

Deborah said, "So what do we do now?"

"Find a way to lobotomize the good doctor . . ."

Deborah looked at him to see if he was joking—the stern look on his face was her answer.

When a number of investigators are involved, a tactical plan is developed . . .
—*FM 3-19.13, Law Enforcement Investigations*

30

"I told Toledo to meet us tomorrow morning at the monument to the Mexican Revolution of 1910."

"I thought you wanted someplace less public," Traynor replied, between bites of food.

"This is Mexico and tomorrow is Sunday. If the good people don't show up at mass, the priest will show up at their home later."

"With his hand out, no doubt."

"Most definitely. Rather than have the good padre visit, they'll attend mass."

"How so?"

"If you attend mass, you can leave in an hour and a half, at most . . . if the priest shows up on your doorstep, he'll leave when he wants to—and that could be hours later and with your liquor supply severely depleted."

"Point well made," Traynor said. "What's your plan?"

"Don't have one."

"Now that's as comforting as a one-way ticket to hell."

"Yup . . . and that is exactly what it may turn out to be." Manuel grinned. "So we'd better follow the rules of a gunfight—"

"Gotcha, rule number one: bring all your guns."

"Number two: bring all your friends and all of their guns."

By now Traynor was caught up in the spirit of the game. "Don't forget the most important rule . . ."

"Ahhh, yes. Don't be the one idiot who brought nothing but a knife to the gunfight."

Traynor chuckled. "Okay, let's assume that the gunfight is over and we're still looking at the grass from the green-side down. What then?"

"We make a run for the airport and the corporate jet."

"Could be hairy."

"No doubt it will be. Once word spreads that we have him, three-quarters of the crooked cops in Mexico City will be after us. The reward for anybody who rescues Toledo will be substantial."

"So far, I'm with you. However, we both know the teachings of the great prophet Murphy. What do we do if we can't catch our plane?"

"Then we run north . . . try to cross the border somewhere between Tijuana and Matamoros."

"If I recall my junior-high geography correctly, that's the entire border between Mexico and the US."

"I figured I'd leave us some room to improvise."

"You are a truly gifted strategist, Manuel."

"You think?"

"No." They were grinning like a couple of teenagers plotting to skip school.

"But either way, you got to promise me something," Traynor said.

"Like what?"

"You won't get your ass killed. With my knowledge of Spanish, I wouldn't make it to the nearest street corner."

Still grinning, Manuel said, "I'll try my best. What will you do if my unfortunate demise becomes imminent?"

"Then like women in the old west used to tell their men—save your last bullet for me."

"Hmmm, sounds tempting, but there's only one problem."

"Which is?"

"I'm told you never hear the one that gets you. I might be dead before I can fulfill my promise. Then what?"

"You got a point. Fortunately, I have until tomorrow morning to figure something out. Maybe even become fluent in Spanish."

Manuel burst out laughing. "Become fluent in Spanish overnight? That I would love to see, *amigo*."

"Well, you know what they say."

"They say a lot of things."

"I'm thinking of Plato, who said: *Necessity is the mother of invention.*"

Each member of the . . . team should know the scope and extent of the crimes and activities in which the suspects are involved.

—*FM 3-19.13, Law Enforcement Investigations*

31

The morning broke crisp and sunny. Nevertheless, humidity and haze hung over the mountains surrounding the city and promised extreme heat for later in the day. The streets of Ciudad de México were for the most part empty; it was still too early for the market places and businesses to be open. The plaza and parking area around the monument to the Mexican Revolution of 1910 were vacant and Manuel and Traynor had the place to themselves. While Manuel roamed around—probably checking fields of fire and escape routes— Traynor strolled over to the old steam railroad locomotive that sat across from the monument and pondered what role it had played in the revolution that had taken place just over a century ago.

After several minutes, he lost interest in the old train and walked into the arch, once again reading the plaque dedicated to Pancho Villa.

He contemplated how many North Americans knew Villa had been much more than the border bandit depicted in the movies. In reality, Villa was a revolutionary who advocated for the poor and wanted agrarian reform.

Traynor's reverie was interrupted when Manuel called to him, pointing to the street that led into the parking lot. Their guests had arrived . . . and it was time to get down to the business at hand.

Traynor's first impression was that they were up to their asses in snapping alligators. Toledo's men came in two stretch limos—it would be an exercise in futility to try to estimate how many them there were. He turned to Manuel. "Got any ideas?"

"Yup."

"Such as?"

"Shoot first . . . and shoot often."

"Sounds like the best plan you've had yet."

Five goons, dressed in their Sunday-morning finery, exited the second limo and immediately set up a perimeter around the plaza. Each bore a small automatic weapon; several appeared to be Uzis. "That's one hell of a lot of firepower," Traynor muttered.

"I saw. We need to even the odds a bit."

"How do we do that?"

"We have to lure Toledo inside the arch, where we'll have some cover."

Toledo and two more of his security guards appeared from the other limo. The bodyguards also carried automatic weapons, but Traynor didn't have time to care what type of weapons these were . . . He was too busy trying to come up with a way to cover his ass.

"So much for trusting those with whom you do business," Manuel muttered. He raised his arm in greeting. *"¡Buen día! Señor Toledo."*

Toledo approached but said nothing. He stopped before them and seemed wary. "I see no *portfolio*."

Traynor was bewildered. Was Toledo expecting drawings or architectural plans? Manuel did not miss a beat and said, "The briefcase is inside the arch."

"You left that much *dinero* unattended?"

Manuel was as cool as an ice mine in Antarctica. "Of course not. There isn't anyone else here this early on a Sunday." He made a point of removing a handkerchief and wiping his brow and the back of his neck. "*Madre de ¡Dios*, it is hot. Shall we continue our business in the shade of the arch?"

Toledo glanced at the monument and then nodded to one of his goons, who turned toward it. Traynor followed and before he had gone two steps, Toledo said, "Still there is no trust . . ."

"Of course there is," Traynor replied, "as much as you have for us." He pointed at Toledo's guards. "Honestly, Señor, seven men, all armed with automatic weapons. Is that your idea of trust?"

Traynor followed the armed hood into the arch. Toledo's man looked around the interior for several moments and then gave him a menacing glare before returning to his *jefe*. He spoke softly into Toledo's ear and the drug boss's face grew hard.

"Esteban tells me there is no portfolio there."

"Of course there isn't," Manuel said. "As you yourself pointed out, it would be *estúpido* to leave so much money in a public place."

Toledo looked as if he were about to bolt but stayed in place when Manuel said, "It is in our truck." He turned to his partner and said, "Señor Traynor, if you would bring the case."

Traynor walked across the plaza and down the tree-lined street to where their SUV was parked in the shade. He was surprised that Toledo had not sent one of his henchmen to accompany him—in his place, he would have.

Traynor unlocked the truck and at the last second, decided to change the plan. Rather than bring the briefcase—with the million dollars of play money—he was going to bring the truck. They might have to make a quick getaway.

He gets campaign contributions from the rich and votes from the poor on the pretense that he's protecting each from the other.

—English adage

32

Engle had once again gone out on a limb for McMahon and obtained the home phone and address of "Just Call Me Larry" Provost. Over breakfast, Deborah had come up with a tactic that surprised McMahon, while at the same time impressing him with her deviousness—if not her capacity for treachery. "Let's spook him out," she had said.

"Sounds good. What you got in mind?"

"A couple of phone calls."

"One will be to Provost, no doubt. Who will the other go to?"

"To that deceitful bitch I think set up my sister—Celia Doerr."

McMahon heard the venom in her voice and saw the hardness in her eyes. He knew Deborah had always been a tough woman—she had to be if she was to successfully run an international conglomerate—but this level of vindictiveness was something new. She had undergone a meta-morphosis since she had arrived in Los Angeles. He felt sorry for anyone who crossed her in the future.

"What do we say?" he asked.

"Not much. Only: *We know what happened to Mindy.* Let the murdering bastards figure things out for themselves."

"It might work," he said. "If nothing else it may spook them enough to run to Skidgel. Hell, they may get scared enough to call a meeting with the entire crew. When do we make these calls?"

"Most people are at home on Sunday morning . . ."

"And it's Sunday morning . . . How about we do it while sitting outside one of their homes?"

Deborah gave him a knowing smile. "I vote on her place."

"Any particular reason?"

"I want to be there to observe her reaction. Also, Provost is heavily involved in the governor's reelection campaign. The last thing he or the governor wants is a scandal."

"Deborah, the more I get to know you, the more I'm glad you're on my side."

———————

Traffic was light and in less than an hour, McMahon and Deborah were parked down the street from Celia Doerr's house in Simi Valley. Deborah took a cell phone out of her purse.

"She's probably got caller ID," McMahon said.

"No doubt. That's why I bought this disposable phone last night."

He chuckled. "So this is not something that you came up with this morning."

"Hardly. By the way, when we drove by, did you notice what's parked behind her house?"

"Yep, a shiny new Jag. This guy thinks he's smart. Unfortunately for him, and fortunately for us, he's dumber than a cow pie."

Deborah called information and asked for Celia Doerr's number. When she was prompted to hit a key to dial the number, she did so. She waited for a few minutes, listening to the ringing of the phone. "Either they're sleeping in . . . or giving each other some early-morning delight."

Not wanting to be heard should the phone be answered, McMahon swallowed his laughter.

After several tense moments, someone answered.

Deborah lowered the tone of her voice and mumbled, "We know what you did to Mindy." Then she broke the connection. "Now," she said, "I guess we wait."

"We wait," McMahon said softly. "Early-morning delight. Woman, you amaze me." He laughed.

"Stick around, *big boy*," Deborah said, doing a passable Mae West. "You ain't seen nothin' yet."

Do unto others—only do it first.
—Perversion of the Golden Rule

33

It took all of Traynor's resolve to keep the SUV's speed at forty-two kilometers per hour—or as he thought of it, about twenty-five miles per hour. He wanted to stomp on the accelerator and send a couple of Toledo's thugs to hell. Even though it was a great fantasy, it was hardly a smart tactic. Instead, he opted to use the truck to divide and conquer. He wanted to park it in a manner that would block out two or more of the perimeter guards, which, he hoped, would render them reluctant to shoot until they knew where their boss was located. Then, hopefully, he and Manuel could deal with the other four. Regardless, it was a gamble, but letting Toledo learn that they had no money was a bigger one.

Traynor drove into the plaza and stopped close to Manuel, Toledo, and the two gunsels. He took his nine-millimeter pistol out and when he opened the door, aimed it at Toledo and said, "How's this for trust, shithead?"

Manuel pressed his pistol against Toledo's head and said, "I'd tell your boys to back off, amigo. If they try anything, you'll be the first to go."

Toledo spoke in rapid Spanish and his entourage raised their hands.

"Tell them to drop their weapons," Manuel ordered him. "If one of them so much as farts, I'll blow your brains across the plaza."

Traynor heard the clatter of weapons falling to the pavement.

"Now, I want them together where I can see them—all of them."

The six men kept their hands raised and walked to the center of the plaza. "Keep him covered, Ed. If he flinches, shoot him."

"It will be a pleasure."

Manuel quickly and professionally frisked Toledo. A knowing smile crossed his face when he discovered a small pistol and a nasty-looking switchblade. "It appears as if you didn't trust us all that much either, *amigo*."

Traynor opened the console between the SUV's seats, took out a pair of handcuffs, and tossed them to Manuel. Once Toledo's hands were shackled behind his back, Manuel opened the back door and forced him in. Keeping his eyes on the clustered goons, Manuel jumped through the open door into the seat beside their prisoner. "Let's get the fuck out of here."

Traynor stomped the accelerator and the tires screeched as they leaped forward. In the rearview mirror, Traynor saw Toledo's men scrambling for their weapons and dashing for the limos. "Which way?" he asked Manuel.

"Take the next left."

They raced through the city streets, which were starting to come alive with early risers and churchgoers, many of whom shouted as they sped by.

Traynor kept a wary eye on the mirrors but saw no sign of pursuit. "I don't see his goons."

"I'm certain they're about. They're probably on their phones, rallying the troops as we speak. They'll have men headed for the airport and train station in minutes."

Manuel's cell phone rang. He answered, listened for several seconds, and said, "Thanks, I thought as much."

"More trouble?" Traynor asked.

"Nothing I didn't expect. The Mexico City police have shut down the airport. It's over land."

In his rearview mirror, Traynor saw one of the limos appear, skidding around a corner a couple of blocks behind them. "They're on us," Traynor said.

"Take the next left . . . Let's get off the main thoroughfares."

"Won't it take us longer to get to the airport?"

"Forget the airport—we'll never make it."

"You will not make it anywhere," Toledo interjected.

"That will be a bad thing for you," Manuel said. "The last thing I intend to do before I die is kill you."

"And if he doesn't do it, I will," Traynor added. "So just sit back, shut your yap, and enjoy the ride. It could very well be your last."

In the mirror, Traynor saw Toledo glaring at him. "If it's money you want—"

"We don't want your money," Traynor answered.

"Then what is it?"

"Your ass strapped to a table waiting for a lethal injection. So, just relax and try to remember a recent production of your movie company."

Toledo looked at Traynor as if he was delusional. "What? You speak riddles, gringo."

"Since you seem to be so slow, I'll give you a hint . . . *The Black Orchid*."

Toledo's eyes widened and Traynor believed he finally got the answer to the riddle.

"Who are you people?"

"Friends of the family," Manuel said.

"Whose family?"

"The star of *The Black Orchid*. The young lady came from a wealthy and influential family, and they have spent lavishly to bring their daughter's murderers to justice," Traynor said.

Manuel looked out the back window, making Traynor look into the side mirror. The limo was racing down the narrow street, closing the gap between them.

"Turn into the first street or alley," Manuel instructed Traynor. "Then stop."

Traynor saw the mouth of a narrow street approach on their right and put the SUV into a tire-screeching drift that almost rolled the vehicle. Once it was inside the lane and out of sight, Traynor stomped on the brakes. With his hands shackled behind his back, Toledo could not brace himself and he slammed into the back of the front seat. When he bounced back, blood was streaming from his nose.

"Just so you don't get any ideas—" Manuel hit him alongside his head with his pistol. Toledo slumped over onto his side. "That should hold him," Manuel said. He leaped from the SUV and ran to the back. He lifted the hatch and raised a secret compartment from which he withdrew a military-grade rifle, one that had a grenade launcher underneath the barrel. "Don't go anywhere—I'll only be a minute."

As much as Traynor wanted to say something pithy, he was speechless. Manuel had obviously planned this caper in much greater detail than he'd been led to think. He watched in amazement as Manuel stepped out into the street, in what Traynor assumed to be the path of the charging limo, and fired a grenade. A loud bang rolled down the street; the buildings that lined the sides served as an amplifier and the sound tsunami shattered windows and shook the SUV. Within seconds, Manuel had jumped back into the truck, grinning. There was a broad smile on his face when he said, "That ought to keep them occupied."

In the city, it's too easy to lose the subject due to traffic jams and lights . . .
—*Private Eyes: A Writer's Guide To Private Investigators*

34

Manuel directed Traynor to Highway 15 and told him to stay on it until they came to Guadalajara. Toledo regained consciousness as they passed out of the city limits. A half-hour later, blood was still trickling from the small wound where Manuel had hit him. He said nothing, but his malevolent glare was message enough. It was an hour before he spoke, and when he did, Traynor wanted to tell him to shut up.

"You are *muerto!* Dead! You have no hope of getting out of Mexico alive."

Manuel silenced him when he said, "The same thing is true of you. In case you didn't think I was serious before, let me assure you that I am."

"You will never get me to the border, let alone cross it."

"Really?" Traynor answered. "What makes you think that?"

"By now my people will have alerted my organization throughout the country."

"We can deal with that," Manuel said.

"Possibly . . . but have you thought about the policía and my rivals? The cops will want the reward for my rescue, and my rivals will want me out of the picture so they can take over my business."

Suddenly, Traynor realized just how monumental their task would be. "He does have a point."

"Yeah, we may have to avoid the large towns as much as possible."

"We should dump this truck," Traynor said. "I'm sure a description of it will be broadcast everywhere. According to the GPS, it's about a five-hour drive to Guadalajara. If we're lucky, we can make the switch before anyone gets wise."

Manuel was quiet for several moments and then said, "We could call Deborah and have the corporate jet meet us there."

"It's worth a try," Traynor answered.

A dilemma (Greek: δί-λημμα "double proposition") is a problem offering two possibilities, neither of which is practically acceptable.

35

Within fifteen minutes of receiving the call, Provost and Celia Doerr burst out of her house and leaped into the Jag. They backed out of the drive and were already accelerating when they passed McMahon and Deborah. They were in such a panic that McMahon was certain they hadn't noticed they were being watched. McMahon, on the other hand, got a close look at their faces. Doerr looked terrified and was obviously the more upset of the two; she was shouting at Provost. When they turned the corner, McMahon started the car and did a U-turn. "Now," he said, "let's see where they lead us."

As they entered the Reagan Expressway, Deborah's cell phone rang. She listened for several moments and then said, "I'll take care of it and will call you back."

When McMahon glanced at her, she said, "Ed and Manuel have Toledo."

"That's great."

"There've been some complications, though. They weren't able to get to the airport and are driving north to Guadalajara. They want me to have the corporate jet meet them there." Without saying anything further, she called Hollis International's Mexico City office. She explained the situation and then hung up. She turned to McMahon and said, "They're working on it."

Within minutes her phone chimed and she answered. Once again, she listened. "I'll pass that along." She dialed another number. "Ed? It isn't good news. The authorities in Mexico City have impounded the plane—you'll have to bring him out via land . . . Call the Guadalajara office." She relayed a phone number. "Tell them to meet you with a clean car. Tell them to provide anything you need. Let me know if I can do anything else."

McMahon's face was grim as he stared through the windshield. "I gather they're taking the long way home."

"They have no other option. Well, maybe one, and if things get rough, I hope they take it. They can always kill Toledo and hope that takes the heat off."

"Either way, they'll be running a gauntlet—with crooked cops on one side and who knows how many different criminal factions on the other. They could very well find that they're the filling in a shit sandwich."

The first rule of life: Shit happens.

—Old adage

36

"The Mexican authorities have impounded the jet," Traynor informed Manuel.

"Shit."

Traynor tossed Manuel his cell phone and a small notebook and then repeated the number Deborah had given him. He said, "Make a list of anything you think we'll need. Hollis International has been given instructions to provide it."

"One thing we could use is a platoon of Marines." Manuel spent several minutes developing his list and made the call. When he was finished, he handed Traynor back the phone and said, "Drive through the city and take Route 54 north. They'll be waiting for us there."

At a quarter to two, they reached Route 54. Traynor followed Manuel's directions to a small, unpaved road that meandered along the banks of a river—or more accurately, a trickle of water drifting through a dry gulch.

When Traynor saw a white Ford Expedition with dark, tinted windows, he pulled in behind it. They got out and slowly approached. A young man got out of the Ford and met them near the back. He raised the hatch, and Traynor saw six five-gallon gas cans lined up against the back of the rear seat. In front of the cans was a wooden box similar to a military-issue footlocker. The young man raised the lid and spoke rapidly to Manuel.

Manuel patted him on the back, and he and Traynor walked around to the front of the Ford. "Everything is set. Give Mendoza the keys to the Excursion and bring our passenger."

Traynor threw the Excursion keys to the driver and then opened the back door. Toledo gave him a surly look and said, "This will be of no help. My people will still find us."

"For your sake, you'd better hope they don't," Traynor said. "In California, you'll probably get twenty-five to life.... If your people show up, Manuel and I will make sure that life becomes a very short sentence. Now, shut your mouth and get out before I drag you out."

His hands were still cuffed behind his back, and Toledo stumbled and almost fell on his face when he slid off the seat. He lurched forward a couple of steps, regained his balance, and gave them a dirty look.

"Cool dance," Traynor said, "but I don't think it will catch on."

"*Bastardo.*"

"Now let's not bring my parents into this." He shoved Toledo into the backseat of the Ford and when Manuel got into the driver seat, got in beside him. Toledo once again glared at Traynor and said, "I have been shackled for six hours. My hands are numb."

"Just think," Traynor said, "eventually they'll become gangrenous and fall off and then you'll lose the handcuffs. Until then, shut your mouth and enjoy the ride."

"I'd like it better if his goddamned mouth was numb," Manuel snarled.

Traynor looked at Toledo and smiled. "I got a dirty sock I could shove in his mouth."

"How dirty?"

"I've worn them all day . . . if I know my feet, the smell will be enough to knock a buzzard off a gut wagon . . ."

When Manuel said, "Sounds like a plan to me," Toledo shut up and looked out the side window.

Manuel waited for the young driver to depart in the Excursion and drove after him. "If we try and avoid the toll roads, it will take us two or three days to reach Juárez."

"How much cash do we have? According to the travel guide, it costs forty-three of our bucks in tolls between Mexico City and there."

"Not to worry, Deborah has been ahead of us. She knew we'd need cash and sent a thousand dollars in pesos."

"Then by all means, take the toll road. Secondary roads down here are for shit. The sooner we're back in the good old US of A, the better I'll feel."

"Sit back and relax. If all goes well, it's a seven-hour drive to Durango."

Traynor stared out the window, making it a point to ignore Toledo when he would sigh or moan in a futile attempt to let them know of his discomfort. As they drove north along the toll road, he was surprised by the countryside. Rather than a cactus-filled desert, it looked more like central Texas or the plains of Kansas. The rolling hills were grass covered and as they passed through a myriad of small farming villages, Traynor saw fields of cactus that appeared to be cultivated. "What are these fields?" he asked.

Toledo looked at him as if he were the most ignorant person he had ever met. Traynor was getting tired of his act, and it took all of his will-power to keep from punching him.

"That's *nopal*," Manuel answered. "It's a staple of the Mexican diet. Two nights ago, you ate a nopal salad at the hotel."

"Is that the stuff that tasted like green beans?"

"Yeah."

They rode in silence for several minutes and then Traynor asked, "You give any thought to what we're gonna do with old Holy here when we stop?"

"Haven't thought much about it."

"I know one thing," Traynor said. "If I have my way, we aren't gonna drive all night. You and I have been up for over twenty-four hours and we need to sleep—and I, for one, don't want to spend hours trying to sleep crammed into a truck seat."

"I'm with you. We'll find a place in Durango. We can take turns guarding him."

"Great, not only is he the biggest pus-bag on earth, but he's the only one who'll be getting a full night's sleep . . ."

Traynor heard Manuel chuckle. "I wouldn't worry. I've dealt with pricks like him all my life. They're gutless and only fight with their money. With an army of paid muscle, they're pretty brave—but by themselves, they're softer than shit and twice as useless. But, if it makes you feel better, we can wake him up every hour to check his hands . . ."

Traynor glanced at Toledo, saw an almost petulant look on his face, and knew that Manuel was right—at least as far as Holy Toledo was concerned. All of a sudden, he was looking forward to the night.

The Second Rule of Life: Shit happens every day.

—Old adage

37

McMahon and Deborah followed the Jag through Santa Susana Pass and into Los Angeles. Provost was headed someplace, but it was not his estate. "You don't suppose," McMahon mused, "that we've gotten lucky and he's leading us to someone else in this chain?"

"How many others can there be?"

"We still haven't identified the cameraman. The film was pretty good quality, so there could be any number of assholes involved."

"Jack," Deborah asked, "what do you think our chances are of getting them convicted and sent away?"

"With that DVD as evidence, the odds should be good."

"That's what they thought about O. J. And just recently, there was that case in Florida . . ."

"Nothing is certain once you turn it over to a jury."

She stared pensively at the freeway for a few seconds and then said, "Not if I have anything to say about it."

US residents should avoid traveling to the states of Chihuahua, Durango, San Luis
Potosi, Sinaloa, parts of Sonora, Zacatecas, and others.
—US Department of State, January 9, 2014

38

Manuel and Traynor arrived in Durango just after nine at night. They found a small hotel on the northern edge of the city and checked into a single room. The room was passable: two single beds, but it did have a shower and hot water. The furnishings were more suited to a patio than a hotel room, but Traynor realized the heavy metal tables would work in their favor. "I'll get us some food," Manuel announced.

"I guess that means I'm babysitting," Traynor said laconically.

"I won't be long."

Traynor pushed Toledo toward one of the cast-steel chairs and told him to turn around. He took the handcuff key from his pocket and tested the chair, which was too heavy to use as a weapon. "Sit," he ordered him.

Toledo flopped onto the worn and frayed seat cushion and gave Traynor yet another malevolent stare. "Toledo, if you don't make a serious attitude adjustment, I'm going to start thinking that you don't like me. And I'm not very nice to people who don't like me. Now, I'm going to release the handcuff from one of your hands and fasten it to the chair. If you so much as twitch, I'm going to break your nose . . . am I clear?"

Toledo gave Traynor a grudging nod.

"Bend forward," Traynor said. Toledo leaned forward enough for him to reach around and unlock one cuff, which he fastened to the chair arm. He checked it to ensure it was secured and then stepped back.

Toledo reached as far as the shackle allowed and rubbed his wrists. Traynor grinned at him, knowing how much pain there would be as the blood flowed into his hands and woke them up.

"How much?" Toledo asked.

"How much what?"

"How much money will it take for you to let me walk out that door?"

"You don't have enough."

"I'm a man of substantial means—"

"No doubt you are, but there isn't enough money in the world for me to allow a maggot like you to go free."

"They'll find me. My men will not stop looking until they free me and kill you and your amigo. I will take great pleasure in making sure that you suffer greatly before you die."

"You talk pretty fuckin' big for a man with a loaded gun to his head." Traynor sat on the edge of the bed farthest away from Toledo and removed his shoes and socks to allow his feet to cool. "Remember, if anything happens to either Manuel or me, you get it next. If it's up to me, I'll shoot you in the gut first and then in both knees. You'll suffer more and it will take you longer to die that way."

Toledo settled back in the chair and snorted. It was a divisive sound.

After several moments of silence, Traynor asked, "How many of you were involved in making that movie?"

"I have no idea. I only financed the filmmaking."

"So, Skidgel is the brains behind the production."

He snorted again. "Skidgel does nothing more than entice the 'star.' He is our procurer—no better than a lowly pimp, if you prefer."

"Then who's the brains behind the production?"

"A person who is well known throughout the American movie industry. If you let me go, I'll give you his name."

"Before this is over, you'll give us whatever names we want. You bastards are all alike. You'd sell your wife and kids to drop a couple of years from your sentence."

Toledo's face flushed with anger. "I am going to take great pleasure in killing you."

"You'd better bring some heavy artillery, because I'll use my last ounce of energy to cut you down. Now, shut up. I'm tired of listening to you talk out your ass." Traynor lifted up one of his socks and smelled the sour reek of foot odor. He showed it to him and said, "Or else—"

Manuel returned with the Mexican equivalent of fast food and several bottles of soda. "We got any ice?" Traynor asked.

"Remember what I said about no ice," Manuel grumbled.

Traynor's watch said two in the morning when Manuel woke him up. He reached for the lamp and Manuel hissed, "No. We have company." Traynor slid from the bed and looked to their prisoner. He could see Toledo in the ambient light that glowed through the partially closed drapes. He lay on the floor with most of his body hidden in the shadow of the bed. All that was visible was one arm, which was still shackled to the metal chair.

"Who?"

"Local cops."

Traynor moved to the window and peered through the gap at the side of the blinds. Two men in tan uniforms were studying the Ford closely, inspecting it from all angles. One of them walked back to their dented and dusty squad car and spoke into the handset. He was either running the plates or notifying someone of their presence. "What do we do?" he asked Manuel.

"I'm going out to talk to them. You get Toledo ready to move."

When Manuel stuck his nine millimeter into the back waistband of his trousers, Traynor asked, "Is that wise?"

"No, but it's probably smart. Be ready to move on my signal."

Manuel opened the door and stepped out into the night. He was easily visible in the light from the bare bulb in the fixture beside their door. Traynor heard him greet the cops in Spanish.

Traynor shoved his bare feet inside his shoes, drew his pistol, and kicked the bottom of Toledo's foot. He placed a finger over his lips and aimed the pistol at his head. He motioned for him to get into the chair, and then stood back. Once he was settled, Traynor said in a low voice, "One fuckin' peep out of you and you'll be trying to convince Saint Peter not to send you to hell. You got me?"

He nodded. Traynor motioned for him to twist sideways and unlocked the cuff from the chair. He felt Toledo tense, so he touched his ear with the muzzle of his gun. "Go ahead . . ." Toledo settled and Traynor cuffed his wrists behind his back. He paused and then got one of his more devious ideas. He returned to his bed, picked up his soiled socks, returned to Toledo, and pinched his nostrils closed. In less than a minute, Toledo's mouth opened and Traynor pushed the socks in and released his grip on his nose. "There. Now I don't have to worry about you calling them. Get up and move over by the side of the door."

Toledo shook his head, trying to dislodge the socks. Traynor placed a hand on his head, stabilizing it. He shook his head and said, "You wouldn't want me to have to bust you up, now would you?"

Toledo stopped moving and looked at Traynor like he was going to cry. Traynor mocked him. "You know, Holy, whoever started your reputation as a badass must not have met you in person. For a big-time drug dealer, you got to be the biggest damned wimp I ever met."

He heard a brief scuffle outside and then Manuel said, "Bring him out."

Traynor led Toledo through the door and saw the two cops shackled together, back to back, with handcuffs. The microphone to their radio lay on the pavement, its cord ripped out of the transceiver.

Manuel pushed the cops toward the now vacant room. They looked comical as they shuffled sideways, banging each other against the sides of the doorway as Manuel shoved them inside.

Manuel turned his head and asked Traynor, "You get everything?"

When Traynor nodded, he locked the door, sealing them in. He looked at the black socks hanging from Toledo's mouth. "You didn't . . ."

"Couldn't risk him shouting for help."

"Those aren't a clean pair, are they?"

"Nope, need *them* for my feet."

Traynor heard him chuckling softly. Manuel walked to the police car and got behind the wheel. "I'm gonna put this out of sight. You get him into our car and be ready to go when I get back." Manuel looked at Toledo once again, shook his head, and laughed as he drove the police car behind the building.

In minutes, Traynor had Toledo in the front passenger seat, his hand-cuffs threaded through the handgrip above the window, and was behind the wheel with the motor running. Manuel came running around the building, paused for a second when he saw Toledo in the front, and then jumped in the back.

As Traynor accelerated out of the parking lot, he looked at Manuel in the rearview mirror and said, "I figured that if he's up here, we can take turns sleeping back there. The GPS calculates a nine-hour drive to Juárez, and we can take turns at the wheel."

"We should avoid Juárez. The drug lords up there have the *policía* under siege."

"Is there any place in this fuckin' country that's safe?"

"Sure, parts of Acapulco—if the gangs of street kids don't rip you off. Cozumel, and most of the resorts are pretty safe."

Traynor drove out of the city and when they were in the primordial dark of the rolling hills, asked, "How are we going to get this piece of shit across the border?"

"Not sure yet. You have any ideas?"

"You're the guy who knows the turf down here."

"I'll call Deborah and tell her we need someone to meet us at a place to be determined." Manuel chuckled. "It looks as if we're about to become wetbacks."

Incidents have occurred during the day and at night, and carjackers have
used a variety of techniques, including roadblocks, bumping/moving vehicles
to force them to stop, and running vehicles off the road at high speeds.
There are indications that criminals target newer and larger
vehicles, especially dark-colored SUVs.
—Mexico Travel Warning, issued by the United States Department
of State, dated January 9, 2014

39

"Which way?" Traynor asked Manuel.

"Stay on Route 23. There aren't that many major roads in this country and anyone looking for us will be able to watch them easily."

"That's not what I wanted to hear . . ."

"I know, but it's what you needed to hear. We have to stay away from the toll roads as much as possible. By now every toll-taker in Mexico has been alerted to the reward that's been offered to anyone who spots us."

"You know," Traynor said, "a few days ago, this caper seemed so easy, but it sure as hell got complicated fast."

"We haven't seen anything yet."

Manuel looked at Toledo and said, "Is he turning blue?"

Traynor glanced at their passenger. "A bit."

"Either the dye is running out of your sock or it's poisoning him."

"You think?"

"I think."

Traynor turned his head and said, "If you keep your food-trap shut, I'll take those things out . . . but if you so much as say one goddamned word, I'll put them back in. You got that?"

Toledo nodded.

Traynor pulled the socks from his mouth and offered him a bottle of water. "Drink?"

Still secured to the handgrip, Toledo was unable to open the bottle, so Manuel took the water, removed the cap, and held it in front of Toledo's face. The drug kingpin leaned forward, took the bottle in his lips, and when Manuel tipped it, guzzled water down.

Traynor glanced over, saw water trickling down Toledo's chin, and drove on into the darkness of early morning.

I may be getting old, but not foolish.

—Elia Kazan

40

Deborah was already eating a light breakfast of yogurt and coffee when McMahon entered the dining room. She looked as fresh as the early-morning dew and was once again dressed in jeans, ready for wherever the day took them. They had watched the majestic house into which Doerr and Provost had taken refuge until 2:00 a.m., and when McMahon had shaved that morning, he had not liked what he saw in the mirror. His face sagged and his eyes were bloodshot; he thought that he looked older than last week's weather report. His first reaction had been to say, "There has to be a better way of dying than this gettin' old shit."

He sat across from Deborah and when the server appeared, ordered coffee. "Kondrat Jabłoński," she said.

"What the hell is that?"

"I guess you don't follow the Hollywood scene much."

When the server returned and placed a steaming mug of coffee before him, McMahon smiled at her. As she walked away, he watched the exaggerated sway of her ass in her tight, short skirt and then turned to Deborah. She grinned at him and he felt his face flush. "What can I say?" he said. "I like women."

"I'm not surprised. Nevertheless, you had that wistful look old men get when they see an attractive young woman."

Considering his earlier concerns, that hit too close to the mark and he knew he sounded defensive when he said, "Hey, I'm not *that* old."

Deborah sipped her coffee and said, "Who are you trying to convince—me or you?"

Rather than dig himself in deeper, he changed the topic, "No, I don't follow the Hollywood scene."

"Kondrat Jabłoński is the hottest director in town right now. Three of his last four movies were nominated for Oscars—one even won best director."

McMahon sat back, all thoughts of his age gone. "There is no way someone that well known would direct anything like *The Black Orchid*."

"Don't be so sure. Jabłoński is a Polish ex-patriot, and when he arrived here from Poland, he was all but a nobody. To fend off starvation, he directed several financially successful pornos before he got the chance to make any mainstream films. He is also a very close friend of Larry Provost. Engels told me they're often seen together hitting some of the clubs."

"So, there is something of a track record here."

"Yup . . . and who knows what someone like Toledo may have on him."

Mexico is facing clearly the most severe security challenge it has experienced in nearly a century. You're looking at battles between the government and the drug cartels, among the various cartels themselves, and violence inflicted by organized crime groups against civilians.
—Fred Burton, former deputy chief of the counterterrorism division of the State Department's Diplomatic Security Service

41

Traynor was sleeping on the backseat when the surface of the road got rough. Manuel had to slow down to control of the vehicle as he navigated along the many ruts and potholes. "Where are we?" Traynor asked.

"We just left Route 23. This secondary road will take us north to Route 45, which will take us out of the state of Durango and into Chihuahua."

Toledo was slumped against the side window, and when they dropped into a deep rut that cut across the unpaved surface, his head banged against the glass and he woke up. He shook his head a few times to clear it and blinked his eyes against the early-morning light.

Once again the early haze promised a torrid day—even the country-side had changed. The land through which they drove was mostly high desert, with scrub brush and a small population of tropical palm and cactus trees; on all sides, mountains were visible against the horizon. "Where are we?" Traynor asked.

"The Sierra Madres. We've been driving through them since we left Durango. You couldn't see them in the dark."

Traynor studied the terrain and wished he had a hot cup of coffee. To take his mind off his body's desire for caffeine, he commented, "Looks like it's gonna be a hot day."

"It may not get as hot as you think—maybe the mid- to upper eighties. We're more than six thousand feet above sea level here—it doesn't get all that hot. Wait until we get into Chihuahua . . . that's some real desert."

Toledo said, "I have to *meada*."

"What does he want?" Traynor asked Manuel.

"He has to take a piss," Manuel said.

The road was empty and the countryside uninhabited, so Manuel pulled over, stopping beside a ditch that ran alongside the road. Traynor got out and opened the door for Toledo, who smiled sweetly at him and rattled the handcuffs, which were still threaded through the hand-grip located near the window. Traynor stepped back and said to Manuel, "Undo him."

Manuel gave him an incredulous look. "What do you mean *undo him*? He can get his own dick out."

"Not if you don't unlock his handcuffs," Traynor added.

"You probably should have said that in the first place," Manuel grumbled.

To ensure that Toledo was a good boy, Traynor took his pistol from the holster suspended from his belt and aimed it at him. "Get out."

Toledo stepped to the edge of the ditch, rubbing life back into his wrists. He looked up at the sky and said, "A beautiful day . . . no?"

"Yeah," Traynor said. "It shows promise."

"Yes, much too splendid a day for dying."

"If I were you, I'd hold that thought. Now do your thing."

Traynor stepped back so that he was out of range. He would not have put it past Toledo to stumble or falter, spraying him. Once he was finished, Traynor motioned him back into the truck with the pistol. Manuel secured him to the handhold once again and exited the SUV. As they stood side by side, doing their bit to irrigate the sandy soil, Manuel stared off at the mountains.

"Looks peaceful out here," Traynor commented.

"Don't become complacent. The state of Durango has the second highest number of gang killings in Mexico. We're in the middle of one of the busiest drug routes in the world."

"Which state is number one? Sonora?"

"Nope, Chihuahua."

"Terrific. Right along our escape route."

In the distance Traynor saw a small aircraft circling over the mountains. Each loop seemed to bring it closer to them. "Does that plane look as if it's coming this way?" he asked.

Manuel looked in the direction he was pointing. "Zip up and get in the truck."

Mexico's murder rate has doubled over the past five years, to nearly nineteen per 100,000 people per year.

—Economist.com

42

"What do we do now?" Deborah asked without taking her eyes from the windshield.

"We wait and watch. We don't have anything on Jabłoński—yet. Who knows, we might get lucky. They may decide to call a meeting of all the crew."

"Why don't we squeeze Skidgel, or even the Doerr woman?"

"Oh, I don't think that will be necessary. Once Ed and Manuel get Toledo out of Mexico, I wouldn't be surprised if the bastards don't trample all over each other trying to cut a deal."

"What if they decide to go down together?"

McMahon sipped from a takeout coffee cup. "The odds are against that. One of them will want to avoid the slammer."

Deborah's cell phone rang and she answered. She listened for a few moments and then said, "You're sure it was *his* men?"

She listened again.

"Okay, keep me in the loop."

She disconnected the call and slumped in her seat, letting out a long sigh.

"Problem?" McMahon asked.

"The driver who took the company SUV to Ed and Manuel didn't make it back to the office."

"Any idea what happened?"

"They found his body outside Guadalajara. I'm assuming Toledo's men got him. They didn't go into detail, but they said it's almost certain that whoever snatched him now knows everything he knew."

43

The plane came in low, no more than fifty feet off the ground. It passed them and then looped back. This time it was lower— low enough that Traynor could make out the pilot's face. When Toledo looked up, he was most definitely recognized. The plane sped ahead and made another turn. It stayed low, and as it passed on the left, an automatic weapon opened fire on them. The bullets walked across the sandy soil, kicking up small clouds of dirt as they hit. Manuel cursed as the gunner zeroed in.

He turned the wheel, left the road's surface, and raced across the bumpy terrain. Scrub brush and bushes scraped the side of the Ford and several disappeared beneath the undercarriage. The rasping sound, accompanied by the bouncing vehicle, made Traynor pray that they would not lose the oil pan or do so much damage that the truck would be unusable.

Manuel aimed for a small copse of trees. The plane passed overhead, and several rounds popped through their roof, hitting the seat mere inches from Traynor's leg and letting in small dots of sunlight. "Christ, Manuel, step on it!"

They stopped inside the grove of trees and Manuel popped the hatch. He and Traynor scrambled from the Expedition. Manuel raced to the back of the truck, tore open the wooden crate, and threw Traynor an assault rifle and two magazines.

Traynor shoved one of the magazines into the receiver, hit the bottom to ensure that it was seated properly, and then pulled the operating rod, loading a bullet into the chamber. He took cover behind a tree, switched off the rifle's safety, and searched the sky for the plane. The Piper was in the middle of yet another turn, and when it straightened its flight path, it aligned itself for a run on the trees in which they had sought shelter. Traynor aligned his sights, leading the aircraft slightly to allow for its speed. When it was alongside the grove, he opened fire. As the plane passed, bullets perforated its thin skin. One of the heavy rounds must have hit the shooter as well as the motor, because the automatic weapon that had been firing at them fell to the ground and smoke erupted from the engine cowling. The plane was too low for the pilot to glide far, and it flew into the ground, tumbled several times, and then settled on its back, bursting into flames.

Toledo stared through the window, his face pale. Traynor opened the door and said, "Looks like someone in your organization is attempting a hostile takeover."

"Possibly it was not *my* people. They would not do anything that would get me killed. I believe it's one of the gangs that compete against me—possibly the Sinaloa Cartel."

"Either way," Manuel said, "we're fucked. They know where we are now."

"Well," Traynor said. "We have enough of a head start that we may be able to outrun them."

"No doubt he contacted his people . . . and we can't outrun a radio." Manuel returned to the Ford. "Route 45 is this road's only outlet and they'll seal it off before we reach it." He climbed into the driver's seat and Traynor jumped into the back.

"Are we going to check for survivors?" Traynor asked.

"Why? We'd just have to shoot them. If anyone survived, let them take care of themselves."

They returned to the unpaved road, bouncing across the open ground, and turned north.

A stationary or fixed surveillance is conducted to observe a home, building, or location to obtain evidence of criminal activity or to identify suspected offenders.
—*FM 3-19.13, Law Enforcement Investigations*

44

McMahon and Deborah had been watching the mansion for six hours, and no one had come or gone. She shifted in her seat, wiped her palms on her thighs, and sighed. "My butt is sore from all this sitting."

"Stakeouts usually become an endurance test."

Deborah poured the last of the coffee from their thermos and said, "I know you don't want to hear this, but I have to pee."

"It probably wouldn't hurt to change locations. We've been here a long time. You take the car and go take care of nature's call. I'll stay here and find a new focal point."

When he opened the driver's side door and got out, she rounded the vehicle and got behind the wheel. "How will I find you?"

"I'll be close to here. All you have to do is drive up the street and I'll find you. If all else fails, we each have a phone."

"Okay, give me twenty minutes," Deborah said.

"While you're at it, refill the thermos."

She passed an electronic camera with a large zoom lens through the window. "If anyone shows, you'll want this."

He took the camera and after she turned the corner and disappeared, walked along the sidewalk. As he strolled, the camera swung from the strap around his neck, acting as a metronome to help him keep his pace under control. To a casual observer, he appeared to be a tourist out for a stroll, taking pictures of southern California's rich and famous. He reached the corner and looked back at the estate. The view from there would allow them to keep their vigil. He strolled back, and when he reached a large willow, he slipped into the obscurity of its hanging branches. He stayed there, not leaving the tree's shelter, until Deborah drove down the street and stopped beside him.

He got in on the passenger side and settled back. "We'll park on the corner up there." He pointed to the new vantage point.

"Anything happen?"

"No. We'll give it a while longer and then possibly revise our strategy."

"Any sign of Skidgel?" As if it had a psychic connection, the transceiver that monitored the tracking devices on Skidgel's cars began to chirp.

"I'll be damned," McMahon said.

"What?"

"Unless I miss my guess, he's less than a mile away."

"At last," she said softly, "all of the vultures are convening."

"I'd like it better if Ed and Manuel were with us," he said.

"I'm sure they'd rather be here than where they are." She drove to the new outpost and pulled alongside the curb.

McMahon raised the camera to his eye and adjusted the lens to ensure that any photos they took would be useful. When the distant gates appeared in the reticule as sharp as if they were mere feet away, he said, "This rig must have cost you a bundle."

"About the same as Daddy's weekly booze bill."

McMahon whistled. "That much?"

According to a study by the international think tank, Institute for Economics and Peace, northern Mexico continues to be the region most affected by drug-related violence; this is due to its proximity to the United States, the region's most important market for illicit drugs.

45

They made first contact with the opposition in midafternoon. Their antagonists were clustered around two parked Chevy SUVs blocking the road. Several of the men wore law-enforcement uniforms and held shotguns. Manuel stopped a couple hundred yards short of the roadblock. He surveyed the scene for several tense moments and said, "I wish I knew who in the hell we're dealing with. If it's douche bag's people we could hold a gun against his head and force them to let us through. On the other hand, if they're the opposition, that would only make them act sooner."

Manuel studied the terrain on either side of the road—a lot of scrub brush and patches of dry, brittle grass; this time there was no convenient grove of trees. "Not a lot of cover if we have to make a fight of it."

Toledo inclined toward the windshield and through the dusty glass tried to determine who they were. "You could let me go and end this."

"Like we said, that might work if those are your people," Traynor said.

"Who's to say that they aren't Sinaloa?" Manuel added. "They have a presence in seventeen states. They may have put up a reward larger than yours to anyone who gets you—preferably dead."

"I'll take my chances," Toledo replied. "This is Mexico and money talks."

"Sure," Traynor said, "and once you're free, you'll give us safe passage."

"Of course."

"Will you be upset if I tell you that you're full of shit?" Traynor said.

"I am a man of my word."

"You *are* full of shit," Traynor said. Manuel seemed to have made a decision and spun the wheel to the right. Once again they left the road and headed cross-country.

As they left the thoroughfare, Traynor watched the assembled mob. "They're running for their trucks," Traynor said.

"They can't go any faster than us on this surface. Maybe we can make it into the mountains and make a stand."

"Great, just what I want . . . to be part of an Alamo reenactment."

"Maybe it will be San Jacinto. The Texans won there."

"I hope we find something," Traynor said. "It'll be hard to circle the wagons with only one wagon."

The ground rose, and when they dropped down the other side, they lost sight of their pursuers. Manuel suddenly turned the Expedition in a tight circle, stopped, and pressed the release button, raising the back hatch door.

"What are you doing?" Traynor asked.

"There are times when the best defense is a good offense . . . we're going to take the fight to them."

Traynor lowered one half of the backseat, gaining access to the material in the rear. He moved the gas cans to one side, pushed the wood crate aside, and checked the rifle to ensure he had a full magazine. "Okay, now what?"

"When I pass through them, you open fire."

Traynor was not exactly sold on this plan, but it was better than anything he'd been able to come up with. He slid through the opening and lay in a prone shooting position. When Manuel accelerated, Traynor began to slide toward the open hatch, and he had to use his toes to grip the top of the lowered backseat to keep from sliding. The Ford rose over the swell and accelerated toward the oncoming SUVs. Manuel armed himself with a pistol, and as they closed in, Traynor heard shots. Suddenly the Chevrolets flashed by and were behind them. Traynor fired an enfilade of 7.62 mm bullets into the cloud of dust that came from rear of each SUV. When the strong wind blew away the dust, he saw one of the trucks attempt to turn and its front wheel sink into the soft ground, flipping it over.

The second Chevy slowed, safely turned, and then raced after them. Traynor aimed at where he thought its grill would be and fired several rounds, hoping to hit the radiator. When the truck appeared out of the dusty contrail, he saw that one of its headlamps was smashed and there were flashes coming from the left side window. Whoever was shooting was good. One of the rounds snapped as it passed over him and blew a spiderwebbed hole in the windshield. Traynor adjusted his line of sight and shot three bullets into the windscreen on the shooter's side. Steam and smoke began to flow out of the hood, and the Tahoe slowed as the driver attempted to stop and turn off the engine before it overheated and seized up. Manuel drove away, leaving them in a cloud of dust.

Traynor scrambled into the backseat and held on as Manuel careened back onto the road and raced north. Toledo's face was as white as a sheet. "Whoever that was," Traynor said to him, "they weren't overly concerned with your well-being. It gives me a bit of consolation to know that even though a shitload of people want us dead, even more seem to want your hide hanging on their barn."

Toledo gave Traynor a look that said he did not understand the euphemism. Traynor decided to let him ponder it.

Manuel pulled to the side of the road. "Close that hatch, will you, Ed?"

"Sure." When Traynor was back in the truck, Manuel pulled back onto the road and accelerated.

"Where are we?" Traynor asked.

"The GPS says our next turn, which is Highway 45, is in fifty-seven miles."

"About an hour, huh?"

"If we don't run into anymore road hazards."

Traynor patted Toledo on the back of his head and said, "Starting to look as if we're gonna make it, Holy." For some reason, Toledo did not seem pleased by the news.

––––––––––––

As the sun was setting, they crossed into Chihuahua, refueled, keeping the empty cans for refilling later, and Traynor took over the driving. "We'll spend the night in Hidalgo Del Parral," Manuel said.

"Is that wise?"

"Probably not, but it's about two hundred kilometers to the next town of any size. We need some food, gas, and showers wouldn't hurt. I, for one, must smell like a dead dinosaur."

Once again Traynor was surprised by the terrain. Here it was mountainous and forested. "This dispels all the myths I believed about Mexico," he said.

"No doubt," Manuel responded. "As we go north, we'll run into more of what you expect. We will soon be in the Chihuahua Desert. These forests and mountains are its western border."

Toledo, who had gotten quieter the farther north they progressed, snorted derisively. "You *Norte Americanos* are ignorant of anything you don't see on your television or in your cinema."

Traynor sat back and remained quiet; for the first time Toledo had said something with which he could not argue.

Hidalgo Del Parral was larger than expected. It was located in a valley surrounded on all sides by the foothills of the Sierra Madre Mountains (which, Manuel explained, were actually two mountain chains: the Sierra Madre Occidental in the west and the Sierra Madre Oriental in the east. The first extended from the state of Chihuahua into the far southern tip of the state of Durango; the latter ran from the state of Coahuila into the state of Nuevo Leon). Traynor made up his mind that one day he was going to return to this magnificent country and explore it in more detail.

They found a small hotel in the southwest corner of the city, along Highway 24. Manuel informed Traynor that, after a night's sleep, they would follow 24 to Highway 23 and from there, make a dash for the US border somewhere between Douglas, Arizona, and Columbus, New Mexico.

"How are we gonna get over the border fence?" Traynor asked.

"It's not complete through that stretch—and may never be as there are no towns there. We shouldn't have to worry about the border patrol either, there ain't a lot of illegal border crossings through that stretch."

Once inside their room, Toledo was once again shackled, this time to a thick cable that secured the antiquated TV from theft. Traynor took a quick shower and then watched Toledo while Manuel did the same.

"I, too, would like to clean my body," Toledo said in the whiny tone that had become his norm.

Traynor opened his valise and took out a stick of deodorant and some aftershave and tossed them to him. "You'll have to make do with these," he said. "At least you'll smell a bit better."

Toledo caught the hygiene products with his free hand and gave him an angry glare. Traynor flopped onto one of the beds and crossed his arms under his head.

When Manuel walked out of the bathroom, he saw Toledo holding the aftershave and deodorant and asked, "What's up?"

"Ole Holy, doesn't like the arrangements I made for his personal hygiene."

Manuel walked across the room and unlocked Toledo's handcuff. "We're only hurting ourselves . . . He smells like day-old roadkill."

He led Toledo into the bathroom and Traynor heard Toledo whine, "I can't remove my clothes with these on." The handcuffs rattled.

"Tough shit," Manuel said. "Your clothes stink too. Shower with them on."

Traynor heard Toledo muttering in Spanish, and although he did not understand what he was saying, by the tone he knew that it was not complimentary. He turned the television on and tuned it to what he assumed was a local news and weather forecast; at least a buxom young woman was reading something in Spanish. Over her shoulder he saw a weather map of Mexico and the southern United States. Centered in the blue expanse of the Gulf of Mexico was the winged circle symbol, showing the position of Hurricane Fredericka. Several lines with arrowheads showed the predicted possible tracks the storm could take; one of them pointed toward northern Mexico.

"That," Manuel said, "could be a problem."

Traynor had not heard him come back in and turned to him. "Is she saying what I think she's saying?"

"If you think she's saying that Fredericka may come this way . . . then the answer is *yes*."

He was quiet for several seconds and then shook his head. For the first time since they had met, Traynor detected worry in Manuel's demeanor. "What is it?" he asked.

"That's a strong storm. Right now it's a category four, but could be a five before it makes landfall."

That made Traynor worry; he was no meteorologist, but knew that a category five storm meant winds in excess of 155 miles per hour. He also knew that category five hurricanes had a nasty habit of spawning tornadoes along their leading edge.

Unattended parked surveillance vehicles may create suspicion
or become the target of criminal activity.
—*FM 3-19.13, Law Enforcement Investigations*

46

Skidgel arrived and drove through the gate. He parked in front of the tall white mansion and went inside without knocking. McMahon snapped several pictures and lowered the camera. "So," he said, "the plot sickens."

Deborah ignored his play on words and said, "If we had any doubts about Jabłoński's involvement, they're gone."

He nodded. "Yup, seems we now have the producer, the casting agent, and the director."

"I need to look at that video again," Deborah said.

"Once wasn't enough?"

"Oh, it was more than enough to disgust and shock me. This time, however, we need to concentrate on Provost. I think he was the butcher.

We need to determine whether or not there are any marks or features that will help us to positively identify him . . ."

" . . . Or them. We still don't know exactly what Doerr's involvement is."

"We can't stay here forever," Deborah said. "Why don't we get some dinner and then go to her house? I want a few minutes alone with that bitch." Her face hardened, and McMahon was certain that if Doerr knew anything, Deborah would get it out of her.

Provost dropped Celia Doerr at her home just past nine that evening. Rather than stay, he left. Once Celia was inside and Provost was out of sight, Deborah opened her door. "You coming with me?" she asked McMahon.

He replied, "I'll come in once you're inside. If she sees me, she might be reluctant to let you in."

"Okay."

Deborah was standing beside the car when she heard McMahon call to her. She bent over, her head inside the door.

"You may want this." He offered her a pistol.

"I don't need a gun to deal with the likes of her."

"All right, it's your call . . . just be careful."

"Always."

She walked to Doerr's house and rang the doorbell. It took several moments for the door to open as far as the security chain would allow. Doerr peeked at her through the narrow opening. "Yes?"

"Ms. Doerr, Celia Doerr?"

"Yes, how can I help you?"

"I'm Deborah Hollis . . . Mindy's sister. I've come to LA to take her home. The men we hired to find her said that she had been living with you, and I've come for any of her things you may have."

"It's quite late—"

"I know and I apologize for that, but I'm flying home in the morning and this is the first chance I've had to come for her things."

"I suppose it will be all right."The door closed and Deborah heard the security chain slide and the door open, letting her in.

"Thank you." Before she entered she glanced back and saw McMahon get out of the car.

Inside, Doerr offered her a seat and said, "After your men were here, I realized that someone would be coming for her things, so I took the liberty of packing them up. If you'll excuse me, I'll only be a few moments."

"Of course."

Once she left the room, Deborah opened the door and let McMahon in. They both sat on the couch and waited for her to return.

Doerr walked into the room carrying a cardboard box. She saw McMahon and stopped. "What is this?"

"I believe that you and Mr. McMahon have met," Deborah announced. "I think you'd better sit down and talk with us."

"About what? I already told him and the other man everything I know."

"How about," Deborah said in a flat voice, "your relationship with Larry Provost and Vernon Skidgel?"

"I have no idea who those people are."

McMahon saw the box Doerr held and asked, "What is that?"

"Mindy's things," Deborah answered.

"Really?" McMahon said. He turned on Doerr. "When we first met, you said that she tool all of her things when she moved out."

Doerr tried to cover her tracks. "I found these after you left . . ."

Deborah's eyes narrowed and her lips stiffened into a straight line. "Let's not play games, Ms. Doerr. We've been following you. Larry Provost spent the night here and you and he abruptly ran out and drove to Kondrat Jabłoński's home when I phoned you—"

"That was you?"

Deborah gave her a coquettish smile and said, "We also know that Provost is more than casually acquainted with Skidgel. We've seen them together."

Doerr's face blanched and her eyes darted from side to side. Deborah thought she looked like a cornered rodent.

"Vernon Skidgel, also known as Vincent Beneventi, entraps young women into making pornographic movies. Am I getting through to you Celia?" Deborah smiled and in a pleasant voice added, "It is all right if I call you Celia? You can call us Deborah and Jack."

Doerr began to pace back and forth, wringing her hands as she did. "I had no idea what they had planned—"

"What's Jabłoński's role in this?" McMahon asked.

"He directed that disgusting film."

"Why," Deborah interjected, "would he become involved in something like that?"

"Kondrat Jabłoński is possibly the worst of all of them," Doerr answered. "They have home video of him having sex with minors and he's a cocaine addict and dealer. Nevertheless, I think he'd do it even if none of that were true. He's scum."

Neither Deborah nor McMahon said anything, allowing Doerr to bare her soul. "When this gets out," she said, "and I'm sure it's about to, I wouldn't be surprised if he isn't on the next plane to some country where there's no extradition treaty with the United States. He would have no problem leaving the rest of them to take the fall."

"*Them?* I think *us* would be more appropriate." Deborah's voice was fraught with contempt.

"No, *them* is the correct word. I had nothing to do with that movie. Why would I be held accountable?"

"Let me put this in words even you can understand," McMahon said. "This is not going to be a morals charge. Mindy was murdered and everyone who knows anything about it will be arrested and charged as an accomplice. In your case as an accessory either before or after the fact, or possibly the lesser crime of aiding and abetting—either way, you're looking at some serious jail time."

"But I did nothing—"

"Exactly," Deborah said. "You did nothing . . . nor did you do anything to stop it."

"What if I testify against all of them . . . Would that get me anything?"

"The word of one person, who I might add is trying to save her own neck, against that of who knows how many people . . . at least one of whom is very influential," McMahon said. "How much value do you think that will have in court? You'll be lucky if the DA even considers you as a potential witness."

Doerr flopped into an easy chair. "What can I do? I'll give you anything you need."

"The names of everyone involved," Deborah said. "And I mean everyone, even the people who cleaned up the cabin after . . ."

"You know where *that* is?"

"Celia," Deborah said, "you have no idea how much we know."

47

The sun shining through the small window in the door woke Traynor. He heard the toilet flush and a few seconds later Manuel walked into the room, wiping his hands with a towel. "Good morning," he said.

Traynor nodded, too groggy to say anything. He looked around the room; he'd been in so many strange rooms the past week that it took him several seconds to remember where they were. Toledo lay on the floor, shackled to one of the legs of Manuel's bed. Traynor stood and slid into his trousers. "It's almost five in the morning. Why didn't you wake me for my watch at three?"

"You've been doing most of the driving and will continue to do so, so I figured I'd let you sleep. I'll be able to nap in the truck."

Traynor nodded toward Toledo. "He give you any trouble?"

"Nah."

Traynor smelled coffee and saw that Manuel had made some in the room's small coffee service. He walked to it and poured a cup. "I've been thinking . . ."

"I thought I could smell wood burning," Manuel quipped.

Traynor looked at the steaming cup of coffee for a second, and then asked, "Does heating the water for coffee make it safe to drink?"

"No, you need to boil it for twenty minutes at least to kill all the micro-organisms. Don't worry, I used bottled water, so you should be okay."

Traynor sipped the coffee. It wasn't gourmet, but it was hot and full of caffeine, which was good enough. "As I was saying, I've been thinking. Are we on a fool's errand?"

"In what manner?"

Traynor nudged Toledo with his foot. "Shithead here. If all he did was finance the movie and wasn't even in the US when it was made, what can he be charged with?"

Manuel checked how secure Toledo's handcuffs were and motioned for Traynor to follow him outside. Once the door was closed behind them, he said, "For the movie, probably nothing. For trafficking in illegal drugs, he'll do a long stretch. The DEA has been after him for years."

"So we continue risking our lives to bring him north? Manuel, don't tell me you have a hidden agenda here."

"Such as?"

"I don't know—maybe balancing the books from your stretch undercover?"

"No, I'm not. But taking a major player out of the picture is fulfilling."

"That doesn't seem like much of a consolation to me. You and I would be facing kidnapping charges down here."

"Murder charges."

"Murder? Anyone we killed was trying to kill us. In any court, that's self-defense."

"Remember, this is not the US, so get your bribes in early . . . and often."

Traynor sipped his coffee, letting the brilliant sun warm him. "This is nuts. We race across half of Mexico and if we do get him across the border, he can afford to hire some high-priced mouthpiece who'll probably fix it so he walks to the nearest airport and buys a first-class ticket home. Am I right?"

"No." Manuel turned and put his hand on the doorknob. "If he goes home, it will be in either an urn or a coffin."

Traynor let that one ride and followed him back into the room.

An hour later, they were back on the road. Toledo was once again securely chained to the handgrip near the top of the passenger-side door. "I'm hungry," he announced.

Traynor held his hand out. "Glad to meet you, Hungry. I'm Ed."

Toledo turned his head and stared out the window.

Manuel threw a chocolate bar into Toledo's lap. "Put that in your mouth and shut up."

Toledo looked over his shoulder and scowled at Manuel. He picked the candy up with his free left hand and said, "I can't open it with one hand."

"Use your fuckin' teeth," Manuel growled.

Traynor switched on the radio. "Let's see what Fredericka is doing."

All they picked up was static.

They stopped on the outskirts of a small city named Janos, population about two bricks shy of a full load. Manuel exited the truck, placed his hands on the small of his back, and stretched. Traynor too got out and circled the vehicle.

"You want me to drive for a while?" Manuel asked.

"Naw, I just need a short break. How far is it to the border?"

"Two and a half, maybe three hours." Manuel inhaled deeply. "From now on, we're deep in cartel country."

"I gather you're telling me to keep a weapon handy."

"And have it loaded and cocked. If they don't already have us pinpointed, I'll be surprised."

Traynor stared at the morning sun and arched his back, feeling his vertebrae shift, and his road-weary muscles stretch. "Well," he said, "I guess this is why we make the medium bucks."

"We need to watch closely from here on. There isn't a town big enough to have a welcome sign between here and Agua Prieta."

"That where we're headed?"

"No, they'll be watching the border crossing between there and Douglas, Arizona. Not far from there is an old mining road that ends close to the border. We'll ditch the truck at the mine and walk about a mile, give or take, to the border."

Traynor remained silent, processing what Manuel had said. It made sense not to try and cross at any established crossing; even a Cub Scout would know enough to report them.

"What do you think our chances are of making it across without being found?"

"About the same as Charles Manson's chances of getting into heaven."

"That good, huh."

"Maybe even less . . ."

"Well, if I'm going to hell, at least this trip has got me acclimated to the heat."

Manuel grinned and gave him a tap on his right biceps. "C'mon, let's get this over with."

Before heading through town, they took care of nature's business and made sure that Toledo did the same. He was even more surly than usual. Traynor didn't know if it was from proximity to the border or the fact that if they did run into anyone, they would most likely not be concerned with his health and well-being.

Traynor studied the landscape and found it to be more hills and scrub brush. He hadn't seen a real tree in so long that he vowed to stop at the first one they encountered and sacrifice a goat. A flash of light attracted his eye, and he said to Manuel, "Try to be as nonchalant as you can and look at that bluff to the east."

Manuel shifted, trying not to look directly at the location. "What do you see?"

"I caught a flash of light on the top of the smaller of the ridges over there."

As if on cue, the flash showed itself again. "I think they've found us," Manuel said.

"Terrific."

"They know that we only have two options once we arrive in Janos. We can go east to Juárez or west to Agua Prieta. They'll be waiting for us on Route 2, which is the only road of any substance between the two." He turned toward the truck. "Like I said, keep your guns handy . . . and loaded."

Investigators often believe they can "pretend" to care about the suspect's situation in order to gain his trust.
—*FM 3-19.13, Law Enforcement Investigations*

48

McMahon decided that it was time for him to poke a stick into the varmint's den and see what scurried out. The tracking device on Skidgel's car indicated that he was back at the estate. Rather than breeching the walls a second time, he drove through the gate to the front door.

When he rang, Skidgel answered. He gave McMahon a hard look and said, "What you doin' here?"

Without waiting for an invitation, McMahon walked into the house. "Nice place. Helluvalot better than that apartment you keep as a front, that's for sure."

Skidgel closed the door and scowled at his uninvited guest. "You got brass balls, buddy. This ain't my place. I'm the head of security here. All I got to do is call my people and you're dead."

"I've already met your security people, and they didn't impress me much. Now how about you knock off the bogus tough guy routine and sit down before I knock you down."

Skidgel deflated, and he turned and trudged deeper into the house. Following close behind, McMahon studied the décor; it was impressive to say the least. The furnishings were expensive: two of the gilded chairs that lined the foyer's walls probably cost as much as his car. An ornate crystal chandelier was suspended from the ceiling, but he couldn't even estimate its worth. They walked through a long hallway adorned with artwork, mostly landscapes and several seascapes. The passage led them to a colossal living room in which an enormous leather couch, with matching chairs, faced a marble fireplace that was so large McMahon thought it was ostentatious. Without waiting to be offered a seat, McMahon dropped into one of the chairs.

Skidgel tried to keep as much distance between them as possible and sat in a chair on the opposite end of the couch. "One of my guards was found dead in Topanga Canyon," he said. "You know anything about that?"

McMahon leaned back and said, "As I said, your security team isn't very good."

"Okay, you got the floor. You still haven't told me why you're here."

"After living in a place like this"—McMahon looked around the room—"sharing a nine-by-twelve cell with some gangbanger named Bubba is going to be a rough transition."

Skidgel shrugged as if he was unconcerned at the thought of prison—but the sudden drop of his jowls said otherwise. "That ain't been determined yet. I got friends," he replied. McMahon knew that he was speaking with more bravado than he felt.

"Oh, I think a lot more has been determined than you think. As much money as this place cost, it's just a shack compared to where Jabłoński and Toledo live. You do know that we have Toledo?"

Skidgel paled. "I don't know any of those names."

"Bullshit. I saw you enter Jabłoński's estate yesterday. I also saw you meet with Provost. You're all up to your armpits in quicksand . . . and there ain't nobody around to throw you a rope."

Skidgel sat back, looking the same way he had in the apartment the day they found his video library and the copy of *The Black Orchid*. Even though his swagger had left, he still tried to sound tough. "Ain't no big deal. I'm sure a lot of people know those guys, it don't mean nothin'."

"We also got somebody—I won't give you the name—who is willing to turn state's evidence. Now, think about this. If some heavyweights like Jabłoński and Provost are faced with doing time, who you think they're gonna roll over on? Hell, I wouldn't be surprised if Jabłoński isn't on his way back to Poland as we speak."

"You still ain't told me what you want."

"Nothin', I just like to watch assholes like you shit razor blades." McMahon stood. "It's been a pleasure visiting with you, Vern . . . or do you prefer Vince? Don't bother gettin' up—I know the way out."

As he walked through the hall to the foyer, McMahon finally allowed himself to grin. Now, he thought, let's see who rolls over on whom . . .

The northern Mexican border state of Chihuahua and the southwest state of Guerrero tied for highest murder rate in the country in 2012.

—*Insightcrime.org*

49

They stopped in Janos long enough to refuel and for Manuel to get an update on Hurricane Fredericka's progress. It was not encouraging. The maelstrom had slammed into Mexico between Matamoros and Tampico, pummeling the coastal towns with an eighteen-foot storm surge. Hundreds of homes were demolished and more than a thousand people were either missing or dead. The forecasts were still undecided about its track. One model said it would take a sharp right and cross into the US near Laredo, Texas; another said it could head west, sending some much needed rain to Chihuahua and the American southwest.

Although it was obvious that the gas station attendant was trying hard not to show any sign that he saw Toledo handcuffed inside the truck, Traynor knew that they had been spotted. If he had any doubts that they were on a major drug trafficking route, the way that the attendant ignored the weapons that were on the backseat and on their hips was all the proof he needed. In north Chihuahua, silence was not only golden, it was a means of survival.

Giving Traynor a break, Manuel drove and they were back on the road in no time, fully aware that if the flashes they had seen earlier were binoculars and the person using them was either one of Toledo's people or a member of the local cartel, they were about to enter another confrontation. An hour later, the pursuers made their move.

"We got company," Manuel said, his eyes never leaving the rearview mirror.

Traynor turned and looked through the back window. "Could be anyone, maybe some local farmers?"

"Not in three matching SUVs."

Traynor picked up his assault rifle and made sure it was in operating condition. He laid the seat back down again; if it came to a running fight, he wanted a clear field of fire. He reached into the wooden crate and removed two additional full magazines and placed them beside his shooting position. He was ready for whatever was about to happen . . . or so he thought.

The pursuing vehicles were steadily closing the gap between them, and any doubts Traynor harbored about their intentions were removed when one of the trucks pulled abreast of the first, effectively sealing the road behind. Traynor slid through the gap left when he had reclined the seat and prepared to fire as soon as Manuel popped the hatch open. He heard Manuel say, "Sonuvabitch . . ." and slid back and looked out through the front window. Driving straight at them were two more SUVs, also traveling abreast of each other. They were trapped in between.

"Can we get off the road?" Traynor asked Manuel.

"No. The ground around here is like dry quicksand—we'd bog this thing down as soon as we hit the sand."

"Any ideas?"

"Yeah, forget about the guys behind us . . . try to take *them* out." He pointed at the trucks bearing down on them from the front.

Traynor rolled down the window directly behind Toledo and said to him, "I'd keep my arms inside if I were you," and then leaned out. Holding the rifle steady on any single target was more of a chore than he had realized. Although the road surface was relatively smooth, there was still enough vibration and bouncing to make aiming a weapon a tricky situation; still, he did his best. He aimed for the front tire, but the bullet smashed the windshield between the men occupying the front seats. It was doubtful that he had hit anyone, but it startled the driver enough that he yanked the wheel to the left, hitting the vehicle in the next lane. The vehicles bounced off each other, and they both corrected, drifting onto their respective shoulders. Dirt, dust, and rocks flew from their tires and the drivers' faces were tense as they fought to maintain control of their vehicles.

Manuel took advantage of their plight and moved to the center of the road. When they raced between the SUVs, Traynor tried to shoot the tires out from under the one on his side. He was not successful. In seconds the road ahead of them was open and Traynor felt his body being pulled back as they accelerated away. Through the hatch window, he saw the two trucks skid to a halt. Once the three pursuing vehicles dashed past them, they returned to the pavement and took up the rear.

Manuel glanced at Traynor in the rearview mirror. "We havin' fun yet?"

"Nope."

"Well," he said, with a devil-may-care attitude, "let me know when we start . . . I never know these things."

"Just get us the hell away from that motorized army back there—then we'll worry about having fun."

Manuel reached over and punched Toledo in the arm. "How 'bout you, Holy? You havin' fun yet?"

Toledo winced and glowered.

"You got nothing to say, Holy?"

"I don't like being called that."

"Okay," Manuel said, continuing to aggravate his prisoner. "Would you prefer something else?"

"My name is Giuliano Olivas Toledo. I prefer to be called Señor Toledo."

"*I* have a problem with that," Manuel said in Spanish, without taking his eyes from the road. "Señor is a title of respect and you're lower than a pile of whale shit on the ocean floor. I think I'll call you Señor *Mierda*."

Toledo's head snapped to the side, and he gave Manuel another scathing look. He clenched his free hand into a fist, and for a moment Traynor thought he was going to punch Manuel. Traynor was not sure what had been said to piss him off, but he didn't think it was wise to distract a man driving almost 180 kilometers per hour. He touched the muzzle of his nine millimeter automatic to the back of Toledo's head. "Holy," he said, "don't let a few seconds of pleasure fuck up the rest of your life."

Toledo relaxed and said, "It is bad enough to be kidnapped and dragged across half my country without being insulted as well."

"We aren't asking for much," Traynor said. "All we want is one little reason to blow the top of your head off. The only thing stopping me from offing you this very minute is that it would be too fast. I want you to suffer like Melinda Hollis did."

"I have told you that I do not know this woman."

"Melinda—better known as Mindy—was the star of your latest cinematic venture. A distasteful piece of schlock entitled *The Black Orchid* . . . need I say more?"

"I will pay you anything . . . I will even sign over my ranchero to you, if you set me free."

Suddenly, Traynor tired of speaking with him. He turned to Manuel instead. "How about we cut our losses, Manuel? I can put a bullet in his skull, and we can roll his corpse onto the road. That might even satisfy the vultures behind us."

"It might . . . but not until they run him over a few times to make sure he's dead."

Toledo began to perspire profusely, despite the blasting air conditioning. Sweat ran down the side of his face and across his neck, soaking his shirt collar. Traynor tapped him on the back of his head with the pistol muzzle a few times and gave him one last barb. "The only thing that would stop us from capping you is a guarantee that there is a cell waiting for you. You'll enjoy being a bitch for the Aryan Brotherhood . . ."

Toledo's eyes grew to the size of a peso coin, and Traynor sat back in his seat. It was all he could do to keep from laughing.

Guerrero and Chihuahua were also the two most dangerous states in Mexico in 2011, with homicide rates of 70 per 100,000 and 126 per 100,000, respectively.

—Insightcrime.org

50

Traynor, Manuel, and Toledo had gone less than ten kilometers when another wave of vehicles appeared before them. Manuel did not hesitate. He left the pavement and headed for a nearby range of bluffs and mountains. When the big Ford began to bog down in the sand, Manuel said, "We're gonna have to ditch the truck and make a run for the border on foot."

Traynor remained mute, staring at the landscape. Hardscrabble sandy soil, cactus, and brush were not his idea of terrain suitable for a standoff against who knew how many armed thugs. But rather than complain, he got busy and opened the wooden treasure chest that had thus far contained everything they had needed. Whoever had packed it had thought about every possible scenario. Along with the weapons and ammunition, it contained several canteens and water bottles, and a couple of backpacks. But what really amazed him was the inclusion of two pairs of hiking boots—one of which looked to be his size. "What size boot do you wear?" he asked Manuel.

"I wear an eleven in American sizes."

"What about Mexican?"

"That would be a ten. Why are you asking about shoe sizes?"

The truck bounced and slid on the rough terrain, and it took Traynor several attempts to grab the second pair of boots and check the size. They were a ten. He threw the boots into the front seat between Manuel and Toledo. "Looks as if our benefactors took every contingency into consideration."

Manuel glanced at the boots and said, "The smallest things are sometimes the biggest miracles. This terrain is not suited for street shoes."

Traynor sorted the contents of the crate into two piles—one to take and the other to be left behind. The only things missing were hats to protect them from the desert sun; still there was enough essential equipment to give them a chance of survival. He held up a pair of plastic raincoats and debated whether or not to take them. The truck bounced again and as he threw them into the leave-behind pile, he hoped he was not making a mistake.

"How far are we from the border?" he asked as he replaced his street shoes with hiking boots.

"About twenty-five, maybe as much as thirty miles."

Traynor tried to calculate how long it would take to walk that distance. He didn't like the result. On a paved sidewalk, he could walk approximately five miles per hour, which meant somewhere from five to six hours. However, they were going to be doing it in mountainous desert, with a bunch of cutthroats and mercenaries—all of whom probably knew the area—chasing them. He didn't like their chances.

Traynor looked at their passenger. From the look on his face, he knew that Toledo was not looking forward to the trek. This turn of events had the drug-lord so scared he would probably crap a soft stool.

"Sucks, doesn't it?" Traynor asked him.

"What?"

"Having all that money and realizing it won't do you any good." Traynor motioned toward the convoy that chased them across the sunburned, broken land. "In fact," he added, "I think your chances of survival are less than ours. Those guys will probably let us walk—it's you they really want."

"If they are my people, they will kill you."

"True. But, I think they'll kill you first . . . even if they are *your* people. Surely you're not naïve enough to believe there isn't someone in your organization who wants to take your place at the top. On the other hand, if they aren't your guys . . . well, I don't have to go into detail."

"They will still kill you."

"At least we'll go quickly. It wouldn't surprise me if they take their time with you. I'm sure there's a lot of information they want. You know, bank account numbers, stuff like that."

The ground sloped upward, the tires bit into the soft soil, and the truck's rear end fishtailed as they fought for traction. Traynor took a last look at their pursuers and estimated they were a half, possibly three-quarters of a mile behind. He began getting ready to leave the mechanized cavalry and join the infantry.

Manuel drove down a small ravine and aimed the SUV toward a line of stunted trees on the opposite side. The tires began spinning and Traynor felt the four-by-four's rear axle dig into the sand. They had gone as far as the truck was going to take them.

They leaped out, and while Traynor unloaded the equipment he had identified as essential, Manuel changed his footgear.

It took only a few minutes for Manuel to finish, and then he and Traynor quickly divided the equipment between them before pulling Toledo from the vehicle. Manuel spun him around and snarled, "I'll end this the second you try to slow us down. So if you have any plans to do so, remember that."

Manuel walked to the front of the truck and raised the hood. A few seconds later he reappeared, carrying a handful of rubber cables, which Traynor immediately identified as the spark plug cables.

Toledo made one last chance at sounding tough. He looked at Traynor and said, "This gringo doesn't have the cojones to shoot me."

"Maybe not," Manuel interjected, "but if I was you I wouldn't push my luck—because I, for one, sure as hell think he does." He pushed Toledo up the hill.

Traynor took out his cell phone and checked the signal strength—no bars. He shoved it into his pocket and scrambled after them.

"Life is what happens to you while you're busy making other plans."

—Allen Saunders

51

Angela Engle joined Deborah and McMahon for dinner. The first fifteen minutes of the conversation consisted of McMahon updating her on what they had learned and done—he omitted the incident with the security guard—thus far.

When they had finished, Engle said, "We still don't have much on them."

"What about the cabin?" McMahon asked. "Did the forensics people find anything there?"

"That place had been sterilized. They must have hired someone with experience cleaning up crime scenes."

"We have Celia Doerr," Deborah said.

"I've met her," Engle said. "A good defense attorney will eat her alive. All they need to do is play up her relationship with Provost. It shouldn't be hard to convince a jury that she's nothing more than a jilted girlfriend who's trying to get back at him. She saw nothing, which means anything she can testify to will be considered hearsay. Keep in mind, Provost's connections go to Sacramento and beyond." She turned to McMahon. "What about Skidgel?"

"He's too scared of the others."

"Any chance that Provost or Jabłoński will roll on the others?"

"I doubt it," McMahon answered. "Provost will be too worried about what would happen to his job as the power behind the governor if he admits to being a part of it. As for Jabłoński, it wouldn't surprise me if he's halfway across the Atlantic by now."

"I know for a fact that he isn't," Engle said. "He's three weeks into filming a big-budget project for a major producer. If he left them high and dry, it would kill him professionally."

"Maybe," McMahon mused, "I should pay him a visit."

"Won't be easy," Engle said, "he's filming on location in Vancouver."

McMahon looked at Deborah.

"The corporate jet returned from Mexico today. You can fly to Vancouver in the morning," Deborah reported.

"I'm not sure that's wise. If I confront him, he'll be on the next plane out."

"I agree with Jack," Engle said.

"Then," Deborah amended, "don't confront him. Keep an eye on him and if he tries to leave North America, take action."

McMahon turned to Engle. "Can you find out where he's staying? I doubt they'll let me just wander onto a movie set."

"I'll try. While you're there, be careful," Engle said.

McMahon gave her an inquisitive look.

"Whatever you do, don't let them know you're from the Boston area. They're a bit sensitive about that since the Bruins knocked the Canucks off in the Stanley Cup Finals."

Students must pass a Board approved fitness test at the 40th percentile based on age and gender norms. The following three (3) test items constitute the physical fitness test: Maximum Push-Up test (untimed); One Minute Sit-Up test; and 1.5 mile run.
—Physical Fitness Test, Maine Criminal Justice Academy

52

B y the time they reached the trees near the top of the ravine, Traynor was sucking wind. He remembered how easily he had passed the PFT in police academy—then realized that had been more than twenty years ago. He got some consolation when he saw that Toledo's face was red, and that he collapsed to the ground and hung his head forward as he gasped for breath. Traynor was not about to give him the satisfaction of seeing that he was in a similar condition, so he avoided him and joined Manuel, who was studying their back trail. Manuel also showed the effects of the climb. Sweat plastered his shirt to his back and he breathed heavily.

Between deep draughts of air, Traynor asked, "What now?"

"We have to slow them down."

"Okay . . . how do we do it?"

"One of us stays behind, while the other drags Mary Alice here"—he hooked a thumb over his shoulder in Toledo's direction—"or we take turns."

"I'm more inclined to take turns. If you stay behind, I don't know my way around well enough to get to the border . . . and assuming I survive, the same holds true if I stay," Traynor said.

"All right, who covers our rear first?" Manuel asked.

"I will."

"Okay, give us about five minutes start and then follow. I'll mark the trail somehow."

"In this soft soil, I should be able to find your footprints."

"Yeah, but so will they."

Manuel didn't have to tell Traynor who *they* were. He peered around the brush they were hiding behind, and saw the first of the black Chevrolets stop behind the Ford Excursion they'd abandoned. "What you figure the distance is?"

"About three hundred meters."

"So"—Traynor raised his AK-47—"they're within range."

"Yuh."

"Okay, you grab shithead and take off. I'll be along shortly."

Traynor settled in behind the scrub brush and watched as the remainder of the convoy reached the disabled Ford. It didn't help his confidence when each of the five vehicles discharged four armed men. They looked up the slope in his direction and then must have agreed on a strategy. The occupants of two of the trucks jumped back in and drove around the abandoned Ford, following the ravine north. Traynor quickly took aim and fired a burst of rounds at them. The first of the two trucks took the brunt of the enfilade, and Traynor knew that he had either hit the driver or startled him enough that he hit the brakes; either way, he swerved into the path of the second Tahoe. They collided with a resounding crash. Both vehicles looked as if they would be out of commission for a while.

Traynor turned his attention to their abandoned and disabled truck and saw one of the men sitting in it. He saw him slam his hands against the steering wheel and then get out and run to the front. He lifted the hood, looked at the motor, and slammed the hood back down. He ran for cover, yelling to his comrades. Traynor fired another burst of rounds—this time aiming at their vehicles. When he saw puffs of smoke, he knew they were returning fire, and soon he heard the angry snap of bullets flying past. Crouching down to make as small a target as possible, he ran after Manuel and Toledo. Dashing across the sandy ground, he kept his eyes on the trail of footprints.

As he ran, he hoped they had enough ammunition to engage in a running firefight for thirty miles.

No sight that human eyes can look upon is more provocative of awe
than is the night sky scattered thick with stars.

—Llewelyn Powys

53

They traveled north as long as the light would allow. As the sun dropped below the peaks, the world seemed to turn purple as the waning daylight illuminated the sage. Although the valley was immersed in deepening shadows, the peaks of the mountains that surrounded them still basked in the setting sun. It was a sight worthy of a calendar picture.

"We'll stop here for a couple of hours," Manuel said.

"A couple of hours," Toledo protested, "I cannot go on, especially in the dark."

Manuel ignored him, but Traynor saw his shoulders tense. He, too, was tired of Toledo's constant whining. "I think," Traynor said, "that if I were you, I'd shut up before someone shut me up."

Toledo looked at him and then flopped down on the sand. "I'm hungry."

"No fire," Manuel said.

Traynor dropped the pack that contained their supplies and grabbed a couple of energy bars, one of which he tossed at Toledo's feet.

Toledo stared at the bar for a second and then at Traynor. He opened his mouth to protest, but before he could say anything, Traynor cut him off. "You complain and I'll take it back."

"I am going to enjoy killing you," Toledo said.

"Shut the fuck up. I'm tired of listening to you say that. You're getting to be a bore," Traynor countered.

Manuel chuckled and lay down using his pack as a pillow. "You know," he said, "I think when we move out we'll put both packs on ole Holy . . . let him be our pack mule."

"That sounds like a plan to me. Why should we carry everything?"

Toledo did not look happy as he ripped open the energy bar with his teeth.

When Manuel warned them, "Check the ground for scorpions before you sit down," Toledo jumped to his feet.

"Don't worry," Manuel assured him, "only the female is deadly."

Still surveying the ground, Toledo said, "Who's going to pick them up, look between their legs, and tell me when I'm in trouble?"

"Then," Manuel continued, "there are the tarantulas and the fire ants."

Even though Traynor did not show it, he was no happier to hear this than Toledo was.

The moonlight made the desert look silver. The brush and cactus cast menacing shadows, but there was ample light to see by. Manuel kicked the bottom of Toledo's left foot until he woke up. "Time to get moving," he said and walked away.

Before Toledo could whine about breakfast, Traynor said, "We'll eat later."

They pulled Toledo to his feet and checked that his handcuffs were still secure. Traynor inspected his wrists and saw that three days in shackles had rubbed the skin raw and his wrists were crusted with a ring of blood. "That must hurt," he said with a broad smile.

Toledo mumbled something under his breath, and Traynor shoved him forward, slid his pack onto his back, and picked up his rifle. "Hey, Manuel, were you serious about using him as a pack mule?"

"Maybe later . . . when it gets really hot."

"I can hardly wait," Traynor answered.

Manuel turned and looked at Toledo. "Beware of the rattlesnakes. They like to lie on rocks because they hold the warmth of the sun."

Toledo looked terrified as he searched the immediate area for serpents. "Is there anything in this godforsaken desert that won't kill you?" he asked.

Traynor shivered in the night chill. For the first time he experienced the desert's drastic contrast—blazing heat during the daylight hours and frigid temperatures at night. All day long Traynor had prayed for a break from the sun and heat, but now at three in the morning, he was wishing for daylight and some warmth. It was so cold that even Toledo's mouth seemed to have frozen shut; either that or he was too occupied searching every rock and bush for a sidewinder poised to strike. Either way, Traynor thought it was better than his perpetual whining.

They walked until the sun crept over the peaks to their right. Cresting a small hill, Manuel immediately dropped onto his stomach. He motioned for them to do likewise and Traynor pushed Toledo onto his face. He urged the captive ahead of him until they had crawled beside Manuel. Venturing a look down the hill, Traynor saw what had alarmed Manuel.

One of the black SUVs was parked below them; an armed man sat on its hood, smoking a cigarette. "Looks as if I didn't knock out all of their trucks," Traynor whispered.

"I'd have been more surprised if you had," Manuel replied.

"Now what?" Traynor asked.

"We try to work our way around them."

They slid backward until they were below the crest of the hill and stood. Manuel hunched over and jogged toward the rising sun. Traynor grabbed Toledo by his shirt collar and whispered in his ear, "One peep out of you and I'll kill you before they can locate us—you got that?" When he nodded, Traynor pushed him forward and followed Manuel.

A chance encounter between the undercover investigator and the suspect may occur on the spur of the moment or be a well-planned maneuver, either of which should appear to the suspect as a natural chain of events.
—*FM 3-19.13, Law Enforcement Investigations*

54

After a three-hour flight, the Gulfstream G500 landed in Vancouver, British Columbia. McMahon was impressed by what he saw out the window as the plane dropped toward the runway. The fjords and the Rocky Mountains created a panoramic view that was breathtaking in its rustic beauty. Several bush planes equipped with pontoons raced through the harbor as they attained a speed suitable for takeoff.

McMahon had traveled light and was through customs in minutes. In less than an hour, he was in a rental car and driving toward the city.

As he drove, it became evident to him why the Vancouver area had become Hollywood North. The city offered a number of photogenic neighborhoods, from Gas town, which reminded him of an American street at the turn of the twentieth century, to a Chinatown that would rival any outside of China itself.

Then there was the seedier side of Vancouver. McMahon knew that the east side of the city was a mecca for sex workers. Prostitutes openly paraded up and down Seymour and East Hastings Streets, and drug addicts and the homeless lived in the empty buildings that lined the sidewalks. There had been a major cleanup attempt made when the 2010 Winter Olympics were held in the city, but once the heat was off, things returned to normal in short time.

McMahon followed the GPS as it led him along the Stanley Park Causeway into North Vancouver and then along Route 99. He followed the shore of Howe Sound for an hour until he came to Squamish. He cruised along the length of Cleveland Street, which was the main drag, looking for a restaurant or bar where he might tap into the local gossip. He narrowed his selection down to either the Dairy Queen or a restaurant called the Howe Sound Inn and Brewing Co. He opted for the inn.

A bar ran the length of the room and there were fifteen or twenty tables filling the rest of the space. Believing that he had a better chance of striking up a conversation at the bar, McMahon slid onto a stool. The bartender came over and asked, "What can I get yuh?"

"What's a good local beer?"

"We brew our own, We call it Garibaldi Honey Pale Ale."

"I'll try one."

"I hope you're thirsty."

The comment puzzled McMahon until the bartender placed a frosty one-liter bottle with a flip-top in front of him. "Most folks can't drink it all at once," the bartender commented. "The flip-top allows you to reseal it and take it with you."

McMahon took a drink. The ale was cold and he found it bitterer than his palate was accustomed to. The server stood in front of him, a look of expectation on his face. "What you think?" he asked.

"Not bad, not bad at all."

"You don't sound like you're from around here."

"I'm visiting from LA. Just got into town this morning. Maybe you can help me."

"I can try."

"My fiancée is here, making a movie with the famous director, Kondrat Jabłoński. I hoped that someone might know exactly where they're shooting."

"Only movie anyone's making, that I know of, is back toward Vancouver. You come up ninety-nine?"

"I did."

"Then you drove past it. It's a house by itself, out on a point into the sound. Just look for a bunch of cars and trucks."

"What does a bunch of trucks mean to you?" McMahon asked.

"Up here, anything more than two." The bartender laughed and then walked down the bar.

McMahon retraced his route along Howe Sound. The scenery was breathtaking. It was early September in the low country, and the summits of the Canadian Rocky Mountains were snow-covered. The white peaks stood out in stark contrast to the crystal clear blue skies that seemed to rest atop them. He descended a long, winding slope and saw an impressive house perched on a point that jutted out into Howe Sound. The drive was filled with trucks, which made him certain that he had found the location of the movie shoot.

He parked on the shoulder along the highway and walked up the drive, hoping he could get close enough to the house to see what was going on—maybe even be able to identify some of the people. A security guard stopped him about a hundred yards short of the wide parking area. Several other people stood along the barriers, all of them rubbernecking in hope of spotting a celebrity. There was also the chance—albeit a remote one—that one or more of them would be selected as a walk-on. McMahon stood along the barrier close to the security guard, assuming she could be a useful source of information.

A tall, lanky man walked out of the house, apparently headed for one of several trailers that were sitting on the periphery of the set. "Who is that?" McMahon asked the guard. The woman turned and gave the man a cursory look. "Rock Stone," she answered.

"I've never heard of him," McMahon commented. "Is he one of the stars?"

"It doesn't surprise me that you've never heard of him. He's one of those Hollywood-types who think they're a hell of a lot bigger than they are. If you bought him for what he *is* worth and then sold him for what he *thinks* he's worth . . . you could retire to your own private island in the South Pacific."

"He does look familiar, though."

"Jabłoński has a stable of would-be stars who work cheap . . . I guess they find it better than working for a living. He casts them in most of his movies. Without him, they'd probably be living on the streets."

"Really?"

"Yup. Now you take Stone, he's the lousiest actor I ever saw. I think he has compromising pictures of Jabłoński . . . That's the only reason I can think of for him being in every Jabłoński epic."

McMahon wondered what Stone had done to earn the security guard's disdain. He studied the actor, wondering if he had found Mindy Hollis's costar. His reverie was broken when a white-haired man of medium build stormed out of the house with two people on his heels. One was an attractive woman.

"If it ain't the *great one* himself," the guard commented.

"Is he the star?"

"That's Jabłoński."

"Who's the woman?"

"Abigail Allen, Jabłoński's assistant. It looks like she's gonna have to earn her money today—he's pissed about something."

"How can you tell?"

"Three, four times a day he storms out with his ass-kissers in tow. Notice how his face and neck are red? Whenever his face gets that red, you know he's pissed."

McMahon studied the renowned director and thought: *He looks like a pimple that's ready to pop.* Jabłoński pointed at the observers gathered along the barriers and then stomped back inside the house. Abigail Allen, who had been silent throughout his harangue, walked off the deck and crossed the yard, stopping about ten feet short of the barrier. She scanned the people standing outside the perimeter, her gaze stopping on McMahon. She walked to him. "You interested in making a few quick bucks?" she asked him.

"Sure, why not."

"What's your name?" Allen asked.

Her question caught McMahon off guard and he said the first thing that came to mind, "Peter Puller."

She looked at him for a few seconds. "You serious—Peter Puller?"

"Yeah. Believe me, I learned to fight at a young age."

Allen said, "Well, your name won't appear on the credits anyhow, and if it does, no one will stay around long enough to read them." She said to the guard, "Let him in." She turned on her heel and took several paces, then stopped. She looked over her shoulder at him and said, "What are you waiting for? Follow me."

Her tone was sharp and authoritative; obviously she was used to having her orders obeyed without question. He fought back his resentment over her abrupt manner and moved quickly in order to walk beside her. "What," he asked, "do I have to do?"

"Play dead."

"I can handle that."

Jabłoński met McMahon and the woman when they were halfway across the parking lot. In the murky light of the approaching sunset, it was difficult to make out his features. But his heavily accented English left no doubt about his Polish heritage. "Who is this?" he demanded.

"Our corpse," the woman replied.

Jabłoński stepped back and studied McMahon as if he were lining him up in the reticule of a camera. "*Tak.* We will shoot his scene first thing in the morning." Without saying anything further, he spun on his heel and stormed back toward the house.

McMahon looked at the woman. "*Tak*?"

"Polish for yes. You just passed your screen test."

"Must be a major part."

"Be hard to have a murder mystery without a murder, now wouldn't it?" She appraised him for a few seconds. "All you got to do is lie in a pool of fake blood and look murdered . . . I think that even you can handle that."

"Probably, I have some experience—"

"With what . . . being murdered?" She cast him a wary eye and added, "Or murdering?"

"Neither. I was a cop for three years—I've seen more than my share of murder vics."

"Hmmm"—she gave him another appraising look—"maybe Kondrat should consider *you* for Rock's role."

McMahon decided to act as if he had no idea who she alluded to. "Who's Rock?"

"The supposed star."

"Oh, him. I think I saw him in a movie once . . . wasn't a very good movie."

"Rock's not a very good actor," she said, with animosity. "Maybe you aren't just a handsome hunk after all."

"Why does Jabłoński keep using him?"

"If you find out, tell me, okay?" She gave him a catty smile. "Come on, I'll show you to the trailer where you can sleep tonight."

55

They crept through the early-morning light, trying to circumvent the lookout sitting on the hood of the truck. To ensure that Toledo kept his mouth shut, Traynor periodically nudged him with the muzzle of his rifle. During their sojourn together, Traynor had come to believe that Toledo was not the brightest crayon in the box, but he seemed to get the message.

They had not crept more than a hundred feet when Toledo tripped over a rock and fell with a loud thud. In seconds, Traynor heard voices speaking in Spanish and knew that somebody would be coming to discover the source of the noise. Manuel turned and said, "Take him and head north. I'll catch up with you once I've taken care of things here." He immediately ran to the top of the rise and dropped onto his stomach. He aimed his rifle at something on the other side and fired. He must have scored, because Traynor heard a grunt, followed by more excited

Spanish. He grabbed a handful of Toledo's shirt and pulled him to his feet. "For your sake, I hope that fall was an accident," he snarled.

Toledo's eyes shone white in the approaching dawn and it was evident that he was scared out of his senses. Traynor pushed him forward and warned him, "All I need is one reason . . ." He led Toledo through the scrub brush and cactus, keeping the slit of light that split the angry red sky above the eastern horizon to their right. Another shot, followed by an answering shot, broke the morning stillness.

"Your amigo will be killed," Toledo said.

"For both of our sakes, you better hope he isn't."

"I will pay you more than you ever dreamed of making—"

Traynor cut him off. "That hasn't worked yet, so shut up about it." He pushed him forward and said, "Run."

Several more shots rang out and it seemed to add impetus to Toledo's awkward gait. Traynor knew running while his hands were handcuffed in front of him was not easy, but he showed Toledo no mercy and pushed him to run faster.

The soft, sandy, soil was anything but conducive to a sprint. It did not take long for the effects of the past few days to catch up with Traynor. He was soaked with sweat and his breathing became labored. He knew that Toledo was in no better shape and that they both needed a break. He motioned for Toledo to stop by a large patch of bushes and they dropped to the ground without worrying about snakes or scorpions. Traynor inhaled deeply and almost had a heart attack when Manuel appeared like an apparition.

"Jesus! I almost shot you," he gasped.

"You wouldn't have had the chance. The two of you made more noise than a pair of skeletons screwing on a hot tin roof."

Traynor knew he was right, but rather than leave himself open for another evaluation of his escape and evasion skills, he changed the subject. "You get them?" he asked.

"I hit two of the three, but don't think I killed them." He studied the sky for a second. "They no doubt know where we are and will concentrate their efforts."

"I'm assuming you're alluding to the possibility of an aerial search."

"It isn't a possibility—it's a sure thing."

Manuel must have been a prophet, Traynor thought, because no sooner had he finished speaking than they heard the unmistakable beat of a helicopter's rotor blades.

"Quick," Manuel said, "follow me."

Manuel led them off course, to the northwest. They both grabbed a handful of Toledo's shirt and hauled him along. "There's a narrow pass through the mountains about a mile from here. If we can get in there the chopper won't be able to land."

"Yeah," Traynor answered, "but won't it allow them to concentrate their efforts?"

"There's always a critic . . ."

The way the undercover officer conducts himself during a chance meeting with a suspect will determine his acceptance or rejection by the suspect
—*FM 3-19.13, Law Enforcement Investigations*

56

McMahon stood off to the side, watching the camera crew and technicians ready the set for his cinematic debut. He drank from a disposable cup of coffee and yawned. He stared through a large picture window at the dark waters of Howe Sound. He'd had no idea that most movies and TV shows were filmed at the ungodly hours around sunrise. The woman who had selected him from among the onlookers suddenly appeared at his side. "You ready for your fifteen minutes of fame?" she asked.

"Yeah." He smiled. "You know, you and I have been talking off-and-on since yesterday afternoon and I still don't know your name."

"It's Abigail Allen. I'm Kondrat's assistant."

Their discussion was interrupted when Rock Stone entered the set with the air of a king. "Well, now that the Great Ham is on set—it's time for me to get to work," she said.

Before she could approach him, Stone walked over to them. He gave McMahon a critical look, as if he considered him a rival for his leading role. "And who do we have here?" Stone asked Abigail.

"This is Peter Puller. He's Kondrat's latest discovery."

Stone stiffened and looked around the room, obviously searching for Jabłoński. McMahon was amused at how Stone so obviously lacked confidence in his own abilities as an actor. During his years in LA, he had come in contact with a number of celebrities, and it always amazed him how fragile their egos were. Stone was more nervous than most, but then, according to Allen, he had no acting skills. Still, he had to learn what Stone's hold was over the director.

Allen studied McMahon for a moment. "We'll have to come up with a better name for you than Peter Puller, if you want to get anywhere in this business."

"Do you mean something sexy . . . like Rock Stone?"

Stone's smile was smug. "Yes, I came up with that on my own."

"No doubt," McMahon answered.

His sarcasm seemed to go over Stone's head, but Allen picked up on it and looked as if she would explode as she struggled to suppress her laughter. When Stone wandered off, she let out an explosive breath. "Touché," she said. "His stage name sounds as hokey as his acting. Still it's an improvement over his true name."

"Which is?"

"Cupido Pugliesi."

"You have to be shittin' me."

"Nope." She took him by the arm and said, "C'mon, let's go over your big role."

"If I'm to play a crucial role in this movie, maybe I ought to know its title?"

"You're going to be the first victim in *Murder by Moonlight*."

McMahon lay on the floor, soaked in fake blood, which had started to congeal around him. *Thank God, they gave me these clothes*, he thought. His musing was interrupted when Jabłoński shouted, "Action!"

The script called for the corpse to have its eyes open, so McMahon could see Rock Stone's inept investigation. He was not sure if the movie crew included an advisor on police procedure, but if it did, Rock was evidently not about to worry over authenticity. The pseudo-detective approached the corpse and without putting on latex gloves, immediately knelt down in the pool of blood.

Stone looked at the red stain on the knee of his trousers and said, "Shit."

Jabłoński erupted like a volcano that had been building pressure for millennia and shouted, "Cut!"

McMahon stood and turned to the director. "Don't you have a consultant on police procedures?"

Jabłoński, who was not accustomed to being questioned on his sets, seemed to back up, as if repelled by McMahon's challenge.

Unable to stop, McMahon pushed the issue. He pointed at Stone. "Ole Rock here made at least three *major* mistakes in the last three seconds."

"What?" Stone stepped forward as if he had been personally attacked.

Jabłoński held up a hand in Stone's direction, silencing the affronted actor. "What were these mistakes?"

"For starters, he isn't wearing protective gloves. Any investigator worth a nickel knows that contaminating a crime scene is a cardinal sin. *Always* wear gloves. In fact it's advisable to wear a minimum of two pairs, one over the other."

Jabłoński became interested and said, "Why is this important?"

"To keep from contaminating the scene by leaving fingerprints all over the place."

"Ahh, I see."

"Then there's the problem of biohazards, like AIDS and HIV . . . the gloves offer some personal protection."

"How is it you know so much about this?" Jabłoński approached McMahon with an entirely different attitude.

"I was a cop."

Jabłoński raised his voice. "Take a break." When all of the crew and cast except Stone began walking away, he said, "You too, Rock." To McMahon he said, "You stay."

Stone began to protest, but the director raised a hand, cutting him off. "I said, *take a break.*"

The actor walked away, his shoulders slumped like a chastised child's.

"I think you hurt your superstar's feelings," McMahon said.

"Hah!" Jabłoński waved his right hand back and forth as if he were shooing a fly. "He is of no consequence. Besides, his talents are more suited to pornographic films."

McMahon's internal alarm system went to condition red. He stared after the departing actor. "Has he made porn?"

"Several. It's the one thing he is equipped for."

... a tempestuous noise of thunder and lightning heard.

—William Shakespeare, *The Tempest*

57

The wind picked up and Traynor looked to the east. An ominous bank of dark clouds rolled at them, turning the sky an ominous purple-black, like bruises on a battered boxer. "What you make of that?" he asked.

"That," Manuel answered, "is the last thing I want to see."

Traynor studied the dense blanket of clouds as it rolled toward the northwest, obliterating the blue sky in its path like a tsunami. A vortex dropped from the maelstrom's black bowels, and he realized that he was watching the birth of a tornado. . . . As pants-shitting scary as it was, there was a violent, hypnotic beauty to it. There was no doubt that Fredericka had caught up with them. Traynor didn't know about the others, but he'd been praying that it would follow the computer model that predicted it would turn right and head away from them, giving Texas some badly needed rain.

"In a few hours," Manuel said, "all of northern Chihuahua is going to be one gigantic mud-pie. It appears that our luck has run out."

"When I saw it on TV, I knew we'd be caught in it . . ." Traynor muttered.

Manuel cast him a quizzical look.

"If it wasn't for *bad* luck . . . I'd have *no* luck . . . and *that* is some serious bad luck."

"I wish you'd told me that before we left LA."

"Don't blame me," Traynor retorted. "You shoulda asked."

One minute it was dry and the day bright, the next they were in the middle of a wind-swept deluge in late twilight. The wind was so powerful that brush and cacti were torn from their tenuous grip on the soil and whipped through the air. A large tumbleweed rolled into Toledo, knocking him off his feet.

Manuel turned his back to the wind and yelled something that Traynor could not hear over the raging storm. Dirt, gravel, and grit pummeled them and he began to feel as if he were being sandblasted.

Toledo curled into a fetal ball and tried to protect himself from the elements. Afraid that he would get away in the storm, Traynor grabbed him by the waist of his pants and pulled him to his feet. By the time Toledo regained his feet, Manuel had staggered his way back to them. "We have to find some shelter," he shouted.

It was all Traynor could do to breathe in the sand-filled wind—so rather than answer him, he nodded. His feet sank into the wet ground, and when Manuel turned and motioned them to follow, Traynor lifted one of his now fifty-pound feet and walked like a zombie, pushing Toledo ahead of him.

Suddenly a figure appeared on the rise to their left. The figure bent forward against the wind and when it tried to raise what looked to be a weapon, Traynor released his grip on Toledo, shouldered his rifle as he spun, and fired. Either he hit the shooter or else he was pushed back over the dune by the tremendous gust of wind that blasted into them.

The gale was so strong that for every two steps they took forward, they took a couple sideways. Traynor's skin felt as if it were being scraped away and the heavy rain drops mixed with hail, pounding their heads like steel ball-bearings being hurled from some hell-born machine. Just as Traynor became certain that they were going to be flayed to death, a line of large boulders appeared and Manuel turned toward them.

The rocks served as a windbreak and though they were still getting drenched, they were at least able to be heard above the storm. They settled down, sitting against the wet rock, trying to minimize their silhouettes and hunching over to protect their faces from the driving rain. Traynor began to shake and shiver violently, and he realized in that moment that it was possible for any one of them to die of hypothermia. Manuel crawled over and settled beside him. His features were barely discernible in the primordial dark. "You okay?" he asked.

"Hell if I know. Ask me when this is over."

Lightning flashed, revealing a scene worthy of inclusion in the Chamber of Horrors at Madame Tussaud's Wax Museum. The trio looked like the survivors of a terrible shipwreck, coated in mud and grime, and Toledo's and Traynor's hair was gnarled into filthy tangles. Toledo fared worse than Manuel and Traynor: at least they had boots. Toledo had lost his shoes—a pair of expensive Gucci loafers—somewhere along the way the sucking mud had taken his socks. He sat barefooted, staring into the torrential downpour.

Manuel broke Traynor's trance when he said, "The storm seems to be moving fast, shouldn't last but a few hours."

"That's supposed to make me feel better?"

"No, but think of it this way: the guys who are chasing us won't be able to use their vehicles or aircraft in this."

"That does make me feel better," Traynor shouted against the wind. A gust of wind curled around the boulder, and in a flash of lightning, Traynor spied a rattlesnake trying to swim against a surge of water that raced down the mountainside like a swollen stream. Suddenly, he became more worried about being bitten by a panicked reptile than he was about the storm. Toledo must have seen the snake, too; he shouted in alarm and pulled back against the rock. Manuel grabbed him by the arm and said, "Where you think you're going?"

Toledo's eyes were open wide, shining like beacons in the storm. He stammered when he pointed past Traynor, saying, "S-s-snake . . ."

"Don't worry," Manuel said, "it has bigger things than you on its mind."

Traynor found it slightly calming to know that at least one of them was more scared than he was.

A typical tropical cyclone will have an eye of approximately twenty to forty miles across, usually situated at the geometric center of the storm.

58

The storm raged on for three more hours. Water formed into rapidly moving streams and washed dirt and debris down the mountainside. As Traynor hunched over in a lame attempt to protect his face and keep his weapons as dry as possible, he kept remembering the raingear that he had left in the truck. But then, as suddenly as it had hit, the wind died away and the storm abated. "Is it over?" Toledo asked.

"The leading edge is," Manuel replied. "We're in the eye. In a few minutes—maybe as long as an hour, depending on the size of it—we'll be in the trailing edge. The wind and rain will return, only from the opposite direction." He stood up and wiped his muddy hands on his trouser legs—but as far as Traynor could see, all this did was smear more mud.

"We should move," Manuel said. "Use the reprieve in the storm to put some distance between us and them . . . and see if we can't find better shelter."

Ever the optimist, Toledo whined. "What kind of shelter will we find in this wilderness?"

"We'll know when we find it." Manuel turned and slogged through the mud and muck.

Walking was a battle against the elements. The heavy mud clung to their feet like a prisoner's ball and chain. It did no good to shake it off, because as soon as their feet hit the ground, the clinging mess covered it again. Toledo slipped and fell face-first into the mire. He sat up and cursed. "You could at least remove these fucking shackles so I, too, can climb."

Traynor was in no mood for his perpetual pissing and moaning. It was taking every bit of his own willpower to keep climbing the mountainside. He doubted they would ever reach the top; it seemed as if they would take three steps forward and slide back two. Remembering that their pursuers were faced with the same challenges was little, if any, consolation. As they climbed, they were forced to hold their rifles high to keep them as dry and clean as possible. Thus they used their feet and free hands to crab up the slippery slope—an act that he knew made them look like three-legged donkeys . . . with the exception of Toledo. With his hands shackled, he looked like a two-legged platypus in a mud wallow.

Traynor tried to keep his anger out of his voice when he said to Manuel, "Why didn't we wait until the storm passed?"

"A couple of reasons. First, I thought we'd be able to outrun it. But, and more importantly, I didn't set the agenda—Holy did that."

"One more reason why we should shoot the sonuvabitch," Traynor complained. Rather than continue his harangue, he trudged on. He needed all of his strength to overcome the greasy mire and keep moving forward.

Toledo stumbled again and fell on his face. As he slid down the slope, Traynor stopped him by putting a foot on his ass. When his weight pushed against the foot, Traynor's other one slipped, threatening to send him down the slope too. But he braced himself and was able to maintain his balance.

Manuel turned sideways and half walked, half slid to them. He grabbed Toledo by his collar and lifted his face out of the mud. "If I thought you kept falling to slow us down, I'd step on the back of your head and drown you in this shit."

Toledo's face was coated in muck and he looked completely dejected and defeated. He didn't even protest when Traynor said, "Hell, we should do it anyway."

Toledo tried to get up, but lost his purchase again and slammed back into the mud. He looked as helpless as a cow on a frozen pond and Traynor laughed. He ignored the fact that the drug lord had a reason for falling so much: walking while wearing boots was tough enough, let alone doing it barefoot.

Manuel and Traynor each grabbed one of his arms and pulled him up. Toledo's hair was soaked and matted with sludge and grime. He looked about as happy as a cat that had been thrown in a river.

They shoved him forward. "Move," Manuel ordered him.

As they trudged on, Traynor thought that if his current profession didn't work out, Manuel could get a job as a weatherman. About forty-five minutes after they had first noticed the calm, the storm came raging back with even greater ferocity. Traynor, for one, had had his fill of being soaked and wearing a suit of armor made of Mexican mud. Similar to Toledo, he too was getting frustrated and entertained thoughts of giving up. It was then that he heard the loud crack of a bullet breaking the sound barrier near his head. In the howling wind and rain he had no idea where the bullet was when it reached its final destination. Simultaneously, lightning flashed and he turned and saw a new man shouldering a rifle. The shooter tried to aim at them while maintaining his balance on the slippery slope. Traynor did not hesitate. Once again, he lost his footing and as he dropped onto his butt, he fired three rounds at the gunman. Like before, he didn't know if one of the bullets hit the assassin or if the wind knocked him down; either way the shooter fell onto his back and slid down the slope. Traynor lost sight of him in the torrential rain and clawed and scrambled to his feet. Manuel and Toledo had turned and were looking in his direction. Traynor knew that if he said anything they would never hear it against the gusting wind, so he waved to let them know he was all right. Without any fanfare, Manuel grabbed Toledo and they turned back to their ascent.

Traynor soon lost all sense of time; he had no idea how long they were crawling toward the mountain summit, but they finally reached it. Breathing in the howling wind and whipping rain was near impossible. Even though the storm was no longer a category five, it was still a raging bull. Traynor believed the wind was still in excess of one hundred miles an hour, and their bodies acted like sails as they stood fully exposed to its force. It pushed them off the summit and down the leeward side.

As difficult as climbing had been, the descent was infinitely worse, albeit faster. One by one, they lost their footing and went sliding and careening downhill. Traynor was the first to lose his footing, and he slid down until he collided with Toledo. Toledo and Traynor then crashed into Manuel and the trio began a ride down the slope that would make the designers of an amusement park flush with envy.

Manuel rolled to the right, leaving them to continue down like a two-man bobsled team. Traynor grabbed onto Toledo's shirt, hoping that their combined weight would slow them. It did not help—if anything, they accelerated. Toledo must have been of a like mind, because he spread his legs wide, in a futile effort to regain some control of their slide. Thus far in their adventure, Traynor had felt no sympathy or compassion for him whatsoever, but when their combined weight and momentum slammed Toledo's groin into a Saguaro cactus hard enough to demolish the prickly plant, even Traynor winced. No sooner had they stopped than Toledo rolled onto his side and grabbed his crotch, which served only to push the sharp spines in deeper. He was in such pain that he could not speak. His mouth was wide open, yet no sound came from it. Traynor fought back the impulse to laugh at his agony.

Manuel slid about twenty feet beyond them, stopped, and scrambled back. He saw Toledo writhing and quickly assessed the situation. "*Now*, we're having fun," he said with a sadistic grin. Adding: "I'll bet right about now he wishes he had a couple grams of the shit he pushes."

After the first contact, the undercover investigator is immediately faced
with the problem of avoiding suspicion.
—*FM 3-19.13, Law Enforcement Investigations*

59

McMahon picked up his cell phone and hit speed dial number two. Deborah answered on the second ring. "Hey," she said. "You gotta love that caller ID, huh?"

She ignored his attempt at humor. "How you making out?" she asked.

"Great, just great."

"You make contact with Jabłoński?"

"Sort of."

"You want to explain what that means?"

"I got a part in his movie."

"You're kidding me."

"Not in the least."

"Have you ever acted before?"

He thought about some of the acts that he had put on when meeting women in clubs and bars and decided they did not count. "No."

"So he gave you a bit part?"

"The male lead."

"You're shitting me!"

"Not at all." He leaned back in his recliner and studied the interior of the trailer he had inherited from Rock Stone. He grinned as he recalled the look on the ham's face when Jabłoński informed him that his role had been changed Stone was now playing the corpse—and because of his change in status, he would have to give up his trailer to the new leading man: McMahon.

"When you try to get close to someone, you don't fool around, do you?" Deborah said. He thought he heard a new level of respect in her voice—or was it possibly something stronger?

"I gotta be truthful . . . I was just checking around and they offered me the part."

Deborah chuckled. "How much longer will you be up there?"

"The shooting schedule originally called for three weeks—one of which has already passed. Now, however, we'll have to reshoot the scenes in which my predecessor had my part. We should be done with the location shoot and back in LA in two and a half to three weeks."

Deborah chuckled again. "Damn," she said, "you even got the talk down already."

"I guess I'm just a born star."

"More like a shooting star."

Deborah turned serious. "Jack, watch your ass—something about this stinks."

His voice was grim when he said, "I thought so too. No way in hell am I a Lana Turner."

"Who's that?"

"Actress from the forties. The legend is that she was discovered working at the soda counter at Schwab's drug store."

"Really?"

"Yeah, only she had better legs than me."

Deborah took it upon herself to keep tabs on Celia Doerr and Lawrence Provost. She went to great lengths to remain undetected. She even went so far as to rent a different car each day. Neither of her subjects did anything out of the ordinary, although Doerr's continued meetings with Provost concerned her. As she sat in the early-morning light, sipping takeout coffee, she mentally processed Doerr's actions. Was Doerr a good enough actress to hide from Provost the fact that she was willing to sell him out to save her own neck?

Thinking of Doerr as an actress made her think of McMahon. The way in which he had fallen in with Jabłoński so quickly amazed her—and at the same time—alarmed her. It wouldn't surprise her if he turned out to be a halfway decent actor—stranger things had happened.

Her reverie was interrupted when Provost left Doerr's house and climbed into his Jaguar without as much as a cursory inspection of the area. He backed out of the drive and turned toward Los Angeles. *Maybe*, Deborah mused, *McMahon is not the only actor involved in this*. Doerr certainly seemed to be holding her own. The woman seemed content to remain secluded in her house, so Deborah followed Provost.

McMahon stepped from his trailer and grunted. He did not like this early morning shit. He walked toward the house, knowing that Jabłoński would already be there. As he stepped onto the deck that spread toward Howe Sound, the day was calm and the water so smooth it looked like a glass floor he could walk across.

Abigail Allen saw him through the sliding glass door and walked out onto the deck. She handed him a cup of steaming coffee and asked, "So, you all set for your big moment?"

"I was up most of the night studying the script."

"Hmmmm, if I'd known you weren't sleeping, I would have stopped by."

He looked at her with a new interest. "I thought . . ."

"That I was in a relationship with someone?"

"Well . . . yeah. You seem to hover very close to our director."

She smiled, emphasizing a pair of thin crow's feet by her eyes. He thought the small marks of years past made her even more alluring. "My job is to be his gofer. Other than that, Kondrat has certain interests . . . interests that I don't want any part of."

"Such as?"

"He's into pain . . . only not his."

"So he's fond of S and M?"

"More S than M. Besides, what's the old axiom about only a fool drills for oil in a company well?"

Movement caught his eye, and he turned his attention to the interior. Jabłoński was motioning urgently toward him. Allen also noticed and said, "Looks like you're on."

As McMahon reached for the door, she touched his arm. "Maybe if you have another sleepless night, I'll drop by with a bottle of wine and we can pass the time together . . ."

"That," he replied, "sounds like a plan to me."

The Juárez Cartel is responsible for smuggling tons of narcotics from Mexico into the US throughout its long and turbulent history, and the group's intense rivalry with the Sinaloa Cartel helped turn Juárez into one of the most violent places in the world.

—*Insightcrime.org*

60

The storm abated with the arrival of daylight. After a day of heavy, low clouds, the sun seemed brilliant as it crept over the summits of the mountains to the east. After Toledo's encounter with the Saguaro, they had continued down the slope until Manuel stumbled upon an abandoned mine. Traynor never thought a hole in the side of a mountain could look so welcoming.

Traynor stood and stretched, wishing he had a cup of coffee to jump-start his fatigued body. His clothes had dried; however, they had become so stiff, that they weren't much more comfortable than they'd been while soaked. He took quick stock of their appearance and knew that if they were to walk into a town like this, anyone they encountered would assume they were living out of Dumpsters and sleeping in alleys. The mud that coated his clothes had dried to a concrete-like hardness and broke off in chips when he wiped at it. He had not shaved in three days, and when he touched his face he felt balls of dirt clinging to the bristles. The tightness of his face and scalp suggested that they too were coated with grime.

Manuel came out from the bowels of the mine, and one look at his appearance told Traynor that his assessment had been accurate. "Do I look as bad as you?" Traynor asked.

"Worse."

"Thanks."

"Let's get him up and move on," Manuel said.

Manuel walked to Toledo's still form and nudged him with his foot. Holy groaned and sat up. He hissed and inhaled sharply.

"When you pulled the spines out of your balls, you musta missed a few," Manuel said. "You better find them and pull them out before they get infected."

Traynor turned and walked to the mouth of the mine. He stared through the entrance of the abandoned mine and thought: *There is something about the aftermath of a big storm. God can be unpredictable, angry, and lethal one minute and then calm, serene, and nurturing the next.* That morning it was as if God had cleaned the air to make amends for this latest rant. The sky was cloudless and the deepest azure he had ever seen.

He looked over his shoulder and laughed out loud. Toledo had dropped his trousers and undershorts and was delicately inspecting his genitals for any cactus spines he had missed last night. He must have found some because he plucked at something, and from the way his face curled in on itself, it was anchored pretty deep. Traynor couldn't help thinking, *Better him than me.*

Manuel walked over and stood beside Traynor. He stared out at the valley that they had to cross.

"Beautiful morning, huh?" Traynor said.

"Yup, gonna be hotter than a brush fire by midday, though."

"Ain't you just a breath of fresh air?"

Manuel chuckled, checked on Toledo, and said, "If we're where I think we are . . ." He pointed in the direction Traynor took to be north. "The border's about twenty miles that way."

"So if all goes well, we should be back in the States by nightfall?"

Manuel turned and walked back toward Toledo. "If all goes well," he said.

The only thing that bothered Traynor was that thus far not a hell of a lot had gone right. After all, he believed that Murphy was an optimist.

In spite of the storm's deluge, the desert was fast turning into a huge concrete tarmac. It was almost like walking on crusty snow, their feet breaking through the hardening surface with each step. Looking behind them Traynor saw a line of footprints that anyone could follow.

They had only been on the march for about an hour and Traynor was already soaked—only this time it was with sweat, which had flowed down his body and concentrated in his groin, which was chafed and raw. Each step was becoming agony as his body salt stung the tender flesh. Traynor began to dream of a long, hot shower. If there was any consolation to be had, it was that Toledo was not doing any better. He walked as if he had just spent three days in a saddle that was too wide for his short legs.

Manuel, on the other hand, seemed to be doing fine. Traynor could not help but envy his stamina. He knew that if he was not careful, that envy could turn to resentment. But it never got the chance. Out of nowhere, a pair of helicopters appeared and dropped to the ground, one in front of them and the other behind. When several heavily armed men leaped from them, Traynor knew their trek was over.

"These your people?" Manuel asked Toledo.

Holy sounded like a man who had just learned he was scheduled for a life review at the entrance to heaven when he gasped, "No . . ."

Knowing that they had no chance, Manuel dropped his weapons and raised his hands, so Traynor did likewise. Toledo, on the other hand, dropped to his knees and hung his head—apparently, his admission through the gates had been denied.

Traynor woke up lying on a hardpan dirt floor. The events of the last few days had left him aching and sore. He groaned as he rolled off his back and sat up. The room's only light came in through a small opening high up on the wall; it was too small to call it a window and it barely illuminated the chamber to the level of twilight. He saw Manuel sitting in a corner with his back against the adobe wall.

"It's about time you woke up," he said.

"Have I been sleeping long?"

"About three hours. Since we were in the helicopter . . . you nodded off within ten minutes. Our little adventure seems to have exhausted you."

"But not you."

"I'm so tired that I could sleep through a tornado."

Traynor got to his feet, crossed the small room, and dropped back down beside Manuel, assuming a posture similar to his. "You got any idea where we are?" he asked.

"Juárez, maybe Agua Prieta. Or we could be in Chihuahua City itself."

Traynor studied their less-than-elegant accommodations. "Ain't exactly five stars, is it?"

"Ain't even one fifth of a star."

They sat quietly for several minutes, neither willing to give voice to the question that was on their minds. Finally, Traynor could stand the suspense no longer. "What's our prognosis?"

"Ain't good."

"Toledo's?"

"Even worse. He might even be dead by now."

Traynor let his head drop back until it touched the stucco and he looked at the rough-hewn wooden rafters that supported the ceiling. He exhaled with more force than necessary, his breath making a whooshing sound as it escaped his lips. "This is one of those times when I wish I had embarked on a career in the wonderful world of fast food, rather than law enforcement."

Manuel chuckled. "A burger and fries *would* be nice about now."

The levity stopped when they heard a door open and then slam shut.

"Sounds as if we got company," Manuel announced.

"Yeah."

Two linebacker-types, led by a nattily dressed man, approached their cell. The clotheshorse reached into his pocket and took out a set of keys. He opened the door and the goons aimed a pair of pistols at them.

The men motioned for them to turn, cuffed their hands behind their backs, and ushered them out of the cell. As soon as they were secured, Traynor felt the unmistakable roundness of a gun barrel shoved into his back, and he walked toward the blazing light that poured in through the door.

The sun was in their eyes and beat down on them like an open flame as they were led from the cool, dimly lit interior of their jail, into a treeless, bare dirt courtyard. On the far side, Traynor made out the forms of several men sitting in the shade of a hacienda. After the gloom of the cell, the sunlight was like looking into a strobe light. He blinked, trying to adjust his eyes so he could identify the men. Traynor was about three-quarters of the way across the courtyard before his vision returned to normal—and then, he wished it hadn't.

Toledo was sitting to the right of a large, middle-aged man, with two pistols on the table before them. Traynor wondered if this man was to be their judge, the jury, or the executioner—or possibly all three. He had a bushy black mustache, and Traynor thought that he looked almost like Hollywood's version of a *bandito*. Their escorts pushed them into chairs that had been placed so that the sun would be in their eyes. They removed the handcuff from one of Traynor's hands, fastened it around the chair's arm, and then did the same to Manuel.

The fat man spoke in Spanish and Manuel answered him in English. "Please speak *Inglés, por favor*. My compadre has as much right to be a part of this as I."

The inquisitor nodded. "Of course. He has as much right to plead his case as you." He turned his attention to Traynor and said, "Please, señor, be so kind as to tell me why I should not kill you?"

"Because," Traynor said, "we've done nothing to you. Hell, I don't even know your name, let alone anything else about you."

The big man chuckled and his stomach bounced, reminding Traynor of the usual depiction of Santa Claus. However, this Santa was probably not so much jolly as he was lethal.

"This may be true," the bandito answered. "But I don't know you either, so whether you live—or die —is of no consequence to me."

He then addressed Manuel. "You think I don't know, eh? Well, I do. I know who you used to work for." He turned to Toledo and said, "You did not know that he was once DEA?"

Toledo started and it was then that Traynor realized that maybe his earlier worries were misdirected—Toledo was still wearing handcuffs. Rather than being an honored guest, he too was a prisoner of Santa.

"However," Santa turned his attention back to Traynor and Manuel, "whether by intent or by accident, you have provided me with a great service." He picked up a ledger and said, "I now control all of the drug traffic from Mexico City to Juárez." He picked up one of the pistols, turned, and aimed it at Toledo's head.

Traynor jumped in his chair. As much as he detested Toledo and all that he stood for, they had been companions on this journey and in spite of all the times he had threatened him, the thought of him being so coldly and dispassionately executed enraged him. Santa pulled the trigger. A loud click sounded and Toledo rocked so far to the side that his chair fell over. Traynor heard him sobbing.

Santa smiled at them and said, "I never liked him. He is always whining and complaining, no?" Then a stern look came over his face. He stood, walked around the table, and approached Manuel. Traynor jumped up and, with his free hand, he grabbed the chair and held it poised to strike. Santa said something in Spanish and one of the thugs who were guarding them handed him the largest and no doubt sharpest knife Traynor had ever encountered.

"Ed, sit down," Manuel ordered.

"And if I don't?"

"He will carve you up and take great pleasure in slowly flaying you alive. So sit down and control yourself. All is not lost . . . yet."

Undercover officers sometimes develop actual friendships with these criminals.
—Police Procedure & Investigation: A Guide For Writers

61

McMahon settled back to enjoy the sight of the full moon sparkling across the surface of Howe Sound. He opened a can of beer and raised it to his lips. Before he could take a drink, a voice said, "You got a spare beer?"

"Nope. They only come twenty-four to the case. You're welcome to one, though."

Rock Stone took a bottle from the cooler and dropped into an empty chair. "I saw you talking with Miss *Everything* this morning."

"Yeah, you have a problem with that?"

"She needs someone to breed her, maybe take some of the starch out of her spine."

McMahon felt his face flush with anger. "And I suppose you're just the man to do it?"

"Naw, too much work to train one like her. I like mine to be a bit more . . . shall we say . . . knowledgeable."

"Sounds as if you have quite a bit of experience."

"Ever hear of a movie called *Slaves Of Desire*?"

"Sounds like a porno to me."

"It is. Not just any run-of-the-mill one though. Jabłoński directed it—"

"And you starred in it?"

"Male lead . . . Emma Ho got top billing." He looked into the distance, a wistful expression on his face. "God, that woman was built . . ."

McMahon fought back the urge to immediately ask if Stone knew anything about *The Black Orchid*. But he didn't want to burst his bubble—not until he had the information he needed. He was certain that if he was patient, Stone's ego would provide him with everything he needed to bring him and Jabłoński down.

"I made some damned good pornos. They actually had a plot—a real storyline," Stone said. "I never understood why I couldn't make the transition—"

"Not many actors successfully make it from adult to mainstream film," McMahon commented.

"Yeah, but when you got as much charisma as me, I knew it was only a matter of time before Hollywood came knocking . . ."

Too bad, McMahon thought, *Hollywood didn't knock you on your ass.*

Stone continued his soliloquy of self-importance. "Yeah, the girls in the valley were heartbroken when ole *Rock Hardon* made the big-time."

"The *valley*?"

"Yeah, the San Fernando Valley. We filmed all our adult movies there."

"I gather that you were Rock Hardon?"

"My stage name . . . what else could you call a man who's—"

"I get your point," McMahon interrupted. "I'm surprised that Kondrat got involved in that stuff."

"Jack, you got no idea of some of the shit that Pollack is into."

"Such as?"

"Any fuckin' thing that'll make him a buck. Believe me, the last thing you ever want to do is get between him and a dollar bill. He'll run you over to get to it."

Stone chugged down his beer, wiped his mouth with the back of his hand, and stood. "Well, I gotta get some shuteye." McMahon kept a straight face when Stone looked at his quarters with envy. McMahon had spent his first night on set in the trailer that Stone's demotion had placed him in—it was so small a preschooler could tow it with a tricycle. "How you like these digs?" Stone asked.

"They're okay."

"Well, enjoy it while you can. You fall a lot quicker than you climb in the movie biz. I learned a long time ago to never forget the people you meet on the way up . . . because you're gonna pass them again on the way back down."

"Sounds like good advice to me—no matter what you do in life."

Stone walked to the edge of the light and said, "We ought to do this more often." He waved and disappeared into the darkness.

When his guest was out of sight, McMahon gathered up the empty bottles and the cooler and went inside the trailer. He had just finished putting everything away when there was a knock at the door. He opened it and Abigail Allen stood at the foot of the steps. She was barefoot, wearing a loose-fitting robe, and holding a bottle of wine. "How about a nightcap?"

Nighttime surveillance presents unusual problems . . . because of darkness the suspect is able to view any vehicle following him due to the presence of headlights.
—*FM 3-19.13, Law Enforcement Investigations*

62

Deborah followed Provost into Canoga Park, where he turned into the parking lot of a strip club. As much as she hated losing sight of him, there was no way she was going into a place like that. Not that she was a prude or felt herself too good for such a place, but because she knew she would stand out like a moose in a mall parking lot. She parked across the street and settled in for what she hoped would not be a long night. She turned on the satellite radio and listened to oldies music. It was not long before her eyes closed.

She woke to a rapping on her window. Deborah blinked her eyes, trying to erase the effects of sleep, and glanced at the digital display on the car's radio: it was two thirty in the morning. The rapping was repeated. Still groggy with incomplete sleep, she lowered the window.

A hand reached in and grabbed her shoulder. She tried to pull away, but the grip tightened. She turned her head and stared into Larry Provost's face.

"You want something, lady?"

"N-n-no . . ."

"Then why have you been shadowing my every move for the past few days?"

"I-I haven't—"

"Get out of the car. You're coming with me." He pushed a small handgun through the window. "Do it quietly and don't let a bad decision affect the rest of your life." He said, "Keep both your hands where I can see them."

Deborah stared at the angry maw of the pistol, realized that she'd never get the handgun out of her bag without him seeing, and knew she had no recourse but to follow his instructions. Moving slowly, she placed both of her hands on the top of the steering wheel. Then, Provost reached through the open window, and unlocked her door. He stepped back and motioned with his free hand. "Get out."

She unhooked her seat belt and slid out. Provost motioned for her to walk forward and when she did, he closed the car door and positioned himself behind her. "Cross the street." His order was terse and having no other option, she complied.

He forced her across the street and into the strip club's parking lot, where he led her to his Jaguar. He motioned for her to get in on the passenger side. One look at his face told her that if she got in that car, it could very well mean the end of her life.

"I said get in."

Just as Deborah reached for the door handle, a loud whoop sounded, followed by a flash of blue lights. A police car pulled into the parking lot and slid to a halt behind the Jaguar.

Deborah saw a brief look of fear flash across Provost's face, only to be replaced by a look of cocky self-assurance, and she stepped back.

Angela Engle, in uniform, got out of the police cruiser and with one hand on her sidearm, she stepped toward them. "Is everything okay?" she asked.

Provost saw a second cop exit the cruiser and quickly slid the small pistol into his jacket pocket. "Everything is fine, officer. My friend and I were just heading home."

"Is that why you took her out of her car?"

Provost knew that he had been observed, so he fell back on the one thing he had always been able to rely on—his political reputation. "Officer?"

The second cop, a large well-proportioned male, walked around the cruiser and positioned himself so that Provost was in front of him. The cop's hand hovered close to his service pistol.

"Engle."

"Officer Engle, I'm—"

"I know who you are, Dr. Provost. That's the only reason you aren't being handcuffed as we speak. Now, in the interest of all parties, why don't we all forget about this incident and go our separate ways?"

Deborah saw him stand in place for a second, as if he was trying to determine how trustworthy this cop was. It was obvious that the last thing he needed was for the tabloids to learn that he was picking up women at a strip club. Engle took the decision from him when she said, "Or we can go to the station and work this out . . ."

Provost held up his hand in defeat and circled around his car. Before getting in, he looked across the roof at Deborah and said, "Call me, darling . . . we need to discuss this." He climbed in, started the engine, and backed out, burning rubber and almost clipping Engle's car as he sped away.

Deborah turned to Engle and said, "Thank God you came along, Angela."

"I didn't *come along*. I've had your every move under observation since you started trailing him. One of our patrol cars called me to tell me where you were—and that you were sleeping in your car. Do you have any idea how bad this neighborhood is?"

Deborah scanned the area and said, "No."

"It's no place for a young woman to be sleeping in her car, that's for sure."

Deborah looked embarrassed in the stark blue light that oscillated from atop the police car.

Engle took her by the arm. "I want you to go home." She turned her head to her partner. "I'll be right back."

Once Deborah was safely behind the wheel of the rental car, Engle leaned in the window. "Deborah, don't be stupid. I know you want the guys who murdered your sister, but getting yourself killed isn't the way to do it. Now, go to your hotel and wait there until I call you this afternoon."

"I know what I did was stupid and that I should let the pros do it, but I can't just sit around waiting for Jack, Ed, and Manuel to return."

"I understand that, which is why we're going to put our heads together and determine what *we* can do. Deal?"

"Deal."

"I want you to keep one thing in mind. As of right now, we got nothing on Provost, other than that he knows Skidgel. You keep doing what you're doing and he'll run like a jackrabbit. You got a good team of professionals working this—let them do what they do best, okay?"

When Deborah nodded, Engle smiled at her and said, "Now get outta here and go back to your hotel."

The Juárez Cartel has a large and longstanding transportation, storage and security operation throughout the country. It counts on its ability to co-opt local and state law enforcement, especially the judicial or ministerial police (detectives) and the municipal forces.

—Insightcrime.org

63

They were taken back to their cell and left alone. "Who in the hell is that sonuvabitch?" Traynor asked.

"Joaquin Sevilla Fitzpatrick."

"*Fitzpatrick?* You know him?"

"In the early eighteen hundreds, a lot of Catholic Irish from English Protestant-controlled Ireland came down here. They fought against the Americans during the Texas Revolution as well as during the Mexican-American War. As for how I know him . . . every DEA agent in Mexico knows who he is."

"So what is his place in the overall scheme of things?"

"He runs one of the largest drug cartels in northern Mexico. Once he's done with Toledo, he'll probably run the largest drug business in all of Mexico, if not North America."

"That bullshit with the pistol," Traynor said, feeling renewed anger and indignation, "was sadistic."

"But it was psychologically effective. We both know that Toledo is softer than a shit-milkshake. In fact, I wouldn't be surprised if Toledo isn't singing an aria as we speak."

"Will it buy him anything?"

"No doubt he thinks it will." Manuel flopped to the dirt floor and leaned back against the adobe wall. "The best Toledo will get is a quick death." He considered a moment, then said, ". . . Or a slow one, if he suddenly grows a pair."

"So, either way, Toledo's ass is grass . . ."

"And he's directly in the path of a lawn mower."

They sat in silence until Traynor finally asked, "How are we going to get out of this?"

"That," Manuel said, "is what I'm trying to figure out."

"What if we try to bargain with him? Tell him we work for a wealthy American who will pay him for our release?"

"Maybe . . . but only as a last resort. The only reason we're still alive is because Fitzpatrick has some use for us. For instance, if he thinks someone will ransom us, he'll take the money and send them our bodies in return."

Traynor stared up at the few stars he could see through the small portal. "What do you think will happen tomorrow?"

"One of three things," Manuel said. "One, they let us walk. Two, they don't. Three, they kill us."

"Wonderful. . . . I vote for option one."

The chamber was so dark that Traynor couldn't see his companion. From the dark he heard Manuel say, "Me too, only this ain't a democracy—it's a dictatorship and we got no say in the matter."

Police officers are human. They have emotions . . . and they can become
sympathetic or emotionally attached to their target criminals . . .
—*Police Procedure & Investigation: A Guide For Writers*

64

Allen left McMahon in the early morning hours, sometime between two and three. He barely stirred when she rolled out of the bed, wrapped her robe around her, and disappeared into the frosty Canadian morning.

She crossed the lot to the house where Jabłoński was staying, stepped onto the deck, and walked to the dark, shadowy figure sitting by the railing. "Well?" Jabłoński asked.

"I learned nothing. But no way in hell is his name Peter Puller. I'm certain that he's the guy we were told about."

"Hah!" He spat over the rail.

"There's always tonight," she said. "And the next . . ."

Jabłoński reached out and gently stroked her right buttock and thigh. His fingers trailed across her body in slow, sensuous circles. A shudder of pleasure coursed through her body; he must have felt her respond to his touch, because he said, "Abigail, be careful that you do not enjoy your work too much . . ."

"Don't worry, Kondrat. I read Skidgel's message too."

"It was too bad he did not sent a photo."

———————

McMahon stood in the dark and watched Allen rendezvous with her boss. Maybe Jabłoński was shrewder than he had thought. He obviously did not trust easily, and maybe he wanted to keep an eye on McMahon as much as McMahon did him. He turned back to his bed to get another couple of hours' sleep. They had a five o'clock shoot.

———————

They ended the day's shoot just after three in the afternoon. McMahon watched Allen as she returned to her trailer. Throughout the day he had observed the interactions between her and Jabłoński. If he had not witnessed their late-night rendezvous, he would have assumed that their relationship was strictly business. Rather than being upset about the way she had manipulated him, he found it amusing. He knew when she showed up barely clothed, with wine in hand, that she had some ulterior motive.

He liked to think of himself as an attractive man. He was aware that his six-foot two-inch height, broad shoulders, and narrow waist were appealing to many women; he knew that from experience. His face was not a detriment either. His square jaw and dark brown hair gave him a Christopher Reeve look. But he had no delusions about a woman like Abigail Allen throwing herself at him the way she had. On one hand, the brazen seduction flattered him; on the other, it made him suspicious. Did Jabłoński know more than he was letting on? What was Allen's role in the production of *The Black Orchid*? She had already stated that she knew Kondrat made porn movies and that he had a sadistic mien to his sexual preferences. He had also learned firsthand that she was aggressive in bed and enjoyed rough sex.

He strolled across the parking area, using the time to survey the lot. He had not seen Stone since they wrapped their last scene together. That was another thing that was eating at him. Stone had accepted his demotion too easily. If all McMahon had been told about Stone's ego was true, he ought to have been madder than hell. In his place, McMahon would have done everything in his power to undermine the inexperienced usurper to his throne. He figured that he must be up against at least a triumvirate and that they knew more about him than he was comfortable with.

He entered his trailer, filled his cooler with beer and ice, and then returned to his seat under the awning. As he sipped the cold brew, McMahon wondered if he would have guests again that evening.

He didn't have long to wait before Rock Stone flopped into one of the vacant chairs. Already so drunk that he was unsteady on his feet, Stone pointed to the cooler that was centered between the chairs. "You got any more?"

McMahon reached out with his right foot and raised the lid. "Help yourself."

Stone pulled out a can of Labatt's and popped the top. When a mound of foam appeared through the opening, he sucked it into his mouth and took a drink. "I see you had a visitor last night."

McMahon stared at his guest. "You keeping an eye on me?" He sat back and folded his arms across his chest.

"Be careful with that one," Stone warned.

"Oh?"

"Back when I was a little kid, I heard this song about a woman who finds a venomous snake on a freezing day. She takes it home and thaws it out, saving its life. As soon as the snake thaws, she picks it up and it bites her. When she asks why, the snake replies, 'Because I'm a snake, what did you expect?' Abigail is one of those snakes. Her beauty makes her even more deadly because you let your guard down around her."

McMahon wanted to probe further into the topic. "Maybe you could be a bit more specific."

"She's Kondrat's blitzkrieg. When he wants to invade, she's the storm trooper. Within minutes, he'll know anything you say and do."

"I did get the impression that there was more going on between them than meets the eye. Are they lovers?"

"Of the craziest kind. They're bonded to each other, but both are sexually . . . shall we say . . . liberated? Neither of them worries about the other's fidelity."

"You sound as if you're talking from experience."

Stone drained his beer, belched, and said, "That's no shit . . ."

McMahon opened the cooler and indicated for Stone to help himself. "Would you care to elaborate?"

Stone settled back in his seat. "I'm only telling you this because, in spite of what's happened here, I like you. I'd hate to see you eaten alive by those two . . . like I was."

McMahon remained stoic.

"I was married when I first met them. I loved my wife as much as any man can love another person. But, when I fell into Shelob's clutches—"

"Shelob?"

Stone gulped another mouthful of beer. "I gather you're not a fan of Tolkien, huh? Shelob was the gigantic spider that lived below the ground, protecting some tower or something. Anyone attempting to enter the tower using the subterranean stairs would be caught and devoured by her. Abigail won't eat you, but she will sexually devour any man with whom she comes in contact."

"I get your point."

"Before she and Jabłoński were through with me, my wife found out I was fuckin' them and making porn and left me."

"*Them?*

"Hey, it ain't only women who have to spend time on a director or producer's couch to get a job. Jabłoński enjoys sex in any and all forms. Anyhow, my wife was raised in a devout Protestant home; she couldn't take it. I haven't heard from her since." He got a wistful look. "I've tried everything to reach her . . . thus far, nothing has worked."

McMahon thought Stone was about to cry.

"Once they entice you into their web, they're relentless. No matter how hard you try to free yourself from their clutches, they hang on. Even if you do succeed in driving them off, you're still stuck in the web. They won't stop until they've sucked the life out of you—and you end up, like me, a no-talent actor who's stuck with them."

"You were forced into making adult movies?"

"Yeah, sounds stupid, doesn't it? A man blackmailed into screwing beautiful women on screen? Trust me when I tell you, bein' Dick Hardon ain't all it's made out to be."

"I don't understand . . . this isn't the 1960s. Making porn and being AC/DC isn't a big thing."

"Tell that to my wife—she thought it was."

Since its beginnings, the cartel has focused on drug trafficking, but has expanded into other criminal activities such as human trafficking, kidnapping, local drug distribution, and extortion.

—*Insightcrime.org*

65

It was still dark when they came. Once again, Fitzpatrick was sitting at the table in the courtyard. He ignored Traynor and said to Manuel, "If I were to have my people . . . shall we say . . . *interview* you, what could I learn about DEA operations in Mexico?"

"*Nada*, but I doubt that will stop you."

The drug lord laughed and once again his ample stomach shook. "You have cojones anyway. That's more than can be said for the soon to be dead Señor Toledo."

Traynor's eyes narrowed.

"You going to kill him?" Manuel asked.

Fitzpatrick said, "When he is of no further use to me. Once I have all the information I need to take over his business."

Traynor caught the implication, but noted that he did not answer his question. Either way, he felt his face burn with indignation. He glanced at Manuel and saw that the news had angered him as well. If Fitzpatrick killed Toledo, they would lose an important witness against the makers of *The Black Orchid*. His musing stopped when the drug lord said, "Now, I must decide what I'm to do with you."

He stood and walked around the table, stopping before Manuel. "I can't help but wonder how much you know about DEA actions along the border."

"Nothing," Manuel answered. Traynor was impressed by the way he kept his cool. Especially since he knew, better than anyone, what lay in store for him if Fitzpatrick thought he held any valuable information about anti-cartel operations. "I've been away from it for over five years."

Fitzpatrick stiffened and then slapped him. "I think you bullshit the bullshitter, eh?"

"I'm no longer a member of the DEA; therefore, they don't consult with me much." Manuel spoke through clenched teeth. Blood trickled from one corner of Manuel's mouth and Traynor could see that Fitzpatrick's slap had enraged him.

"You expect me to believe that you came to Mexico and grabbed Toledo on your own?"

"No, I don't. My current employer is a wealthy American. His daughter disappeared and he sent me and my companion to find her."

Fitzpatrick's eyebrows furrowed as he absorbed this information. "Obviously, you were unsuccessful."

"She was dead when we found her," Traynor interjected.

The drug lord turned his attention to him.

"She was killed in a snuff film," Traynor added.

"What did Toledo have to do with this . . . snuff film?" he asked.

"He was the money behind the production," Manuel said.

Fitzpatrick seemed to be pondering what they had told him. "Our friend, Toledo, is lower than I thought." He turned his attention back to Manuel. "You swear that you know nothing about any DEA agents in Mexico?"

"I haven't since they pulled me out over five years ago."

Fitzpatrick returned to the table and sat behind it. Traynor was beginning to think of that chair as his throne. After studying them for several long moments, he said to his henchmen, "Take them back. I have to think on this turn of events."

Once again they stood in the courtyard, under the baking sun. Fitzpatrick was nowhere in sight. A white commercial panel truck pulled into the courtyard. "Looks as if we may be going for a ride," Manuel said.

"I hope that is meant in the way one usually thinks of it," Traynor whispered to him.

"Prepare for the worst and if it doesn't happen, it will be a blessing."

"And if it does?"

"At least we'll be ready for it."

The driver and two other men exited the van and entered the hacienda. It was a matter of minutes before they returned and the two goons grabbed them, marched them to the van, and shoved them inside. The side door of the truck slid closed, and in minutes the interior was like an oven, the heat like a blistering wall. There were no seats, just a roll of canvas lying along one of the sides.

"You'd think," Traynor commented, "that they could at least turn on the A/C for what may be our last ride."

"*Fam hacer callar!*" one of the guards said.

"What the hell is he saying?" Traynor asked.

"He said shut up," Manuel replied.

"Oh."

They sat side by side with their backs against the van's metal wall. Traynor studied the rolled tarp lying against the opposite wall and decided that it offered a softer seat than the plywood that covered the van's floor. When he moved across the small confines and sat on the rolled the tarp, it groaned. He bolted up, hitting his head on the van's ceiling. He looked at Manuel while rubbing his skull. "You hear that?"

Manuel reached over, grabbed the edge of the canvas, and pulled. The tarp unfurled like a window shade, revealing Toledo. His face was a mass of bruises and lacerations, and when he opened his mouth, Traynor saw that his top front teeth were missing.

"I'll be dipped in shit," Traynor said.

"He wasn't what I'd call eye candy before this," Manuel said, "but those missing teeth make him really ugly."

Traynor slid down and sat beside Manuel. Toledo opened his eyes and stared at them in disbelief. "Where are we?" he asked.

"Somewhere between the grinding wheel and the millstone," Manuel answered.

Toledo's tongue darted through the gap in his teeth. Traynor supposed he was only just discovering that his appearance had been altered. He gave them a questioning look, similar to the one Traynor's dog once gave him after his first encounter with a skunk. "Do drug lords have dental insurance?" Traynor asked.

Toledo rolled onto his side with his back to them. He began to shake.

"You think he's crying?" Traynor asked Manuel.

"If he isn't, he will be once we tell him where we are and what our chances of survival are."

Toledo lay with his back to them. At least fifteen minutes passed by until finally the van lurched, and Traynor looked through the heavy grill that separated the driver from the cargo section. They had turned off the paved road and entered a dirt lane that appeared to lead into the desert. He made a vow that if he got out of this alive, he was never leaving New England again.

The road was hard and they bounced each time the truck hit a hole or depression in the packed sand surface. Toledo sat up and morosely stared off to a place only he could see. Each time the van bounced, his head banged against the metal. More so than at any time since Traynor had met him, Toledo looked as if the spark of life within him had died out.

Traynor ventured a look at Manuel. The former DEA agent sat with his arms resting on his knees, hands limp, and his head was turned forward as he stared out the front windshield. It suddenly dawned on Traynor that of the three, he probably had the least knowledge of what the cartel had in store for them.

Manuel slid down and used the rolled tarp as a pillow. After a few minutes, he appeared to be sleeping, which Traynor doubted. No way in hell could anyone sleep while being tossed around the interior of a moving vehicle. Traynor occupied his mind trying to figure out a way to escape the deadly fate he was sure lay in store for them.

Suddenly, the van slowed and the driver and guard got out. It was time for their sentence—whatever it was—to be carried out. After a few seconds, the driver opened the side door and stepped back, letting Manuel and Traynor out. The other guard stood off to their left, pointing an automatic weapon at them.

The driver did the talking. "The border between Mexico and your country is ten kilometers in that direction." He pointed a thumb over his shoulder and then removed Manuel's and Traynor's handcuffs, leaving Toledo's in place. "Start walking," he said.

Traynor looked at Manuel, wondering if they should stand their ground or if they should follow his instructions, which would leave them open to being shot from behind. Manuel shrugged and Traynor interpreted that as saying: *What the hell, we're probably screwed either way.* Manuel looked over at Toledo still in the back of the van, but stopped short when the guard with the Uzi shook his head no.

"Let's go," Manuel said.

As he and Manuel passed the gunman, Traynor counted paces as he walked—all the time his shoulders were tensed against the bullets he was certain were coming. He jumped when there was a short burst of gunfire. Tensed against the impact of the expected bullets, he looked to his left, fully expecting to see Manuel lying in the blazing sand.

Manuel was in turn looking at him.

They heard the slam of the van's doors and exhaled explosively. They kept walking until they heard the truck moving, at which time they turned and watched it drive away. A pile of stuff laid where the van had stood and Traynor went back. On the ground lay their passports, keys to the handcuffs, and two handguns with magazines lying beside them. Traynor opened the first passport, saw it was Manuel's, and handed it to him. He loaded the pistols and passed one to him.

They watched the van do a tight U-turn and race back toward them. Traynor raised his pistol and aimed it at the truck. Manuel grabbed his arm and said, "Don't. If they were going to kill us, they'd have already done it."

The truck skidded to a stop about fifty yards from them. The driver turned until it was beside them and the sliding door opened. Toledo came flying out of the door, landing on his stomach. The gunman jumped out and pulled him to his knees. "Don Fitzpatrick says you can have him!" Then he took a shiny, chrome-plated pistol from his belt and shot Toledo in the back of the head. As he jumped back in the van, he shouted, "Don't leave your garbage lying around my country." The van accelerated and drove away in a cloud of dust.

Traynor ran forward and fired his pistol at the rapidly retreating van. After he'd taken several steps, he realized that Manuel was not with him. He stopped and looked at his companion. "What the hell just happened?"

"I guess Fitz figured he had nothing to gain by killing us, but he was never going to let Toledo leave here alive—he knew too much about too many people's business. Our friend was not overly brave and once he was in DEA hands, he'd have spilled his guts," Manuel said. He didn't seem especially surprised, or perturbed. "What's really fucked up about this is that Joaquin Sevilla Fitzpatrick was Toledo's cousin."

"What are we gonna do about him?" Traynor asked.

"We're goin' to leave him."

They began walking north, Traynor spit into the sandy soil, and said, "If I'd known it was going to turn out this way, I'd have shot the sonuvabitch in Mexico City."

"Why the hell would we have done that?" Manuel said.

"Would have saved us a lot of trouble, that's for sure."

The safety and physical well being of . . . police and other individuals in and around the crime scene, is the first priority of the first responding . . . policeman.

—*FM 3-19.13, Law Enforcement Investigations*

66

Angela Engle met Deborah in the hotel dining room. "You heard anything from the guys?" she asked.

"I spoke with Jack yesterday. However, I haven't heard a word from Manuel and Ed."

Angela peered out the window at the rain that ran down the glass. "Two days ago, this was Hurricane Fredericka and it raced across northern Mexico before being downgraded to the tropical depression we're experiencing."

"You think they got caught up in it?"

"Most likely."

"Still, it seems they would have called."

"Cell service down there is spotty in good weather. It's probably nonexistent in a storm."

Deborah picked at the omelet on her plate. "You want something to eat?"

"Coffee's fine with me."

"So what are we going to do?"

Engle stared at the rain again. "That's the question of the day, isn't it?"

Deborah pushed her plate away and said, "I wish the guys were here."

"It would make our lives a bit easier. In the meantime, we need to keep Doerr and Provost under surveillance."

"Something I'm not very good at."

"I think that it's time we started to put some pressure on Provost," Engle said. "He's the one with the most to lose, as well as the most to hide. Public knowledge of his involvement in a film of this nature would be professional suicide for him."

"How can I help?"

"Hollis International," Engle said, "does it have any pull with the media?"

"We own a number of television and radio stations."

"In California?"

"One of each in LA, San Francisco, and Sacramento."

"Perfect. Here's what I think we should do . . ."

Deborah and Engle stood on the front porch of Celia Doerr's house. They rang the bell and waited several seconds, listening for any indication of occupancy. "Maybe," Deborah said, "she's out."

Engle raised her right foot and took a .32 caliber hideaway pistol from her ankle-holster. "Her car is in the drive."

"She could have gone with someone else."

"Then again, she may not have." Engle turned the knob and the door opened. "That worries me," she said.

Cautiously, Engle led the way into the house. The living room was as neat as it had been the last time Deborah had been in it; nothing seemed out of place. A cursory search showed no sign of Doerr. They walked to the kitchen; other than some dirty glasses on the sideboard, it too seemed to be in order. Engle turned and motioned for Deborah to follow her down the hall, in the direction of the bedrooms.

Engle pointed her pistol toward the ceiling and held it near her right ear as she reached for the doorknob. She slowly turned it and pushed the door open. They stepped into what appeared to be the guestroom and Angela immediately crouched into a shooting position with the pistol pointed forward. She panned the gun from right to left.

Deborah studied the small room and wondered if it had been Mindy's. She watched in silence as Engle gave the room a short but professional inspection. Backing away from the miniscule closet, Engle said, "Well, only the master bedroom and bath left."

"Lead on," Deborah said.

They crossed the hall and stopped before the entryway to the final bedroom. Deborah cast a nervous look at Engle. "For what it's worth," she said, "I'm glad you're with me."

Engle smiled at her and stepped inside. Once again she swept her pistol from side to side. "Nothing in here, either," she pronounced.

Deborah gave the closed bathroom door a hesitant look. "That's all that's left."

"Unless this house has a basement." Engle stepped in front of Deborah and opened the door. She turned on the light and stiffened. "Don't come in here," she warned.

Deborah's curiosity got the best of her. She peered over Engle's shoulder. The shower curtain was pulled partially across the tub and the surrounding area was streaked with red trails and splotches. The thick coppery smell of blood assailed her and she sputtered, "I'm going to be sick." . . ."

Engle spun around and pushed her toward the living room. "Not here," she said, "we have to preserve the crime scene."

Deborah dashed through the house and vaulted into the front yard. She bent forward and vomited. Sweat dripped from her brow and she remained in place for several minutes, until the waves of nausea passed. Once she was under control, she turned back to the house and saw Engle standing in the door. "You okay?" the cop asked.

"I-I think so."

"Stay there while I call 9-1-1."

Another wave of dizziness swept through Deborah. "Don't w-worry, I'm not going anywhere."

"Get yourself together. I don't know Celia Doerr from Eve. You'll probably have to do a preliminary ID on the body."

Deborah bent over, resting her hands on her knees, and when she turned her head, Engle was no longer in the door. "ID the body," she whispered, "now that's a chore I'm *really* looking forward to." Her stomach heaved again, but nothing came up.

Deborah watched the EMTs slide the gurney into the back of the ambulance. She stood in the middle of the small patch of dry grass that passed for a lawn in Simi Valley, while Engle talked with two plainclothes cops. When the California State Police detectives got in their cars and drove away, she went to Deborah. The two women stood side by side, Engle looking professional and unbothered by what they had found. On the other hand, Deborah stood with her arms folded across her chest as if she were cold. "They found what they think is the murder weapon," Engle said, "a butcher's knife. Apparently, the killer tried to clean it up, but you can never get rid of all trace evidence."

"Where was it?"

"He put it back in the wooden block with the rest of the knives in the set."

Deborah was fixated on the front of the house. "That was the most horrid thing I've ever seen," she said.

"It *was* bad," Engle said.

"How do you deal with these things?"

"Fortunately, I don't have to deal with this type of crime on a regular basis."

Deborah could not get the image of Doerr's corpse out of her mind. "Why did the killer cut her so many times?"

"That level of brutality usually indicates an extreme level of rage. The type one might feel if they thought the victim had betrayed them."

"You don't think—"

"That Larry Provost murdered her? Yes, I do. If he learned that she had agreed to work with us, he'd have more to lose than any of the other conspirators."

"But," Deborah said, "I thought you guys felt she'd be a shaky witness at best. In fact, I had the impression that everyone thought the DA would discount her completely."

"Maybe we should have told that to Provost."

Deborah faced Engle. "I don't think I'm up to this anymore." She thought about the death of Skidgel's security guard and realized that she had never before been exposed to violent death, but since she had come to the West Coast, this was the third brutalized body she had encountered.

"We're getting close to bringing your sister's killers down," Engle said. "It's too late to stop now."

Deborah inhaled deeply. "I know."

———

When the ambulance took Celia Doerr's remains to the morgue, Deborah and Engle followed the Simi Valley police to the station. They parked in the lot reserved for police officers and entered the building, stopping before the watch commander's desk. One of the officers who had been at the crime scene guided them inside to a small conference room and left them alone.

The women sat alone for no more than five minutes before an officer wearing a business suit walked in and introduced himself. "I'm Sergeant Arreola. . . . I run the Violent Crimes Division of the Detective Unit. How is it that a member of the LAPD finds a murder victim in Simi Valley?"

"We knew Ms. Doerr," Engle said, "from her involvement in a case we've been working."

Arreola turned to Deborah. "What is your involvement in this?"

"The victim of the open case was my sister. I came out here to find out what happened to her."

Arreola sat back in his chair and said, "Maybe you should tell me everything you know."

Keep your friends close and your enemies closer.

—Sun Tzu

67

Abigail Allen was waiting on the deck when McMahon arrived for the morning's shoot. She handed him a steaming cup of coffee and he took it and leaned against the railing beside her. "Today should wrap it up," she said.

"I thought there were a couple of weeks to go."

"There are, but we won't need to shoot them on location. We'll finish filming on the sound stage in LA."

McMahon sipped his coffee and pondered his next course of action.

Jabłoński appeared in the sliding-glass door and motioned for McMahon.

"The master beckons," he said. He handed his mug back to Allen, opened the door, and walked onto the set.

McMahon tossed his suitcase into the trunk of his rental car. He grabbed the lid, preparing to slam it down, but stopped when Allen came up from behind and said, "Can I catch a lift to the airport with you?"

He turned and said, "Why not?" She was dressed in a white blouse, tight jeans, and the whitest sneakers he had seen outside of a shoe store. He looked over her shoulder and saw two stagehands struggling to keep pace as they each carried two gigantic suitcases. "What you got in them? Bodies?"

"Hardly. It's easy for you guys to make jokes," she countered, "but it takes a lot to keep us girls looking good."

He stepped aside while her "porters" placed her luggage in the trunk and then walked to the right side door and opened it for her. "Your coach awaits, Your Majesty."

"Very funny." She got in and fastened her seat belt.

When McMahon sat behind the wheel, buckled his seat belt, and started the motor, she said theatrically, "To the airport, James."

He chuckled and drove out of the parking lot.

They rode in silence until they were on Route 99, headed toward Vancouver. Out of nowhere, Allen asked, "Who are you anyway?"

"Peter Puller. You know that."

"Don't get cute. You know what I mean."

He resisted the urge to look at her, keeping his eyes on the twisting road ahead. "I'm a disgraced LA cop, who thought he'd take a vacation to British Columbia. I heard about the movie and thought I'd drop by and watch the goings-on."

"There's only one word to describe that story: bullshit," she said. "You aren't telling me everything."

"That's all you need to know."

"Humor me."

"Why, so you can tell your *lord and master*?"

She picked up the emphasis and distaste in his voice. "It's Kondrat you're after, isn't it?"

"How many of his movies have you seen?"

"All of them."

"The pornos too? What about a disgusting piece of shit called *The Black Orchid*?"

"I'm not a prude, you should know that. But no, I've never seen that one."

"Maybe once we're back in LA, I'll arrange a screening for you."

They rode in silence for several minutes.

"My turn to ask you a question," he said.

"Okay, I won't promise you an answer though."

"Your refusal to answer could be an answer."

The road curved and he saw snow on the peaks that surrounded Howe Sound. The white shone brilliant between the light blue sky and the deep blue water. The landscape reminded him of the White Mountains, only with seashore. It was breathtaking.

"Okay," he said, "what does Jabłoński want? I'm not buying that he thinks he found a heretofore undiscovered talent in me—everything happened too easily to be happenstance."

"I have no idea."

That, he thought, *is the biggest line of bullshit I have heard from you.*

"Do you mind if I smoke?" Allen asked.

"Crack a window."

McMahon and Abigail Allen retrieved their checked baggage and exited the terminal. They stood on the sidewalk as McMahon flagged a cab. "You need a lift?" he asked.

"No, here's my ride."

McMahon watched a familiar Porche 9-11 pull alongside the curb and Vernon Skidgel stepped out of the car. He smiled at McMahon and said, "Well, if it ain't my favorite ex-cop."

McMahon's jaw clenched and it took all of his will power to refrain from punching Skidgel. Instead he said, "Yeah, ain't it funny how we keep running into each other."

Skidgel kissed Allen on her cheek and picked up her bags. He walked around the car, opened the trunk, and put the suitcases inside. He then opened the passenger door for Allen and closed it once she was seated. He turned back to McMahon and with a cocky smirk said, "I'd offer you a lift, but as you can see there's no room. Be seeing you."

"You bet your ass we will," McMahon muttered in reply.

"What have you heard from Ed and Manuel?" McMahon asked.

"Nothing in the last four or five days," Deborah answered.

"Well, let's hope that no news is good news. Now, bring me up to date on the Celia Doerr murder."

"There isn't much to fill you in on. The Simi Valley police have jurisdiction and due to Angela's involvement in the case, they haven't been forthcoming with much information. I have my own theory though."

"Which is?" McMahon took a drink of coffee and, over the rim of the cup, stared intently into Deborah's eyes.

"I have no doubt that Provost did it," she said.

"Not that I don't agree with you, but elaborate as to why you think that, please."

"Because I also believe he was my sister's butcher. He is, after all, a medical doctor—a surgeon. He has definite political aspirations, which would take a kick in the pants if his participation in a murder was to ever be discovered."

"If that's the case, why risk filming it?" McMahon asked.

"Well, I think his risk is minimal. I haven't had the stomach to watch the entire movie, but what I did see only showed the killer's hands. Angela has her own theory about why he would do it."

McMahon was certain he knew what Engle's theory was, but opted to hear it from somebody else. "Which is?"

"She feels that similar to a serial killer taking souvenirs, he wants to revisit the crime scene. What better way than to watch it whenever he gets an urge?"

"I'm inclined to believe you," McMahon said. "Now, if we can connect him to Jabłoński and Abigail Allen, we could probably tie this thing up."

"We already know that Provost is involved with Skidgel, and Allen is too. I'm hoping that Skidgel will help us there."

"But we still can't connect him directly to Jabłoński."

"I think Angela may have done that too."

McMahon leaned forward. "Oh?"

"She has learned that Jabłoński and Provost worked together on television ads during the governor's last election campaign."

"Wow, if we could only inform the governor that Provost is a person of interest in Celia Doerr's murder."

"That," Deborah said with a conspiratorial smile, "may be easier than you think. Hollis International was a major contributor to the governor's campaign."

Poor Mexico, so far from God and so close to the United States.
—Attributed to Porfirio Díaz (1830–1915)

68

After a three-hour hike, Traynor and McMahon came to a paved road and saw a sign that announced that Agua Pietra was ten kilometers away. Traynor wondered how much credibility anyone give to them. They were filthy. Their clothes were stained with mud and marked by rings of sweat; exposure to rain, mud, and swirling dust had made them formless and loose. He could not see Manuel's face but knew it was streaked with furrows where sweat had cut through the dirt and dust; his hair looked dull and was matted with clumps of desert soil. Traynor figured that he probably looked even worse.

Ten kilometers was about six miles and it took them almost another three hours to reach the outskirts of Agua Pietra. Several times they encountered vehicles going in their direction, but one look at the pair of them and the drivers kept on driving. One old man in a flatbed truck slowed, but when he spotted their guns, he too, thought better of stopping.

"I wish Fitz had returned my cell phone," Traynor said.

"What would you do?" Manuel asked. "Call us a cab?"

"I don't need a phone for that."

"You don't?"

"Nope. *We're a cab.*"

Manuel shook his head. "As a comedian you make a good cop ... don't quit your day job."

Manuel and Traynor looked at each other and began snickering. Then Traynor bent over and laughed like a maniac.

It was midafternoon when they reached the border crossing. They stood a couple of hundred yards away and waited for traffic to die down. As they walked across the border to US Customs, Traynor said, "I never thought it was possible to look worse than the picture on my driver's license. I hope they'll be able to match us with the pictures in our passports."

───────

Manuel and Traynor checked into a local hotel where the clerk gave them dubious looks. Traynor knew that if their positions had been reversed, he would have been hesitant to accept a credit card from two men who looked as if the best accommodations they had seen of late was the inside of a gila monster den. Once they checked in, their next stop was a department store for new clothes and toiletries. Their purchases complete, they returned to the hotel where Traynor spent twenty minutes in a hot shower, trying to remove several pounds of Mexican dirt from his body.

As soon as he was assured that he no longer smelled like a dead dinosaur, he called Deborah and updated her on their status. She was not pleased to learn of Toledo's fate. When he explained that they had nothing on him in regard to the making of *The Black Orchid*, she said she understood, thankful that he and Manuel had survived the ordeal.

She, in turn, apprised him of the events that had occurred since they had last spoken. It was obvious to Traynor that the situation in California had escalated. She said, "Ed, we need you and Manuel here as soon as you can get back." She informed him that she would make arrangements for the corporate jet to pick them up at the nearest airport with a runway capable of handling the Gulfstream. She told him that she would call back as soon as she had arranged things.

Manuel and Traynor were eating their first decent meal in days when the desk clerk walked into the small café and handed Traynor a message. The Gulfstream would pick them up in Tucson at three that afternoon. "Well," Manuel said, "it seems that our vacation is over."

"Apparently," Traynor replied, "I wonder if there's a rental car office close by . . . I've done enough walking for one day and it's four or five miles to the airport."

"I ain't gonna say it," Manuel answered.

"I know, call us a cab . . ."

Talk low, talk slow, and don't say too much.
—John Wayne, on acting

69

McMahon got to the set early and was greeted by Abigail Allen. At the back of the sound stage, he saw Jabłoński in what seemed to be a serious conversation with a man that McMahon could not see.

"I want to apologize," Allen said.

"For what?"

"Leaving you at the airport like I did."

McMahon glanced at Jabłoński and saw that the conversation appeared to be at an end. He almost left Allen when he saw Vernon Skidgel walking rapidly to the nearest exit. *Maybe*, he thought, *the rats are about to depart the sinking ship.* Jabłoński cast a worried look in McMahon's direction and turned away.

Allen was saying something. McMahon turned his attention away from the obviously worried director and said, "I'm sorry, I didn't hear all of your last comment."

"I said the man who picked me up was an old friend."

"Abby, I wasn't upset. Who you see is none of my business. Now, what's the shooting schedule?"

She consulted her notebook and said, "We're shooting the final scene today."

She walked toward the cameras and he followed. As he neared Jabłoński, the director gave him a look that McMahon thought was filled with suspicion and caution. McMahon had no delusions about whether or not Jabłoński knew who he was—the director's recent discussion with Skidgel had removed any possibility of anonymity. He knew that the final scene was an action scene involving a shootout between McMahon's character—the protagonist—and the antagonist. He thought about the possibility of someone changing the blanks in the villain's gun for live ammunition and decided to be even more vigilant than usual.

———

Engle and Deborah were in a rental car and had spent the morning watching Provost. Deborah had to admire the audacity of his actions; he went about his business as if nothing out of the ordinary had happened of late. "You have to hand it to him," she commented, "he's very calm and collected. If my lover had been murdered, and I thought that I was the prime suspect, I'd be a nervous wreck."

"Political connections and clout will do that."

"You know what amazes me?"

"That the governor isn't running from him as if he had the plague?"

"That too, but what truly amazes me is his arrogance. He obviously believes that he's untouchable."

Provost's car turned into the parking lot of an upscale restaurant and Deborah followed, passing their quarry and turning into a row several behind him. They parked in the first spot they found and watched as he exited his car and walked across the lot, disappearing through the door. "I think," Engle said, "it's about time we put the fear of God into him."

"How do you intend to do that?" Deborah asked.

"Wait here. I'll let you know if it works."

Engle followed Provost into the restaurant and immediately spotted him sitting alone at the back of the dining area. "May I help you?"

Engle turned toward the voice and saw the maître d' standing behind her. "I have a lunch appointment with Dr. Provost." She saw indecision on the woman's face and took the initiative, walking into the dining room on a collision course with Provost's table.

When she dropped into the chair across from him, Provost gave her a questioning look. He obviously did not recognize her in her civilian garb. She stared at him and said, "Don't you remember me?"

His only response was to continue staring at her.

"You're probably confused by the jeans," she said. "But we met several nights ago . . . only I was in uniform then."

His eyes widened with recognition. "Ah, yes, the cop."

"Yeah, *the* cop," she said. "I'm also the cop who is going to bring you down for the murder of Celia Doerr."

"Really?" He took a sip from his water glass. "Best of luck there. . . . I didn't kill anyone."

Engle gave him a coy smile and stood up. "Really? Well, time and good investigative work will tell. Won't it?"

"Obviously, you don't have any idea who I am, not to mention how much pull I have."

"Obviously, you have me confused with someone who gives a shit."

Provost sat back and met her glare with one of his own.

Suddenly, Engle's face softened into a coy, seductive smile. "Enjoy your lunch, Doctor."

Provost smiled as if they had been having a friendly discussion. "See you around, officer."

Engle stood and turned away. She walked several paces, stopped, turned, and made a gun with her right forefinger and thumb. "You bet your ass . . ."

A man travels the world over in search of what he needs . . .
—George Moore

70

Manuel and Traynor arrived in LA in the early evening and drove straight to Deborah's hotel. She met them in the bar, and Traynor was surprised by the many changes that seemed to have come over her. Gone was the inexperienced young woman; she'd been replaced by one with a much more cynical view of the world. His first thought was that dealing with assholes would do that to anyone.

Once they were settled in and drinks delivered, she said, "You've both lost weight. I gather your trip to Mexico was more strenuous than any of us expected."

"I've had better vacations," Traynor answered.

"What about Toledo? Did you learn how he was involved in this?"

Traynor deferred, saying, "I'll let Manuel fill you in on that."

Manuel spent twenty minutes updating her on their experiences, ending by saying, "Toledo invested the money for the movie. He convinced me that he had no idea what type of film it was and was never actively involved. He was a drug dealer looking for a way to launder money—not necessarily a maker of porn and snuff films."

"And this Irish drug lord had him killed?"

"Yeah," Manuel answered. "But Fitzpatrick is Irish in name only. He's Mexican in every other way."

"So that's that?" she inquired.

"You want the truth?" Manuel answered.

"Will I like it?"

"Probably not," he replied.

"Tell me anyway."

Manuel looked at Traynor as if he wanted assistance.

"Don't look at me. You're the one that opened this can of worms," Traynor said.

Manuel turned back to Deborah. "Had we gotten Toledo to the border, he'd probably have been exchanged for one of our citizens being held in a Mexican prison. Once he was back there, he'd have easily bought his way to freedom."

Deborah stiffened. It was obvious that she was not pleased. "So the trip down there was for nothing."

"Toledo did tell us that it was Provost that he handed the cash to," Manuel answered.

"Now," Traynor interjected, "all we got to do is tie this up and bring these assholes down."

"I'm working the Provost angle," Deborah said. "It's only a matter of time before the floor drops out beneath that scumbag."

Her language made Traynor smile. "So, all we need to do is gather everyone together and come up with a plan."

Deborah looked at Traynor. "Something still seems to be bothering you."

"Yeah, something is. Fitzpatrick—one of these days I'd like to take him down."

He saw her quizzical look and said, "Toledo might have been a pus-bag, but he was our pus-bag and I don't like the fact that all we did was lead him to his execution."

"Well," Deborah said, "there's nothing to be done about now."

"But one day . . . in the not too distant future," Traynor said. He looked at Manuel, who nodded.

They gathered in a conference room at Hollis International's LA Office. After greetings had been exchanged, Engle was the first to get down to business. "It appears our man Skidgel has disappeared."

"What about the others?" Traynor asked.

"I can assure you that Jabłoński is still here," McMahon said. "We finish shooting in a week and after that there's the editing to do."

"I wouldn't be too sure that he too won't run," Manuel said. "He has assistant directors who could do the editing. Hell, with overnight couriers and the Internet, he could still be involved with it—even after pulling a Polanski."

"Well," Deborah said. "It'll be up to Jack to make sure that Jabłoński doesn't run."

McMahon leaned back in his chair and nodded. "I got it."

"Now," Deborah asked, "what are we going to do about Skidgel?"

"I'd like to deal with him," Traynor said.

"Okay," Deborah said. "Who is going to handle Provost with me?"

"He's never seen me," Manuel said. "I'll take him."

Traynor looked worried, and Deborah said, "Something on your mind, Ed?"

"Other than that I know more about the streets of Singapore than I do about Skidgel?"

"I may be of help there," McMahon said. "He was very, very friendly with Jabłoński's assistant, Abigail Allen. She might have some idea of where he ran off to. I'm fairly certain that he's in the US, though, because the court made him turn over his passport."

"With enough money, a passport can be bought," Manuel said.

"Either way," McMahon answered, "I'm of the opinion that Skidgel is hot for Allen. He'll want to stay in touch with her."

"Why," Traynor asked, "would she help us?"

"In her own way, Abigail is as big a predator as he is. She'll do anything if she sees a profit in it."

Deborah sneered and said, "I never understood why people will do some of the things they do for money."

Traynor wanted to say: "That's because you've always had it," but for once, he kept his mouth shut. He turned his attention to McMahon. "Can you put me together with her?"

He shrugged. "I don't see why not."

With that, their strategy session was concluded.

When Traynor walked out of the conference room, he saw McMahon return his cell phone to his pocket. "You up for a drink?" McMahon asked.

"It's been a long day . . ."

McMahon took Traynor by the arm and led him toward an open elevator door. "C'mon, Abigail is meeting us."

"That was fast."

Now there are five sorts of secret agents to be employed. These are native, inside, doubled, expendable, and living.

—*The Art of War*

71

Abigail Allen met them at a bar on Van Nuys Boulevard. After some of the joints Traynor had visited in Mexico, this one seemed very upscale—almost too yuppie for his taste. She sat at a table and smiled when she saw McMahon. "One thing about you, Peter, is that you're punctual. I like that in a man." She spent a few seconds appraising Traynor. Her scrutiny was so intense he felt as if he were in a lineup. "Who's this?" she asked.

"Abigail, this is Ed Traynor. He's an old friend. Ed, this is Abigail Allen."

Traynor nodded and said, "Pleased to meet you."

"Ohh . . . and he's polite too."

McMahon sat in a chair to her right, and Traynor took the one across from her. A waitress appeared and they ordered drinks. When Traynor ordered a club soda with a twist, Allen gave him a quizzical look. "I've been traveling all day," he said. "If I have a cocktail, I'll be on my ass."

"Oh, I hope you were someplace exotic."

"Mexico. On business."

"And what business might you be in?" she asked.

"Security. High-level execs hire me to ensure they don't get snatched while in Mexico City on business."

"Is it that bad down there?" He saw that she was truly interested.

"Some people consider Mexico City the most dangerous city in the world."

"Really? I wasn't aware of that."

"But based on my experiences, I'd argue that of late Juárez and some of the border cities are much more dangerous."

"Of course. The drug cartels . . ."

Their drinks came and the subject turned to McMahon's sudden stardom. Allen smiled at Jack and said, "He's really quite good—in fact, he's far better than I thought he'd be."

Suddenly she became quiet and looked from McMahon to Traynor. "I don't believe that you showing up in Vancouver was a coincidence. To be quite frank, I've never believed your name to be Peter Puller, either."

McMahon shrugged his shoulders and said, "Cards on the table, Abigail?"

She looked at Traynor and then turned back to McMahon. "Cards on the table, whatever your real name is. Do you want to start by telling me what this is about?"

McMahon decided it was time to hit her with the reason they wanted to meet with her. "Okay. First, my name is Jack McMahon and I work as a security specialist for Hollis International, a worldwide conglomerate. Ed and I are on a special assignment for the corporation." He gave her a second to let that sink in and then said, "Do you know what a snuff film is?"

"Isn't that a movie in which they actually murder someone? They're a myth . . ."

"I'm afraid they aren't a myth, and several of your close friends made one, maybe even more," McMahon said. "Included among them are your boss and the greaseball that picked you up at the airport."

Her face became ashen. "I swear that I had nothing to do with it. I don't believe that Kondrat would be involved with anything that sick."

"Settle down, Abigail," McMahon said. "Nobody is accusing you of anything. Nevertheless, you came onto me quite hard in Vancouver—as much as I'd like to believe that I'm irresistible to women, I know I'm not *that* attractive. Now suppose you tell us what that was all about."

"Kondrat sent me to you in Vancouver," she said to McMahon. "He wanted me to keep an eye on you. He said that he'd got a message from Vern Skidgel warning him that there were people looking to . . ." She paused and then said, "Fuck him over."

"What put you—or him—onto me?" McMahon asked.

"You were the only person who fit the description we had."

"Actually," Traynor said, "it's not so much Jabłoński as it is Skidgel that we're interested in at the moment. He seems to have disappeared. You wouldn't have any idea where he went, would you?"

She looked surprised by the news. *She's a natural actor too*, Traynor thought. He decided to play his trump card. "The victim of the film in question was a member of the Hollis family. As you might imagine, they are wealthy and influential. . . . I'm sure they will gladly compensate you very well if you are able to help us."

If she'd been the old cash register in the corner store where Traynor grew up, her bell would have rang when the drawer opened. Without hesitation she said, "Kansas."

"Kansas?"

"He grew up in Kansas. He told me that his grandmother was very ill and he was going to see her before . . ."

"The town, Abigail," McMahon said, "what's the name of the town?"

"He never said. When anyone asked where it was he always laughed and said, 'It's easy to find, halfway between nowhere and who cares.'"

"Did he say anything else that might help us narrow it down?" Traynor asked.

"I don't know if it helps or not, but he said it was near an army base."

He was not what he seemed to be. He was a psychopath, a cold-blooded killer.
—Paul Doyle, former undercover DEA agent

72

Provost drove through the gates that protected him and his estate from the unwashed masses. Manuel followed him out of Brentwood and into the Hollywood hills. When they were deep in one of the canyons, Manuel cut his quarry off on one of the narrow hairpin curves that were cut from the walls.

He got out of his car and strode to Provost, who had gotten out of his own vehicle. His face was flushed with anger. "Are you nuts or something?" he shouted at Manuel.

Manuel closed in on the indignant man and grabbed his shirt. He snarled through clenched teeth, "You and I need to talk."

Provost tried to pull free but Manuel tightened his grip and held him fast.

"I . . . I d-don't kn-know you," Provost stammered.

"No, you don't, but I know all about you, Jabłoński, Skidgel, and *The Black Orchid*."

Provost's face lost its flush and turned pale. "I-I d-don't kn-know what you're talking about—"

"I also know what you did to Celia Doerr." Manuel shook Provost back and forth. Each time he yanked Provost forward, the fist that held Provost's shirt hit him in the face—a technique Manuel had learned watching hockey fights. "You're dead meat, buddy. Skidgel has already hauled ass, and if Jabłoński hasn't done the same, he won't be far behind."

Provost's eyes widened.

Manuel laughed at him. "What? They didn't tell you that they're leaving you to take the fall?"

Provost tried a new technique to deal with this threat: bravado. "I have no idea who those people are, or what the fuck you're rambling on about."

Manuel had to hand it to the man; he was making a valiant effort to keep up the act.

"For what it's worth, the young woman you butchered was from a prominent, wealthy family. So wealthy they can afford to track you guys down anywhere in the world—you'll have no safe haven. So, why don't you just 'fess up now?"

"You're insane."

Manuel pushed him away and he toppled into the ditch. Water splashed as Provost fell. "You're an arrogant fool, Provost," Manuel said.

Provost's head snapped up. "Who are you and how do you know my name?"

"I'm the guy who's gonna to be all over you like a case of the shingles."

Manuel took a couple of steps toward his car, then stopped and turned back. "Oh yeah, you might be interested to know one other thing. Do you recall that influential family I told you about? The Hollises have major business holdings in California and for obvious reasons were major contributors to the governor's last campaign. It wouldn't surprise me if they have contacted him already. You could become one of California's fifteen percent unemployed . . ."

The investigator may be able to speculate as to the suspect's motivation and present a hypothesis.

—*FM 3-19.13, Law Enforcement Investigations*

73

McMahon saw Jabłoński smile and lean back in his chair. He felt relieved when he heard the director say, "That's it," to Abigail Allen. "It's finished—in the can as they used to say."

McMahon walked toward them and when Jabłoński saw him he said, "I got to hand it to you, Peter. You're a natural."

"Well, it wasn't as if I don't have a lot of experience at being a cop."

"Still, actors usually tense up and stop being natural the first time they face the camera."

"Ever talk to an undercover cop, Kondrat?" McMahon asked.

"Just you."

"That what you think I'm undercover?" McMahon felt his guard go up.

"I don't know. But I'm not entirely buying your story that you just happened to see us shooting on Howe Sound and stopped in to see what was going on. I think you were bound for our set all along."

McMahon flopped down in the vacant seat to the director's left. "Well, I did see one of your films and became a fan."

"Oh? Which one?"

"*The Black Orchid.*"

For an instant, Jabłoński looked frightened. But he quickly recovered and said, "That's not one of my films. You must have me confused with somebody else."

"Oh, you directed it all right."

Abigail coughed lightly, shuffled her feet, and said: "I have things to do." Without waiting for her boss to dismiss her, she fled the scene.

Once she was out of earshot, McMahon looked Jabłoński in the eye. "Now that the hired help is gone, let's you and I stop the bullshit and be honest with each other."

Jabłoński returned McMahon's stare and said, "Yes, why don't we?"

"I'm not alone in this. You fucking morons picked the wrong woman this time. She wasn't some runaway from Buttfuck, Iowa. She was from money—old New England money and lots of it. There are some serious badasses working this case and everything points to three scrotums—Larry Provost, Vernon Skidgel, and you."

Suddenly, Jabłoński looked scared.

McMahon immediately picked up on the director's fear and pressed on. "I can tell you this, Kondrat." McMahon stood and glared down at him. "Should you try to fly off to Europe, or anywhere short of Mars, there's enough power and money behind this operation to find you. We've already got the moneyman from Mexico City in custody—and Provost and Skidgel won't be far behind," McMahon lied. "We know all about the movie—from the financing to the filming. We're even fairly sure that it was Provost who did the killing. So you see, it's only a matter of time before you'll find yourself being a codefendant to the charge of murder one. Since the movie was distributed outside of California—making this a federal case—you could be riding a hot needle before all is said and done."

Jabłoński sat as still as a statue. McMahon could see fear in his eyes. "If you talk with your partners, emphasize to them that they fucked with the wrong woman this time." McMahon paused. "Too bad this movie will never be finished. I think it could have been a blockbuster. By the way, if it does make it to the big screen, instead of Peter Puller, use my real name—Jack McMahon."

Jabłoński was still sitting in his director's chair when McMahon left the set.

Sometimes a suicidal person may ram his head into a wall or in some other way create enough impact or crushing force to cause fatal injuries.

—*FM 3-19.13, Law Enforcement Investigations*

74

Traynor made two phone calls and learned that the only US Army base of any size in Kansas was Fort Riley, near Junction City. The nearest airports of any size were in Kansas City or Wichita, both a couple of hours, drive away. There was, his source informed him, an airport in Manhattan, but it was so small he doubted a jet could land or take off there. So Traynor booked a United flight to Kansas City.

Driving west on I-70 left him with one impression. God knew what he was doing when he put tornadoes in Kansas—there was nothing there for them to hurt. The landscape consisted of rolling hills and grass that had turned brown in the late-summer heat. Junction City was a typical military town. The local economy was geared toward taking care of the thousands of soldiers stationed at Fort Riley. A friend of his had lived there thirty or forty years ago, when her husband was in the army. She'd described Junction City as having two businesses: bars and prostitution. Although he was sure both were still thriving, the latter seemed to have been driven underground.

Traynor checked into a local chain hotel and was given a room with a beautiful view of the local Super Walmart—the largest store in town.

Traynor grabbed the local phonebook and thumbed through the listings. Angela Engle had been able to use LAPD resources to check into Skidgel's background. He had been pleased to discover that the grandmother was on his father's side. There was only a single Skidgel listed, a Franklin, with a Madison Street address. He consulted a street map and saw that the address was at most a three-minute drive from his hotel.

He took a quick shower and was outside the Skidgel house in less than five minutes. He cruised along the tree-lined street, studying the post-World War II houses and pausing briefly when he saw a Porsche with California plates in one of the driveways. Junction City was right in the middle of the US, and he wondered how fast Skidgel had to drive to make it there so quickly; one thing was certain, he had driven straight through the night. Skidgel was smart, but when it came to covering his tracks, he was dumber than dirt. A Porsche was not a car that helped one fade into the wallpaper. He wondered what Provost's reaction had been when he'd learned that his security chief had run off with one of his expensive sports cars.

Traynor circled the block, found a vacant parking spot on the street with a clear view of the Skidgel house, and settled in to watch and wait for Vernon to appear. He sipped from the cup of coffee he'd bought at a local convenience store and decided that if Skidgel did not appear by nine or ten that evening, he would go back to his hotel and get some much-needed sleep.

It turned out that he did not have long to wait. A few minutes past seven, Skidgel came out of the house and got into his car. He backed out and headed south along the street, a route that would take him past Traynor. He paid no attention as he drove by, most likely feeling secure. Traynor watched him in his mirror and when he turned left, Traynor followed.

Skidgel turned onto Washington Street and stopped at the first liquor store he came to. Figuring that he would not be recognized in the rental, Traynor pulled into a spot where he could watch the door and the Porsche at the same time.

In less than five minutes, Skidgel exited the store carrying a paper bag. He stopped beside his car, put the sack inside, and lit a cigarette. That was when he spotted Traynor. He tried to act cool and collected as he got into the Porsche but gave himself away when he drove onto the street and floored the accelerator, heading toward the highway. Traynor cursed his stupidity for parking where Skidgel could get a good look at him. He put the car into gear and went after him. He knew that he had to head Skidgel off before he reached I-70; there was no way he was going to keep up with a 9-11 in a Dodge Charger.

Skidgel sped down Washington Street, and Traynor raced after him, barely making a stoplight before it turned red. He kept glancing in his mirrors, looking for a cop. If stopped, he would have to explain that he was a skip-tracer and Skidgel was wanted back in California for jumping bail. By the time he finished, Skidgel would be halfway to Missouri.

As it turned out, the local police did not make an appearance—at least not then. Traynor saw the highway overpass and Skidgel was almost to the on-ramps. Traynor was surprised by what his quarry did then. The westbound on-ramp split off at a forty-five degree angle and at the speed he was traveling, Skidgel would have an easier time entering the highway. However, Skidgel opted to go east—and that ramp was a much sharper ninety-degree turn. The Porsche flipped, rolling in the air and landing on its roof. The car was a convertible with a canvas top, and when it finally settled, Traynor knew that there was no way Skidgel could have survived. He locked his brakes, hearing his tires squeal as he skidded to a stop, and rushed to the pile of twisted metal and plastic that had moments before been a Porsche. He dropped to his knees and peered at the crumpled interior of the convertible. He saw Skidgel and knew he was already dead. His head had been crushed between the steering wheel and the ground. Traynor could smell the distinct odor of whiskey and knew that the liquor bottle Skidgel had bought must have shattered during the crash. He heard sirens in the night and returned to his car to await the arrival of the local police. In minutes a Junction City patrol car arrived and minutes later a Kansas state cop came off I-70. They interviewed Traynor, who told them that the Porche had flown by him, weaving as it raced to the on-ramp. The cops smelled the whiskey and in no time wrote the accident off as caused by a driver under the influence.

An honest politician is one who when he is bought stays bought.
—Attributed to Simon Cameron (1799–1889)

75

Provost stared across the table at Jabłoński. "I don't like us meeting in public," he complained.

"I understand why you feel that way, but I need to talk to you. I don't trust telephones and things have changed. The authorities have Toledo and even though he doesn't really know much, he's probably telling them everything he does know."

Provost said, "The cops are yanking your fucking chain. I have it from a reliable source that Toledo is dead—killed by a rival gang in Juárez." Despite his confident words, Provost was worried.

"I heard that Skidgel's dead," Jabłoński said.

"That was an accident."

"Not the way I've heard it," Jabłoński replied. "He was being chased by one of the people who are prying into every aspect of the film."

Provost's interest overcame his worry. "What do you know about these people?"

"I know nothing, except they have enough money behind them to hound us for years."

"Well, let me tell you what the security firm I hired learned,"Jabłoński said. "They are a team—a dedicated and professional team consisting of a disgraced LA cop, a former DEA agent, a private detective, and the sister of the woman—"

"Killed," Jabłoński said.

Provost leaned forward, dropping his voice to an angry, threatening rumble. "Shut the fuck up, Kondrat. We don't know who is listening. You're sure you weren't followed here, right?"

Jabłoński suddenly looked concerned. "I'm fairly certain. But then, I'm not an expert in these matters."

Provost leaned back and didn't hide his contempt for Jabłoński when he said, "There are times when I wonder just what in Christ's name you are an expert in."

Jabłoński acted as if he were ambivalent to Provost's anger. "Who else is involved? They seem to know a lot about us."

"I've been told there are one or more members of the LAPD aiding them." Provost grew pensive. "We need to find out the names of the local people. I can put political pressure on any local cops who are involved."

Their conversation was interrupted when Provost's cell phone rang. He looked at the display and said, "Shit," then flipped the phone open. "Yes, governor."

He listened for several seconds and said, "Yes, sir. I'll be there this afternoon." He closed the phone and told Jabłoński, "I have to be in Sacramento by three." He motioned for the check.

Provost strode into the governor's office with his usual air of superiority and immediately knew he was in trouble. There was no preliminary greeting from the chief executive of the State of California. "I've gotten some disturbing news," the governor said.

"Oh? What about?"

"About a major scandal that's about to break."

Provost felt his stomach sink. "What can we do to head it off?"

"I have to cut off all association with the object of the scandal. A major donor to my reelection campaign has already threatened to cease contributions if I don't."

Knowing the answer to his question, Provost still asked, "Who is it?"

The governor slammed his fist on the top of his desk. "Don't play dumb with me, Larry. How could you be so fucking stupid? A snuff film for Christ's sake!"

Provost felt his face redden and did not dare look in the eye of the man he knew was about to become his former boss.

"If I had one shred of evidence, I'd have the state police in here placing you under arrest as we speak."

Provost stood up. "I can fight it, make it go away."

"It's too late for that. I *cannot* allow myself to be associated with anyone who is even rumored to be involved in something like this."

"I understand. I will resign immediately."

"There's no need for you to do that—I've already announced that I've terminated you."

Provost turned to leave. He stopped and turned back when the governor said, "Larry."

"Yes, sir."

"If I find out that you were involved in this, I will do everything in my power to see that you get strung up by your balls. If I don't, on election day, my opponent will be in this office fifteen minutes after the polls close. Now, get out of here—I have a shitload of damage control to do."

Provost turned and left the office.

Native agents are those of the enemy's country people whom we employ.
—*The Art of War*

76

Traynor was back in LA at noon on the day after Skidgel's demise. Deborah and Jack picked him up at LAX. As they drove into the center of the city, they discussed the situation. "The cops wrote it up as a DUI," he said. "The only mention of me is that I witnessed the accident."

Deborah turned and looked back. "Ed . . ."

"I know what you're about to ask," he said. "Yes, it was an accident. Now, what's been happening on this end?"

"I approached Jabłoński," McMahon said, "and Manuel did the same to Provost."

"And?"

"They tried to play it off as if they were clueless about the whole thing, but this morning they met for breakfast."

"So we can at least prove that they're acquainted."

"Yes," Deborah said, "and I think Larry Provost had a bad day. Hollis International contacted the governor and threatened to pull all campaign donations if Provost was involved with his reelection campaign in any manner. We were told that the governor had summoned Provost to a meeting in Sacramento."

"That must have rattled Provost."

"Of that I'm certain. Manuel followed him to the airport, where he took a flight to Sacramento, and then Manuel waited for his return. Provost booked his flight through a travel agency that Hollis owns. So we knew his itinerary. To cut to the chase, Manuel said Provost did not look happy when he deplaned."

"Good," Traynor said. "It's all coming together. In short time the heat is gonna be on high and Provost and Jabłoński are going to be in a pressure cooker."

"We still don't know who the rest of the crew were. There had to be at least one other to run the camera."

"Once we get Provost and Jabłoński in a cell, they won't be long in rolling over on everyone involved," Traynor said. "All we need to do is ratchet up the heat another notch or two."

How easily murder is discovered.
—William Shakespeare, *Titus Andronicus*

77

Traynor tagged along with McMahon while he shadowed Jabłoński. The director spent the morning inside the editing studio. "Probably trying to figure out a way to cut all my scenes out," McMahon lamented.

"That would be more than a little difficult seeing as you were the lead."

"Yeah, I suppose. However, if it wasn't for the fact that a lot of money has been spent on it, he'd probably scrap the entire project."

"You know, Jack," Traynor said, "you're even starting to sound like an actor. How much are they paying you for this anyhow?"

"They promised me a percentage of the gate. I got to admit, I did enjoy it."

"Who knows, if the movie is a success you may have a new career."

Their discussion was interrupted by the ring tone of McMahon's phone—it was the sound of a machine gun firing. He checked the display, said, "Angela," and answered.

For several seconds Traynor listened to one half of the conversation, and while he was not certain of the exact words, he knew something had happened. McMahon finally broke the connection and started the car. Without taking his eyes from the road, he said, "The tests on the knife they believe was used to murder the Doerr woman came back. Larry Provost's DNA is all over it. It looks as if Jabłoński may have to be moved to the backburner for a while."

"So we're going after Provost?"

"Yes, we are—along with the Simi Valley police and who knows how many other law enforcement organizations."

"I guess we now know who cut Mindy up."

"Looks that way."

Provost turned onto the street leading to his LA residence and stopped the car. There were four or five police cars blocking the gates to the estate. He did a quick U-turn and left the area. In spite of the cold air blasting from the Jag's air conditioning, he began to sweat. His hands shook as he tried to control the greatest fear he'd ever felt in his life. His first instinct was to try to figure out who had dropped the dime on him. The list of suspects was not very long; the entire production crew of *The Black Orchid* was only five people. He checked them off in his mind: Skidgel, Jabłoński, Doerr, the cameraman, and himself. Of the five, one was dead, and he doubted that either Skidgel or Jabłoński would have the balls to do it—after all they were in this up to their assholes, too. That left Darren Hale, the cameraman, who strangely enough had remained unscathed and out of the spotlight. Did Hale strike a deal with the cops? Provost made up his mind to find out as soon as possible.

Once he was safely out of his neighborhood, he stopped at the first ATM he came across. If the cops were looking for him, it would only be a matter of time before they got a judge to lock all of his accounts—and he needed all the money he could his hands on.

Provost sighed with relief when the ATM spit out the maximum withdrawal allowed. He would have to find a branch office and go in and clean the money out of as many of his accounts as he could.

His thoughts returned to the last thing the governor had said to him, and he knew that every cop in California and the surrounding states would now be looking for him. Leaving the country for Mexico was out of the question—they would surely have notified ICE to be on the lookout for him. His mind raced as he tried to think of where he could go.

He tuned the radio to an all-news station, and in short time knew he was the subject of a massive manhunt. Somehow or another, they had evidence that he had done in Celia Doerr.

Strangely, he was not concerned about the authorities. It was the Hollis woman and her band of vigilantes that truly concerned him. The cops would be bound by Miranda and the US Constitution—the Hollis bunch would have no such restrictions. He recalled his conversation with the former DEA psycho and broke out into another heavy sweat. Never before their meeting in the canyon had he looked at someone who could kill another human being as easily as he believed that man could.

He saw a branch of his bank and turned in. After making a furtive search of the parking lot, he darted inside.

Provost parked in a visitor spot behind Hale's apartment. He entered the square and then circled the outdoor pool that was in the open center court of the complex. He stopped before a sliding door near the middle of the western side and tapped on the glass. He ignored several screaming kids who were playing in the pool. Suddenly, the drapes were pulled aside just enough for the apartment's occupant to see who had rapped on his door. The latch clicked open and the glass pane slid apart until there was enough space for Provost to slip inside.

Darren Hale looked like an advertisement against the use of drugs and alcohol. His eyes were bloodshot and watery, he had not shaved in at least a week, and his T-shirt looked like it held remnants of his entire diet for the past week. From what hair he had, it was evident that it had not seen a comb since he had last shaved. "You look like shit," Provost said.

Hale shrugged as if his appearance was of little, if any, concern to him. "What the fuck you want, Larry?"

"We got problems. That last movie—"

"I told you guys that I didn't want anything to do with you after that."

"Well, here's the scenario. The woman's family has money—more money than they know what to do with—and they hired a bunch of mercenaries to deal with everyone involved in the filming."

Hale's face turned ashen. "Christ, man, all I did was operate the camera. You were—"

"It doesn't matter to them. They'll say maybe you didn't *do* her in, but you didn't stop it either."

"What about the others?"

"That's the really bad stuff. Celia and Skidgel are dead, and Jabłoński is about to run out on us. That leaves only you and me."

"But my name isn't on that film—not even a fake name."

Provost looked at Hale as if the man was dumber than an amoeba. "Don't you wonder what Doerr and Skidgel might have told them?"

Hale dropped onto his couch and held his head between his hands. "Oh man, what the fuck are we gonna do?"

"I don't know about you, but I'm on my way out of town. I cleaned out my bank accounts and I'm headin' south."

"South?"

"Yeah, Brazil or maybe Argentina."

"I ain't got enough money to take it on the lam like that. If Jabłoński talks, I'm dead meat."

Provost said, "Exactly."

Hale looked up to see the flash of light on the knife blade a microsecond before it was driven into his chest. He grunted with pain and fell onto his side. There was a quizzical look on his face as he asked, "Why? I won't say nothin' to anyone . . ."

Provost pulled the knife free and drove it into Hale again. "I know that . . . now."

Provost straightened up and turned toward the door. Before he exited, a female voice called from the bedroom, "Darren, are you okay?"

Cursing under his breath, Provost walked toward the voice.

An officer may make a warrantless arrest for a felony as long as he has sufficient probable cause to believe a felony has been committed and the person he's arresting is actually the person who committed the felony.

—Police Procedure & Investigation: A Guide For Writers

78

Traynor was eating lunch when McMahon walked into the dining room and flopped down at his table. He immediately saw that something was on his mind. "What's up?"

"Maybe nothing, maybe something."

"Okay, so why don't you tell me what it is that might be something or might be nothing?"

The hostess approached the table and McMahon ordered coffee. When she left, he turned back to Traynor. "Angela called."

"And?"

"This morning LAPD got a call from someone in the valley . . ."

"Which valley? This place is full of them."

"San Fernando."

"Okay."

"They answered the call and walked into a double murder."

Traynor was still unable to determine why this would be of importance to them.

However, McMahon wasted no time in clarifying.

"The victims were a guy named Darren Hale and his girlfriend. Hale was a cameraman, and he'd made several pornos with Jabłoński."

"You think he was behind the camera?"

"There's one other fact that makes me think that."

The waitress returned, placed his coffee in front of him, and quickly departed.

McMahon took a conspiratorial glance around the room and then said, "A new Jag was seen leaving the scene around the time that the crime scene techs think it went down."

"Provost."

"Yeah, Just Call Me Larry fuckin' Provost. He must be running scared."

"No doubt. Well, this changes things," Traynor said.

"I know. Jabłoński is the only one left who can identify him as the man under the hood in *The Black Orchid*."

"Does Manuel know about this?"

"If he doesn't, he will in a few seconds."

Traynor looked up as Manuel and Deborah took the remaining chairs at the table. "You heard?" he asked them.

Deborah nodded. "Angela just called."

"So," he asked, "what now?"

"We let the cops worry about finding Provost," Manuel said. "We'll go after Jabłoński."

"Ahhh," Traynor replied. "Another case of 'if the mountain won't go to Mohammed . . .'"

"Exactly."

Rather than send McMahon after Jabłoński, they decided to approach him together. Manuel opted to go to the director's home while the rest of them went to the studio. When they arrived, Engle and another cop met them at the gate. The security guard smiled at McMahon and then gave his entourage a look of concern. "I'm afraid I can't let all of you in, Mr. Puller," he said.

Engle wasted no time in putting him in his place. "You either let *all* of us in, or I arrest you for obstruction."

For a few seconds, the guard looked confused and then decided to find a way to pass the buck. "Let me call—"

"You'll call no one," Engle said. She motioned her partner forward. "Officer Diaz, make sure that he stays off the phone." She turned to her companions and said, "Let's go get him."

They passed through the gate and headed for the studio where McMahon believed Jabłoński would be editing the movie he had just finished filming. As they walked, Engle looked at McMahon and asked, "Who the hell is Mr. Puller?"

"My screen name is Peter Puller."

Her mouth fell open and then she started giggling as they walked. "Peter? Puller? Sounds like—"

"I know, I know. But I had to come up with something fast."

Engle shook her head and said, "For the rest of our lives I'll think of that every time I look at you and it'll be all I can do not to laugh."

McMahon looked at her. "Do you want to?"

"What, laugh?"

"Look at me for the rest of our lives . . ."

They neared the door to the studio and Engle said, "Once we finish this job . . . well, all I'll promise is that we'll talk."

McMahon smiled. "Can't ask for more than that."

He reached out and turned the handle, opening the door. "Ladies before gents."

They barged inside and found an assistant editor hard at work. Startled by their sudden entrance, he turned to face them. "Hey, Pete," he said, "what's up?"

"Where's Kondrat?" McMahon asked. He glanced at Engle and saw that she was still clenching her lips, trying to hold back a laugh.

"Don't have a clue. He called in this morning and told me that he wouldn't be in and for me to start editing the soundtrack."

Rather than reply, McMahon took out a cell phone and hit speed dial. When Manuel answered, he said, "Hey, it's Jack."

Behind him McMahon heard the assistant ask, "Who's Jack?"

"Him. His real name is Jack Ash," Engle answered.

"Jabłoński isn't at the studio," McMahon said, ignoring the conversation behind him.

"I know, he's still at home. Hold on a minute."

After several tense moments, Manuel came back on the line. "It looks like he may be bolting. One of his hired flunkies just backed a car out of the garage and put some luggage in the trunk."

"Keep him there," McMahon said, "we're on our way with the cops."

"He isn't going anywhere. Trust me."

Manuel parked his SUV across the drive, blocking the gate so that it would be impossible for anyone to get by him. He got out of the truck and leaned against the door, watching the front of the house. In minutes, one of Jabłoński's staff came down the drive and stopped before him. He was a large man and Manuel was certain that he was hired security; if nothing else, the telltale bulge under his left arm advertised that he was armed.

"Who are you?" the man asked.

"The guy who's gonna make sure that your boss doesn't leave the property."

"You the cops?"

"No, I'm not, but they aren't far behind me." Manuel straightened up and said, "Don't reach for that piece unless you got enough life insurance to support your family."

The bodyguard raised his hands and said, "I'm paid to keep intruders out, not to interfere with the cops."

"Smart idea. Now, why don't you go back inside and tell Jabłoński that there's been a change to his travel plans?"

"No sweat." The man turned away, walked a few steps, and turned back. "You *ex*-cop?"

"Spent some time with the DEA."

"I figured you must be some type of cop." He walked up the drive.

The use of trickery, deceit, ploys, and lying is legally permissible during the course of an interrogation (under certain conditions) . . .
—*FM 3-19.13, Law Enforcement Investigations*

79

Kondrat Jabłoński was sweating like the proverbial pig. The entire troupe had descended upon him and he was not happy about it. He was especially unhappy about Engle's presence—her uniform made things official. They had been "interviewing" the director for the better part of an hour, and Traynor, for one, was becoming weary of his incessant, bullshit denials. "Look, Jabłoński," he said, getting up close to his face, "you may as well open up—we have your entire crew identified. Toledo, Skidgel, Doerr, and Hale, your cameraman, are all dead. That only leaves Provost loose and he's on the run. He'll be caught and then he'll be rolling over on you like a runaway truck."

"I think I want my lawyer," he replied.

"Officer Engle, would you step outside please?" Deborah asked.

Engle got up from the easy chair where she'd been sitting and walked to the door.

"You can't leave me with these people," Jabłoński cried. "You're responsible for protecting me . . ."

"I don't have any responsibility unless a crime has been committed, and so far I haven't observed anything but a discussion among a group of friends."

"These people are not my friends! They are trespassers—burglars who have broken into my home."

"That isn't the way I saw it," Engle replied. "I saw your security people open the gates and let them in—right before they took off." She smiled and left the room.

They listened until the sounds of her footsteps died away. Deborah grinned at Jabłoński. It made her look like a cat playing with a mouse it had trapped. "Your lawyer may be needed later on," she said. "But before you see hide or hair of him, you're going to tell us what you know—even if that means I have to turn these men loose on you."

Jabłoński looked at McMahon and saw the stony mien on his face. It was obvious there would be no help from him. He then turned to Manuel. And Traynor knew that scared the shit out of him.

The director lost his bluster. In turn he made eye contact with each of them and saw not a single sign of mercy in any of them. He reached for his cigarettes; when he tried to get one out, his hands shook so hard he scattered the smokes across the small coffee table. Traynor reached over and handed him one.

Jabłoński thanked him, retrieved a shiny Zippo lighter from his pocket, and then ignited it—it took him three tries to light his cigarette. Traynor was unsure if it was the nicotine fix he got when he inhaled the smoke or if he decided to make one last futile attempt at being tough, but he sat back and in a defiant tone said, "I still have no idea what you're talking about."

"Bullshit!" Traynor went on the attack. "We know all about you and your so-called career. You came here after several failed movies in Europe and made porn for over a year. During that time you somehow became involved with Doerr, Skidgel, and Provost. We also know that you have made at least one snuff film, possibly more. You used Skidgel, who was nothing more than a shill for you and Provost, to entrap young women into making your films." He decided to lie and see how Jabłoński would react. "We can prove that you were the director and what Skidgel's role was. We want to know how Celia Doerr fit into this and who the killer was." Traynor was careful not to divulge the fact that they were certain that Doerr's only part in the scheme was to keep tabs on Mindy and ensure that she did not change her mind about making what she probably thought was a run-of-the-mill skin-flick. They were also about 80 percent certain that Provost was the sadist wielding the knife. The problem was that unless one of them broke, they had no hard proof.

Manuel took matters in hand and reached across the coffee table, grabbing Jabłoński by the front of his shirt. The startled director dropped his cigarette into his trousers and began shouting as it burned a hole in his lap. He beat at it with his hands before Manuel pulled him across the table and the smoldering cigarette fell to the floor.

"If you don't tell us what you fuckin' know, I'm gonna bust your face so bad, your own mother won't recognize you."

"I . . . I'll sue you!"

"You're welcome to try," Manuel snarled. "But it won't be easy with no witnesses."

"You have a police officer with you." Jabłoński's eyes turned to the door through which Engle had departed. "She will have to protect me."

Engle must have been listening because suddenly the front door closed with a resounding bang. "Looks as if your police protection has gone to lunch," Manuel said.

"Mr. Jabłoński," Deborah said in a voice filled with reason, "we are going to find my sister's killers. To be completely frank with you . . ." She stood and strolled to the window. Her back was to them when she said, "We will do whatever it takes to resolve this issue." When she turned and glared at him, she was cold, hard, and resolute. "You better pick up that cigarette," she said. "It's burning a hole in the carpet."

"Kondrat," McMahon said, "looks to me that the script has been changed—and anyone can see that you're royally fucked. Why don't you relax, accept the inevitable, and tell us what we want to know?"

"I can't," Jabłoński said, "it would destroy me."

"You've already got one foot in a prison cell and the other on a banana peel. Your career," McMahon replied, "is already over. You aren't up against a bunch of irate citizens with no power. You're up against a multinational corporation that owns everything from computer companies to newspapers and entertainment businesses."

"Many producers and directors in California have made adult films," Jabłoński said.

"We're not talking about porn," McMahon answered. "We're talking about multiple murders and snuff films. I would venture that the next camera you see will be that of a news broadcast exposing you to the world."

The director's shoulders slumped and his head dropped. He was defeated and he knew it. Suddenly, he looked like an old man. "It was Provost," he said. "The man is a cold-blooded killer . . ."

"How many snuffs have you made?" Deborah asked.

"Three. Provost was the killer in each."

Offer the enemy a bait to lure him; feign disorder and strike him.

—*The Art of War*

80

As much as he hated to do it, Provost knew that he had to get rid of the Jaguar. It was too easily spotted. He had no delusions about his plight. The police would have a BOLO on him by now and all things considered, he was most likely the number-one priority of every law enforcement agency in the state. He fled LA, driving east on secondary roads until he felt the city was far enough behind that he could stop.

When the sun dropped below the western horizon, he found a no-tell motel in a no-horse town on the edge of the Mojave Desert and checked in. The Desert View Motor Inn was a throwback to an earlier time when motels consisted of small, one-room cabins barely big enough to hold a single bed and a cubicle that served as a bathroom. However, it had two things in its favor: the parking area was hidden from the highway behind the cabins, and it looked as if he had been the first customer since the Gold Rush of 1849.

Provost still had one major factor to deal with: his face. As an integral part of three gubernatorial campaigns, he had been interviewed any number of times. Even if he were being grandiose, he believed that he was one of the most recognizable nonentertainment figures in southern California. He stowed his meager luggage in the cabin and returned to the office.

The same old man who had checked him in was sitting behind the counter, listening to a Los Angeles Angels game on an old AM radio. He looked up when his only guest entered. "How c'n I he'p yah, Mr. Hefner?" he asked, using the alias under which Provost had checked in.

"I got a splitting headache. Is there someplace where I can buy something for it?"

"I got some asp'rin. Yore welcome to take some."

"Aspirin won't be strong enough. These things really kill me."

"Well, they's a Supermart about a mile east. They got just about anything you could need. It's a good thing, too. There in't nothin' else b'tween here and Nevada."

"I'll try that, thanks."

Provost exited the office and paused on the steps. A large mart could be a magnet for cops. The problem of the Jaguar popped its head again. He turned and poked his head through the door. "I shouldn't drive with this headache—it hurts so bad, my vision blurs."

"Yuh, I get them ever' now and then—usually when my sperm count gets higher than my blood pressure." The old man laughed at his own joke.

Not seeing the humor in the statement, Provost said, "Is there cab service around here?"

"Kinda. Elwood Pearson runs a service, if you can call one cab and a cell phone a service."

"Would you arrange for him to pick me up?"

"Yup."

"Tell him I need to go to the Supermart and I'd like for him to wait and bring me back."

"No problem, but knowin' Elwood it'll be expensive."

"Can't be as expensive as a car accident," Provost replied, backing out of the door.

"I wouldn't count on that." The old man laughed again.

An hour later, Provost was back in his cabin. He placed the hair color he had bought on the sink and peered into the mirror, checking his jowls with his hand. He wished he could grow a beard on demand. *Well, if I can stay hidden for a few weeks, it'll grow out.* He stripped off and stepped into the shower.

───────────

Engle arrested Jabłoński and led him to her cruiser. Traynor turned to the assembled group and asked, "Okay, the only one left is Provost. What's our plan of action?"

"We find him and bring him in, one way or another," Deborah answered.

Traynor looked at her and said, "I would assume that my part in this is over. You hired me to find your sister and we have."

"You've been in this since the start," she said. "I would like you to stay on to the end. Don't worry about the money."

"I'm not worried about my fee; in fact, from this point on, my services are pro bono."

"That isn't necessary. I'm more than willing to pay you."

"Manuel and Jack aren't receiving anything, other than their salaries. I feel like a mercenary."

"Manuel and Jack will be receiving bonuses for their work." She addressed all of them. "You guys have exceeded anything I had imagined when we started this."

Traynor turned to McMahon and asked, "How do we go about finding Provost?"

"He could be anywhere by now. He has the financial resources to hide for a long time."

"Engle will be monitoring whatever the police get and she'll let us know," Manuel added. "Nobody can stay underground forever—especially someone who likes being in the limelight as much as Provost does. All we need do is wait. He'll show up somewhere, and I'd stake my salary that it will be sooner rather than later."

Manuel was quiet for a few moments and then said, "Maybe we can help him along."

"How so?" Deborah asked.

"Earlier today, Jack said something that caught my attention," Manuel replied. "He said Jabłoński was the only person left who can put Provost under the hood. What if we were to let it be known that he has been arrested for suspicion of murder, is out on bail, and was looking to make a deal with the DA?"

Traynor said, "It may draw Provost out to tie up his only loose end."

"Yeah," Manuel said. "Only we'll be here to tie *him* up."

What goes around, comes around.

—English Adage

81

Provost threw the half-eaten piece of chicken into the takeout box and stared at the television in disbelief. The reporter stood before the LA Federal Court Building, reporting on a situation that made a chill run up his spine. The authorities had Jabłoński in custody and he was singing an aria. Of everything she said, the phrase that cut him deepest was when she said, "Sources have reported that, based on information provided by Kondrat Jabłoński, a well-known social and political figure has been named a person of interest in the murder of Melinda Hollis, the daughter of a powerful and politically connected East Coast billionaire. It has also been conveyed to this reporter that Ms. Hollis was murdered during the filming of a pornographic snuff film . . ."

He leaped to his feet and paced around the small motel cabin. The sonuvabitch was about to sell him out—if he hadn't already done it! The reporter's voice drew his attention back to the broadcast: "Jabłoński has turned State's Evidence in return for a reduced sentence. I have also learned that, apart from the undisclosed person of interest, Jabłoński is the only surviving witness who can identify the killer. My sources have informed me that the person of interest is none other than political king-maker, Lawrence (Larry) Provost, who is currently being sought for questioning about the murders of Celia Doerr, whose body was recently discovered at her home in Simi Valley, and of Darren Hale, believed to be the cameraman on the film, and his companion, Erica Lang. Their bodies were found in Hale's San Fernando Valley apartment earlier this week . . ."

The anchor cut in and said, "Maria, were you given any indication that the police are closing in on this person of interest?"

"No, Cliff. But my source inside the LAPD has told me that a manhunt covering the states of California, Oregon, Arizona, and Nevada is underway and they hope to have the suspect in custody very soon. Maria Esteban, reporting live from LAPD headquarters. Back to you in the studio, Cliff."

Provost switched the television off and picked up the fifth of whiskey that sat on the small table that abutted the bed. He drank straight from the bottle and cursed. He had to get back to LA. Jabłoński had to be dealt with before he could testify. His mind turned to the problem that the Jaguar presented. He had to get rid of it, but if they knew who he was, they'd be watching for it. Selling it to a dealer was out of the question; once the sale hit the DMV the cops would know it. He had to dump it out in the desert where it could go undiscovered for weeks, months if he was lucky. He gathered his belongings and left the cabin.

Provost left the paved road and followed a dirt lane leading deeper into the desert. As he drove through the night, his mind raced. Dumping the Jag was going to be the easy part; getting back to civilization presented an entirely different set of problems. First, he had to walk back from wherever he left the car and then he would have to get some form of transportation. Buying a car from a dealer was out of the question—it required too many forms and he would have to provide some identification to the dealer. He was still pondering his situation when his headlights illuminated an abandoned farm. He turned off the road and followed the short drive to the barnyard. He stopped before a dilapidated barn and studied it before deciding it would be as good a solution as he would find.

Before he stepped from the car, he checked the ground around the vehicle. Stories of snakes lying in roads at night filled him with trepidation. The worst thing he could do now would be to step on a sleeping rattler and get bitten out here in the middle of nowhere. He took a flashlight from the glove compartment and swept the beam back and forth across the ground. Satisfied there were no venomous reptiles, he got out of the Jag and approached the barn.

He raised the beam of light from the ground and into the interior of the worn-out building. The exterior of the barn was gray with age and the wood was warped and twisted from years of exposure to the sun. He wondered for a few seconds what would make anyone think they could scratch out a living by raising crops in such an arid, desolate place—but he dismissed the thought and accepted the former owner's stupidity as a blessing.

He swept the light around the inside and saw a setting perfect for a hack-and-slash horror flick. Spiderwebs arched between the beams, and old, worn-out farm implements were scattered around. Even though the place had obviously been abandoned for years, he could still detect a foul hint of animal urine and manure. He stepped inside, ducking beneath two worn six-by-six beams that had fallen across the entrance. He turned the shaft of light to the upper end and supposed he could push them aside enough to allow him to drive the car inside without the whole building collapsing around him.

He swept the light across the surface of the old wood to ensure it was free of black widow spiders and scorpions. Satisfied that that all was safe, he set the light down. Suddenly, he heard something scurrying through the debris and old dry straw that littered the stalls and he froze. The furtive sounds ceased, and he dismissed them as those of small rodents fleeing.

He grabbed the board and pulled. A load screech filled the air as he pulled the rusty, aged spikes from their resting place. The beam yanked free and he lost control of it. An avalanche of rotted wood and dust cascaded from the loft and he knew that he had made a major miscalculation. The unwieldy beam kicked to the side, hitting him in the shin. He cried out in pain and fell backward as the heavy post dropped, driving him to the floor, and shattering his tibia. The second post also fell, dropping across his already broken leg. Provost screamed in pain before passing out.

When he regained consciousness, he found himself pinned to the sandy floor like a butterfly in a display case. He lay back and fought against his desire to cry in frustration—then he heard the ominous rattling near his left ear.

All's well that ends well.

—William Shakespeare

82

Two days after they had leaked Jabłoński's arrest to the press, Deborah woke Traynor with an early-morning phone call. He was usually slow to wake up, preferring to ease into the day, but what she said brought him to his feet instantly. She said, "They found Provost. We're all meeting in the dining room at eight."

He showered and dressed in record time but was still the last to arrive. He sat and poured coffee from the carafe that sat in the middle of the table and asked, "Have they got him in custody?"

They all turned to face Engle, waiting for further information.

"An old man who runs a motel in the desert saw the newscast and called the information hotline. By the time the local cops arrived, Provost was gone, so they started an air search. His car was spotted in the yard of an abandoned farm in the desert. Provost was inside the barn. It appears a beam fell on him, breaking his leg."

"Where is he now? Do the local cops have him?" Traynor urged.

"He's in the local morgue. When he was pinned by the beam, he must have disturbed a sleeping rattlesnake—it bit him near his carotid. He was probably dead within minutes."

"Too bad," McMahon said. "I was looking forward to bringing him down."

"It's probably better this way," Deborah said. "The courts would have given him life—this way he got death."

"Yeah," Manuel intoned, "only it would have been nice to know that every night his cell mate was doing to him what he did to Mindy . . ."

"Better this way," McMahon said. "They'd have kept him in solitary confinement."

"So," Traynor asked Engle, "where does that leave Jabłoński?"

"He says Provost blackmailed him into making the movies—"

"Movies?" Deborah asked.

"They made three of them, using young girls who had just arrived in LA. As we knew, Skidgel was the recruiter, Jabłoński the director, and Doerr the matron who kept them at her home until their debut." Engle looked at Manuel. "If it gives you any consolation, he's confessed, and by this time next week, he'll be either in Folsom or San Quentin."

"Like they'd have done with Provost, he'll be in solitary," McMahon said. "If they put him in with the general population, he'd be killed in no time . . . if not by some inmate, then by suicide."

"Then, it's over," Deborah said. "Now we can all go home and I can bury my sister and hopefully get on with my life. It's strange though—I thought I'd get more satisfaction from bringing these degenerates down. Instead of feeling jubilant, I just feel empty."

All farewells should be sudden.

—Lord Byron, *Sardanapalus*

83

Traynor stepped out of his SUV and saw McMahon walking toward him. "You back to being the would-yuh?"

"More or less. How you been?"

"I can't complain."

"Good thing," McMahon said. "Nobody wants to hear you whine anyhow."

Traynor grinned. "How's the movie doing?"

"Well, as you can see, I haven't quit my day job yet. There hasn't been a line of agents and producers at the door either."

"You should talk to Deborah. Maybe she can bring the power of Hollis International into the equation."

"Truthfully, acting is hard work. The hours are crazy and then there's all that envy and backstabbing shit that happens on the set. Not to mention that my experience with Jabłoński and his ilk kind of soured me on the industry. You better head out back—the duchess awaits."

Traynor circled the mansion and found Deborah sitting at the same table under the same umbrella; again she was flanked by Cyril and Marsha Hollis. Strangely enough, the old man looked sober and Mrs. Hollis did not look like she had a metal shaft up her butt. Byron Moore sat across from Cyril, looking his usual stiff self.

Without waiting to be piped aboard the USS *Hollis*, Traynor stepped onto the deck and sat under the parasol. The first thing that impressed him was that the cold, imperial attitude with which they had greeted him on his last visit was gone—in fact, in their own stuffed-shirt way, the old man and woman seemed positively amiable.

Marsha was the first to speak. "Good afternoon, Mr. Traynor." Before he could reply, she said, "I want to apologize for the way my husband and I behaved during your last visit."

As much as he wanted to gloat, Traynor took the diplomatic route. "No apology needed, Mrs. Hollis. You were all under quite a bit of stress back then."

A servant—not Manuel—stepped up to the table and asked if he would like a refreshment. He ordered iced tea, unsweetened with lemon. Turning to Deborah, he asked, "Where is Manuel?"

"He is no longer with us," Deborah said.

"Oh?"

"He was paid a substantial bonus after . . ." She paused. ". . . we returned from the West Coast. He decided it was time to return home."

"Good for him." He studied the Hollises and decided to get to the point. "Why did you want to see me?"

"It has been brought to our attention," Cyril said, looking at Deborah, "that you went way beyond the normal scope of what we asked you to do . . . to the extent that you put your very life at risk."

Still unsure of where this was headed, Traynor downplayed it. "I didn't give it a thought. I guess you might say it's an occupational hazard."

"I doubt that," Marsha said.

"Mr. and Mrs. Hollis, what happened to your daughter was despicable. In my career in law enforcement, never before have I had to deal with anything like this. Those people were lower than whale shit—you'll have to pardon my vernacular, but what happened to your daughter still enrages me. My only regret is that they didn't get a worse fate."

"I was told," Cyril said, "that the actual killer died a horribly painful death."

"Maybe so, but Manuel and I would have stretched that death out from minutes to hours, maybe even days."

"Still," Hollis said, "Deborah . . ." He amended what he was about to say. "*We* would like to extend an offer to you."

"What sort of offer?"

Deborah took over. "I'd like you to be our head of security. The compensation package would be quite generous and the salary in the mid-six figures."

Traynor had to admit the prospect of a high-paying steady job was enticing. Then he realized it also meant that he would lose his professional freedom—not to mention he thought it could be pretty boring. "Deborah, Mr. and Mrs. Hollis, I'm very flattered by the offer. However, I have to decline."

Moore seemed shocked that anyone would turn down such a job. "Why in heaven's name would you decline?"

The servant appeared and placed Traynor's beverage in front of him. He took a sip. "For twenty years, I worked inside a bureaucracy—namely the New Hampshire State Police. After I retired I looked into several options, even running for a county sheriff position somewhere in the state. In the end, I realized that I wanted the independence to take what cases I wanted, without having to deal with a lot of politics. So, I opened my own agency."

"You would have absolute authority over all security matters," Deborah said.

"Deborah, Hollis International is an entity unto itself—therefore it thrives on policies and procedures. That is not my thing. However, I will offer my services as a security consultant on an as needed basis."

Deborah seemed to ponder his answer for a few seconds. "I'm sure that can be arranged."

"Why don't you offer the job to Jack?"

"I'm certain he'll be pursuing an acting career."

"Have you asked him?"

"No, I haven't. But now that he and Angela are considering reconciling, I assumed he'd be going back to California."

"If he and Angela are thinking of getting back together and you offer him the same package you were going to offer me, I'm sure he'll convince her to join him over here."

"But," Deborah said, "Angela seemed determined to have a career in law enforcement."

"So, hire her too. They're really a good team—besides can you think of anyone else more capable of making him toe the line?"

She smiled. "No, I can't—and it would certainly keep things from getting dull."

He gulped down the iced tea and stood. "Again, I thank you for the offer. I'm truly flattered."

They all stood and shook hands. "Now, if you'll excuse me," Traynor said. "I have to get back to my office."

When McMahon met him by his truck, Traynor asked, "What's this I hear about you and Angela?" He grinned.

McMahon actually seemed to blush. "We've decided to give it another try. We're still debating where we want to live."

"Well, that decision may become a lot easier."

"Oh?"

"They offered me a job."

"I knew they were going to." But still, his face showed his disappointment that he hadn't been given a shot at the position.

"Well, I'm not the corporate type. You, however, might want to update your résumé." Traynor got in his truck, took out his cell phone, and placed it on the console.

"You expecting a call?" McMahon asked.

Traynor grinned. "No, but you never know when a billionaire might need your services."

AFTERWORD

Definition of a snuff film, according to Kerekes and Slater in their book, Killing for Culture: Snuff films depict the killing of a human being—a human sacrifice (without the aid of special effects or other trickery) perpetuated for the medium of film and circulated amongst a jaded few for the purpose of entertainment.

The snuff film is an urban legend. There has never been a single one found and the few that have proclaimed to be such have been consistently proven to be fraudulent. However, we only have to take a trip to our local video store or movie theater to be confronted with our society's fascination with violence and gore. I recall the first time I saw Sam Peckipah's *The Wild Bunch*. I had returned from a year serving with the Marines in the Republic of South Vietnam. During the first shooting scene I recall thinking, *I just spent a year in a combat zone and didn't see anything like this!* What has followed over the years has made that classic movie seem tame.

Somewhere along the way, our society has come to believe that we have to *see* the weapon hit home. We seem to overlook the power of our imagination. Truly, one of the most disturbing scenes ever filmed was the infamous shower scene in Alfred Hitchcock's classic *Psycho*, based on the 1959 novel by Robert Bloch. Audiences recoil in horror as a deranged Anthony Perkins attacks an obviously nude Janet Leigh as she showers. However, the power of the scene is not in what it shows, but rather in what it doesn't show and how our imaginations fill in the gaps. For many years, I believed that Hitchcock showed the knife strike; it was only years later when I watched the film as an adult that I realized that nothing could be further from the truth.

However, the fact that there has never been a snuff film made for commercial distribution does not mean that such an event has never been captured on film. (Remember the famous photo from Vietnam of a security officer shooting a Viet Cong in the head? That photo turned the nation against the war.) Each and every day we learn of new levels of depravity inflicted by one human being on another.

I pray that we never find out.

Vaughn C. Hardacker
March 2016

ACKNOWLEDGMENTS

As is always the case when one finishes a work of fiction, I owe thanks to many people. To list a few: My domestic partner, Jane Hartley. During the course of a long northern Maine winter, when cabin fever threatened to make us both homicidal, she read the finished manuscript (several times) and was always willing to tell me what I needed to hear; not necessarily what I wanted to hear.

Thanks are also owed to Linda (Lockhart) Hamilton and Penny (Monteith) Celino who were there at the beginning. Avid readers of my sophomoric writing in Caribou Junior High School, they cornered me at the thirty-fifth reunion of our high school graduation asking, "Why haven't we seen any of your books?" I couldn't answer their question and turned to my wife for support. She said, "Why haven't they?" So I got off my keester and wrote them. Thank you, ladies; without your encouragement it might never have happened.

To be successful, a new writer needs a strong critique group of writers who are willing to read the bad stuff and to be strong enough to give the writer constructive, honest criticism. I have been fortunate to be involved with the Breathe group in Maine. Thanks are due to Wendy, Heather, Vince, Larry, and Michelle for their invaluable feedback and input.

Thanks are also owed to several former members of law enforcement and authors in their own right, Brian Thiem (former commander of the Homicide Section of the Oakland, California PD), Bruce Hoffman (fellow Marine, who served with me in Vietnam, Captain on the Hillsborough County Florida Sheriff's Office), Paul Doyle (retired DEA agent), and Lee Lofland (former police detective). Paul's memoir of his years as an undercover DEA agent in Boston (*Heavy Shots and Heavy Hits: Tales of An Undercover Drug Agent*) is a fascinating look into the life of an undercover agent. It helped me to understand the many challenges faced by the men and women who perform this vital function, not to mention the stress they face daily (both personal and professional). Lee's *Police Procedure & Investigation: A Guide for Writers* didn't leave my side as I worked through the manuscript . . . It is a *must have* for anyone who writes crime and thriller fiction.

Special thanks are owed to my agent, Paula Munier, and my editor and her team at Skyhorse Publishing, who spent a great deal of time and effort overcoming my love for ellipses while copyediting the work. You've got to hand it to a couple of women who will tell you to delete that wonderful scene you wrote (but that truthfully belongs in another book) and when you balk say: "Just do it!"—especially when you're working overtime trying to find ways out of it!

This book is a work of fiction and any mistakes within are entirely the fault of the writer.

BIBLIOGRAPHY

The following listed sources were of invaluable assistance to me in the writing of this novel:

1. *Private Eyes: A Writer's Guide To Private Investigators*, Hal Blythe, Charlie Sweet, and John Landreth, ©1993, Writer's Digest Books, an imprint of F&W Publications, Inc.
2. *FM 3-19, Law Enforcement Investigations,* January 2005, Department of The Army, Approved for public release, distribution is unlimited.
3. *Police Procedure & Investigation: A Guide for Writers,* Lee Lofland, © 2007, Writer's Digest Books, an imprint of F&W Publications, Inc.
4. *Heavy Shots and Heavy Hits: Tales of An Undercover Drug Agent,* Paul E. Doyle, © 2004, Northeastern University Press.
5. *STP 21-1-SMCT, Soldier's Manual of Common Tasks,* October 1987. Approved for public release, distribution is unlimited.
6. *The Tempest,* William Shakespeare, *The Complete Works of William Shakespeare,* ©1994 Barnes & Noble Books.
7. *The Art Of War,* Sun Tzu, Translated and with an introduction by Samuel B. Griffith, © 1963, Oxford University Press.
8. *Clicking Mics,* Bruce Hoffman, ©2015, Hoffman Books.

ABOUT THE AUTHOR

Vaughn C. Hardacker has published three novels and numerous short stories. He is a member of the Mystery Writers of America, The International Thriller Writers, and the Maine Writers and Publisher's Alliance. His first two novels, *Sniper* (a finalist for the 2015 Maine Literary Award, in the Crime Fiction category) and *The Fisherman* were published by Skyhorse Publishing, Inc. and are available through all outlets.

He is a veteran of the US Marines and served in Vietnam. He holds degrees from Northern Maine Community College, the University of Maine, and Southern New Hampshire University.

He lives in Maine and at this time, is working on another Ed Traynor thriller.